CIRCLE OF FEAR

PINNACLE BOOKS HAS SOMETHING FOR EVERYONE –

MAGICIANS, EXPLORERS, WITCHES AND CATS

THE HANDYMAN (377-3, $3.95/$4.95)
He is a magician who likes hands. He likes their comfortable shape and weight and size. He likes the portability of the hands once they are severed from the rest of the ponderous body. Detective Lanark must discover who The Handyman is before more handless bodies appear.

PASSAGE TO EDEN (538-5, $4.95/$5.95)
Set in a world of prehistoric beauty, here is the epic story of a courageous seafarer whose wanderings lead him to the ends of the old world – and to the discovery of a new world in the rugged, untamed wilderness of northwestern America.

BLACK BODY (505-9, $5.95/$6.95)
An extraordinary chronicle, this is the diary of a witch, a journal of the secrets of her race kept in return for not being burned for her "sin." It is the story of Alba, that rarest of creatures, a white witch: beautiful and able to walk in the human world undetected.

THE WHITE PUMA (532-6, $4.95/NCR)
The white puma has recognized the men who deprived him of his family. Now, like other predators before him, he has become a man-hater. This story is a fitting tribute to this magnificent animal that stands for all living creatures that have become, through man's carelessness, close to disappearing forever from the face of the earth.

Available wherever paperbacks are sold, or order direct from the Publisher. Send cover price plus 50¢ per copy for mailing and handling to Pinnacle Books, Dept. 721, 475 Park Avenue South, New York, N.Y. 10016. Residents of New York and Tennessee must include sales tax. DO NOT SEND CASH. For a free Zebra/Pinnacle catalog please write to the above address.

CIRCLE OF FEAR

JIM NORMAN

PINNACLE BOOKS
WINDSOR PUBLISHING CORP.

PINNACLE BOOKS are published by

Windsor Publishing Corp.
475 Park Avenue South
New York, NY 10016

Copyright © 1993 by Jim Norman

Excerpted material from *The Looking Glass War* by John Le Carré used with permission of The Putnam Publishing Group.

Excerpted material from *Scoundrel Time* by Lillian Hellman used with permission of Little, Brown and Company.

All rights reserved. No part of this book may be reproduced in any form or by any means without the prior written consent of the Publisher, excepting brief quotes used in reviews.

If you purchased this book without a cover, you should be aware that this book is stolen property. It was reported as "unsold and destroyed" to the Publisher and neither the Author nor the Publisher has received any payment for this "stripped book."

Pinnacle and the P logo are trademarks of Windsor Publishing Corp.

First Printing: June, 1993

Printed in the United States of America

Acknowledgments

This book is for Peggy, who, believing, made it possible.

A large debt of gratitude is owed the following good people: Pat Evans, for early encouragement, comments, and moral support; Ronda Wanderman Young, for seeing the possibility the first time and for wearing numerous hats; Charlie Young, for friendship; Tom Johnson, for wizardry and kind words; Beth Lieberman, for seeing the possibility the second time. Thank you.

"The belief in a supernatural source of evil is not necessary; men alone are quite capable of every wickedness."

—Joseph Conrad. *Under Western Eyes.*

"Do you know what love is? I'll tell you: it is whatever you can still betray.

—John Le Carré. *The Looking Glass War.*

"I do not believe in recovery. The past, with its pleasures, its rewards, its foolishness, its punishments, is there for each of us forever, and it should be."

—Lillian Hellman. *Scoundrel Time.*

PART I

SYMPTOMS

A man dressed in a cowled black robe stood before a rough-cut stone altar. On the altar lay a young woman. Her hair spilled in chestnut waves over the stone, and she wore no clothes. In her raised hands she balanced a battered gold-colored chalice. The man poured a dark liquid into the chalice, and he spoke clearly in a deep, resonant monotone. His words were in a strange, foreign-sounding tongue.

Behind him stood perhaps fifty people—men and women and even a few children. The cowls of their coarse robes were pulled low, obscuring their faces. Occasionally, the group repeated a phrase spoken by the leader.

Smoke rose from braziers set on either side of the altar. It gathered in the high ceiling of the room; the walls and ceiling and corners and windows were lost in the shifting smoke.

The leader softly spoke a phrase. The gathering repeated it. Slightly louder, the leader repeated the same phrase. The gathering echoed it. The rhythm and volume of the recitative increased, becoming urgent, like lovers laboring toward climax. As the chanting grew louder still, the smoky haze over the dais filled with a frenzy of shadowed activity. Smoke swallowed up the leader and the altar and the woman on the altar, replacing them with monochrome shapes and indecipherable movement.

The leader no longer spoke, the recitative now entirely taken over by the gathering and repeated louder and faster, increasingly urgent. Finally, there was no longer a demarcation between one repetition and the next, and the chant became a toneless roar.

Then it stopped. Echoes of the last syllable seemed to hang in the smoky air and reverberate from the stone walls.

The absolute silence of the gathering was shattered by a wild shriek from the altar. It went on for long seconds, then died. The room was once again filled with a hollow silence. The shapes within the smoke seemed to withdraw. As the onlookers watched, breathless and still, a faint sound infiltrated the quiet . . . the sound of slow dripping. The eyes of the group moved to the base of the altar. Something wet and slick was dripping onto the stone floor. Something red, like blood.

Chapter 1

Week 1: Monday, July 31

Sarah Johnson checked a temptation to look out the window. Six years as a therapist had trained her not to let her attention wander. Too many missed cues and vacant stares, and people got the impression that you'd rather be somewhere else. And that was not the right message to send. But something was different today. Perhaps it was the storm front moving in from the mountains. Sarah wanted to watch the purple and gray thunderheads she could just see through the window. She forced her attention to the woman sitting on the other side of her desk.

"Francis, I'm very proud of you," she said. "We've been seeing each other for three months now and that's the first time I've heard you sound excited about something."

"You know, you're right. I feel like I've been in a cave for the last year. It's good to feel like life has some fun in it again." Francis Jenkins smiled. "Thank you."

"Well, you've done all the work. But you're welcome. If you need anything, just call. See Margie on the way out for our next appointment."

The woman left, closing the door behind her. Sarah walked over to the window and looked out on the parking lot. *More rain,* she thought. *Well, that's okay. It'll cool things off and I won't be tempted to work out in the yard. Maybe Mark will be home early and we can relax a bit before dinner.* She took a deep breath and stretched, then absently ran both hands through her chin-length brown hair.

The door to Sarah's office opened, and she turned from the window. Sarah's secretary Margie, a short, slender woman in her mid-twenties, peered around the door.

"What's up?"

"We've got a walk-in." Margie nodded toward the door. "I know it's late, but she said she really wanted to see you. She seems kind of upset."

"What the heck. Tell her I can see her for a few minutes. If we need it, I'll let you do an intake when I'm finished."

"No problem, boss." Margie smiled. "I knew you'd see her."

"Give me a minute, then send her in."

Sarah sat at her desk. She pulled the computer's keyboard toward her, typed in a command, and inserted a tape cartridge into the slot at the front of the machine. When her backup of the day's work was finished, she removed the tape, stuffed it into a plastic box, and dropped it in her purse. Margie sometimes accused Sarah of being fanatical about her computer backups, but she had learned the hard way that always keeping a copy off site was the only sane insurance against loss of information.

The office door opened. Margie stepped aside to allow the woman to enter.

"This is Diana Smith," Margie said.

Sarah stood, offering her hand, and regarded the stranger. She was dressed casually in jeans and a crisply pressed cotton blouse. She carried a functional-looking gray bag. *More like a camera bag than a purse,* Sarah thought. Diana Smith was of medium height, five-six or seven, slim build. She was quite attractive, especially her face and deep-set blue eyes. Shoulder-length hair, very blond. *Artificial,* thought Sarah, glancing at the crown of the woman's head.

"I'm Sarah Johnson." Sarah offered her hand. The woman shook it firmly. "Please have a seat."

"I really appreciate you seeing me with no notice."

"That's all right. What can I do for you?"

"Well," the woman paused, glancing around the room. "Now that I'm here, I don't know what to say."

"Why don't you just relax for a minute. Do you smoke? Please feel free."

The woman nodded. Sarah opened a desk drawer and removed an ashtray. Diana lit a cigarette, inhaling deeply.

"Would you like one?"

"I'd love one," replied Sarah, "but I quit a few years ago."

Sarah paused a moment and watched the woman settle into the chair. "Diana—may I call you Diana? Good. Diana, how did you find me?" Sarah hoped a neutral subject would help her relax.

The woman smiled shyly. "I found your office listed in the Yellow Pages. To be honest, I just liked the sound of your name. That, and the fact that you were obviously a woman."

"You feel more comfortable talking to a woman?"

"Yes."

"That's fine. Tell me, have you ever been in therapy before?"

Diana shook her head.

"Do you feel ready to tell me a little about yourself?"

"Actually, I feel a little silly. There's really nothing much the matter. In fact, I'm not entirely sure why I came." The woman shifted nervously in her seat.

"That's okay, Diana. As long as you're here, it won't hurt to talk things over a bit."

"I guess I've been kind of down lately," she said,

and glanced up at Sarah. "It's strange. I feel like I don't have any energy."

"Uh-huh. Have you seen your doctor about this?"

"Yes, I have. I thought at first that maybe I had mono or something. So I went to my doctor. He ran some tests."

"And?"

"Nothing. But there's more to it than that."

"Please go on." Sarah looked up from her notes.

"Even though I'm really tired, I wake up in the middle of the night and can't get back to sleep."

"I see. Any dreams?"

"No, none that I can remember. But I wake up sweating and my heart is beating like ninety miles an hour."

"How long ago did this start?"

"Maybe four or five months."

"I see. How's your appetite? Any changes? Eating more, eating less?"

"Uh . . . well, maybe eating less. I've lost ten pounds over the last month or so. But that's the good news. I don't mind that at all." Diana smiled for the first time, and Sarah found herself liking her new client.

"Anything else?" Sarah asked. "For example, headaches? Difficulty breathing? Problems concentrating?"

Diana looked startled. "Yes."

"Problems concentrating?" Sarah asked.

Diana nodded. "And headaches."

"Okay, we'll come back to that," Sarah said. "You say you've felt kind of down lately. Tell me a bit about what you mean. Physically tired, maybe? Mentally?"

The woman nodded. "Both. You know the expression *I've got the blues?* That's the way I feel *all* the time, you know?"

"Feeling mentally as well as physically down can mean a lot of things. Sometimes people feel so bad—

have the blues, as you put it—they even think about harming themselves."

Diana paled and averted her eyes. She stubbed out the butt of her cigarette, fumbled in the folds of her bag, and eventually produced another one. Finally, she found her matches. Only after the cigarette was lit did she meet Sarah's gaze.

"I've had thoughts like those," she said softly. "Do you know what's wrong with me?"

"I'm not sure anything is wrong with you. So far you sound very normal."

"Really? I didn't think normal people thought about . . . well, about killing themselves and being buried and things like that?"

Sarah frowned without thinking. "Did you say *being buried?*"

"Yes. I sometimes can't stop thinking about it. It's almost like I can feel myself in a coffin. And I'm terrified. When I think about the coffin, I feel like running away. I've only thought about suicide a couple of times. And that was pretty intellectual. I mean, just a way out."

"A way out of what?"

Diana looked puzzled. "I don't know," she said. "A way out of all the confusion. The mess, you know? Sometimes, it's like I'm in a maze and I can't find my way out."

Sarah regarded her client in silence. This woman was depressed, certainly, but there was something else, something different about her. Sarah followed her instincts in therapy, sometimes even when they ran contrary to accepted practice. Her instincts were throwing signals at her now, but the message was confused. *Caution,* maybe? *Be careful? Take nothing for granted? Danger?* She didn't know. To give herself time to think, she picked up a legal pad and jotted down notes for several minutes.

"Diana, I would very much like to see you again."

The other woman frowned. "Do you think there's something wrong with me?"

"I would hate to draw any conclusions until we've spent some time together. But I think you are somewhat depressed, and I believe you could use a little help to get back on top of things. What do you think about that?"

"I think that's fine. I'd like some help," Diana smiled hesitantly. "There's something else I need you to understand."

"All right," Sarah said. "What is it?"

"Whatever you might conclude about me—about what's wrong with me—I don't want to have to take any drugs."

"May I ask why? Not that that's something we would even consider at this point."

"I just don't like them. The whole idea of drugs." The blonde stubbed out her cigarette with unnecessary force. "It's just something I feel strongly about."

Sarah nodded. "That's fine for now. We might want to talk more about it another time. Anyway, I'm going to let Margie set up an appointment and get some information from you. She'll also discuss fees with you. In the meantime, if you need somebody to talk to—for anything—call me."

Sarah stood and pulled a business card from the plastic holder on her desk. Usually, she was reserved in offering her time outside of scheduled sessions. She encouraged her clients to limit contact. What was it that made her feel that this woman might need her? The mention of suicide, surely, but then Diana had minimized that and Sarah believed her. What then? Instinct was sometimes a disturbing adviser.

"If you need anything . . . okay?" Sarah said, handing Diana the card.

The other woman smiled uncertainly and stuffed the card into her bag. "Sure. Thank you."

But Sarah was not assured.

* * *

Sarah reversed the Oldsmobile into the driveway, easing it in next to her husband's aging and battered Volvo. *Soon,* she thought, *we'll be ready to add another set of payments to the current crop and Mark will have something decent to drive.* Mark had quit his job some months before to try his hand as a self-employed computer and data processing consultant. So far, they hadn't gone hungry, but the returns left a lot to be desired.

Mark waited on the back deck as his wife got out of the car and made her way up the short steps. Sarah set the small bag of groceries on the patio table and hugged her husband. Mark Johnson kissed her. After five years of marriage, Mark and Sarah were still in love. A lot of passion had been replaced by affection, but neither were complaining. They had both seen plenty of marriages where passion was replaced by boredom, or bitterness, or nothing at all. They had had their hard times, too, times when both had wondered whether they would make it. But they had weathered the storms.

"How about a drink?" Mark asked.

"Sure. Give me a minute to change and put these groceries away."

"You get changed. I'll put the groceries away and fix us a couple of drinks. It's my night to cook. Hope you like stir fry."

"Great."

Mark was back in his chair on the deck, drink in hand, when Sarah stepped out from the kitchen, her working clothes replaced by jeans and a T-shirt. Mark handed her a drink and she sat in the remaining chair.

"Thanks," Sarah said, accepting the sweating glass. "How was your Monday?"

"My Monday was great. I installed a couple of new systems today and picked up some new work."

"Honey, that's wonderful." Sarah made a face as

she took a sip of the drink. "Whew, this is strong stuff."

"You looked like you could use a stiff one. Tough day?"

"Actually, no. It was a pretty good day. Long, but good. I picked up a new client today myself."

"Hey, great. Anything interesting, or just the normal run of everyday craziness?"

"Oh, nothing special. Depression, I think. Although there was something different about this one. Something that didn't quite fit right . . ." Sarah frowned, and her eyes focused on the distant horizon.

"Hello. Come back. Anybody in there?" Mark waved his hand in front of his wife's eyes.

"Oh, sorry. Just daydreaming for a moment." Sarah smiled at her husband. "Hey, do you remember me telling you about the woman who hadn't left her house in two years? I started working with her about six months ago?"

"Yeah, I remember."

"Well, she's doing great. She's driving herself. She's lost weight. She's wearing makeup and dressing nicely."

"Sounds like a success to me."

"I think so."

"I keep telling you you're good. One of these days you're going to start believing me."

"I tell you the same thing, but do you believe me? No."

Mark smiled. "I'll start believing you when I start contributing to the budget again."

"So, that's bothering you, is it? I was wondering when that was going to hit."

"No, it doesn't really bother me. I knew going into this that it would take a while to start seeing a return. Actually, I think I'm doing pretty damn good. I just hope that we can hold out long enough to see it all pay off."

"Honey, I'm just proud of you for trying. Quitting your job and starting your own business takes guts. What's the worst that can happen, anyway? If it doesn't work, it doesn't work. And don't worry about the money. We're doing fine."

"Thank you. That's nice of you to put it that way."

Sarah stretched luxuriously and smiled at her husband. "I love you, you know."

Mark smiled back. "I love you." He pushed himself out of the lawn chair. "And on that note, it's time for me to start dinner."

"That's right. Off to work, you galley slave."

"You mean *love slave,* don't you?"

Sarah laughed. "That comes later."

Chapter 2

Week 1: Tuesday, August 1

Sarah Johnson pulled into the office parking lot, noting with satisfaction that her secretary had already arrived. Margie's pickup truck was parked in its usual spot.

As Sarah entered the office, she found Margie pouring water into the coffee maker they had dubbed "Old Faithful," so named not only because of its utter reliability in times both bad and good, but also because of the explosive wheezing sounds it made at regular intervals while brewing the essential beverage of the mental health profession, caffeinated coffee.

"Good morning, lady. You're here awfully early," Sarah said.

"Yup. You know me. . . . Just can't stay away."

"Right . . . uh-huh. Where's your calendar?" Sarah sifted through the clutter on Margie's desk.

"It's right there. Just dig down a layer." Margie was indisputably the best organizer Sarah had ever had the good fortune to employ. She kept the office neat and on schedule. Her desk, however, was a chronic disaster. Sarah was certain, though, that in spite of appearances, Margie knew precisely where every paper clip was on that desk.

"Thanks. I just want to see what we've got on tap."

Sarah located the calendar book and thumbed it open. She glanced over Margie's neat handwritten notations. "What's this one at three? It looks like a *D* and an *S*."

"Oh, you got me before I could clean that one up. That's the woman you met with yesterday. What's her name—Diane? Diana. Diana Smith, right? We didn't have anything else open this week, so I set her up for today. Okay?"

"Sure. Boy, she's going to think that we run some outfit. Just walk in off the street and get instant service. That's good. What else do we have?"

"Just the regulars, I think, and nothing until nine. I'll bring you a cup of coffee when it's finished."

"Thanks, but you don't have to do that. I can get it myself."

"Yes, I know. Next month we move the machine into your office and you can bring *me* coffee. Would that make you feel better?" Margie pointed a mocking finger at her employer. "Now get in that office and make us some money."

The day passed swiftly. Things were so busy that both Sarah and Margie ate lunch in. Sarah had finished the notes to her first afternoon session and was reviewing Margie's intake on Diana Smith when she glanced at her big wall clock. It was almost three o'clock. As she was about to get up, Margie stepped into the office.

"Ready for your three o'clock?" the secretary asked.

"Sure. Is she here?"

"Just came in."

"Good. Let me get a cup of coffee, and I'll be ready."

Sarah got her coffee, and Diana followed her into the office. Both women seated themselves. Sarah had already arranged her legal pad and yesterday's notes. She took several sips from her mug, then set it down and smiled at her client. Diana Smith returned the smile.

"How did you sleep?" Sarah searched tentatively for a way to get the woman to open up. "I seem to remember from yesterday that you have had some problems sleeping. Any trouble last night?"

"Actually, yes. I woke up again in the middle of the night and couldn't get back to sleep."

"Do you remember what time it was?"

"About three o'clock, I think."

"Do you remember what woke you up?"

"No, I don't."

"Bad dream, or a noise maybe?"

"I don't remember any dreams. And if there was a noise, I don't remember that, either."

"This is probably a stupid question, but you don't have a clock that chimes on the hour, do you? It was close to the hour when you woke up."

"No, I'm sorry, I don't have any clocks like that." Diana shook her head.

"Do you remember any dreams at all from last night?"

"No, I don't."

"That's interesting. Do you remember dreams as a rule?"

Diana closed her eyes for a moment. The lashes were long and dark.

"No, to tell you the truth, I hardly ever have any dreams."

Sarah smiled. "That's probably not quite accurate. You almost certainly are dreaming, you just don't remember. That's all right. A lot of people have difficulty recalling dream content. How did you feel when you woke up?"

"I felt absolutely panicked. My heart was racing and I was in a cold sweat. I know this sounds strange, but I felt like I was running, trying to get away from something. I don't know why."

Sarah nodded. "Do you usually feel like that when you wake up in the middle of the night?"

"Sometimes."

Sarah jotted down the phrase *middle sleep disturbance* and then added *anxiety attack? blocked dream recall?*

"You know, we sort of have gotten off on the wrong foot. Usually, I try to learn something about my clients before we go into detail about what's troubling them. Why don't you tell me a little about yourself. What do you do for a living?"

"I'm a photographer," Diana said.

"Portrait, or journalism, or something else?"

"Free-lance. I sell most of my stuff to the local newspapers. I'm also putting together a book."

"Really? What's the subject?"

"It's just a collection of city scenes. Both architectural oddities of the city and people shots. I'm calling it *Richmond Works.* It's a spare time project, but I do have a local publisher interested."

"That's wonderful. Will it be color or black and white?"

"Oh, definitely black and white. Color is just too expensive to produce. Also, I work almost entirely in black and white."

"I'd love to see your work. Perhaps you'd bring some in sometime?"

"Okay."

Sarah consulted her notes. "Let's see, Diana. You mentioned yesterday that there were some other things that bothered you. Why don't you tell me about them."

"I don't know. I just feel so tired lately. Like I could sleep all day. Sometimes I come home in the afternoon and take a nap. I've never done that before." She paused.

"This is difficult," Diana exhaled suddenly, and Sarah sensed her exasperation. "Everything seems so hopeless lately. I feel this sort of weird guilt that doesn't really have to so with anything specific. If I get sick, I feel guilty. If I take a nap, I feel guilty. If I have a fairly good day, I still feel vaguely guilty for some reason. Does this make any sense?''

''Don't worry about whether it makes any sense. It's more important that you are in touch with how you feel and can verbalize those feelings. You're doing a great job.''

Diana nodded gratefully.

Sarah glanced over her notes again. ''Are there any other symptoms or problems that you can think of? Please tell me anything you think of, no matter how trivial or silly it might seem.''

''Like I said yesterday, I feel like I can't concentrate as well as I used to. I mean, it's like everything's in slow motion or I'm looking at everything from a distance.''

''Yes.''

''As a photographer, I have to be really sharp. If I don't feel well, it's hard to see the pictures.'' Diana paused, searching for the right words. ''To take a good photograph, you have to be able to *see* what it will look like. And you've got to be able to react quickly to whatever's going on around you. I don't feel like I can do that anymore.''

''Have you managed to keep selling your work since you started feeling like this?''

''Yeah, but it's mostly schlock stuff. Filler. You know, cute shots of kids in the park and ducks in the pond. Nothing really good, for the most part.''

''Okay. Why don't you tell me a little bit about your relationships. Family and friends. That sort of thing.''

''I don't have any family,'' Diana said, and her voice was toneless.

''No? How about parents?''

''They died a few years ago.''

''I'm sorry. Any brothers or sisters?''

''No.''

''Okay, how about friends?''

''I have friends.''

"Of course you do," Sarah said. "What I mean is, has anything about your relationships with your friends changed?" *Strange response,* thought Sarah. She scribbled the word *friends* on her yellow pad.

"I guess maybe I haven't been particularly interested in keeping up with them. I stay pretty busy. I'm afraid I don't have a very active social life."

"I see. What do you do for entertainment?"

"Oh, the usual stuff, I suppose. I read a lot. Watch television. I do a lot of darkroom work in the evenings. Go out once in a while."

"When's the last time you went out?" Sarah looked up from her note-taking.

"It's been a while."

"I see."

"Look, I've answered a lot of questions. Maybe you'll answer one of mine," Diana said, a sudden tone of determination in her voice.

"I will if I can," Sarah said.

"Good. What's wrong with me?" The tone of her voice was both plaintive and determined.

Sarah hesitated before answering. "I'm not sure that's one I should try to answer, but if you insist, I'll tell you what I think so far. These are your symptoms—I hate that word, it makes everything sound so precise and medical, and that's not often the way things work. But anyway, see if these sound right . . ." Sarah flipped back to a previous page in her notebook and began scanning. "Middle sleep disturbance, or insomnia; diminished appetite; fatigue and possible daytime hypersomnia; feelings of guilt, inadequacy, and despondency; gastrointestinal disturbance; diminished social interaction; and difficulty concentrating. Plus there's one other that we haven't talked about today." Sarah looked up from her notebook. "Suicidal ideation. How does that sound?"

"It sounds pretty bad." Diana averted her eyes. She added quietly, "It also sounds pretty accurate."

"Please don't be embarrassed. There is nothing unusual about what you're going through. Look, I'm not in the habit of handing out diagnoses during first sessions, but I believe that you're experiencing a major depressive episode. At least that's what they call it in the books. Depression, Diana, is a very common mental health issue. But there is a lot of misunderstanding about depression. People hear the word *depression* and they automatically think of *being depressed,* or *down in the dumps,* or *having the blues.* Amazing all the euphemisms we have, isn't it? But depression is a lot more than *the blues.* It can be a very serious problem."

"Somehow you're not making me feel better."

"I'm sorry, but I want to give you the bad news first. As it turns out, there's quite a lot of good news. But the worst of the bad news is the feeling you have that life isn't worth living. That's the major danger of what you're going through right now."

"What?" Diana asked. "That I might kill myself?"

"Quite frankly, yes," Sarah answered. "That is the single greatest danger of depression. Statistically, even without treatment, persons experiencing major depressive episodes will recover within six months to a year and be at their previous level of functioning. The trick is to keep them from harming themselves in the meantime."

"So you're saying that all this will go away if I give it enough time?"

"No, I did not say that. You've got a problem that *sometimes* takes care of itself. Another statistic is that most persons not treated will experience another major depressive episode. But more important is the good news: Depression is easily and effectively treated."

Diana frowned and a single vertical line creased the space between her eyebrows. "You're talking about drugs, aren't you?" she said, making the phrase as much a statement as a question.

"Well, there are at least two schools of thought on

that one. One says that the new antidepressant drugs are often sufficient by themselves to handle a majority of mild to moderate depression cases. I'm from the other school that says therapy is, if not essential, then highly desirable in almost all except the mildest episodes. Combined with the correct antidepressant, it's an unbeatable combination."

"Look, regardless of anything else, I don't want any drugs."

"May I ask why? Is this a religious objection?"

"No, it's not religious. I'm not one of those fanatics."

"Okay," Sarah said. "I know some people are afraid of becoming dependent. They hear the word *drug* and they automatically think *junkie.* Of course, given the potential for abuse of many drugs, that's not always an altogether bad prejudice. Is it something like that?"

"I guess that's part of it," Diana said. "Look, I just hate pills, I hate needles, I don't even take aspirin."

"Nobody's going to make you do something you don't want to do. But let me tell you a couple of more things. Not so long ago, taking an antidepressant often meant that you would have to be careful about what you ate. Cheeses, for example, could make you very ill. But with most of the new drugs, there are no food contraindications. Also, a lot of people worry about diminished capacity. They think they are going to become stoned-out zombies. That just doesn't happen. Without the drugs they might *act* like zombies because they just don't have much energy anymore. The drugs help prevent that. I will admit that it may take a little experimenting to find the one that works best for you."

"Are you listening to me?" Diana asked, her voice rising. "I said *no* and I meant *no.* I'm not taking drugs."

"All right, then. I'm sorry for the lecture. I just want you to know the facts. If you absolutely insist on not trying the medication"—Diana opened her mouth to speak, but Sarah raised a silencing hand—"if you're not going to try the medication, then my biggest job is helping you to keep from getting so depressed that life no longer seems worth living. Our job together is to get you through this episode intact, and to maybe shed some light on why it's happening and how to cope with it."

Diana nodded. "I think that sounds okay. But there is one thing I don't quite understand."

"What's that?"

"You seem awfully worried about suicide. Like I said yesterday, I've thought about it but not seriously enough to really do anything. I want to live. I want to feel good again."

"You did mention that yesterday." Sarah thumbed through her notes for a moment. "Yes, I believe you said that you thought about suicide as an escape. And also that you thought a lot about being buried. Is that right?"

"Yes, that is right." Diana averted her eyes again, fumbling in her purse for a cigarette. She lit it and looked up. "Is that a part of depression, too?"

Sarah hesitated a moment before answering. "I don't know. That's something I think we need to explore. When do these thoughts occur to you?"

"They come at most any time. And they come out of nowhere. One minute everything is fine and the next I have this overwhelming sensation of suffocating and—and . . . oh, damn, this is harder than I thought."

Sarah watched closely as her client pulled a Kleenex from her purse and wiped at her eyes. She was about to speak when the intercom buzzed. She picked up the phone receiver and pressed the intercom button on the telephone.

"Yes?"

"Sorry to interrupt, but time's up," Margie said.

"Thanks. We'll be through in a minute." Sarah

hung up the phone. "You were going to say something before Margie buzzed?"

"No," Diana said, "not really. Nothing that can't wait."

"You're sure?"

Diana nodded.

"Okay," Sarah said. "I guess that's all for today. I'd really like to see you next week. You will be coming?"

"Yes."

"Good. You still have my card?"

"Yes."

"I'll see you next week, then."

Week 1: Wednesday, August 2

Diana Smith reflexively cradled the big Nikon in her left hand as she jogged across the westbound half of the street. Her right hand rested on the gray canvas of the camera bag, preventing it from bouncing against her hip. She paused at the crossing island and waited for the light to change. Out of sheer habit, she surveyed the scene across the street. Busy pedestrians walked quickly. Shoppers with bundles waited for buses. Professionals rushed from one appointment to the next. Everyone seemed either hurried or restlessly waiting, each engaged in some private internal enterprise hardly related to the bustle of external activity. Diana scanned almost without thinking, waiting for some juxtaposition of objects—a combination of subject and light—to resolve out of the pandemonium of the street.

She spotted an old man sitting on the steps of one of the large downtown buildings that housed state agencies. His elbows rested on his knees and his chin was cradled in the palms of his hands. The early morning sunlight illuminated his face with a clean, golden light.

Diana lifted her camera. She had left the long lens on, for opportunities such as this. Raising it to her eye, she composed the scene in her viewfinder. She pushed the shutter release, hesitated a second while the autowinder advanced the film to the next frame, then made a slight adjustment to the shutter speed setting. Before she could shoot again, a bus roared past. The old man stood shakily, gathering his belongings.

Diana crossed the street and debated which direction to take. She continued south on a side street, heading roughly in the direction of her apartment. It was quieter here, with fewer pedestrians. She stopped for a moment at the mouth of an alley she had never noticed before. The alley was dark, but it looked safely deserted. It would be a short cut to her apartment on Greene Avenue several blocks to the west.

The light all but disappeared as she stepped off the street. On either side, aging brick facades rose five or six stories. Trash cans lined one side of the alley. Amazingly, the alley was cobblestoned. One of the few areas of cobblestone left, Diana realized. Uncomfortable in the stale darkness, she walked quickly. About midway through the block, she glanced up. She found herself looking through the latticework of an old wrought iron fire escape. Through the many layers of iron, she could see the sky between the two buildings. The pattern of light was almost like looking through lace. She lifted her camera to her right eye and peered through the viewfinder. *Wrong lens,* she thought, and replaced it with another from her bag.

She raised the camera again, but the scene suddenly seemed to shift. No longer was she looking at the expanse of sky through a fire escape. She seemed to be looking up through a narrow tunnel. She felt enclosed, trapped inside the darkness of the alley walls and the viewfinder frame. Diana stumbled, overcome by nausea and vertigo, and barely kept herself from falling. She leaned with her back to the brick wall, breathing loudly in ragged gasps. Closing her eyes, she tried to gain control over her dizziness.

Diana fought the temptation to look up again and hurried through the remaining distance of the alley. Emerging into the light, she caught sight of a taxi, climbed in, and gave the driver directions.

Feeling drained, Diana slumped against the doorway upon entering her apartment. After a few minutes, she lay down on the sofa. She briefly considered turning on the television set, then thought better of it. Instead, she rolled over with her face buried in the back of the sofa. She drew her knees up and pulled an afghan off the back of the sofa and onto her legs. She closed her eyes and thought briefly that she probably wouldn't be able to fall asleep. But almost immediately, she did . . .

In her dream, Diana is playing with two dolls. She is an adult and she is in her apartment. Everything seems normal, except that she is on the floor playing with two dolls. The dolls are old-fashioned baby dolls, with large round heads and beautifully made glass eyes. Diana notices that she is wearing a child's fancy dress, with a high lace neck and petticoats. She sees that the dolls are dressed similarly. Why am I dressed like this? she wonders.

A knock sounds at the door. She looks up and feels herself smile, but she does not get up. The knock is repeated. Diana looks down at her dolls and continues arranging their dresses and smoothing their hair. The knocking continues, but it is not like the normal rap-rap-rap knocking of someone politely requesting entrance. This knocking is more like a drumbeat.

Diana continues to ignore the knocking, although it gradually increases in volume. She begins humming a song, and the louder the knocking becomes, the louder she hums. Eventually, the knocking is so loud it cannot be ignored. Disjointedly, Diana thinks, it's so loud it's going to wake me up. But the knocking continues, boom-boom-boom. Diana glances toward the door. She notices that the doorknob is turning. Boom-boom-boom. Someone is rattling the door while the knocking continues. The door begins to shake visibly now. Boom-boom-boom. Diana begins to scream:

No! The screaming coincides with the knocking—boom-boom-boom, no-no-no—until Diana cannot tell which is which. Eventually, she can scream no longer. The knocking stops. Diana cowers over her two dolls and watches as the doorknob continues to turn. She is silent for several moments, then begins mouthing, almost silently, no-no-no. Suddenly, the door is opened with a crash. Diana continues repeating her litany of no-no-no, but this time she says it slowly and nearly silently, almost like a chant.

A figure enters the room. In the indeterminate way of dreams, Diana knows that it is a figure dressed in black, but she cannot see it clearly. She has the impression of a figure in black and an overwhelming sensation of evil and danger and panic.

"You must give me the doll," the figure in black speaks.

A hand, gloved in black, reaches out to her. Diana screams, then suddenly she is on her feet and trying to run. Her dolls are clutched tightly to her chest as she tries to run. Her feet will not work correctly. They feel as if they weigh a hundred pounds apiece. Slowly—too slowly to avoid capture, she thinks—she runs toward the bedroom. The slow-motion sensation vanishes and she is standing before the mirror on her bedroom vanity. She looks at herself in the mirror and then turns to see the figure in black reaching toward her. The gloved hand grabs one of the dolls. She struggles, frantically trying to hold on to the doll. But she is no match for the strength of the figure in black. As Diana screams—No!—the doll is wrenched from her grasp. She sees the doll receding from her in a field of black, growing smaller and smaller and smaller. Diana screams again, and this time . . .

This time she is awake and covered in sweat. She is shivering and her voice is hoarse. *My God,* she thinks, *have I really been screaming?* She gets up shakily and walks into the bathroom. She looks at herself in the mirror. There is something wrong about the image she sees. She cannot place what is wrong. She sits down on the side of the bathtub. *Oh God,* she thinks, *is this why I don't remember my dreams?*

Chapter 3

Week 2: Tuesday, August 8

"I'm very impressed. Not only did you remember a dream, but you've just related it in remarkable detail. That's not an easy thing to do. Do you think it has any meaning?"

Diana took a nervous puff on her cigarette. The ashtray was already half filled with several cigarette butts. "Don't all dreams mean something?" she asked.

"Oh, I'm not at all sure they do," Sarah answered. "I think dreams have meaning if they give us something to think about. Sometimes we dream just because it's pleasant and natural to dream, and sometimes we dream to tell ourselves things or to work through whatever we're feeling. Do you think your dream falls into one of those categories?"

"I don't know. It's so strange. Maybe it doesn't mean anything."

"Maybe. Let me ask you a question. What is your overall feeling about the dream? If you had to sum up the dream as a single feeling, what would it be?"

Although Sarah was no particular proponent of dream interpretation, she had spent the last half hour looking for a way to get her client to open up. Diana had eventually mentioned the dream. She had seemed quite anxious as she recounted it, smoking heavily and holding herself very tightly.

"I would say a feeling of great loss," Diana said. "At the end I just feel incredibly sad. I mean, at first the dream is very frightening, but when the thing takes the doll, I feel so sad. I feel as if I've had something ripped right out of me."

Sarah nodded. "What do you think the figure in black is? Or who?"

"I don't know. I feel like I almost recognize it, like I know who or what it is. Because even though I'm really scared, I'm not surprised by it. It's not like a mugger or an intruder. Does that make any sense?"

"Does it make any sense to you? It all sounds very reasonable to me. But it's what it means to you that's important. Tell me, does the figure seem like it's male or female?"

"Uh . . . that's interesting," Diana said. "I hadn't thought about that. I would say male. Yes, definitely male."

"Let's talk about the dolls. Do they seem to represent anything to you?"

"I don't know. I'm playing with them. I feel very protective toward them. But I guess that's not hard to figure. Just looking at it very literally, they're my dolls and I wouldn't want them to be taken away. You know?"

"Uh-huh. Go on."

"Well, they're just dolls, you know. Nothing special."

"Are they dolls you remember having as a child?"

Diana frowned. "No, I don't think so. I mean, they could be. I just don't specifically remember any dolls. They look like normal dolls, though."

Sarah made a quick notation on her legal pad. "Describe them, please."

"They're just regular dolls. There's really not much to describe."

Sarah looked up and sighed. *I'm starting to show my frustration. Every time I get close to anything, she clams up. I'm doing most of the talking.*

"That's okay," Sarah said. "Tell me what they're wearing. What color are their eyes? Their hair? Do their eyes close when you lie them down? What are they made of?"

"Oh, okay." Diana nodded, and a smile spread across her face as she recalled the details. "They seem to be made out of a really hard material—the heads, that is. They're not like modern plastic dolls. The heads are porcelain, I guess. And the eyes . . . the eyes are incredible. They're beautiful blue eyes, with this amazing detail in the irises. They look almost like real eyes, but I think maybe they really did used to make dolls like that. Hey, maybe they *are* real dolls that I used to have. I don't know."

"You say they both have blue eyes. Are the dolls identical?"

"They both have blue eyes, but no, they are not the same dolls. Of course not. One is . . . uh . . . one is . . . I mean, one has brown hair and one has blond hair. And . . ."

"Wait a minute." Sarah leaned forward in her chair. "You said, 'One is . . . one is,' almost as if you were going to say a name. Do you remember a name?"

Diana frowned. "I don't know. I don't think so."

"That's all right," Sarah said. "I'm sorry I interrupted. You were saying that one had blond hair and one had brown hair?"

"That's right. And they're both wearing these identical white dresses, very lacy and with petticoats or crinolines or whatever that stuff is. Like something you'd see at a rich kid's birthday party. And I'm wearing the same thing."

"So the dolls are identical except for the hair?"

"I guess so. They look the same, anyway."

"They look the same, but they're different. Is that what you mean?"

"Well, yeah, of course they're different."

Sarah paused a moment, wondering which way to take the session. "Which one gets taken by the intruder?" she asked.

"Oh, that's Sissie," Diana's eyes seemed to cloud over and become distant. For a moment, she was silent. "It was the blond doll."

"The blond doll? Sissie. You just called her Sissie."

"I did? Huh, I guess I did. Isn't that strange?" A slight frown creased Diana's forehead.

"Yes, you did," Sarah said. "Do you know anyone named Sissie?"

"No," she answered. "No, I don't. At least I don't think so." She hesitated. "Maybe when I was a kid. The name rings a bell, but I don't remember. I don't remember."

"That's fine. You made a comment when you were telling me about your dream. You said you ran into the bedroom and looked in the mirror. You said something didn't look right, but you weren't sure what it was. Can you tell me about that?"

"Sure. There's not much to tell. I mean, that's about it. You know how it is in dreams. Sometimes you know things for no real reason. You just know them. It was like that. Let's see . . . There I am in my bedroom and I'm standing in front of the dresser. I'm looking at myself. I can see the two dolls. I have them pressed against me like this"—Diana crossed her arms over her chest—"and I can see that I'm dressed in this child's party dress. I'm looking at myself, looking right at my eyes, and I just feel that something doesn't look right. I don't know what it is, though. Just something is not right. But then, the thing . . . the figure . . . comes in the room and I turn away from the mirror. And that's it. Sorry, that's all I remember." She smiled apologetically.

"That's okay. It's probably not important. And if it is, you'll remember it later. Let me ask you a couple more questions, and then we'll leave the dream for today. Do you think the doll that gets taken away represents you?"

"What? How could that be? No, no, I don't think so. Why would you think that?"

Sarah ignored Diana's question. "One more thing. Did anyone ever call you Sissie when you were a child?"

"No," Diana said flatly. "That's crazy, too. I think you're way off base. How did you come up with this?"

"Just a wild guess." Sarah shrugged and smiled. "It doesn't mean anything. I thought maybe you were the doll that got taken away. The doll is blond and has blue eyes. You're blond and you have blue eyes."

"No, that just doesn't make any sense. I don't remember anybody named Sissie, and I don't think it's me who's being taken away."

"Okay, that's fine. I don't want to put more importance in a dream than we ought to. Chances are, it's just that—an interesting dream. There is something I would like to talk about today, though, and that's the comment you made about being buried in a coffin."

Diana looked directly into Sarah's eyes for several seconds. Sarah imagined that she saw something new there. A hardness, *like flint,* the expression leaped into her mind. *What's going on in there?* Sarah thought. *Let me in, will you?* After a moment, Diana's eyes softened.

"Yes, I can't seem to get rid of it."

"Get rid of what?"

"This thought of being buried. It's terrible. I don't know. Sometimes I feel like I can't breathe."

"When do you have this thought?" Sarah asked. "Any particular time?"

"No. It can happen anytime. It happened last week while I was doing some shooting."

"Please tell me about it."

Diana related the incident that had occurred in the alley, as she photographed the fire escape. When she had finished, she looked at Sarah. The therapist had the impression that Diana was mildly embarrassed or, worse, reluctant to say more.

"Okay, you've told me what happened, but you didn't mention being buried. Is there a connection?"

"You're right," Diana said. "But, you see, it's the same sensation I get. I didn't actually see a coffin, but that's the way I felt. Like I was in a coffin. Like I was buried alive and suffocating. Like . . . oh, God, I just can't stop thinking about it. Why? Why?" Diana looked pleadingly at Sarah. Tears were forming in the corners of her eyes. Sarah searched in her desk for a box of tissues.

"I don't know, Diana, but I'd like to find out," Sarah said. She hesitated, wondering what her client's reaction would be to what she was about to say. *It needs to be said,* she thought. *At least once. Is now the time? There's no good time.* "There's something else we need to talk about. Sometimes I get the feeling that you are reluctant to talk to me. If you would rather have another therapist for any reason, I want you to know that's fine. Finding a therapist you trust is very important. I can give you a list of therapists I recommend, if you like."

"All right. That's fine." Diana's voice now had a hard, resolute edge to it. Her sudden air of decisiveness startled Sarah.

"Then you would feel more comfortable with someone else?" Sarah asked.

"Look, if you want to get rid of me, that's fine. I'll find somebody myself. No problem."

Sarah realized she had made a mistake. Something irrational was at work here. She wasn't quite sure what it was, only that her client was expressing something other than her actual concerns and feelings.

"Diana, I am very sorry. There is nothing more I

would like than to continue to work with you. I like you and I think we get along well. I was just concerned that maybe you weren't comfortable with me."

"No, no. That isn't it at all. But whatever you want is fine."

Sarah checked her feelings of exasperation. "Diana, let's continue working together. If you ever decide you would rather work with somebody else, that's fine."

On impulse, Sarah made a comment she would later regard as unprofessional as well as uncharacteristic. Her instincts were more compelling than her sense of professionalism. Diana seemed so young and vulnerable, and Sarah, in her struggle to establish a private practice, had fought her own battles against insecurity. Plus, her instincts still insisted that Diana's problem was not depression but something else . . . something even more insidious. Diana was obsessed about burial and that was *not* a feature of depression. And she had mentioned sensations of detachment. There was something familiar about that, something Sarah could not quite dredge up from the depths of memory.

"Let me tell you something," she said. "I don't ever intend on letting you go unless it's something you want to do. I care about you, Diana, and I want to help you."

Week 2: Thursday, August 10

Diana Smith stepped out of the shower. She pulled a towel from the rack and wrapped it around her freshly shampooed hair. Grabbing another towel, she dried her body quickly and wrapped the towel around her, sarong fashion, then opened the bathroom door to allow the steam from the shower to escape. She removed the towel from her head and began using it to rub strands of her hair. After several minutes of blotting, she wiped the steam off the bathroom mirror. Catching sight of her reflection, she touched one hand to her face, probing it tentatively, almost as if it did not belong to her. Starting at her chin, her fingers moved slowly and gently over her face.

Diana regarded herself with a puzzled frown, as if she were greeting a somehow vaguely familiar stranger. Her fingers touched her cheeks, moved on to the soft skin around the eyes, lingered momentarily over the fine brown lines of her eyebrows, and then rubbed with greater firmness the smooth skin of her forehead. Gently, she touched her hair, running her fingers through its long strands. She lifted the front strands on either side, moving her head back and forth as if trying to catch sight of her profile. She looked closely at her ears, tucking the wet hair behind them. Finally, she looked at her eyes. The irises were blue, flecked with little particles of gold and green. Diana shivered, for they seemed to be the eyes of a stranger. For a moment, Diana felt lost in their depths, drowning in an unfamiliar pool of blue.

She started out of her reverie and suppressed a shudder. Suddenly, she recalled her dream. She saw herself as she had been in the mirror on her dresser, clothed in a child's dress, her face a twisted mask of terror. For a moment she saw that something was wrong. There was something about her face, something different. What was it? Something about the face . . .

Diana felt a stab of pain in her right foot. She looked down and realized she had been standing on tiptoe, with her left foot hooked around in back of her right, leaning into the bathroom mirror. *How long have I been standing here?* she wondered. She eased off her toes, feeling immediate relief. *What's wrong with me?*

She picked up a brush, running it quickly through her pale hair, parting it to one side. She avoided looking at herself in the mirror. Walking into her bedroom, she dressed in faded jeans and a cotton blouse, her usual work clothes. Because she did not wish to confront her reflection again, she decided to leave her hair wet and to go out without makeup. Diana could not remember going out without makeup, at least not for a long, long time. Again, the thought played briefly through her head: *what's wrong with me?* Then, something within her broke, perhaps from the weight of the unaccustomed introspection. *What's wrong with me, indeed?* she thought. *There's nothing wrong with me.* She shrugged, concluding that the thought—her concern that something was seriously the matter with her—had come uninvited and wasn't very important. It had no more weight than the other random thoughts that bubbled, unbidden, to the surface of her consciousness. She decided that this was a very useful frame of mind, this dispassionate recognition and evaluation of thought. Why, nothing was wrong with her. Not really. Not at all. She just needed a little perspective, that was all.

Diana picked up her camera bag. Placing the strap on her shoulder, she opened the bag and did a quick inventory. Everything in place. *Need to pick up more film. No problem. I'll get that now.*

She grabbed a set of keys from the desk. As she opened the door to the apartment, she glanced at the phone on the end table. For a brief, fleeting moment she felt a nearly overpowering urge to call Sarah Johnson. For an instant a feeling of warmth washed over her. *Trust,* she thought. *I trust her.*

As quickly as it came, the feeling vanished. In its place was a dullness. *Now why would I want to call her?* Diana wondered. *I'm not even sure I'm going back. There's nothing wrong with me. Nothing at all. There's nothing wrong with me.*

What's wrong with me?

Out on the street, Diana paused to adjust her camera bag. She retrieved one of the camera bodies, removed the cover, and twisted on a lens. She positioned the strap on her shoulder, noticing that there was a single shot left on the roll.

Diana hailed a cab and directed the driver to a small shopping center where she could buy film. As she stepped out onto the curb, she saw a small crowd of shoppers standing in front of a department store window. Walking closer, she realized what the attraction was. A live mannequin posed in the window display. For long minutes, she held herself motionless; then, with robotic stiffness, she would shift into a new position. Diana wondered whether she could shoot the scene so that both the crowd and the mannequin would be visible. The problem would be glare from the plate glass. Quickly, she fished in her bag for a polarizing filter and screwed it on the lens of her camera. Squinting through the viewfinder, she quickly focused, set the exposure, and composed the picture.

Her finger pressed the shutter release. At the instant the shutter clicked, a man emerged from the crowd, walking toward Diana with one hand raised. *He's just ruined my shot,* Diana thought, *and he's putting his hand up to keep me from taking his picture. Why doesn't he just turn away?*

She dropped the camera from her eye. Her mouth opened as if to say something. But there was something vaguely familiar about the man, and this uneasy recognition silenced her. Did she know him? She didn't think so. She didn't know very many fifty-five to sixty-year-old men who dressed in thousand-dollar suits. So who was this guy?

The man dropped his hand as Diana dropped her camera. He smiled at her and crossed the sidewalk in several quick strides.

"Pardon me, miss," he said as he came close.

"Yes . . ." Diana said hesitantly.

In one fluid motion, the man stepped up to Diana so that they were inches apart. At the same time, he leaned his face toward her left ear in a practiced, intimate gesture. Diana's impulse was to back away, to repel this uninvited stranger. But before she could move, the man grabbed her arm in a crushing grip. His face was now next to her ear. Diana thought crazily that he was going to kiss her. Instead, the man whispered.

Instantly, Diana's face went slack. She seemed to slump, but the man stepped around her and supported her with an arm across the small of her back. Again he put his mouth next to Diana's ear and whispered. Her eyes cleared and she straightened her back. She glanced quickly at the man beside her and laughed. Her laugh was loud and hearty. She kissed him briefly on the cheek in the manner of old friends, then skipped lightly from his grasp. The man smiled at her, then turned his gaze to quickly survey the crowd of shoppers. He turned back to Diana, nodded briefly, and walked away.

Diana turned away quickly. Blending into the crowd of shoppers still watching the mannequin, Diana unshouldered her camera and stuffed it into her bag. She pushed through the knot of people, walking past the department store and the entrance to the camera shop next door. This brought her out to a side street, where she managed to hail a cab. She climbed into the cab and was gone.

Chapter 4

Week 2: Friday, August 11

The phone rang as Bill Travers was trying to force his eyes open with the morning's first cup of coffee. He was not a morning person, and the ringing of the telephone felt like a knife cutting through the front of his skull. Travers knew before lifting the receiver who was calling. Nobody at the university ever called him at home in the morning; it was just too damn unproductive. Which meant it had to be the cops, since they *never* learned. Besides, Travers made a little extra effort to be responsive to the cops. After all, they paid him consultant's fees. The consulting gig was lucrative, interesting, and utterly dependent on the whim of the accountant's red pencil.

Travers snatched up the phone on the fourth ring. "What?" he asked.

"This is John Fisher."

"Oh, Sergeant Fisher."

"Right."

"What's up?"

"Can you meet me in half-an hour or so? I've got something for you to look at."

"Where?"

Bill Travers wrote the address on the back of one of the test papers he had been trying to grade. He took off his glasses, rubbed his face, and sighed. The cops—meaning Fisher, usually—always called at the worst damn times. Travers looked guiltily at the pile of ungraded papers on the kitchen table and shrugged. Whatever Fisher had on his mind would be more interesting than wading through a stack of freshman anthropology exams.

Consulting with the Richmond City Police Department was a sweet deal when you really came down to it. The cops called him a "Consultant Sociologist," which he was willing to live with even if it did offend his sense of professional pride. As an anthropologist, there was a certain irony to being labeled a sociologist. Goddamn sociologists hadn't had an original thinker since Emile Durkheim. Of course, the greater irony was that he was retained as an expert in the occult and other "atypical sociological phenomena." Now that was a real hoot. But "Consultant Sociologist" had to be a hell of a lot easier to justify to the bureaucrats as a budget line-item than "mumbo jumbo expert," which was pretty much how most of the force regarded him. *Funny,* he thought. *When he'd made his doctoral thesis a study of a local coven of self-styled witches, he'd never dreamed it would represent a future meal ticket.* But here he was, more by default than intention, expert in the weird and the occult.

Travers drained his coffee, then stood and stretched, and finally walked back to the bedroom to put on his shoes. He tended to work barefoot.

Forty-five minutes later he parked his aging Ford outside the gates of a cemetery. *Cemeteries, always cemeteries,* he groaned. Half the cases he was called in on seemed to involve desecrations or evidence of ritual activities, usually committed by teenagers dabbling in the occult. *Christ-on-a-crutch,* he thought, *doesn't anything ever happen outside of cemeteries?*

He walked up to the gate, noticed it was open, and slipped inside. The air was cooler. Tall oaks lined a walkway, and beneath them he felt a breeze stir.

"Over here."

Travers scanned the trees in the direction of the voice, which he recognized as belonging to Detective Sergeant John Fisher. On a rise about a hundred yards away, he saw the policeman waving.

Travers panted as he topped the rise of the hill. "What's up?" he asked. "Is that your equipment over there?" Bill nodded in the direction of several men standing around a backhoe another seventy-five yards or so across the cemetery.

"Yeah, we've got an exhumation order."

"I can hardly wait. I hope the departed has been gone a long time." In spite of being out of breath, Travers lit a cigarette.

"Long enough. Seventy-five years or so," Fisher said.

"What the hell are you doing digging up a seventy-five-year-old stiff?"

"We don't think that we're the first ones to do it. Come on, let's walk over there," Fisher nodded in the direction of the workmen.

"We got a call a couple of days ago," the detective explained. "The caretaker had been making the rounds and noticed that the ground looked disturbed around this one plot. He called the owners and they called us."

"So what does *disturbed* mean?"

"Not a whole lot, really. In fact, the caretaker almost didn't notice it. The sod had been cut and removed, apparently, and then every bit of dirt that had been dug up was put back. They must have used a tarp to put it all on, because you couldn't see any dirt at all in the surrounding grass."

"How do you know it wasn't done a long time ago?"

"The grass adjoining the plot was kind of smashed down where they must have laid the tarp. But it wasn't very obvious. I think they raked the grass back into shape when they were finished. And, of course, the sod was still loose."

"So why would somebody go to all that trouble to

dig up an old grave?'' Travers combed back blades of grass with the tip of his shoes, as if he were looking for a lost object.

''I don't have the slightest idea,'' Fisher shrugged. ''That's why we're here. When we couldn't figure out anything else, we got an exhumation order.''

''So why am I here?''

''Well, this sounded like something potentially up your alley.'' Fisher smiled without much humor. ''Look, I apologize in advance if this turns out to be a wild-goose chase. But I figured if we find anything, it'll be when we open the coffin. Since you're our resident expert on this kind of stuff, I wanted you to see . . .'' Fisher paused, ''well, whatever there is to see.'' Before forensics rips it all up, you know. I hope the trip is worth your while.''

''What the hell. You rescued me from another round of freshman exams.''

For the next hour, the two men watched as the workers removed the earth from the site. Finally, the soil was cleared away. The casket had been buried without a vault. The workers rigged ropes around it and hoisted it out of the ground.

The coffin was a surprising affair. It was wooden and very simple in design, almost a proverbial pine box. Except that this box was clearly not made of pine. It was constructed of fine hardwood, lacquered black, with brass hardware for hinges and handles. Although the brass was corroded and rotted, the wood was remarkably intact.

The forensics team had arrived during the digging, along with a couple of uncomfortable-looking men in business suits representing the owners of the cemetery. The investigators examined the box carefully. Bill noticed signs of recently chipped wood between the lid and the box.

''It's beginning to look like something other than

a wild-goose chase," he said. "Somebody's been in there."

When forensics had done its work of photographing and sample-taking and fingerprinting, one of the workmen inserted a crowbar between the lid and the coffin. It raised almost without effort, and two more men lifted the top and placed it to the side. The lid was a single piece, not segmented like modern coffins. Apparently, the hinges had either rusted through or been broken by intruders.

The workmen stood silently looking into the coffin. Travers followed Fisher over to the open casket and looked in. At first he could see nothing but a mass of dark and moldy fabric laid against a surprisingly white satin material. He positioned himself for a better view but could still not make out what he was seeing. Then he realized he was expecting the opposite orientation. He was looking at the foot of the coffin, where he had expected the head. Suddenly, the object made sense. A moldering black suit draped lankly over the frame of the skeleton. A head, mummified by desiccation, the skin like gray parchment stretched over a grinning skull. Travers felt a moment of relief that the sight was not . . . well, less bearable. Digging up corpses before breakfast was not his idea of a good time.

"Looks intact to me," Travers said, backing away as a member of the forensics team pushed by him.

Fisher nodded. "Yeah, looks that way."

The technician was bent over the coffin, examining the corpse at close range. She looked up at Travers and Fisher. "Not quite intact," she said.

"What do you mean?" Fisher asked.

The woman stepped away from the casket and pointed. "He's missing a hand."

Fisher glanced briefly at Travers, then stepped up to the coffin. "She's right," he said.

Travers knelt by the coffin. The left hand *was* missing. There was nothing at the end of the arm but the joint of the radius and a small pile of gray dust on the satin lining.

"Maybe he didn't have a left hand to begin with," someone offered.

"What do you think, Bill?"

"Well, there's some dust here. I'm not a physical anthropologist *or* a forensic anthropologist. I can't tell whether the hand's been removed or not."

Fisher looked around helplessly. "So, does the medical examiner need to see this or not? Can we conclude there's been no disturbance? Did they get inside the coffin?"

Fisher didn't seem to be addressing him directly, so Travers stood and walked around the side of the coffin. He looked down into the empty grave. It sure as hell looked as if the coffin had been opened, and somebody had thought enough of the condition of the plot to order an exhumation, no small bureaucratic feat. And there was something about the hand, something he could not quite remember. Some tiny fact mined from an obscure treatise on the occult, no doubt. Probably not important.

The bottom of the grave was littered with loose soil: clods of red Virginia clay, a few stones, friable hunks of a grayish material. The scraped sides of the grave looked like an illustration from a textbook on Virginia geology. A thin layer of dark topsoil merged into the red clay. Below that were bands of lighter soils, sands and silts in streaks of tan and brown.

So where did the gray stuff at the bottom of the hole come from? Travers let his eyes roam over the walls of the grave again, unable to pick out a corresponding layer in the uncertain, shadowed light. He probably just couldn't distinguish the color through all the shadows cast by the brilliant morning sun. Except . . .

He remembered reading an article several years before, some small town account of an alleged former member of an occult group. Travers recalled discounting the article at the time. Rumors of highly organized cults of demon-worshippers and necromancers had been around for years. Too much of the member's so-called confessions had seemed contrived sensationalism. That, and his accounts of human sacrifices and blood rituals, had just struck Travers as absurd. Still, the man had had a few original twists on old themes. He had claimed that bodies of sacrificial victims were disposed of by digging up old graves and burying the body *underneath* the current occupant's coffin. That way, even if the disturbance were detected, it was likely the more recent burial would go unnoticed.

In spite of the warm summer sun, Travers felt a chill. There was no layer corresponding to the gray chunks. Which meant they had to come from a *lower* layer. And then Travers remembered something from an old demonology text. It was the reference to the hand that he had been unable to recall. You dipped the hand of a corpse in tallow—*the left hand,* of course—and used it to light ritual ceremonies invoking Satan and his minions.

Could the grave had been dug up to hide another corpse? And the hand stolen because even if the desecration were discovered, chances were that no one would be overly concerned about a one-handed corpse?

Travers turned to face Fisher. "I think you're gonna need the M.E.," he said. "Can you get somebody down in the grave to do a little digging? He shouldn't have to go very far."

The digging stopped with a shout twenty minutes later. The worker scrambled out of the hole, his face blanched a pasty white. One of Fisher's forensic technicians climbed into the grave. Using a camel-haired paintbrush, he carefully brushed the dirt away from whatever the worker had uncovered. The technician stepped back and Travers felt the muscles in his stomach tighten violently, involuntarily. He fought the rising gorge. Intruders had been here all right. Intruders had exhumed this coffin. They had removed the left hand of the corpse, which by that time must have been nothing more than leather stretched over dry crumbling bones. Then they had deepened a tiny portion of the grave by a few feet and in it they had left the corpse of an infant.

Week 3: Sunday, August 13

Mark slipped his arms around Sarah's waist as she stood at the stove tending two frying eggs with a spatula. She leaned back against him, turned her head to kiss his unshaven cheek, then turned back to the frying pan.

"Breakfast?" Mark asked. "Real breakfast? With eggs and everything?"

"With eggs and everything. We're good all week. I figured we *needed* a little cholesterol."

"Hot damn."

When Sarah served the food, Mark put down the Sunday paper and stood to kiss her.

"So, what have you got planned today?" Sarah asked.

Mark washed down a mouthful of egg with a sip of black coffee. "Not a thing. I've left Sunday open. No fooling around with computers. No tinkering with the car. No preseason games."

"You left Sunday open for little ole me?" Sarah asked in a mock-southern accent and fluttered her eyelids.

Mark laughed. "We've both been pretty busy lately. I thought it'd be nice to spend some time with my wife."

"I'm flattered."

"Hey, if my business ever takes off, our days together may become a rare commodity again."

"I hope not. It's nice having you around more." Sarah almost added, *Remember when you weren't around so much?* Those had been the times that had threatened their marriage, when Mark's job had so utterly enveloped him that he had had nothing left over. When he had seemed like a stranger, arriving home perpetually late and exhausted. The nice thing about his decision to leave his job and start his own consulting business had been the increased time at home. Sarah had once feared that they were becoming strangers. She had resolved to never let that happen again. A job—either of their jobs—just wasn't worth it.

Mark picked up the entertainment section of the paper. "Say, you want to drive into town and catch a movie this afternoon?"

"Sounds good."

After eating, Sarah cleared the dishes and sat back down at the kitchen table while Mark went off to take a shower. She was browsing through the section covering city news when a headline caught her eye. "Professor Assists Murder Investigation," it read. Sarah folded the paper over and scanned down the column of newsprint. An anthropology professor from the university had been instrumental in the discovery of a corpse in a disturbed grave. *What?* Sarah reread the paragraph. *An anthropology professor consulting with the police in cases of occult crime?*

Sarah read the entire article, shaking her head at the strangeness of it, wondering what things had come to if people hid murdered infants in old grave sites and the city found it prudent to employ experts in the occult.

Week 3: Tuesday, August 15

Sarah glanced at the wall clock and saw that it was almost three o'clock. She held the phone tucked between her neck and shoulder, rifling through a pile of case files as she listened to Jenny Burton tell her about the Caribbean cruise she and her husband had just returned from. Jenny was her oldest friend in the Richmond area. Though they didn't get together as often as Sarah liked, they tried to talk on the phone at least once a week.

"Listen, Jenny," Sarah said, "I've got a three o'clock."

"Just hang up when you have to; I'll keep talking till then." Jenny was used to Sarah's schedule and her five-minutes-between-session phone calls.

"Thanks, I . . ."

At that moment, Diana Smith entered. Sarah's client wore faded jeans, a worn cotton blouse, and a canvas vest. The vest was the kind photographers wear, with pockets sewn on nearly every available space. Her blond hair was disheveled and Sarah noticed that dark roots were just beginning to show at the part. This did not appear to be the same woman she had seen the previous weeks. Sarah put down the phone, hearing Jenny's voice vanish in mid-sentence.

Breathlessly, Diana said, "Sorry I'm so late. I was out on a job and the time got away from me. I would have called, but I figured by the time I found a phone that worked, I could be here. It you want to cancel the session, I understand." As an afterthought, she added, "And please excuse the way I'm dressed. These are my working clothes."

"I'm glad you're here. And we certainly won't cancel the session. It just may be a little shorter."

Sarah nodded to a chair and Diana seated herself.

"I was beginning to worry that you weren't coming today," Sarah said. She did not want to sound accusatory, but she wanted to assess her client's reaction.

"Actually, I wasn't sure myself if I was going to come."

"Oh?"

"I just had some second thoughts, I guess."

Sarah waited for her to continue. Silence was usually an effective way to encourage expansiveness.

"It's just that I thought . . . well, maybe I don't really need to be coming. I mean, it's not like there's anything wrong with me. Besides, you would probably prefer to fill my slot with someone else."

"Why do you think that, Diana?"

"Huh? Oh, I don't know. Forget it, okay?"

Why is trust such an issue with this woman? Sarah wondered. *She must have been hurt terribly.* Sarah knew something about the kinds of hurt that destroy trust and the barriers such hurt creates. And the enormous effort needed to tear the barriers down.

Sarah put down the pen she held and leaned over the desk. "There's nobody I want in this slot more than you," she said. "I think we can do good work together. I care about you." *Well, that was not the most professional way to put that,* Sarah thought, *but sometimes a little honesty and friendship is more important than clinical distance.*

Diana smiled, looked at Sarah, then looked away. "Thank you," she said. "I want you to understand something. I'm not used to being dependent on anyone. I'm pretty much of a loner. It's hard to get around that sometimes."

"Diana, I'd like to talk about that a little. Or rather, I'd like to know a little more about you. Do you mind if we talk about the past for a while?"

"No, that's fine."

Sarah thought she heard some hesitancy. "Good. You told me before that your parents were dead. When did they die, if you don't mind my asking?"

"About eight years ago, when I was . . . let's see, yes, I was eighteen."

"I'm sorry," Sarah said. "Was it an accident? They both died together?"

"Yes, they were in a car accident. My father was driving. It was a rainy day, I guess. They just had an accident."

"I see. Were you close to your parents?"

"Well, not really. I was closer to my father than my mother. They were both gone a lot, though, so I didn't really see all that much of them."

"Did they travel a lot? Business?"

"Yes. My father was a businessman. My mother used to spend a lot of time traveling."

"With your father?"

"Not really." Diana smiled hesitantly. "Sometimes, I guess. I think she just traveled a lot."

"Who took care of you when they were gone?"

"Oh, we had a maid. Also, I had a lot of relatives who were always coming and going and would look after me."

"It sounds kind of lonely. Were you happy?"

"So this is where you ask me if had a happy childhood?"

Sarah looked up from her note-taking. She decided that Diana was not being ironic, just humorous. Sarah returned the smile.

"Yes, I guess this is it," she said. "*Did* you have a happy childhood?"

"Sure I did. I mean, I guess so. I don't remember being unhappy, particularly. I remember a lot of good times."

"What's the earliest memory you have?"

"Excuse me?" Diana looked puzzled.

"What is your earliest memory?" Sarah repeated. "What's the first thing you can remember?"

"Gosh, I don't know. Let me think a minute. You know, I'm not sure I have an earliest memory." Diana laughed uneasily. "Is that odd or what?"

"Okay. What's *one* of your earliest memories? Anything at all."

Diana's eyes roamed over the ceiling for a moment. "All right, here's one. I remember my parents had a party. We were living in a big house, then, with a swimming pool. I can remember all these people standing around eating and drinking and talking. I remember running around through the crowds. I don't really remember much else. It's like a snapshot in my head, you know. I don't remember a sequence of events or even anything in particular happening. I just remember this scene, like a photograph, of this crowd of people. Is that the way most people remember? Or is that just the mind of a born photographer?'' Diana laughed.

"I don't know. How old were you then? Do you know?''

"I'm not sure. Let me think a minute. We moved from that house when I was seven or eight, so it had to be before then. But I don't think we lived there all that long. I would guess I was five or six.''

Sarah looked up quickly. Her client seemed serious. *She's not kidding,* she thought. Sarah made a quick notation.

"I see. Now, who is Sissie?''

Instantly, Diana's face darkened. *Hardened,* thought Sarah.

"I told you last time, I don't know any Sissie. I told you I . . .'' Diana became silent, her eyes seeming to search some distant landscape. *What does she see there?* thought Sarah.

"Diana?''

"That's very strange. How could I have forgotten? I remember Sissie. How could I have forgotten? This is amazing. I haven't thought of her for years.''

"You remember someone named Sissie?'' Sarah asked.

"Yes, I do.'' Diana laughed.

She laughs with such surprised delight, thought Sarah. *Curiouser and curiouser.*

"She was my best friend,'' Diana continued. "How could I have forgotten about her?''

"How old were you?''

"Let's see . . . I guess I was about nine when we first met.''

"Would you describe Sissie, please?''

"Sissie's the same age as me and about the same height. She has blue eyes and brown hair. She was a very pretty girl.''

"What happened to her?''

For a brief moment, Diana's face seemed to cloud over and her eyes got that faraway look again.

"I'm not sure. I think she moved away. Yes, she must have moved away."

"When?" Sarah asked.

"That would have been when we were eleven or twelve, I think."

"Did you keep up with her? Do you know what happened after that?"

"No . . ." Diana paused. She looked at Sarah. "Oh, doctor, this is wonderful. I don't know how I could have forgotten, but thank you for helping me remember. Thank you."

"You're welcome, but you're the one that's doing the work, not me. And please call me Sarah."

"Okay. Thank you, Sarah."

"What can you remember about you and your friend?" Sarah pressed.

"I remember lots of things . . . now," Diana added. "Isn't that strange. Does this kind of thing happen a lot?"

"Sometimes," Sarah said. *But not that I've ever seen before,* she thought. *What the devil is going on here? One minute the girl's a blank, a stone wall. The next, she's ready to go tripping down memory lane.* Sarah felt uneasy. She was missing something. What was it? *No time to look over the notes now. Just take good ones,* she thought, *and think about it later.*

For the next half hour, Sarah jotted down notes while her client recalled a series of childhood memories spanning perhaps three or four years: Diana and Sissie going on picnics; Diana and Sissie playing dress-up on rainy days; Diana and Sissie at parties and alone. At times, Diana's face almost glowed with the recollection of happy times. Sarah was certain that this nearly rapturous joy and the unself-conscious sharing of memories were uncharacteristic of Diana Smith.

The memories themselves were unremarkable

enough—typical childhood stuff. But Sarah still felt something was wrong, and she was still just as unable to put her finger on it. Aside from the fact that her client had gone from a nearly total blank to detailed recall, what else was there? *Maybe it's just the sheer volume of such ordinary memories,* she thought. *Maybe it's a little bit like listening to a distillation of the experiences of typical children. Or not typical children at all. Stereotypical children. Real children recalled breaking an arm, or an angry parent getting carried away disciplining, or a birthday when they didn't get a present they particularly wanted. This is like watching television. Yes, that's it. TV kids, storybook kids. Leave It to Beaver meets Lassie meets Rebecca of Sunnybrook.*

Okay, Sarah thought, *I believe all this happened.* There was no denying the look of delight on the other woman's face. *But what happened to all the other stuff? Where are the bad times? Maybe that fits, though. Could Diana be blocking the unpleasant memories? Not inventing a happy childhood, just editing out anything associated with . . . with what? Well, that is the question, isn't it?*

"Why do you suppose you had forgotten about your friend?" Sarah asked.

"I don't know. I don't see how I could have forgotten. I remember everything so well. And you really didn't do anything." Diana blushed. "Oh, I'm sorry. I didn't mean that you didn't *do* anything. I meant that there wasn't anything . . . well, dramatic. Like hypnosis or stuff."

Sarah laughed. "That's quite all right. You'll find that you're the one who has to do the hard work. I've got the easy job." An idea occurred to Sarah. "You mentioned hypnosis. I'm just curious, but how would you feel about using hypnosis sometime? Not now. Probably not at all. But if it looked like a good idea, what would you think? The idea would be to help you remember other things you might have forgotten . . . like Sissie." Sarah was following her instinct again. It had thrown up warning signals when Diana started recalling her friend. Now her instinct was telling her to use this new mood of her client to gain a future concession. Sarah wasn't sure that hypnosis would be important. Fully qualified and licensed to practice hypnosis, she rarely found use for it in therapy. But something was telling her to get permission now, if she could.

"I don't know. I guess if it looked like a good idea, it would be all right. Do you think there's more stuff I can't remember?"

"Perhaps. Anyway, maybe someday we'll try hypnosis. But not today. Today, you're doing a wonderful job of remembering. Would you like to try some more?" Sarah glanced at her watch. Time was getting short.

"Sure."

"What's the most unpleasant thing you can remember from childhood?"

"Let me think, okay?" Diana crossed her legs. She fished a cigarette out of the pack she had set on Sarah's desk and lit it. "I remember once I fell down and hurt myself. I think Sissie was there. I guess I was nine or ten. I remember running, and slipping, and falling. I don't think I was hurt too bad. I remember lying there on the ground. Except it's not the ground . . ." Diana frowned.

"What is it?" Sarah asked.

"I don't know. I'm looking up, and there are all these people standing around me. And I can't move. I can't move."

Diana's breath was now coming in shallow, ragged gasps. She was breathing very hard, very fast.

"Diana." There was no response, just rapid breathing and that distant look.

"Diana," Sarah said, raising her voice. Still no response. Sarah pushed herself away from her desk and stood up. She knelt in front of Diana and placed an arm across her shoulder.

"Diana, listen to me. You're hyperventilating. Bend over; put your head between your knees," Sarah gently pushed the woman's head down. "Slow your breathing if you can. Relax, just relax."

After several minutes, Diana's breathing became regular. She raised her head and looked at Sarah.

"I—I'm okay." She leaned back in the chair.

"Are you sure?"

"Yes, yes, I'm fine. Thank you." She smiled at Sarah.

Sarah stood and leaned against the edge of her desk. "What happened?"

"I don't really know. All of a sudden, I felt like I couldn't breathe. Like I couldn't move. Was that a memory?"

"I don't know. We'll find out, though. Is this the way you feel when you have the feelings of being buried?"

"Yes. Exactly."

"Look, everything's fine. I think that's enough for one day. Why don't you sit there for a few minutes and relax. Can I get you a cup of coffee?"

"No, I'm fine," she said. "I really should be going now."

Sarah thought she heard something in her client's tone of voice as she watched Diana stand up. *Damn,* she thought, *there's that sensitivity to rejection again. She thought I was trying to get rid of her. Why is she so sure that I'm out to reject her?*

"Abso-damn-lutely great news, babe," Mark Johnson burst through the back door, a bottle of champagne tucked under his arm.

"What? What, what, what?" Sarah laughed, amazed at her husband's sudden display of enthusiasm.

"I just landed a new contract and it's big enough by itself to keep me busy for the next month. Not to mention the follow-up stuff."

"Fantastic, honey. Is this a celebration?" Sarah put

down the measuring cup into which she had been pouring rice. It was her turn in the kitchen, and she had decided to get dinner started before Mark got home.

"You bet it is. Care for a bit of the bubbly before dinner?"

"Sounds dangerous. Let's do it."

After a couple of glasses of champagne, Sarah returned to finishing the preparations for their supper. Mark, by this time feeling no pain, peeked into the kitchen.

"Need some help?"

"No, I'm fine. Why don't you relax?"

"I'd rather watch you."

"Okay, but the floor show doesn't start till seven." Sarah gyrated her hips and did a quick two-step halfway across the kitchen floor. "Care to dance, Bubba?"

"Why sure, sweetie." Mark grabbed his wife around the waist and began to lead a slightly out-of-step waltz across the kitchen.

"Allemande right, baby," he said and suddenly they were doing a drunken square dance.

"All right, all right. Uncle. You win. Let me get back to dinner or we'll never eat." Laughing, Sarah pushed her husband away and walked back to the counter where she had been chopping vegetables.

"Okay. Well, I've told you about my day. How was yours?"

"I had a good day," Sarah said without turning around. She picked up her knife and started chopping again. "It was one of those days that keeps you humble. I did good work, but there were several times when I had the opportunity to look at certain assumptions I'd made and decided that I needed to start over."

"Really? That sounds interesting. As long as you're not going to let me attack you right here on the kitchen floor, you might as well tell me about it."

"Let's see. Remember the agoraphobic client I told you about who was doing so well?"

Mark nodded.

"Well, she backslid quite a bit over the weekend. Had a real panic attack. Started decompensating terribly. The funny thing was that she managed to commit herself. Drove herself to the hospital. That surprised me."

"I'll bet." Mark pulled out one of the chairs tucked under the kitchen table and straddled it backward.

"The one that bothers me, though, is the new client I started working with. I thought it was a pretty straightforward case of depression. Now I'm not so sure."

"How come?"

"Oh, it's just that she's presenting in some ways that don't make sense for depression."

"Presenting," Mark said in mock disgust. "The terms you guys use—decompensation, presenting behaviors, schizoaffective bipolar obsessive-compulsive paraphilias . . . God I love it when you talk dirty to me."

Sarah laughed, then turned suddenly serious. "I'm just not sure what to make of this one's presenting behaviors, as you so eloquently put it. I mean, I'm sure she's depressed, but I think there might be more to it. Something doesn't add up." Sarah put down the large cleaver-style knife she was using, placed both hands on the kitchen counter, and leaned forward. She stared with eyes unfocused for several seconds.

"So what do you think?" Mark asked. "What are you going to do?"

"Nothing to do, really. Just wait and see, I guess. That's one I've got to think about. Enough. Are you ready to eat?"

"You bet. Dinner or you?"

"Whichever you wish, dear." Sarah turned and faced her husband. She spread her arms wide. "Whichever you wish."

Dinner was late that evening.

Chapter 5

"Okay, so what's the story?"

Bill Travers paced his living room, cigarette in one hand, drink in the other, telephone pressed between his shoulder and his ear. The room was comfortably cluttered, and Travers traced a circuitous route through a maze of overstuffed chairs, sofa, magazines, books, student papers, and other paraphernalia of the bachelor academic. Travers talked with his hands; this proved dangerous when one contained a full bourbon and water and the other held a lit cigarette. As he walked, flecks of ash leapt off the end of his cigarette. Watery bourbon sloshed over the rim of the squat glass, soaking his hand usually and his feet and the carpet occasionally. Travers licked his drink hand when it got too wet.

"Wait a minute. Say again." Travers had just settled down to a quiet evening of not grading papers when the phone rang. John Fisher was on the line.

"I just got reports from forensics and the medical examiner," Fisher said, not quite shouting.

"Okay, I can hear you. No need to yell. What's in the report?"

"Not a whole hell of a lot. For one thing, no prints anywhere. Nothing else disturbed except . . . well, you saw."

"Yeah. What about the baby?" Travers took a sip of his drink.

"Male, about six months. In good health at the time of death. No signs of chronic abuse. Death was caused by a wound to the heart from a thin, sharp object. We assume it was a knife. Oh, yeah. Whatever it was had an edge on both sides."

"Like a dagger," Travers suggested.

"Right, that's what we think," Fisher agreed.

"Time of death?"

"No way to know, really, or at least with any accuracy."

"Why?"

"The baby was embalmed."

"What?"

"You heard me." Fisher cleared his throat. "A real professional job, too. Makes determining time of death pretty tough, you know. Roughly, sometime within two weeks to a month."

"Any idea when the coffin was dug up?"

"Yeah. Fortunately, our folks took some good sod and earth samples. We got the university to look at them. Judging by the way the roots were cut and then started to grow back, they make it less than two weeks. That's not definite. Anywhere from a week to three weeks, they said."

"Anything else?"

"No. Hell no." Travers thought Fisher sounded tired. "Does any of this make sense from your end? How the hell did you know to look under the coffin?"

"Something I read and didn't believe at the time. An interview with a guy who supposedly defected from a cult of Satan worshippers."

Fisher groaned.

"Yeah, well, that's how I felt about it, too," Travers said. "Now I have to wonder. Anyway, the guy claimed that this cult was not just a casual gathering of Saturday night thrill seekers. He said it'd been operating for years, conducting human sacrifices and disposing of the bodies in all kinds of unique ways. The most creative being the digging up of an already-occupied grave and . . . well, you saw."

"Yeah, a grave within a grave. So what the hell does this mean, Bill? Have we got crazed Satanists on the loose here?"

"Maybe somebody read the same article I did."

"You got any other ideas?"

"Just one. The wound sounds like it could have been made by an athame."

"A what?"

"Athame. A—T—H—A—M—E. It's a kind of knife used in rituals."

"What kind of rituals?"

"Oh, hell, anything," Travers said. "Black magic, white magic, witchcraft, satanic rituals . . . you name it."

"You got one of these knives?"

"Yeah, I think I've got one around here somewhere." Travers cast a doubtful eye around the room. "I'll drop it by if I can find it."

"Thanks. I'd appreciate that. Tell me something else. Why the hell bury the body in the first place? Seems like more trouble than necessary?"

"They needed to get rid of it someplace. What's better than a grave that hasn't been disturbed in seventy-five years? It's an old cemetery, isolated. And it would have worked, too, if it hadn't been for a caretaker with sharp eyes. Think about it."

"I suppose that makes sense."

"You know what really bothers me, though?" Travers drained the last of his bourbon.

"What's that?"

"This isn't just some amateur setup. And it isn't just some lone crazy, either. Digging up a grave without detection and making it look like nothing was touched is no mean feat. That had to take several people. Plus, you say the body was professionally embalmed. This definitely ain't the heavy metal crowd."

"Yeah, that's what I was thinking, too," Fisher agreed. "Listen, thanks for your time. I'll keep in touch, let you know if we come up with anything. We're still looking for missing babies and that kind of thing. If you think of anything, give me a call."

"You bet. And, John? Get some sleep," Travers suggested. "The job's not worth it."

Week 3: Thursday, August 17

By the time Mark Johnson finished running the coaxial cable through the building's drop ceiling, he was tired, sweaty, and dirty. Mark stood on an aluminum stepladder and pulled the final run of coax through the tiny hole he had punched in the office ceiling tile. When he had pulled sufficient cable through the hole, he stripped the cable with a pair of wire cutters, being careful not to nick the central copper conductor. He fished a heavy chrome-plated connector from his shirt pocket and twisted the connector onto the cable. He then threaded the cable through a maze of wires terminating in the back of a putty-colored computer dominating the office's desk. Mark twisted the connector onto the back of the computer and stood up, flipping the power switches on the computer and the monitor.

While the computer ran through its start-up routine, Mark stretched, then wiped his face with a handkerchief. Checking the progress of the computer, he pulled up the desk chair and sat down. He typed several commands on the keyboard and smiled in satisfaction as the network software behaved as he expected it to. He settled back in the comfortable chair, leisurely typing on the keyboard and watching the effect on the monitor. *This is a strange business,* he thought. *Eighty percent of the time you're sitting at a desk, typing away, absolutely seden-*

tary. The other twenty percent, you're lugging around equipment or fishing cables through some god-awful crawl space.

Of course, that's presuming you have any business.

The last year had been tough. Mark had walked away from a secure job as a programmer for a large insurance company. It was a job he had found easy, lucrative, and terribly boring. He'd started up his own company with a handful of contacts in the local business community and had watched as his income took an immediate nosedive.

But things were starting to look up. This customer had been a godsend. Out of nowhere, *he'd* called Mark, which was the way things were supposed to work but rarely did. He'd purchased all his new computers through Mark, and then had retained Mark to set up a local area network and develop a complex company database. Money was starting to flow in for a change. The only bad thing, Mark realized, was that when business was slow, he was always home when Sarah arrived from work. It had been nice, for a little while at least, to bail out of the rat race of sixty- and seventy-hour work weeks, dinners caught on the fly, stranger to your spouse except on weekends. Still, it was good to be busy again.

"Having fun?"

Mark swiveled his chair to face the office door. John Beiderbeck stood there, grinning. Beiderbeck was a trim, good-looking man in his mid to late fifties. He was dressed in an expensive charcoal-gray suit. He brushed a hand over carefully styled hair turning silver. Laugh-lines around his eyes crinkled good-naturedly; the eyes themselves seemed alert and intelligent, the eyes of an amiable hawk.

"Good timing," Mark said. "I just got the last one hooked up. Come in and let me show you what we got."

"Sure. Hey, why don't I get Rose to come watch, too. She's going to be working with this stuff, after all."

"That's a great idea," Mark said. "Sounds like a twofer to me."

Mark stood, and when Beiderbeck returned with his secretary, he offered the chair to the woman. She politely refused until he explained that it was his policy to have his customers actually operate the machines and software he installed. It was much more effective, he said, than having the customer watch him.

After half an hour of instruction, Beiderbeck excused his secretary to go home for the day. When she had left the office, Beiderbeck motioned to Mark to take the chair. Mark sat, leaned back, and laced his fingers behind his head.

"Mark, we're very pleased with the work you've done."

"Thanks. You've got some good people here, and that makes my job easier. I don't think you'll have many problems getting everybody up on the network and using the new software."

"You're right about having good people," Beiderbeck smiled. "But you're going to be around for a while yet, right?"

"Sure. I've finished installing everything, but I still have a few finishing touches to do on your database. And then I'm essentially on call. If you need me, I'll come running."

"Oh, I think we can do better than that. I have some ideas for overhauling our accounting system I'd like to discuss with you. Know anything about accounting?"

Mark nodded. "I took almost as many business courses as I did computer courses. I've written custom accounting systems before."

"Great. If you're finished, I'm ready to call it a day. Can I buy you a drink?"

Mark groaned silently. It was hard to turn down an offer to socialize with the CEO of what was rapidly becoming his major customer. Still, he had promised Sarah he'd be home early.

"John, can I take a rain check? Ordinarily, there's nothing I'd like better, but my wife's expecting me."

Beiderbeck's eyes narrowed and for just an instant his face became very hard. Mark wondered if he'd made a fatal mistake. Then Beiderbeck smiled and clapped Mark on the shoulder. "You bet," he said. "It's very important to tend to your home life. I'm glad you know that."

Mark relaxed. "Wonderful."

"You know, I'd really like to meet your wife someday. What kind of work did you say she did?"

"She's a mental health therapist."

"Ah, yes. That must be terribly demanding and terribly rewarding. I suspect she puts in a few late nights herself?"

"A few."

"All the more important, then, that you get home. Please say hello to—Sarah, wasn't it?" Mark nodded, impressed that Beiderbeck had remembered her name. "Please say hello to Sarah for me."

"I certainly will," Mark said. "You know, I'm awfully glad you asked me to put in a bid." He stood up, allowing Beiderbeck to usher him out of the office. He remembered a question he'd been wanting to ask for some time but had never had the right opportunity. "Tell me something. Exactly how did you get my name, anyway?"

"I think one of my salesmen mentioned you to me, if I remember correctly."

"I'm glad he did," Mark said.

Mark left the office. Beiderbeck held open the outside door for him and both men said good night. Walking to his car, Mark balanced the big tool case and other paraphernalia with one hand while searching his pants pockets for the car keys with the other.

He put the equipment in the car, climbed into the driver's seat, and coaxed the old Volvo into starting. As he pulled away from the curb, he thought about

Beiderbeck's comments on his referral. *That's odd,* he thought. *I'm sure I don't know any of John's employees.*

Sarah looked up from her notes and glanced at her watch. *Oh, no,* she thought. *It's six o'clock.* She reached for the phone, impatiently dialing her home number. Mark picked up on the third ring.

"Hello?"

"Hello, Mark. How are you?"

"Fine. Where are you?"

"I'm still at work, and I have some more stuff to do. I'm sorry, but the time just got away from me. Can you put up with me being late?"

"Sure. I was just getting ready to start dinner. You want me to fix a plate to warm up later?"

"That would be great. But only if it's no trouble."

"No trouble."

"I miss you."

"Miss you, too. Hurry home when you can."

"I will. I love you."

"Love you. Bye."

Mark Johnson placed the phone in its cradle on the kitchen wall. He looked at the nearly empty drink in his hand, then looked at the steaks he'd put on the counter for dinner. He picked up the steaks and put them back in the refrigerator. He contemplated his empty drink for a moment, then reached toward the cupboard where the liquor was kept.

"To hell with it," he muttered, pouring a double shot of bourbon.

Week 4: Sunday, August 20

Diana lay down for a quick nap after finishing an early lunch. She had felt so tired, even after a good nine hours sleep the night before. But lately, that was just how she felt much of the time. Tired. Like moving through Jell-O. Almost too tired and worn out to realize how *different* she felt these past six months. *Eventually, you adjust to most anything. Is this what depression is?* she wondered. *I just want to sleep. I don't want to think about it anymore. Just let me sleep and everything will be fine.*

She opened her eyes at one-fifteen, the backfire from a passing automobile having brought her instantly out of a deep sleep. At first she stared, unseeing, at the ceiling. Her eyes were blank, glacial blue. She blinked and some spark, intangible but clearly present, seemed to reinhabit her eyes. She sat up quickly.

"Goddamn it," she hissed, glancing at the clock in the kitchen. "She takes all the fucking time for herself. Let's see what the hell kind of cleaning up I need to do this time."

The woman walked through the apartment, inspecting each room casually. She nodded in satisfaction. Finally, she walked into the bathroom and looked at herself in the medicine cabinet mirror.

"Fuck," she said. She ran thick strands of her ash-blond hair through her fingers, pulling them this way and that, carefully regarding her image in the mirror. She paid particular attention to the quarter inch of brown that had grown out at the scalp. After inspecting herself for several minutes, she picked up a brush and savagely brushed her hair straight back from her forehead.

She opened one of the drawers set into the sink cabinet. Quickly and deftly, she applied a variety of makeup. She had to search for a moment to locate some mascara and eye shadow at the back of the drawer. She applied these in heavy amounts. When she had finished her makeup, she quickly swept all the cosmetics off the counter and into the drawer, which she shoved closed.

Opening the medicine cabinet, she rummaged for a moment, locating a plastic bottle. She opened it, struggling for a moment with the childproof cap, and extracted two small, yellow pills. She washed them down with a sip of water. She glanced at the label on the bottle: "Diazepam 5 mg. Take one tablet twice a day. Linda Janus."

In the living room, she removed her wallet from her purse, looking for money. She thumbed through the thin sheaf of bills, then put the wallet back in the pocketbook and placed the strap over her shoulder. Snatching up a set of keys, she rushed out of the apartment, slamming the door behind her.

She took a cab to a downtown shopping area, instructing the driver to drop her at a drugstore. She hesitated at the store's entrance, noticing for the first time the establishment next door, a small restaurant/bar combination advertising itself with dusty neon as The Seed Pearl. She headed for the restaurant.

Inside, The Seed Pearl was cool and dark. Ten or twelve tables filled a small front room, empty except for a middle-aged man working a crossword puzzle. He glanced up, regarded the woman without interest, and went back to his puzzle. Diana walked across the dining room and through the swinging doors set at the far end of the restaurant.

Four or five people hunched near their drinks at the bar. A few more drinkers sat at tables. The room was dark. Indirect light from behind the bar filtered through bottles of liquor.

The bartender was a large man, dressed in a white T-shirt and a food-stained apron.

"What'll it be?" he asked.

"Manhattan, rocks, please." Diana extracted a five-dollar bill from her purse and laid it on the bar.

The bartender mixed her drink expertly. He set the small glass on a cocktail napkin, took the bill, and rang up change. Diana let the change sit where the bartender placed it. She removed the plastic skewer holding two maraschino cherries, letting the cherries fall back in the drink, then lifted the glass and drained a quarter of it.

For the next ten minutes, Diana sipped her drink. She ignored the efforts of the bartender to engage her in conversation, until he finally wandered to the other end of the bar where several drinkers were discussing baseball. She had just about finished her drink when two men entered from a side door. One of them carried a pool cue, which he leaned against the wall. He walked toward the rest rooms at the back of the bar.

The second man was tall and thin. He had several day's growth of grizzled beard, and his hair was uncombed and dirty. He wore a T-shirt and a pair of dirty khaki work pants.

"Well, well," said the ugly man, looking at Diana. "What have we got here?"

Diana looked up from her drink, turning on the bar stool. She stared directly into the man's eyes.

"Fuck you," she said, turning back to the bar.

The man walked up behind her.

"What did you say?" he asked.

Diana was silent. She picked up her drink, sipped slowly from it, set it back down.

"Hey, lady," the man said, putting his hand on Diana's shoulder.

The instant the man's hand touched her, Diana rotated the bar seat to face him. In a smooth motion, she slid off the stool and raised her knee into the man's crotch. The man's eyes went wide.

"Don't fuck with me, scuzzball," she said.

Diana stepped aside as the man crumpled over the stool she had just vacated. She grabbed her drink, drained it, and then calmly picked up her purse and walked to the swinging doors.

"Keep the change," she said to the bartender. Behind her, she could hear the ugly man moaning softly.

For the first time since she had awakened that afternoon, Diana smiled broadly. She stepped out of the bar, into the bright sunlight, and entered the drugstore next door. She quickly located the items she needed and paid for them. When she hailed a taxi to take her home, she was still smiling.

Back in her apartment, Diana took off all her clothes and went into the bathroom. She brushed her hair, then combed it and divided it into four sections, pulling up each with a plastic hair clip. She laid out her purchases from the drugstore on the counter of the sink, then removed the contents from a box with a picture of a smiling blonde on the front. She poured the contents of several packages into a bottle with a funnel-shaped top. The kit's instructions lay unopened on the sink. After she had slipped her hands into a pair of plastic gloves, she raised the bottle to the brown roots at the crown of her head and began to squeeze the thick blue mixture onto her hair.

When she finished the application, Diana put a stopper in the bathtub and turned on the water. Being careful to move her head as little as possible, she walked to the kitchen and fixed a drink of vodka and ginger ale. Returning to the bathroom, she eased herself into the steaming tub.

She had not intended to fall asleep. An hour after entering the tub, the alarm clock rang. Diana sat up, startled. She looked wildly around the bathroom, noting with dismay the unfamiliar paraphernalia spread out on the counter of the sink. In a panic, she stood up in the tub, nearly slipping as she reached for a towel. She quickly wrapped it around her and stepped from the tub onto the cold tile floor. She stood in front of the mirror, now covered in steam. Grabbing a hand towel, she wiped a swath of steam from the mirror. She leaned forward in wonder, staring at the blue gel in her multi-parted hair.

"What in the name of God have I done?" she barely whispered.

"Diana . . . Diana," she said.

"Who is that?" she asked.

"It's me, Diana. Your friend and bosom buddy. Remember, baby?" she said.

"No . . . I don't know. What's happening?"

"Nothing. Just relax. It's time for you to go to sleep now. You're just dreaming, baby, and woke up too soon. You're just dreaming. Go to sleep."

Her eyes unfocused. A hard glint returned to them a moment later. The woman smiled at her reflection.

"I swear to God she doesn't have the slightest fucking idea," she said, and picked up the now-watery drink from the edge of the bathtub. She drained it, pulled the stopper from the tub, then examined her hair in the mirror. The color at the scalp was a pale lemon-yellow.

"Shit, I've let it go too long," she said, then shrugged. "Oh, well, it'll be all right."

Before the tub had finished draining, she turned on the shower, then stepped in and rinsed her hair. When she finished, she towel-dried quickly, wrapped another towel around her head, then grabbed her empty glass and padded out to the kitchen. She fixed another drink, a double this time.

Later, after she had finished the drink, she went back into the bathroom and applied the contents of another carton to her hair. After half an hour, she rinsed again. She towel-dried her hair and left the bathroom without checking herself in the mirror.

Several hours later, when her hair had fully dried, she returned to the bathroom, more to relieve herself of the many vodkas she had consumed than anything else. She looked at herself in the mirror and picked up a brush. She began untangling the knotted hair, carefully evaluating the results of her work. She nodded in satisfaction.

"Unbelievable," she murmured at her reflection. "Can't even do her own goddamn hair."

* * *

At three in the morning, Diana got out of bed to go to the bathroom. Her head hurt; she felt as if she had a hangover. *I wonder if I'm coming down with a bug,* she thought. Diana glanced at the nearly full trash can next to the sink and noticed a bottle labeled "Ultra-Blond Lotion Lightener" and a box adorned with a picture of a pretty pale-haired model. She read the label—"Perfect Blondings Light Ash-Blond Toner"—but it made no sense to her. Her scalp felt a little tingly, but she saw nothing unusual. She went back to bed.

Week 4: Monday, August 21

"Damn," Sarah cursed as she banged her shin. Mark had left the kitchen light on, but she was trying to make it to the bedroom with as little disturbance as possible and so had not turned on the hall light. Surely, Mark would be asleep by now.

She saw that the bedroom light was on, and she breathed a little easier. Mark must be reading. She hated coming home this late. Family life was very important to her, and lately it seemed that there were just too many opportunities at work that she couldn't afford to miss. Tonight, for example, was the only chance she'd had to meet with the accountant who moonlighted for her on a part-time basis. They had spent four hours going over the books and discussing business plans. And then Sarah had stayed even later, thinking about her cases. Sarah regretted the time she lost away from home. *The price of success,* she thought and sighed.

Entering the bedroom, she saw that Mark had fallen asleep while reading. *Damn, now I'll wake him for sure.* She gently walked back out of the bedroom, found her way to the bathroom by trailing one hand along the wall, and turned on the light. She brushed her teeth and washed her face. Turning off the light, she navigated her way back to the bedroom.

Sarah quickly undressed. She eased the bedcovers down and slipped into bed. Gently, she pulled the magazine Mark had been reading out of his hands. She closed it and set it on the nightstand, noticing that it was a magazine about computers. *How can anyone enjoy reading about computers?* she wondered briefly. She leaned over her husband's sleeping body and switched off the lamp. As she eased herself back onto her side of the bed, she kissed Mark softly on the lips.

"I love you," she whispered.

"Cable cutter," her husband muttered, and almost immediately started snoring.

Sarah lay in the dark, wide awake. Her thoughts seemed to have a life of their own. They kept circling back to her most recent client.

Diana Smith was a very puzzling case. Certainly, depression was the key feature, but Sarah remained convinced that there was more, much more, if only she could break through to her. The list of anomalies in the case seemed to grow with each session. Sarah ticked them off like a laundry list. An aversion to drugs that seemed less than rational. Obsessive ideation concerning burial. Feelings of detachment. Gaps in memory.

Memory, Sarah thought, *now that's really strange. Diana doesn't remember anything until the age of five or six, and after that everything sounds just too perfect, too good to be true. And when she was giving me the family history, it was almost as if she were picking up cues from me: was your father a businessman? Yes, my father was a businessman. Did he travel a lot? Yes, he traveled a lot.*

Something she'd not considered before occurred to Sarah. Post-traumatic stress disorder could account for most, if not all, of Diana's symptoms. Post-traumatic stress disorder was not a popular diagnosis among mental health professionals. It seemed too new, in spite of all the work done with veterans in the aftermath of the war in Vietnam. Somehow, it was still regarded as trendy and exotic and therefore suspect. But Sarah knew that depression was a common feature of the disorder, and that it sometimes caused intrusive and uncontrollable thoughts and images. *Like being buried,* she thought. Recurrent thoughts sometimes plagued the victim; sometimes there were incredibly powerful memories of the stressing event and sometimes the memories were hidden behind symbolic or obscuring images. *Like being buried?*

Sarah thought about Diana's aversion to drugs and remembered that victims tend to avoid or have odd reactions to things associated with the stressing event. She thought about Diana's odd memory lapses. Post-traumatic stress disorder could cause amnesia.

Post-traumatic stress disorder. Maybe. Just maybe. But if so, why the images of being buried? Was there a traumatic death? Or maybe she was sick a lot and thought about death and dying. Then Sarah remembered one more thing about the disorder: It occurred most commonly when the victim had no control over the stressing event, especially when the event was inflicted rather than accidental. Man's inhumanity to man.

Maybe she had been abused. How many of her cases came down to that? She could envision no more heinous crime than child abuse, because it represented the irretrievable betrayal of innocence. Sarah shivered. She knew more about child abuse that she had ever hoped to have to learn. The human capacity to invoke misery seemed sometimes endless.

Eventually, her thoughts slowed, spinning round in ever-narrowing circles like tiring birds, and Sarah dropped off to a sleep filled with dreams she could not remember the next morning.

Chapter 6

Week 4: Tuesday, August 22

"And so how was your weekend?" Sarah asked.

Her client appeared bright and cheerful and well-dressed. *Quite a contrast to the last session,* thought Sarah. She noticed that Diana had touched up the roots of her lightened hair in the last week and that her makeup was modestly and expertly applied. *Inattention to appearance is sometimes a feature of depression,* Sarah thought. *Doesn't seem to apply here. Although, last week she looked pretty rough. Somehow, I think that was unusual; I'll bet Diana is pretty compulsive about her appearance. So is it depression? Post-traumatic stress disorder? Something else?*

Post-traumatic stress disorder is the best operating theory I've got, she thought. *It's exotic and therefore implausible, but it's the best I've got. So where do I go from here?*

"My weekend was fine," said Diana. She seemed more upbeat and positive than Sarah had yet seen her.

"Good. Did you do anything? What did you do Sunday?"

"Sunday I really didn't do anything. I just slept mostly."

"Are you still sleeping a lot?"

"I don't know. I guess so."

"How much did you sleep Sunday?"

"Let me think. I got up around ten and fixed breakfast. After I took a shower, I read the paper till around noon, I guess. I got sleepy and lay down on the couch. I guess I slept the rest of the day."

"Did you get up to go to bed later?"

"I must have, because I woke up in bed."

"But you don't remember getting up and going to bed?" Sarah asked.

Diana looked at Sarah, averted her eyes, then looked back. "No, I don't. I guess that's a lot of sleeping, isn't it?"

To say the least, thought Sarah. "That's not uncommon with depression, Diana."

Sarah had decided to continue treating depression as the basis for the clinical work with Diana. Her rationale was that regardless of the eventual diagnosis, depression was the significant feature of her client's presenting behaviors and therefore the symptomatic basis for treatment. *Until I figure out what else is going on,* she thought.

"Do you remember any dreams?"

"Not really. I vaguely remember a dream in which I was taking a bath, but that's all that I remember."

"What did you do on Saturday?"

Diana answered without hesitation. "I spent most of the day in the darkroom and organizing negatives. Saturday night I went to see a movie."

"That reminds me. You're going to bring in some of your photographs one of these days, right?"

"Right. I'd forgotten about that," Diana smiled.

"Well, I'm looking forward to it. Anyway, it sounds like Saturday was a pretty active day. You didn't feel like taking a nap?"

"No. Saturday was very busy. It was a good day."

"Good. Tell me, what day did you do your hair?" Sarah decided to pursue an instinct. "It looks so nice. Or maybe you have it done? When was that?"

Diana looked at Sarah with an expression of frank

bewilderment. "I haven't had my hair done. I just curl it every morning."

Sarah started to say, *I meant, when did you have the color done?* but stopped herself. She scribbled something on a message pad and tore off the sheet. "Will you excuse me for a second? I want to make sure that Margie runs an errand for me. I hate to interrupt."

Sarah left the office, closing the door behind her. When she returned, she seated herself and smiled at Diana.

"Let's see," Sarah said. "If you don't mind, I'd like to talk a little more about your childhood. You had some interesting memories last session."

"Okay."

"We talked before about your earliest memory. What other early memories can you recall? They don't have to be anything important. Anything at all that you can remember."

Diana paused to light a cigarette. "I have such a problem sometimes remembering things. Oh, I know. This isn't exactly a memory. Well, it is a memory, but it's like a memory of a dream, I think. When I was a little kid. Is that all right?"

"Yes, that sounds fine."

"It's kind of strange. It's a memory of a dream, only it doesn't seem like a dream. It seems very real, only it can't be real. I'm asleep in my dream. Then, all of a sudden, I feel like I'm floating. It's a wonderful feeling. I'm just floating in the dark. I'm light as a feather. But then I look down and I see myself. At first, this scares me, but a voice says, 'Relax, everything is fine.' "

"Excuse me," Sarah interrupted. "What can you tell me about the voice? Do you recognize it? Is it a man or a woman's voice?"

Diana thought for a moment. "It's a man's voice, definitely," she said. "It sounds familiar, but I don't know whose voice it is, if that makes sense."

Diana inhaled deeply on her cigarette and continued. "The voice tells me to relax, and everything seems better. I keep on floating. The next thing I know, I'm way up above our house. I look down, and I can see our house and the neighborhood. And everything is in such detail, it's beautiful. The moon is out, almost full, and the stars are shining. And I have this wonderful feeling, this sensation of flying or floating. And I keep on rising and rising, until finally I can't see anything. Everything is darkness, above me and below me and all around. I start to get scared, but I hear the voice again and it says, 'Look for them, look for them.' So I look around, but I don't really know what I'm looking for. Then I start to see what look like shapes in the darkness. Like shadows, shadows of people. The shadows start coming closer. The shadows are darker than the darkness, and I can make out the shapes of arms and hands. Then that's all I can see, arms and hands everywhere, and they're reaching out for me. I get real scared. Then the hands are about to get me, hands everywhere, and right before they grab me, I wake up."

"You wake up? Where are you when you wake up? You wake up in the dream or you really wake up?"

"What? Oh, I don't know. I mean, I guess I wake up. That's all I remember. The hands are about to reach me, and that's it."

Sarah tapped her pen against the desktop. "What does the dream mean to you?"

"I'm not sure. It does make me feel good, though. I mean, even with these hands reaching out to grab me, which is terrifying, the dream feels good. I think it's the flying part. It's such a wonderful feeling. Did you ever have any flying dreams?"

"Yes, I have, as a matter of fact," Sarah smiled. "Not for a very long time, though. How about you? Do you remember other dreams about flying?"

"Not specifically, but I know I've dreamed about

flying many times before. Like with you, though, not for a long time."

"Okay. In this dream, when you look down at your body, what do you see? Are you sitting up or lying down? Are you asleep or awake? Are you alone?"

Diana paused for several seconds. "All right, I can picture it very clearly. . . ." She closed her eyes, a frown of concentration on her forehead. "I'm lying down asleep. But I'm not alone. I never thought about that before, but I'm not alone. Someone is sitting on the bed next to me." She opened her eyes. "I never thought about that, but it makes sense, doesn't it? That's where the voice is coming from."

"Is this a man or a woman? Can you make out any features?"

"A man, I think." Diana took a drag on her cigarette. "Yes, a man, I'm sure of it. But I can't really see anything. I'm too high and it's too dark. And the man is dressed in dark clothing. And that's really all I can remember." Diana shrugged apologetically.

"That's fine," Sarah smiled. Abruptly, she changed topics. "Diana, do you ever remember being sick or hurt? Maybe going to the hospital?"

"No."

Sarah thought perhaps she replied too quickly; had she really considered the question?

"I don't get sick," she continued, "I know that sounds conceited, but really I don't. At least, not until this . . . uh . . . problem."

"I guess you haven't had much contact with doctors, then. Any memories of doctors?"

"No. Why? Should I remember something?"

"No, of course not. I'm just curious, really. To be honest, I've been wondering why you were so insistent when you first came about not taking drugs." Sarah paused, letting the implied question sink in.

"Oh, well, that's very simple, really," Diana said. "I just haven't been sick much, and so I don't believe in taking medicines. We don't need them, see. I just really don't like them. I don't even take aspirin."

"You said *we,* Diana. Who's *we?*"

"I just meant anybody, really. We . . . people in general, you know."

"Diana, will you tell me something else?" Sarah asked. "How do you think we're doing in therapy? This is our fourth session, I think. Five, really, if you count the day that we met. Are you pleased with what we're doing?"

"Oh, Sarah, I really am."

Sarah was surprised by the enthusiasm in Diana's voice.

"I hope *you* think everything is going all right," Diana added, suddenly sounding uncertain.

She worries so much about what I think, thought Sarah. *So afraid of rejection. Why?*

"I think everything is going fine, Diana. It is you who are coming to me, however, you who are spending your hard-earned money to be here. It's most important you feel that you are getting what you want out of therapy. What is it you want, Diana?" *There, I've said it,* thought Sarah. *How will she answer?*

"What do I want out of therapy?"

"Sure. You're the one who decides whether it's worth coming back week after week."

"I guess what I want is to feel well again. I'm tired of being tired all the time. I'm tired of feeling like everything's so hopeless, you know? I'm tired of feeling so disoriented."

"Disoriented?" Sarah did not recall hearing this complaint before.

Diana nodded. "Yes. Sometimes I feel like I just woke up and I don't know where I am. Like I can't remember what I was doing. Sometimes it's like I'm looking down a long, dark tunnel and I can barely see the light at the other end."

"You haven't told me this before, Diana. At least, not in quite this way."

"Haven't I?" Diana frowned. "Maybe you're right. I have a really hard time talking about some of this. I guess I'm not used to talking about myself. There are things I want to say sometimes, but I just can't bring myself to say them. I think that they are important at the moment, but then I just sort of forget about them and tell myself they really aren't important."

"Diana, I want you to feel like you can say anything here. Try to just say anything that comes to mind and don't worry about whether it's important or not. If it's not important, we'll figure that out soon enough, won't we?"

"Yes, I suppose so. Sarah, thank you. I really do feel like I can talk about things with you. See, in my family, we were taught not to say things to outsiders. We were also taught not to talk unless we had something important to say. We didn't talk about feelings much."

Sarah was suddenly alert to the reference to family life. "Who said not to say anything to outsiders?"

"Oh, everybody, I guess."

"Everybody? You mean both your parents?"

"I mean all of my parents."

"I'm afraid I don't understand. How many parents do you have?"

"I had a lot of parents, I guess. By parents, I mean all the aunts and uncles and everybody that took care of me at different times."

"I see. So your real parents were gone a lot?"

"Yes, my real parents were gone a lot," Diana said in a monotone.

"What do you remember about your aunts and uncles?"

"Not a lot, really. There were so many. They just took care of us."

"Us?"

"Yeah, me and the other kids."

"I thought you didn't have any brothers or sisters."

"I don't."

"Well, where did the other kids come from?"

"Huh? Oh, I don't know. Neighborhood kids, I guess. My aunts' and uncles' kids. We spent a lot of time together."

"Oh, I see." *I don't see a thing,* Sarah thought.

"Yes. But I'm sorry. I've gotten sidetracked. I was telling you about what I want to get out of therapy."

"That's right," Sarah said, jotting down a note to come back to this topic of aunts and uncles and kids. "You were saying that it's hard for you to talk about certain things."

"Yes. But I'm beginning to feel like I can talk to you."

"That's wonderful." Sarah paused, taking a breath. "Diana, before you go, I'd like to ask you something."

"Sure."

"Do you ever have any gaps in your memory? Blackouts or blank spells. Have you ever come to someplace without knowing how you got there?"

Diana Smith frowned. "I do have a problem sometimes with remembering. Like I was telling you. Sometimes I forget what I was doing."

"When was the last time you forgot?" Sarah asked, trying to probe gently.

"I'm not sure." Diana frowned, and Sarah watched sudden tears well up in the woman's eyes. "I may have forgotten part of this weekend. When I told you about Sunday? But I guess not, because I was sleeping. That's right. I was just sleeping Sunday."

"What's the longest period of time that you have trouble remembering?"

Diana stared blankly at the cigarette between her fingers, then brushed at her eyes with the back of one hand.

"Two years," she said.

Margie Powers watched as Diana Smith walked out of Sarah's office. She noticed the smeared makeup and the Kleenex knotted in Diana's hand. Sarah closed the door after the woman left. *Okay, boss, whatever it is, I'll play along,* Margie thought.

"Hi there," Margie said cheerfully. "Have a seat while I check the appointment book." Diana seated herself and smiled at Margie.

"Let's see," Margie said. "Here we are. Same time next week, okay? I assume there's no change?"

"Yes, that's fine."

"I hope you won't be embarrassed, but can I ask you something?" Margie questioned.

"Of course."

"Well, it's just that I've been thinking of changing my hair and I just love your color. Could you tell me what you use on it or where you have it done? I think it's just beautiful." As she delivered her speech, Margie ran her hands through her own hair. "I hope you don't mind me asking."

"I don't mind you asking," said Diana with just the trace of a smile playing about her lips, "but this is my natural color."

Margie suppressed a desire to say *bullshit.*

The other woman continued, "You really have very pretty hair. I wouldn't change it if I were you. I really don't believe in artificial colors. They just don't look natural."

Unable to resist, Margie smiled, "Oh, it's really no big deal. See, this isn't my natural color, anyway." And then she added, "But thank you for letting me ask. You're very lucky. You have gorgeous hair. And, I guess we'll see you next week."

"Yes, I'll see you next week."

Margie knocked lightly and stepped into Sarah's office. "So, I don't really have to change my hair to blond, do I?"

Sarah laughed. "No, I don't think that will be necessary."

"Good. We can carry this company loyalty stuff too far, you know."

"She denied that she colors her hair, right?"

"Right. Which is a bunch of crap."

"Did you have the feeling that she was deliberately lying?"

Margie thought for a moment. "That was weird, all right," she said. "No, I didn't. I mean, she acted like she really believed it. I was almost convinced. What gives?"

"I'm not quite sure myself," Sarah said, "but I'm starting to have some strong suspicions."

Chapter 7

Week 4: Wednesday, August 23

Diana Smith felt well. The sultry August humidity had evaporated overnight. Today, at least, the weather felt like late September and approaching autumn: The sky was painfully blue; the leaves on the trees green and clean; the air crisp and cool. Diana opened all the windows in her apartment. Finishing her second cup of coffee, she tied her hair back with a covered rubber band. The cabinet under Diana's kitchen sink was a virtual supermarket aisle's worth of cleaning preparations. She loaded a number of these, along with rags, cloths, and sponges, in a plastic tray. Then she set about cleaning the apartment.

Diana turned on the big boom box she kept in the living room. It was set to a local FM station, one specializing in classic rock 'n' roll. She was not really familiar with the music. Still, she enjoyed the lively beat of many of the tunes. It was a distraction, something different, something *not her*. It was nice to be distracted. The DJ's voice faded out to the opening beat of an oldie "sent out on the request line." The song made her feel good; it matched her mood. Diana turned up the volume and went back to her cleaning.

She was nearly through vacuuming when she thought she heard the sound of her doorbell. She switched off the old Hoover and walked toward the door. The radio was playing the final notes of a late-fifties love ballad.

She opened the door, peering through the crack afforded by the length of chain on the safety catch. A young man, perhaps in his late twenties, stood in the hallway, smiling.

"Say, baby, what's up?" he asked.

"May I help you?" Diana stammered, confused by the stranger's familiarity.

"Uh-huh. Look at this."

The man brought his right hand up to the door. Something was apparently concealed there, and as the hand rose, he slowly opened it. Seeing the man's palm, Diana's quizzical expression changed to indifference. Or perhaps blankness would be more accurate. For just a moment, her eyes lost their focus. The fine wrinkles in her forehead smoothed out; her mouth became slack. Then she was reaching for the door latch.

The Doors' "Light My Fire" was blaring from the boom box as the man stepped into the apartment. He grinned at Diana.

" 'You know that I would be untrue,' " he sang, " 'you know that I would be a liar.' "

The man continued walking forward as Diana stepped backward, a pace ahead.

" 'If I was to say to you,' " he continued, " 'girl, we couldn't get no higher . . .' "

Sarah sat at her desk, Diana Smith's folder spread out before her. She tapped a pencil distractedly against the edge of the desk. She felt as if all the pieces of a puzzle were arrayed before her, but she had no idea how to go about solving it.

Help, Sarah said to herself. *I need help.*

What have I got? she asked herself. *I've got an attractive young woman with symptoms of a depressive episode. She has an aversion to drugs and is afraid of intimacy. She denies that she colors her hair, and a significant childhood memory is of an apparently dissociative experience of some kind. Recurrent images of burial and possibly of hands. Large gaps in memory. Large gaps in childhood memory, that is, and possibly current memory lapses.*

The premise of post-traumatic stress disorder had released something within her. Once she had conceded *that* possibility, others had occurred to her, possibilities that were no more comfortable than post-traumatic stress, but no less plausible, either. Especially since the last session.

Sarah got up from her desk and walked over to the shelves that filled one wall of her office. She pulled down a large hardcover volume. It was Strauderman's classic *Strategies of Dissociation. Required reading in some graduate course,* she thought. *I knew all these books would come in handy someday.*

Sarah read for the next half hour, glancing occasionally at her watch so as not to be unprepared for her eleven o'clock. At ten forty-five, Margie buzzed on the intercom.

"Yes?" said Sarah.

"Phone call. It's a woman. She wouldn't give her name, but she said she had to talk to you."

Who? Sarah thought for a moment. Then she said, "Okay, I'll take it." She picked up the phone. "Sarah Johnson. May I help you?"

"Dr. Johnson?" a woman's voice asked. "I'm a friend of Diana Smith. She needs your help."

For a moment, Sarah had the eerie impression that she recognized the slightly husky voice. "Who is this?"

"Look, it doesn't matter who I am. Diana is trying to kill herself. You've got to help."

"What makes you think she's trying to kill herself?" Sarah frowned. *Something's wrong here,* she thought. *Who is this?*

"I can't call anybody. Really, I can't. You've *got* to help. Please, for God's sake." The woman sounded very upset now.

"All right. Tell me where you are. Where's Diana?"

"Diana is at home. That's all I can say. I've got to go now. Please help."

"Wait, please. Are you with her? Can you . . ." The phone connection broke off. "Damn," said Sarah. Hesitating for an instant only, she buzzed Margie. "Get in here, quick."

As Margie walked through the door, Sarah tossed her the folder on Diana Smith. Sarah was simultaneously dialing the telephone. "Find the street address and phone number," she said.

"Nine-one-one?" Margie asked.

Sarah nodded. She opened a desk drawer, removed a phone book, and handed it to Margie. "Find the apartment manager or rental office number."

Sarah reported a probable suicide attempt at Diana's address. Immediately, she dialed again. Reaching the management office, she asked to have someone check the apartment, informing the bewildered assistant manager that an ambulance would be arriving in several minutes. Next, she dialed Diana's number. She counted twenty rings before she broke the connection.

"Cancel my eleven," Sarah said to Margie, standing up. "I'll call from her apartment if I can. Thanks."

Then she was gone, leaving Margie with a client folder in one hand and a phone book in the other.

PART II

MEMORIES

Jimmy Jameson was almost shaking with excitement when he reached his destination with the two older men. He felt suddenly older, matured, as if he had at last entered an adult world of secrets and power. Even the two men deferred to him, holding open the door of the Town Car, ushering him by smiles and openhanded gestures down the tree-lined walk.

Jimmy Jameson felt chosen. He had *been chosen, he told himself.*

That he was unique was something he had never doubted. He had always been different, wanting to read a book while his friends played baseball. Choosing the conversations of adults to the pastimes of children. Excelling at the things of the intellect.

And it had been that way on into high school, except that in high school the small-mindedness, the sheer idiocy of his teachers and his classmates had become so clear it was almost painful. Jimmy had stopped excelling. What was the point of succeeding in a boring world where politicians lied, and parents lived frustrated, whining lives, and teachers didn't teach but sought to fill tiny brains with rehashed Sunday school pap?

When Jimmy stopped excelling, the gap between him and his peers widened. Though he had always felt isolated, he had come to enjoy the pedestal of differentness on which the other kids placed him. He hadn't minded so much being called nerd, as long as he was the *nerd.*

Regardless of his withdrawal, Jimmy's intellectual curiosity had never stopped, and he soon found himself increasingly inter-

ested in odd things like psychic phenomena, the supernatural, and the occult. He read everything he could get his hands on, from books with titles like Making ESP Work For You *to the* Tibetan Book of the Dead. *He carried them with him like talismans, open challenges to the narrow intellects of his teachers and his peers. Except that he discovered a very curious underground. Kids who had had no interest in him before and who he, in fact, would have been afraid to approach were suddenly talking to him. Kids who wore leather and long hair were asking him about the books he carried. What did he know about witchcraft, demonology? Did he listen to the music of Black Death? What did he think of the lyrics to "Strangled Goat"?*

Jimmy immersed himself in the new culture, listening to the new music, adopting the new look. He thought he detected a new look of fear in the guarded glances of his teachers, and he liked that. And among his new friends, he found himself able to assert his superior intellect again, but this time to influence, to organize. The lyrics of Black Death and most of the other heavy metal groups were stupid, half-realized occult doggerel, mere empty theatrics. But the writings of Aleister Crowley and Anton LaVey held the promise of real *power. Soon, he and his friends were reciting the Lord's Prayer backward in rural midnight cemeteries and sacrificing cats to passages from LaVey's* Satanic Bible. *And the power seemed real, because he was admired and respected and perhaps even feared by these tough, tattooed friends.*

But there was more. There had to be. Sources from which real power flowed. Jimmy knew that just as there had been an underground of his peers ready to believe in him, there must be a larger underground of the initiated, the possessors of real knowledge. He was sustained by the mystical adage: When the pupil is ready, the teacher will come.

Jimmy followed all leads in search of his teacher. As his midnight exploits became more practiced and more daring, he sometimes noticed strangers on the periphery of his magic circles. These were adults, and they looked at him at first with what Jimmy imagined to be contempt. But their contempt had seemed to give way to curiosity and, finally, Jimmy thought, open admiration.

For following the previous week's ceremony, one of these unsmiling men had approached him and he had been invited.

Invited. They had never said to where. Or to what. Merely, "You are invited." Say nothing, they had told him, tell no one, and we will come for you. And they had. Jimmy had crawled into the cream-colored Town Car with the tinted windows and leather upholstery with a sense of destiny being fulfilled. He had arrived.

They had driven for a long time out to the country. They had parked in a driveway that seemed to lead nowhere. And now they were walking down a path to a destination unknown. The darkness of the night was absolute. Jimmy's boots slapped against the brick or stone-lined walkway and the full-leafed branches of trees arched overhead.

A wall of mortared stone loomed abruptly out of the night, and before Jimmy could take in any detail, a door was opened and he was ushered into darkness down a short flight of stone steps. It was like entering a root cellar. The air was damp and cool, and it smelled of raw earth. Jimmy was prevented from stumbling by the sure grip of the man behind him. A door opened ahead of him and they stepped through into a small, brightly lit room. All the walls were made of stone, and dark, rough-hewn timbers formed the ceiling joists. Jimmy imagined that he was in the anteroom of some ancient castle, except that there were no castles in Virginia. The room was like a dressing room; dozens of garments, both men's and women's clothes, hung from pegs fixed to the walls.

On a bench against one wall sat a man dressed in a chamois shirt and jeans. He smiled at Jimmy as if greeting an old friend. The man was old, Jimmy thought, maybe fifty or sixty, but he looked in good shape, with his full head of silver hair and his well-muscled arms. To Jimmy, the man's intelligence was obvious; he could see it in the shrewd set of his eyes and his knowing smile.

The man waved a hand and Jimmy's companions disappeared behind another door. As the door closed, Jimmy caught a scent like candle wax and burning leaves.

"Come," the man said.

Jimmy walked to him. He was excited but unafraid. He had been invited. This was an initiation, the thing he had sought for so long. Surely the man before him was to be his benefactor.

"It is time we met," the man said.

Jimmy nodded, a little flustered. After all this time, how absurd that he should be shy. "Y—yes," Jimmy managed to stammer.

"Relax," the man said. He began to unbutton his shirt.

Jimmy felt a brief flicker of uncertainty. This wasn't going to turn into some kind of weird sex thing, was it?

The man seemed to sense his concern. "I'm just putting on my robe," he said.

Of course, *thought Jimmy. On the bench next to the man was a folded pile of black cloth.*

"We've watched you for some time," the man continued. "We had to make sure that you were of a like mind before we could ask you to join us."

"Of course," Jimmy agreed, his voice stronger now. Yes! *he thought excitedly.* I knew it.

"We only invite those with exceptional talent." The man pulled off his shirt. The muscles of his chest were well-defined. "And we had to make sure you were ready."

Jimmy felt magic in the air. All his work, all his striving, had been vindicated. He searched for something suitable to say.

"When the pupil is ready . . ." he began.

". . . the teacher will come," the man finished.

Jimmy was delighted. It was *as he had hoped. He had found his teacher. As if reading his thoughts, the man smiled at him, then stood up and walked over to a low table set against one wall. A silver goblet sat on the table, and the man picked it up and carried it to Jimmy. He held it out.*

"We have a short ceremony planned for this evening," he said. "I'd like you to drink this, to get ready."

For an absurd moment, Jimmy imagined that the goblet was filled with blood. He took it carefully and looked in. It was wine, red wine. Jimmy took a sip. He had drunk wine before, plenty of it. But this was not as sweet, and it left a bitter aftertaste.

While Jimmy drank, the man slipped off his jeans and underpants. He paused to watch Jimmy drink. Jimmy inwardly applauded the man's composure, his utter lack of concern at his nudity. As Jimmy finished the wine, the man picked up the folded robe from the bench and slipped it on.

"Hang your clothes there," the man said, pointing to an open hook on the wall. He picked up another robe from the bench, only this one was white. He tossed it to Jimmy. "This is yours."

Jimmy felt a sudden urge to laugh. The wine was affecting him quickly. It seemed to surge through his blood. It was as if he had taken a hit off a super-strong joint. Warmth spread through him, and as Jimmy slipped off his jeans, he realized he had gotten an erection. He looked in embarrassment at his benefactor, but the man seemed not to notice. Jimmy hurriedly slipped into the white robe.

Things rapidly became very disjointed for Jimmy. He felt hands grasp his arms, then realized he had been taken into another, much larger room. The light from a hundred candles formed star bursts in his vision, making it difficult to concentrate on all the other people in the room, all of them cloaked in robes.

I've got to find out what they put in the wine, *thought Jimmy.* It must be some powerful herb. Maybe a hallucinogen of some kind. *He'd thought about using acid in his own rituals but had always been afraid to try it.*

The hands were helping him onto a low platform, where the candlelight was now much brighter. Disjointedly, Jimmy saw an immense slab of stone. That's an awesome altar, *he thought. His arms were becoming very numb; he could barely feel the hands of the men supporting him.*

The altar was closer now, and then the perspective changed. Jimmy was looking at wooden beams, far, far away. He realized he was lying on the altar.

I'm going to be the living altar, *he realized.* But can they use me as the altar and initiate me at the same time? What kind of ritual is this?

Jimmy heard the voice of his benefactor. "We are here tonight to bring power to a brother in need."

A brother in need, *thought Jimmy.* Yes, that's me.

His benefactor spoke again, but the words were not English. The gathering chanted certain of the phrases that the man spoke. Their voices rang out against the stone walls, and to

Jimmy they seemed full of power and mystery. His mind drifted for a while under the influence of the drugged wine.

The next thing he knew, the voice of his benefactor was behind him. Jimmy forced his eyes open. Two hands held a chalice over his head. It was battered and dull, not at all like the goblet from which he had drunk.

Jimmy glanced down. At the far end of the altar, seeming miles away, as if he looked through the wrong end of a telescope, stood a middle-aged man. He was without a robe, perhaps nude, but Jimmy could not see below the level of the altar. His benefactor still recited in that strange-sounding language while the hidden multitude still chanted in the shadows.

Then the chanting became more insistent, and Jimmy felt himself rousing from the effects of the drug. The crowd is getting rowdy, *Jimmy thought inanely, and then glanced overhead at the gleaming silver dagger held aloft in his benefactor's hand.*

The chanting was deafening now, and Jimmy felt a rush of raw panic rip through him. He tried to sit up and was appalled to find himself unable to move. As if in slow motion, his eyes flicked back to the dagger and traced its downward course. It passed below his chin. Jimmy felt a sudden rush of warmth across his neck. His head was tilted back. The chanting had stopped. The realization of his situation was suddenly, irrevocably clear, and he felt another rush of warmth, this time across his thighs, as he lost control of his bladder.

Jimmy saw the chalice pass across his field of vision again as it was handed to the nude man at the foot of the altar. The man raised it to his lips and drank. A thin trickle of blood slipped from the corner of the man's mouth and traced a course down the side of his chin. Jimmy felt the blood escaping down his own neck, even as the first scarlet drop fell off the nude man's chin. It seemed to hang in space for a long time before it faded, like everything else, into darkness.

Chapter 8

Week 5: Tuesday, August 29

"Rest and relax, rest and relax," Sarah chanted softly in the subdued lighting. Diana Smith lay with eyes closed on the leather couch in Sarah's office.

"You are becoming more and more relaxed. Concentrate on your feet. Your feet are becoming very, very relaxed. All tension is evaporating. Your legs are relaxing . . ." Sarah continued the litany, tracing her way up the body, commanding Diana to absolute relaxation.

"You are now completely and totally relaxed," she said. Sarah checked to make sure the cassette recorder was operating properly. Diana had earlier agreed to allow Sarah to tape their sessions. She watched for the movement of the little tape reels, checking that the record button was depressed.

It was their first session since the suicide attempt, and Sarah had gotten Diana to agree to hypnosis without telling her client exactly what she was looking for. Sarah stared at the attractive, relaxed woman sitting across from her now and recalled with a shudder the woman she had found semiconscious on the bathroom floor that day. Sarah had arrived ahead of the ambulance, ignoring the panic of the apartment manager. Diana's pulse had still been strong, but the pill bottle on the floor was empty. Diana's face had been ashen and clammy, her hair stuck to her scalp in strings. Sarah had been trying to rouse her when the rescue squad arrived and took over. She'd followed them to the hospital. After they'd pumped Diana's stomach and put her to bed, Sarah had gone home, feeling weak and exhausted herself.

"The only sound you hear is my voice," Sarah continued. "Concentrate on my voice. I want you to clasp your hands together. Put your hands together."

Slowly, the woman complied.

"When I ask you to try to pull them apart, you will be unable to do so. Imagine that your hands are bound together by steel bands. You can feel the steel bands wrapping around your hands comfortably but snugly. You cannot move your hands apart. Now, try and separate your hands."

Diana's elbows raised, her hands coming slightly apart at the palms but joined fast at the fingers. Sarah allowed her to continue for several seconds.

"All right, relax, relax. You may now release your hands. The steel bands have vanished. Your hands are back to normal. That's good," she said as Diana lowered her hands back to the couch. "Can you hear me, Diana?"

"Yes," Diana replied, slowly and softly.

"Good. You are now very, very relaxed. We are going to go into a state of deeper and deeper relaxation. Listen to my voice. Concentrate only on my voice. As I count backward from five, your trance state will deepen." Sarah paused. "Five. You are becoming more and more relaxed. Four. Deeper, deeper. Three. Relax. Relax. Two. Rest and relax, rest and relax. One."

"You are now in a state of complete and total relaxation. Do you understand me, Diana?"

"Yes," came the response, almost whispered.

"Excellent," Sarah said softly. "Diana, we are going to go back in time. We are going to go back in time to your twenty-first birthday. Do you understand?''

"Yes."

"Good. When I count backward from five, we will go backward in time. You will become younger and younger. When I reach one, you will be twenty-one and it will be your birthday." Sarah paused and took a deep breath, as if preparing to take some literal plunge herself. "Five. Four. Three. Two. One. How old are you?"

After a long pause, Diana said sleepily, "I am twenty-one."

"Where are you?"

"Home." Diana's voice was a reluctant monotone. Sarah observed her eyes moving beneath closed lids.

"Where is home?"

"Ashton."

"And what is your name?"

"Diana Smith."

"Good," said Sarah. "Now we are going to go back farther in time. We are going to go back to your twentieth birthday. When I count backward . . ."

Sarah continued the age regression through a succession of birthdays. Each time she asked the same questions, always ending with "And what is your name?" Sarah knew what she was fishing for, though she wasn't a hundred percent convinced that her hypothesis was correct. She hoped that the age regression would prove her right or, if wrong, give her another clue to the riddle of her client's symptoms and behaviors. Still, when at age sixteen her client gave her name as something other than Diana Smith, Sarah felt the hairs at the nape of her neck stand on end. *I'll be damned,* she whispered.

Diana said, "My name is Nora Entwhistle."

"I see." Sarah took a deep breath and paused,

struggling to keep the excitement out of her voice. "Nora, how old are you?"

"Sixteen."

"And what is today's date?"

"May 16, 1979."

"Is there something special about today?"

"It's my birthday."

"That's right, it's your birthday," Sarah said. "Are you having a party today?"

"No."

"Is there something that you want for your birthday?"

"No."

"What will you do today? For your birthday?"

"Nothing. I'm alone. Birthdays are bad."

"Nora, who is Diana Smith?"

"She's the forgotten one," said Nora Entwhistle.

"Why is she the forgotten one," Sarah asked.

"Because she has been left for us to continue."

"I don't understand. Why is she forgotten?"

"She is the forgotten one. The forgotten one."

Sarah paused for a few minutes, needing time to think. Should she continue with the session now or wait? Perhaps she should wait and use the remaining time to deal with the waking Diana. *I need to do some serious research,* thought Sarah. *This is not your everyday mental health issue.*

Sarah had strongly suspected some sort of dissociative disorder, especially when Diana revealed significant gaps in her memory. That her client might suffer from multiple personality disorder had been a possibility, albeit the last one to be conceded. Even when the pieces began to fall into place—the imagery of hands and confinement, the memory gaps and tunnel vision—Sarah was still reluctant to admit such an exotic possibility. When the suicide tip had come, though, Sarah knew immediately. The voice had been altered considerably: deeper, huskier, a difference in accents.

But listening carefully, Sarah had thought she could detect the similarity. Diana Smith had swallowed an overdose of Valium, and another inhabitant of the same body had called Sarah for help. Perhaps it was this Nora Entwhistle. Or perhaps there were other personalities. The Valium prescription had been made out to a Linda Janus. Linda Janus might be another personality. At any rate, another personality had called, and the case of Diana Smith had suddenly come into sharp focus.

Sarah ticked off quickly the few things she knew about multiple personality disorder. The personalities were likely to be well-defined and distinct. The personality with the presenting symptoms—Diana Smith in this case—was likely to have little knowledge of another personality or personalities. Personalities might have completely different behavior and response patterns; dealing with separate personalities was little different than dealing with separate persons. In some cases, the personalities might have developed to serve a well-defined function, and so might have a limited range of responses and behaviors. In other cases, separate personalities might have well-developed interests and avocations; they might even hold down jobs. Personalities might perceive of themselves with distinctly different physical characteristics. Personalities might even be of different sexes. Most important, multiple personality disorder seemed to always be a response to severe childhood trauma, very often abuse, very often sexual abuse. *MPD is a strategy for coping, for survival,* Sarah thought. *It is not escape in the sense of problem avoidance; it is not chemical imbalance; it is not neurosis; it is not psychosis.*

She knew also that treatment strategies could vary. The cases Sarah recalled seemed mostly to have gradually worked toward a recognition on the part of the dominant personality of the existence of these other selves. In some cases—though not all—treatment worked toward an integration of the personalities into a new, consolidated whole. MPD went by no hard and fast rules.

"All right, I want you to concentrate. We are now going to move forward in time. When I count to five, you will be . . ." And Sarah repeated the process, rapidly restoring her client to the present. Before rousing Diana, she decided to make the trance induction process a little easier next time.

"Diana, in the future, if I say the word *sleep* and clap my hands three times, you will immediately fall into a deep hypnotic state. Do you understand?" Diana nodded, and Sarah repeated the instructions several times.

"All right. When I count to five, you will awake feeling alert, refreshed, and rested. When I count to five, you will awake. One. Two. Three. Four. Five. Awake."

Diana opened her eyes, looking about the room wide-eyed and disoriented. Seeing Sarah, she smiled sheepishly.

"I'm sorry," she said. "What happened?"

"I hypnotized you."

"Oh, that's right. You mean it worked?"

"Yes. You're an excellent subject."

"What happened?"

"Very little, really. This time I just wanted to see how susceptible you are and try a brief age regression. You were under only for about fifteen minutes."

"Did you find out anything?"

Sarah shrugged and smiled encouragingly. "Only that I think we have a lot of work to do together. Diana, what would you think about coming to see me twice a week for a while? I really think it would be a good idea."

"It's fine with me. I'm just not sure I can afford it. I need to figure out what it would do to the insurance, you know."

"Sure. But if finances are a problem, we can work that out."

"You did find something out, didn't you?" Diana asked. "Why are you so concerned?"

"I'm concerned because last week you tried to kill yourself," Sarah said simply, hoping the response sounded adequate. She paused a moment, then continued. "Look, here's what I found out, more or less. I think you are suffering from some sort of dissociative disorder. I'm not sure exactly what sort of dissociative disorder," Sarah lied. "That's one thing we need to find out. But the main reason I think we should meet more often is that you tried to commit suicide. I want to make sure we address that issue so it doesn't happen again."

"But I keep telling you, I didn't try to kill myself," Diana insisted. "I didn't."

"Diana, when they pumped your stomach, you had enough Valium in you to stock a small drugstore."

"But I didn't take them. I swear I didn't."

"I believe you. This is part of the dissociative disorder. It explains why you don't remember taking the pills and why you have lapses in time, gaps in your memory."

"Do you know why I keep losing time? Sometimes I lose whole days."

"Diana, that's what we need to find out about," Sarah said. "If you trust me, I think I can help."

Diana nodded her assent.

"Good. Can you come back Thursday?"

"Yes."

"Will you call me if you need me? Even if you just want somebody to talk to?"

Diana smiled, nodding.

Sarah considered that she had already crossed a few client-therapist boundaries in the short course of their sessions. She decided to cross another. She felt there was a ninety-plus percent certainty that she was dealing with the aftermath of child abuse. She knew virtually nothing about multiple personality disorder, but she knew about child abuse. Trust was going to be a major issue. To hell with client-therapist boundaries.

"I don't just want to be your therapist, Diana. I'd like to be your friend, too."

"Well, if you ask me, I think you should refer her to somebody else." Sarah could almost see Jenny Burton frowning into the telephone. "I mean, *I* certainly don't know anything about it, aside from what I've learned from watching *Santa Barbara,* which I'm certain is absolutely unimpeachable information. But isn't this multiple personality stuff dangerous?"

"No," Sarah said. "Not dangerous to me, anyway. I'm just worried whether I'm qualified to deal with it."

"Oh shoot," Jenny said. "Don't give me that line. I know you. By this point, you've read twenty books on multiple personality syndrome. . . ."

"Disorder," Sarah corrected.

"Whatever. Anyway, you probably now know more than anybody else in the state."

"Well, I'm sure that's not true, but I appreciate the vote of confidence. Anyway, I've got to run. I've got another client in five minutes."

"And you're sure this multiple disorder stuff isn't dangerous?"

"It's multiple personality disorder, it's not dangerous, and I've got to go. Say goodbye, Jenny."

"Goodbye Jenny," Jenny said, and Sarah hung up.

Week 5: Thursday, August 31

"I figured it was about time we met, face to face."

Sarah was startled by the change in Diana's appearance. This new Diana stood before her now in jeans faded nearly white, several rips in each leg showing thread and skin; a T-shirt that reproduced a portion of a Picasso portrait; and a black leather jacket. Her hair was swept off her face, combed straight back from her forehead. She wore heavy eye makeup, which accentuated the startling blue of her eyes, and no lipstick. It was the voice, however, that truly startled Sarah. Gone was the sweetness of the photographer's voice, replaced by a husky, throaty contralto. *A whiskey voice,* thought Sarah.

"We talked on the telephone." She thrust a hand toward Sarah. The therapist took it. The grip was solid and strong.

"Please come in," Sarah smiled. "Miss?" Sarah let the interrogative hang in space.

"Thanks," said the new Diana, the non-Diana, avoiding the question of identity by ignoring it.

"What can I do for you?" Sarah asked.

"Nothing really, honey. Diana couldn't make it today, so I decided to come down and have a look around. Hope you don't mind."

"Not at all. I'm very pleased you came. You say we talked on the phone. You're the one who called and told me Diana was in trouble, aren't you?"

"Yeah, that was me. The little weasel just about blew it, didn't she?"

Sarah felt confused. Was she in some way addressing Diana now? Was she talking to more than one personality or awareness? Were there others "listening in"? Everything she said seemed to have multiple meanings, depending on who might be listening. Sarah nodded.

"She needs me, you know. I keep her out of trouble. Hell, she can't even bleach her own hair."

"You do that for her?" Sarah asked.

"Yeah, you bet. What a pain in the ass, too. I mean, not a thank you. Did you know she thinks that she's a natural blond?"

"How long have you been doing Diana's hair?"

"Oh, for years. Believe me, she wouldn't know what to do without me."

"I'm sure. You know, I'm sorry, but I didn't catch your name."

"I didn't give it, sister. And don't try to trick me, either." Suddenly, her voice rose in volume. *"You hear me?"*

"I hear you," Sarah replied calmly. "Please, there is no need to shout. I simply wanted to be able to call you by name."

"I'll bet you did."

"What's wrong with telling me your name?"

"Names are power, doc. I'm sure *you* know that."

"I'm not sure I do," Sarah said, then added, "and I'm not a doctor."

"That's okay, doc. You don't mind if I call you doc, do you?"

Sarah shrugged. "Sure, you can call me doc. But don't you think it would be fair to give me something to call you? Maybe you could make up a name. It'll just make it easier to talk."

"Okay, give me a minute," she paused, lighting another cigarette. "All right, doc. You can call me Lynn. That's L—Y—N—N."

"That's fine," Sarah said.

"You're not bad," Lynn grinned. "I knew coming down here was a good idea."

"Lynn, I need your help," she said.

"Okay, doc. Shoot."

"Diana is in a great deal of trouble. She needs our help. She needs all her friends to help."

"Hey, I'll do what I can. Like I say, she's a weasel and a wimp, but she depends on me."

"I'd like you to help me keep an eye on Diana. I need you to look in on her whenever you get a chance, just to make sure she's all right."

"You mean so she doesn't kill herself?"

"Yes, I'm afraid so."

Sarah scanned Lynn's face carefully, fascinated by the subtle changes . . . changes that went deeper than makeup. There were differences in the way she moved her mouth, the way her eyes impatiently scanned the room. Even the wrinkles beginning to show around the woman's eyes had changed.

"Okay, I'll help." Lynn glanced at her watch. "Say, doc, I gotta be going."

"So soon?"

"Yes," Lynn said in a tone that brooked no argument.

Sarah felt frustrated. Their contact had been so brief. She needed a way to hold on to this person. Personality. "Lynn, before you leave, take this." Sarah held out one of her business cards. Lynn took it, glanced at it, glanced back at Sarah, then raised one eyebrow questioningly. "I want you to call me, day or night, for any reason. Okay? If Diana needs help or if you just want to talk. I've enjoyed meeting you and I'd love to see you again. You are welcome any time in my office."

Margie looked at Sarah quizzically as she escorted Lynn to the door.

"Was that Diana?" Margie asked when the door had fully closed.

"No," said Sarah, "it wasn't."

Mark Johnson fed a quarter into the pay phone and stuck a finger in his ear in a vain attempt to block out the bar noise. The phone rang several times before it was picked up. The words, "Hi, honey" were on his lips when the recording cut in: "We're unable to come to the phone now, but . . ."

"Damn," Mark said, and slammed the phone into the cradle. Several heads at the bar turned his way. Mark shrugged and walked back to his table. His companion looked up at him, eyebrows arched.

"Nobody home?" asked John Beiderbeck.

" 'Fraid not."

"Look, if you're worried, we can talk some other time."

"No, no. That's not it," Mark smiled. "It's just that that's the third time this week my wife's been late getting home. She's working really hard. I'm just a little concerned about her, is all."

"I understand," Beiderbeck said.

"Well, I'll tell you what. I think I'll have that drink now," Mark said.

"Good deal." Beiderbeck raised an arm in signal to the waitress. He ordered a round of drinks. "So Sarah works late a lot?"

"Not so much," Mark said. "Only lately. She's got a case that's been taking a lot of her time."

"Really? What sort of case? I imagine she has all sorts of fascinating clients."

"You'd have to ask her. It's all psychobabble to me."

Beiderbeck beamed at the waitress as she set the drinks on the table. The waitress smiled back. "You mean she doesn't tell you about her work?"

"Only in generalities." Mark sipped his drink. "Just like I don't bore her with all the details of my day. She doesn't share my passion for computers, which is probably good."

"Oh, but I'd expected *you* to find Sarah's work fascinating. I understand if Sarah is not all that interested in computers; it is, after all, a pretty specialized field. But she deals with the mind. And the mind *is* fascinating, pure and simple."

Mark felt the sting of criticism in the remark. Was Beiderbeck reproving him for not taking a greater interest in Sarah's work? He looked carefully at Beiderbeck as he sipped his drink. Beiderbeck smiled with cheerful interest.

"Oh, she let's me know what's going on," Mark

said, still not sure of Beiderbeck's comments. "This case she's working on now apparently has multiple personalities or something. Weird, huh?"

"Oh my," Beiderbeck laughed. "See, that's what I mean. Fascinating, absolutely fascinating. I think I should have been a psychotherapist. I really *must* meet Sarah. But I can see that this really isn't your interest." Again, Mark sensed a hint of rebuke. Beiderbeck continued, "So let me tell you about the statistical analysis we'd like to do." He picked up a cocktail napkin and began sketching. . . .

Two hours and several drinks later, Mark squinted his eyes in the glare of the early evening parking lot. Where had the time gone? Beiderbeck was certainly an engaging drinking companion. Mark wasn't sure how they managed to kill over two hours talking and drinking, but here it was nearly seven o'clock. Well, maybe Sarah would beat *him* home tonight, just like the old days when he had worked late all the time.

Twenty minutes later, Mark pulled into an empty driveway. *Still not home,* he thought. *Damnit, just once I'd like to have an old-fashioned evening at home. Nothing fancy. Steaks on the grill. A couple of drinks. Listen to a little music. Go to bed early. Make love.*

Mark fixed himself another drink while he broiled a hamburger in the toaster oven.

Sarah was at a loss. When she was in graduate school, multiple personality disorder was hardly acknowledged as a diagnostic category. Certainly none of her professors had first-hand familiarity with it, and most probably doubted that it actually existed. Even the one professor who had discussed it had relegated it to the nether regions of abnormal psychology, along with other oddities like hypnosis and post-traumatic stress disorder.

Following her meeting with the enigmatic Lynn,

Sarah had made a trip to the university library. She had come back armed with half a dozen volumes, which she proceeded to devour. At some point, Sarah recalled, Margie had said goodbye for the day. Sarah had scarcely heard her, so engrossed had she been in her reading. Now she looked up from a work geared to lay readers, *Chambers of the Mind,* and was surprised to find that it was nearly seven-thirty.

Oh God, she thought, *Mark'll have a fit.* She'd worried enough about him back when he'd had to constantly work late. But now that the shoe was on the other foot, Sarah had been surprised to find Mark somewhat less than understanding. After all, they had never been a couple bound to traditional roles in their marriage. They were both professionals, they had both taken turns as primary breadwinners, they shared household chores. Maybe, Sarah thought, he simply didn't want her to go through the same kind of burnout he had experienced.

Sarah pushed the concern from her mind. She still needed to think about this multiple personality business, to consolidate what she'd learned, before heading home.

Her first concern was whether or not to keep Diana as a client or to refer her to someone familiar with MPD. Sarah thought she'd reached resolution on the issue: She had established a sense of trust with Diana, and apparently that was a key issue in the treatment of MPD. MPD is caused by severe abuse, which is the betrayal of very basic forms of trust. Sarah had made some gains there. That seemed to outweigh her lack of experience.

How many personalities was she dealing with? Were Nora and Lynn just the tip of the iceberg? Unknown, Sarah concluded. There were apparently no limits to the degree of fragmentation, the number of personalities, that the multiple might create. Dozens, even hundreds, were possible.

What was disturbing about her research was the lack

of consensus regarding basic issues, especially treatment. Most treatment involved the gradual uncovering of all the personalities and the reliving of the events that had created them. This reliving—abreaction, in psychoanalytic jargon—sometimes resulted in the merger of the alters—short for alternate personalities—with the core personality. But Sarah had read of cases where there was no core personality, where the abuse had been so extensive and had occurred so early that the original personality had never developed. And some multiples resisted the idea of integration. Integration was a kind of death for the alters, even though their memories and abilities were absorbed and not destroyed. Was integration to be her goal with Diana? Sarah didn't know. She supposed that simply trying to understand what had happened to cause the fragmentation would be the first order of business.

Sarah discovered even stranger facts. Different personalities, depending on how developed they were, tended to function as autonomous beings. They might be of different sexes, have different eyeglass prescriptions, even different medical problems and characteristics. Cases had been recorded where one personality was resistant to a particular drug, while another showed a dangerous sensitivity. One might have high blood pressure, but when the shift to another personality occurred, the blood pressure dropped to normal. MPD was a bizarre testament to the power and flexibility of the human mind.

Another amazing discovery was that multiples often went unsuspected for years—unsuspected by spouses, lovers, children, friends, even themselves. In retrospect, some were thought quirky. Or eccentric. Or moody.

An unsettling thought occurred to Sarah. MPD was often difficult to diagnose. Most sufferers—diagnosed sufferers, that is—had been to three, four, or even more mental health professionals before being correctly diagnosed. Depression, post-traumatic stress, borderline personality, schizophrenia, psychosis . . . the list of incorrect diagnoses went on and on. The thought that chilled Sarah was this: Had she herself misdiagnosed clients in the past?

Sarah suddenly remembered Helen Jenner, a severely depressed woman she had worked with a couple of years before. Helen had also complained of being chronically late and feeling as if she were watching things from a distance. She had wild mood swings. Could they have been personality shifts? Helen had been one of Sarah's failures. She had killed herself. Sarah had never been able to fully distance herself from the pain of that failure, the sense of guilt that she knew was irrational and unproductive. That was probably part of the reason, she thought, that she felt so protective of Diana.

But the question remained: Had Helen been a multiple? Sarah wondered whether Margie would remember her. If she remembered correctly, Helen had been a client around the time Margie had first started to work for Sarah.

On the other hand, Sarah thought, *once you start looking for characteristics of MPD, you start to see them everywhere.* For God's sake, her own husband tended to be chronically late because he got so wrapped up in whatever he was doing that time just seemed to disappear. And as for mood swings, Mark got high scores in that arena, too. But then, she probably did, too. *Catch me before my period,* she thought, *and you find an alternate personality for sure.*

The thought of Mark startled her out of her reverie. Sarah glanced at her watch. Another half hour had slipped by.

Another good example of time disappearing, she thought. *So let's not go seeing multiple personality disorder in every case.*

* * *

"Coffee?"

Bill Travers nodded. "Nice room. This is where my tax dollars go, eh?" Travers looked around the conference room.

"Well, they sure don't go into my salary," John Fisher answered. "I'm surprised you've never been in here before. You've certainly logged enough hours at the department."

"As few as possible, I assure you. I guess Captain Larsen believes that rank has its privileges."

"No doubt," said Fisher as he poured coffee into two Styrofoam cups and carried them over to the conference table. He seated himself at the end of the table, catercorner to Travers. "Well, did you bring me that knife?"

"Yep, right here." Travers opened a battered briefcase and removed an ornate brass-handled dagger.

Fisher whistled, "Hey, that's pretty fancy." He turned the knife over in his hands, looking closely at the designs molded into the handle. "What the hell is this?"

Travers laughed. "I wondered when you'd pick up on that. The figure with the horns and the two-foot shlong is the Goat of Mendes, Satan incarnate. The cuties cavorting around him in the buff are worshippers."

"What's this one doing?" Fisher held out the handle with a finger marking the position of one figure.

"That's the notorious *osculum infame,* the kiss of shame. Sort of gives new meaning to the expression 'kiss my ass.' "

"This is disgusting," Fisher laughed. "What's all this engraved on the blade?"

"Magical symbols. The usual stuff."

"Right," Fisher said doubtfully. "You're gonna let me borrow this?"

"Sure, just take good care of it."

"I will."

"I take it you guys haven't uncovered anything else?"

"I'm afraid not."

"Okay." Travers stood. "I guess I'm outta here, then."

"Thanks for coming down. As usual, I owe you one." Fisher stood, too. He rubbed his chin thoughtfully. "Tell me something. In all this occult, satanic stuff, what's the point in killing babies? I mean, it makes no sense."

"Maybe that's the point," Travers said.

"I don't follow."

"A group of individuals performs the most senseless, vile act you can think of. What could be more powerful in binding them together? You're looking for a very cohesive group, my friend. Besides, there's a whole tradition to uphold. You've got Bluebeard in France in the 1400's and Catherine Deshayes a couple of hundred years later. Infant sacrifice or the use of infant blood in the manufacture of sacramental wafers are pretty significant features of the mythology of the Black Mass."

"I'm sorry I asked," Fisher shook his head.

"So what are you going to do, John? Any ideas?"

Fisher stretched and yawned. "No idea. You're supposed to know about these groups. What the hell would you do?"

Travers shook his head. "I still don't know what we're dealing with here. I think we're agreed that this isn't the work of high school kids dabbling in the occult, smoking pot, and listening to old Black Sabbath records."

"So what is it? You still buy your theory of a highly organized cult of Satan worshippers?"

"Hell, it's not *my* theory. I was just telling you about

persistent rumors. I never gave it much thought until now."

"So tell me about the rumors."

Travers pulled his chair back out and sat down. Fisher perched on the edge of the table.

"According to the rumors," Travers said, "these guys have been around for years. They're supposed to be highly organized. According to some—and I don't buy this for a minute—they're tied into day-care centers and child pornography. They conduct human sacrifices and cannibalism."

"Cannibalism?"

"Blood-drinking, eating bits of flesh."

"But why? I don't get it."

"Remember, I'm just playing devil's advocate here. So to speak." Travers sighed. "If you truly believe in Satan, then you do things to please him, either as a form of worship or to curry favor. Satan apparently loves a good blood-letting."

"But cannibalism, for God's sake?"

Travers smiled. "Are you a Christian, John?"

Fisher nodded. "Episcopalian. Why?"

"When was the last time you took communion?"

"What are you getting at?"

"This is my body, this is my blood," Travers said. "We're not as far removed from blood rites as we sometimes like to think."

Fisher looked unhappily at Travers. "You always make me feel so much better," he said.

Chapter 9

Week 5: Saturday, September 2

Sarah laid the book she was reading to the side as her husband came into the living room. Mark glanced at the coffee table, which was covered with more of Sarah's books and pads of legal paper.

"You want to go out tonight?" he asked. "There's a new French restaurant in town."

Sarah shook her head. "I'm sorry, Mark, but I'm up to my elbows in research. Maybe we can do something tomorrow."

Mark's teeth clenched before he spoke. "You're working too hard. You need a break."

"This is something I've got to do. It's important."

"You and I are important, too."

Sarah sighed. "Of course we're important. But once in a while work takes precedence. You know that."

"Once in a while, okay. But this is becoming a habit."

Sudden anger flew into Sarah. "Mark, how many times did I try to tell you the same thing when you were working all the time? It's okay for you, but not for me?"

Mark flushed with outrage, and Sarah instantly regretted her outburst.

"I don't *do* that anymore. I just didn't want you to

go down the same path I took." Mark turned on his heels. Sarah heard the back door open, then slam.

"Damn," she said aloud. She gave him a minute, then followed him out onto the deck. He was standing with both hands clenched around the railing, staring out at the late afternoon.

Sarah touched him gently on the shoulder and was surprised when he flinched.

"I'm sorry," she said. "I think the real problem is that I'm scared."

He turned to look at her. "Scared of what?"

"Scared of screwing up. I've got this client with MPD, and I'm not qualified to work with MPD."

"So refer her out."

"It's not that simple. We've come too far for me to abandon her. All the ground we've covered so far would be lost."

"You're good, Sarah. You're not going to screw up."

"Maybe not. But to make sure I don't, I've got to understand what I'm working with. I need to be a student again, burn a little midnight oil. It won't last forever."

"Yeah, I know," Mark sighed. "I just worry about you."

Sarah hugged him. "Hey, tell you what. It's Saturday. My head's full of psychobabble, as you call it. Why don't you see if you can get us reservations for that restaurant?"

Mark sighed again. "No, that's all right." Sarah thought she heard a note of exasperation in his voice. "We'll do something tomorrow. You do your work now."

"You're sure?"

"Sure."

* * *

Week 6: Sunday, September 3

"So what do you want to do?" Sarah asked.

Mark looked up from the Sunday paper. "Hmm?"

"What do you want to do today?"

"Let's not do anything." Mark turned his attention back to the paper.

"I thought we had an agreement." Sarah put a teasing note into her voice. "An assignation."

"No, that's all right."

"Come on, Mark, you were right. I need to get out. So do you."

Mark looked over the edge of the paper expressionlessly. "I need to get some computer work done. It's okay."

Was he offended by her initial reluctance to go out the night before? Sarah wondered. Mark was slow to anger, but he was also slow to forgive sometimes. Was this a grudge?

"Mark, talk to me. Are you mad at me?"

Mark folded the paper carefully. "No, of course not." He stood up.

"Come on, let's talk," Sarah said, but he had already left the room.

The rest of the day Mark was polite but distant. Sarah tried to draw him out, but he was reluctant to talk. She decided to give him time.

Week 6: Monday, September 4

"I just don't get it," Sarah said, spooning up a mouthful of hot and sour soup. She paused with the spoon poised before her. "Mark's usually not so—so—"

"Childish?" Jenny Burton asked. Jenny had asked Sarah to meet her for lunch at their favorite Chinese restaurant, and Sarah had eagerly agreed.

"Yeah, okay. Childish."

Jenny arched one perfectly sculpted eyebrow. "Men *are* children," she said. "Robert's the biggest baby I know." Robert was Jenny's husband.

"No, Mark's not like that. Not usually. Although it does seem as if he's got this double standard of how devoted we should be to our work. I *know* that as soon as his business picks up, there'll be more late nights and lost weekends. And I don't mind that, as long as I get the same consideration."

"Well, you said it. Double standard is the right term."

"Mark's not like that."

"Right," Jenny said, an infuriating half-smile on her face.

"He's not."

"Uh-huh."

Back at the office, Sarah suddenly remembered her speculations over the last few days about Helen Jenner, the woman she now thought might have been a multiple. She walked out to the receptionist's desk.

"Margie, I've been meaning to ask you. Do you remember a client named Helen Jenner?"

Margie's eyes narrowed as she concentrated. "I don't know. The name sounds vaguely familiar."

"She was a client around the time you started work here. I was hoping you'd remember her."

Margie shrugged. "How come?"

"Oh, just if you noticed anything strange about her. If she reminded you of Diana at all."

"You mean you think she was a multiple, like Diana?"

"I don't know," Sarah said. "It's possible."

"Tell me more," Margie said. "Now I'm interested."

"Oh, it's not important, really. The name doesn't

ring a bell? I could have sworn she was still coming when you started."

"I don't think so. I'm pretty sure she was before my time."

"Oh, well, it doesn't matter."

"Okay, boss."

Margie turned back to the stack of mail she had been opening as Sarah returned to her desk.

Week 6: Tuesday, September 5

At a glance, Sarah guessed that it was Diana who had come for the appointment today. The woman was well-dressed, her cosmetics carefully and conservatively applied.

"Hello, Diana," Sarah risked greeting her by name.

"Good afternoon," said Diana. She sat and lit a cigarette.

"You look rested."

"I am. You know, ever since the . . ." Diana paused. *Had she been about to say "suicide attempt"?* Sarah wondered. "Ever since the hospital, I've felt so relaxed."

"That's good."

"Yes, well, I've maybe been sleeping a little too much. That's why I missed our session last week. I called your receptionist later to explain."

"Do you remember any more about last Wednesday?"

"Only what I told you before," Diana said. "I remember cleaning my apartment. The last thing I remember is vacuuming the living room. After that . . ." Diana shrugged, "it's all a blank. Sarah, I still can't believe that *I* tried to kill myself. I was in such a great mood. If I was going to kill myself, why then? Why not before, when I was really down? And why can't I remember?"

The desire to tell Diana about the others was very strong now. Sarah considered briefly, then rejected the idea.

"Suicide is often more than an attempt to do away with ourselves," she said. "It can be a way of crying out for help or of signaling the need for change in an intolerable environment. At any rate, as time goes by, I suspect you'll remember more about the events of last week. In the meantime, I wouldn't be too concerned about not remembering."

"Sure," Diana shook her head. "And what's to keep it from happening again?"

An excellent question, thought Sarah. *And we don't really know who tried to kill herself. Or himself. Whatever. Quite a situation—sharing your body with who knows how many personalities, persons really, one of whom has a death wish.*

"Diana, do the names Nora Entwhistle or Lynn mean anything to you?" *When in doubt, change the subject,* Sarah thought.

"No, I don't think so. My editor has an assistant named Lynn, but I don't really know her."

"How about the name Linda Janus?"

"No," Diana said. "Who are these people? Should I know them?"

"No, no. I was just curious. The first two are names that you mentioned under hypnosis. Probably not important at all." Sarah waited a moment, watching her client carefully. "The name Linda Janus was on the prescription for the pills you took last week."

"You think this Linda gave me the pills? Who is she?"

Now there's an interesting interpretation of events, thought Sarah. "I don't know who she is. Just a name on a pill bottle." Sarah hesitated. "Diana, I'd like to try hypnosis again."

Diana sighed. "Well, I don't much care for it. But if you have to, I guess you have to. All right."

Sarah said "sleep" and clapped her hands softly

three times. Immediately, the posthypnotic suggestion had its effect. Diana closed her eyes and slumped slightly forward in the chair. Sarah spent the next several minutes increasing the depth of the trance state. Diana was a very susceptible subject, a fact for which Sarah was grateful.

"We are going to go back in time. Do you understand?" Sarah consulted her notes. "The date is May 16, 1979. It is now May 16, 1979. What is today's date?"

"May 16, 1979," was the slow, dazed-sounding reply.

"Yes. What is your name, please?" Sarah asked.

"Nora Entwhistle."

"Hello, Nora."

"Hello."

"Is there something special about today?"

"Yes, today is my birthday."

"I see. Are you having a party?"

"Yes, we are having a party."

"I see," Sarah frowned. *What was it that this Nora had said last time. Birthdays are bad?*

"Describe your birthday party to me, Nora. Tell me about the party."

"Well, Bill Thompson's here. I like Billy. He's my boyfriend. Judy and Mary and Liz came. Tommy kissed me when he came in." Nora smiled.

"I see. Are there presents?"

"Oh, yes. I got clothes and tapes and books."

"All right. Nora, do you know Diana Smith?"

"Yes."

"Nora, who is Diana Smith?"

"She can't come."

"Why not?"

"I won't let her. She doesn't like parties, anyway, see. This is *my* party."

"Where is Diana when you go to the party?"

"How should I know? I have to watch her all the time. But not now. *I'm* at the party."

"Nora, I want you to relax now. We are going to go forward in time. Do you understand? We are going forward in time. We are returning to the present. . . ." Sarah continued the suggestions. When she had restored her subject to the present date, she asked, "Who is this?"

"Nora Entwhistle."

Sarah raised an eyebrow in wonder. She had expected Diana to answer.

"Nora, where is Diana Smith now?"

"Asleep."

"I see. How would you describe your relationship with her?"

No answer.

"Nora, who is Diana? What is your relationship to her?"

Nora spoke slowly. "I take care of her."

"I see. Do you live together?"

"We share the same body. She uses it most of the time."

"Nora, who is Lynn?"

"I don't know."

"Okay. Do you know anyone named Linda Janus?"

"No."

"Does anyone else share the body with Diana Smith?"

"No."

Confused now, Sarah wondered where to take the questioning. *Are the personalities sheltered one from the other? Is there a personality that has an overview, is aware of all the others?*

"Nora, when Diana uses the body, do you watch her?"

"Yes, I watch."

"What happened last Wednesday? Why did Diana try to kill herself?" Sarah bit her tongue, realizing she was phrasing the questions poorly. With hypnosis, it was important not to ask leading questions. The subject was capable of detailed and clever invention in response to the hypnotist's prompting. Sarah resolved to be aware of this in the future.

"She tried to kill herself, yes. She was tired."

"She was tired?"

"Yes. She almost succeeded in taking the body from me."

"What would have happened to you if she had succeeded?"

"She would have taken the body. She has the body all the time, anyway. Then she tries to destroy it."

"Why would she destroy it?"

"I don't know. She needs help. She is very sick, I think."

"What happened after she took the pills?"

"She fell asleep."

"Where were you when she fell asleep?"

"I went to sleep, too."

"I see. How do you suppose she got to the hospital?"

"I don't know."

"Okay, Nora. That's fine. When I count to five, you are going to awake feeling alert and refreshed. Do you understand? When I count to five, you will feel as if you just woke up from a restful and refreshing nap. One. Two. Three. Four. Five. Awake."

Diana opened her eyes. She glanced around the room, disoriented by the transition to wakefulness. She blinked several times, then looked across the desk at Sarah and frowned.

"Well, it's about time we met," she extended her hand. "Nora Entwhistle."

Sarah's eyes widened as she took in the subtle differences. The voice was lilting, more musical in its cadences, slightly higher perhaps. The skin between the eyes furrowed, a wrinkle Sarah was certain she had not noticed in Diana. Sarah extended her hand.

"Very nice to meet you," Sarah smiled. "Actually, we have talked before."

Nora frowned again. "I don't think so."

"Yes," said Sarah. "Under hypnosis. In fact, we talked just a few minutes ago."

"Oh, I see. Just a minute." Nora closed her eyes. The wrinkle between her eyebrows deepened. In a few seconds, she opened her eyes. "Yes, you're quite right. Quite right," she smiled. "I remember now."

"You remember the hypnosis?" Sarah asked doubtfully.

"Yes."

"Could you tell me what we talked about?"

"Surely. We talked about my sixteenth birthday. Then you asked me about Diana's suicide attempt."

"I see. You have a remarkable memory."

"Thank you. In the future, I don't think you will need to resort to this mesmerization," Nora said. "I am available to come to sessions if you wish."

"Nora, I want you to return the body to Diana. I'm afraid she'll be very disoriented if she does not wake up from her hypnosis session."

"Oh, I see. Yes, you're quite right. I'd be happy to. Till we meet again, then."

"Yes, Nora. It's been a pleasure."

Sarah watched her client's eyes lose focus. Subtle shifts in muscle response altered the face. The wrinkle between the eyebrows vanished. The lids of the eyes seemed to relax somehow, giving the face a dreamy quality.

Diana opened her eyes. "Hi," she said. "Did you learn anything?"

"Nothing," Sarah said evenly. "Nothing that I think we need to go into now. Besides, it's about that time."

Diana looked at her watch. "Yes. I suppose I really should be going."

"Will I see you Thursday?"

"Yes, of course. I'll be here."

Will you, indeed? wondered Sarah.

Week 6: Thursday, September 7

"I'd like to speak with Nora, please."

Sarah had induced a light trance state using the posthypnotic suggestion she had given Diana Smith. Hypnosis, she reasoned, was useful in that she could summon the Nora Entwhistle alter without Diana's awareness. She had abandoned the imagery associated with deepening the trance state and now simply asked to speak with Nora.

"Yes, this is Nora."

"What do you think is wrong with Diana?" Sarah asked.

"I think that she is afraid to live. You see, all my life I have had to take care of the really important stuff."

"Why is that?"

"Diana really can't help herself. She just isn't very strong. She needs my help."

"So you would describe yourself as strong?"

"Yes," said Nora.

"Nora, would you describe yourself to me? Physically, I mean."

"You can't see for yourself?"

Sarah realizied her mistake. Whatever appearance Nora Entwhistle might have created for herself, she expected it to be apparent to Sarah.

"Indulge me, please," Sarah improvised. "Sometimes I find it interesting to have my clients describe themselves."

"So I am a client to you now?"

Stepped into it again, thought Sarah.

"My apologies. No, you are not my client. Diana is my client."

Nora closed her eyes for a moment and frowned, then opened them and smiled at Sarah. "I am about five feet nine inches tall and weigh about one hundred thirty-five pounds." Sarah estimated Diana at about five-five, one hundred five or ten. "I have curly brown hair, almost a chestnut color, and brown eyes." Diana, of course, was an ash-blond, with blue eyes. "Let's see, what else can I tell you?"

"Would you describe yourself as attractive?" Sarah asked.

"About average, I think. I'm no knockout, but I'm all right." Sarah wondered how Diana, whom she considered quite striking in appearance, would describe herself.

"Nora, I'd like to ask you about Diana's early childhood, and yours, if I might. You knew her back then, yes?"

"Oh, yes," Nora said. "I've been with her for a long, long time."

"What were her parents like while she was growing up?" Sarah asked.

"I figured we'd get to the developmental issues sooner or later." Nora made a face, wrinkling her nose. "The Mother was very kind to us. She left early on, did you know that?"

"No, I didn't." Sarah scribbled on her pad.

"Oh, yes," Nora continued. "She left when we were . . . oh, I guess we were about five."

"Why did she leave?"

"I don't know. She and The Father fought a lot, I think."

"You say she was nice?"

"Yes, she treated us well. She never hit us."

"And The Father. What was he like?"

"I hate to talk about this." Nora smoothed her skirt, patted her hair. "It's so difficult, you understand."

"Yes. Please, take your time. Would you like some water?" Sarah asked.

"No, that's all right. Just give me a second." Nora paused. Sarah watched the woman's face, fascinated by the differences in expression that she used. The face was Diana's and yet it wasn't. She used it so differently, the musculature exercised in such distinct patterns, that Sarah's certainty that she dealt with whole and separate persons, not just fragments of personality, fortified. She was certain that now if she were to encounter either Diana or Nora on the street, she would be able to identify at a glance the bearer of the body.

"The Father did things to us," Nora continued. "The Father was mean."

"Did he hit you?"

"He hit us, yes. He hit us when we cried. Sometimes, he hit us for no reason. He hit us with his hand. He hit us with his brush." Nora leaned forward in the chair and looked Sarah directly in the eyes. "He hit *me*. Me."

"You said *us* first, then you said *me*. Why?"

"Because Diana left when The Father got mad. She could not take it. I am strong, so I took the beatings."

"That must have been very difficult," said Sarah.

"That wasn't the worst of it," Nora said. "The Father also did other things." She looked down at the hands clutching each other in her lap. "He touched us, too."

"He touched you?"

"Yes, you know. Where you shouldn't be touched."

"Show me where he touched you, please," Sarah said.

Nora closed her eyes and breathed deeply. When she opened them, she nodded at Sarah and, with her forehead knitted in displeasure, placed both hands in her lap, palms down where her legs came together.

"I see. How old were you when he started touching?"

"Three, maybe."

Nora's shy admissions made Sarah feel angry and

disturbed. *This is not my issue,* she reminded herself, *it is my client's.*

"How did you feel about him touching you?" Sarah asked.

"He told me I could never tell anyone. He told me I would die if I told anyone. He said that The Mother would die. He made me afraid when he touched me, when he did the other things, too."

"What other things, Nora?"

"When he put things in me. Hard things, things that hurt. He would put things in me and tell me I was a bad girl."

Sarah felt no need to hear any greater detail at this point. She fought a sudden wave of nausea. "And you say that Diana went away at this point?" Was it really possible that she had found the core set of experiences that had caused the original dissociation of Diana Smith? Diana's father had physically and sexually abused the child. Placed in an intolerable situation, she had created an alternate personality to deal with it. It was a classic scenario for dissociation. *MPD is a strategy for survival,* Sarah reminded herself.

"Yes. Diana went away. I could deal with The Father."

"How did you deal with The Father?"

"By hating him. By not being afraid. Diana couldn't hate him, you see. She was afraid."

"What happened when The Mother left?"

"Then *she* came."

"Who is she?" asked Sarah.

"The Step."

"The Step?" Sarah asked. "Oh, I see. The stepmother. So your father—" Sarah corrected herself, "The Father married again?"

"Yes."

"Where did The Mother go? Did you see her after that?"

"I don't know where she went. She came back once

or twice, that's all." Nora paused. "I think maybe she was afraid to come back."

"Afraid how?"

"Afraid for her life," Nora said. "Afraid of what Diana's father might do to her."

"Is that why she left?"

"I think so. I think The Father beat her, too."

"Nora," Sarah hesitated, trying to compose the question in a way that would not reveal her own emotions, "The Mother left without taking Diana with her. Why do you think that happened?"

Nora's eyes focused on the far wall. She sat unblinking for long seconds. After perhaps half a minute, she turned her head to look at Sarah. "There you have the interesting question, Sarah. We don't know. *I* don't know, surely, and I know Diana has no earthly idea what happened. I think that she's in denial of The Mother, anyway."

"Why would that be?"

"I think she's worked so hard to blank out the memories of those years when The Father first started . . . you know, abusing us, that she honestly doesn't remember anything."

"Back to the question of why The Mother abandoned you"—Sarah looked closely, watching for any effect of the harsher language and the reference to Nora herself, rather than Diana—"can you speculate?"

Nora's face remained impassive. Sarah continued, "Any guesses?"

"Maybe The Father told her she had to . . . that he would kill Diana or something like that."

"Okay. Can you tell me something about The Father? What did he do for a living? What did he look like?"

"Well, first of all," said Nora, "his name was Charles. Charles Smith. He was an architect. He was a very tall man and slender. I remember he had dark hair and pale blue eyes. His eyes were really something. They were a very pale blue, with almost a metallic sheen. When I meet people with eyes like that, I am frightened by them." Nora looked at Sarah. "How's that?"

"Fine. Thank you. What was the stepmother like? Tell me about her."

"The Step was an odd woman," Nora said. "For a while, she was very kind to us. I find it hard to admit, but I guess she was really a very attractive woman. I suppose The Father had been having an affair with her and that's part of the reason The Mother left. I don't really *know* that; it just makes sense looking back."

"You say she was kind for a while. What happened?"

"I don't really know. Well, that's not true. I have a good guess. The Father stopped doing those things to us for a while, maybe a year or more. This was when The Step moved in. But then he started doing new things. He would make us get into bed with him sometimes during the day when The Step was gone. Later, he would make us sleep in bed with them. I think that when The Step realized what was going on, she became jealous."

"That's quite insightful, Nora," Sarah said. "What happened when The Father made you sleep with both of them?"

"He would hold me for a long time. Just hold me, with his arms around my shoulder. He would do that for a long time. But I always knew what was coming. Sooner or later, he would start to move his hand over me. Then he would do other things to me."

"I see. And The Step was in bed, too? What did she do?"

"The Father slept in the middle. I don't remember The Step doing anything, really. Sometimes, I think she would get up and not come back to bed for a long time, till after The Father was finished."

"I see. And how long did this continue?" Sarah asked.

"Off and on for a number of years. Until we were about ten, I guess."

"And what happened then? Why did The Father stop?"

"I don't know," Nora said.

"And after the age of ten or so, The Father left you alone?"

"Oh, he left us alone with the touching and all of that. He still beat us sometimes."

"And The Step? What happened after she realized what was going on?"

"She became very cruel to us," Nora said without emotion. All during the session she had sat motionless, her back straight. *Primly,* thought Sarah. *She sits primly.* Nora continued. "She did not really hit us, at least not very often. But she would yell at us and call us bad things."

"What kind of bad things?"

"Sarah, is it really necessary that I repeat these things? It has been difficult enough telling you about what The Father did. Do you really want to hear what The Step said?" Nora asked.

"Is this uncomfortable for you?" Sarah asked. "We can stop if you wish."

"No, it's not that," Nora said. "It's just that she used such terrible language. Language I would never use."

"We are both adults. I don't think there is any harm in repeating the language of another person. If you don't mind?"

"All right, I guess so," Nora breathed deeply. "She would say things like, 'Fuck you, you little cunt,' or 'You are nothing but a little whore, you fucking little whore.' " Nora pursed her mouth. "Such terrible language."

"How did you feel about The Step?"

"I hated her," said Nora. "I wanted to kill her when she called me names like that."

"What *did* you do when she called you names?"

"Different things. Usually, I would try to ignore her, pretend I didn't hear her. Sometimes, I would laugh. Sometimes, I would wait and get even."

"How did you get even?"

"Oh, like I broke a necklace that belonged to her. I just got so mad, I reached up and yanked it right off her. That was one time she did hit me."

"What did you do then?"

"I laughed. I still had hold of some of the pearls. I held the string up and let the pearls fall to the floor. And I laughed. The Father beat me for that."

"It sounds like you were a very brave little girl," Sarah said.

"I had to be. Diana couldn't take it. She just couldn't deal with it."

"Nora, how do you feel about Diana? I imagine it's not easy always having to be her protector."

"Oh, you're so right, Sarah. It's not easy at all. But you know we all have responsibilities. We all have things we must do that maybe we'd rather not."

"Like what?"

"Like take care of other people. I mean, to be perfectly honest, there are times when I think I'll just leave. Just leave and let Diana take care of herself. But that wouldn't be right. See, as much of an inconvenience as it is sometimes, Diana depends on me. It's like a mother and her children. Sometimes motherhood is inconvenient, but a mother doesn't just leave."

Some mothers do, thought Sarah.

"Unless they have to," added Nora, as if reading Sarah's thoughts.

"Nora, you've just been wonderful. I'd like to spend a little time with Diana before she leaves. Could you give her control of the body now?"

"Of course, Sarah."

"Thank you. I look forward to talking with you again soon."

"As do I. Sarah, thank you for looking after Diana. I know that she is in good hands."

"Well," said Sarah, "thank you again."

Week 7: Tuesday, September 12

"So the name Nora means nothing to you?"

"You asked me that before," Diana said. "Who is this Nora? Why do you keep bringing her up?"

"Diana, this is difficult," Sarah said. "I don't want to hide anything from you. I'm not entirely sure myself who Nora is. Under hypnosis, you recall a person named Nora, that's all. I just wanted to make sure you have no conscious memory of her."

Sarah grappled with the problem of revealing her findings to Diana. Her conclusion was a compromise: Give Diana bits and pieces of information and hope that with time she would become aware of the other personalities by herself. Or at least be in a better position to accept the truth. Sarah wasn't sure what effect the truth would have now, but her instincts counseled avoidance.

"What's so important about this Nora? What do I remember about her?" Diana said. Sarah looked up in surprise at the hard edge in her voice.

"First of all, it's not Nora herself who's important right now. You remembered some things along with this Nora-memory. For example, you remembered that your father remarried when you were fairly young."

"What?" Diana frowned and shook her head. "No, no. That's just plain crazy. My father never remarried. He and my mother died in a car accident. I told you about that."

"It's okay, Diana," said Sarah. "One of the hazards of hypnosis is that the subject will invent memories in an effort to please the hypnotist." *Well,* thought Sarah, *that is true, essentially. But I didn't put Nora into a position to create a false memory.* "What *do* you remember about your parents, Diana? What were they like? Did you get along with them?"

"I've told you most of what I remember as a kid. Which isn't much, I'm afraid. Mostly, I remember them being around, but I don't really remember having a whole lot to do with them. They were nice, as I recall. I—" Diana lifted her hands in frustration, "I really don't remember much."

"That's fine. There's no need to push it." Sarah decided to change the subject. "How have you been sleeping?"

"Very well," said Diana. "No problem at all."

"Good. And dreams?"

"I guess I've been sleeping pretty soundly. I don't remember any dreams. Of course, it's not usual for me to remember dreams."

"I recall you telling me that," Sarah said. "But when you do remember, they're wonderful. I've thought a lot about the dream of the two dolls."

"Oh?"

"Yes. I'm no dream interpreter, so don't get me wrong, but I thought that dream probably had a lot of meaning for you. Have you given it any more thought?"

Diana hesitated. "To be honest, I *have* thought about it from time to time. The strange thing about it is that even though it's a nightmare, thinking about certain parts of it make me feel really good."

"Which parts?" Sarah asked.

"Well, overall I feel good about it because I remember it. I know that sounds strange." Diana paused, frowning. "But it's just so nice to remember a dream. Actually, it feels like more than a dream . . . like I'm remembering something from the past. Like the dream puts me in touch with something I had forgotten, I guess. The other thing that makes me feel good is something about the dolls. I'm not quite sure what it is."

"Don't you think that has something do with your friend Sissie?"

"Who?" asked Diana.

"Sissie. Your friend."

"Sissie? I don't know." Diana looked absently around the office. "Now that you say the name, I do seem to remember."

"Just now you're remembering?" Sarah asked. "You really didn't recall when I first mentioned the name?"

"No, I didn't," Diana said, eyes suddenly filling with tears. "I must be crazy."

"Diana, it's all right. There are good reasons why you have trouble remembering things." Sarah recalled from her research that multiples did not always retain the memories evoked in session. The client started to remember in a clinical setting certain memories that were either buried or belonged to another personality. Then they forgot. It might take quite a bit of re-remembering for the memory to have any permanence. Apparently, Diana had relegated her memories of Sissie back to the hazy mists of amnesia. "You are not crazy."

"Then I'd hate to meet a crazy person," Diana said.

Sarah chuckled, caught off guard by the comment. Diana, perplexed at first, saw the humor in her own remark and joined in the laughter. Sarah and Diana were helpless to stop laughing. It was several minutes before the women regained their composure.

"Sarah," Diana said, "you don't know how good it feels to laugh."

"It's good to hear you laugh," Sarah admitted. "For that matter, I haven't done enough laughing lately myself."

Suddenly, Diana leaned forward, placing her hands on Sarah's desk. "What's your life like, Sarah?" she asked. "What do you do when you leave this?" Diana made a brief gesture that seemed to take in the office.

"I'm taken aback, Diana. No, no, not in any bad way." Sarah saw the sudden look of dismay on her client's face. "I'm very flattered that you are interested in me. I usually don't hear that in my clients." Sarah thought for a moment. On sudden impulse, she said, "Would you like to come out to my place for dinner some evening? I could introduce you to my husband and we could get to know each other a little better." *To hell with the rules,* Sarah thought. *I've followed instinct on this one so far. There's no reason to stop now.*

"Sarah, I don't know what to say," Diana said and coughed. Sarah noticed the sudden hoarseness, a quick wipe of the eye with the back of her hand. "I'd like that very much."

"Good," said Sarah. "Shall we set a time now?"

"Time? Oh my," Diana said, suddenly crestfallen.

"What's the matter?"

"Well, what if . . . I mean, how will I . . ." Diana stopped. "Damn," she blurted out. "What if time goes wrong on me again? What if I black out?"

Sarah smiled gently. "Then we'll reschedule. Don't worry about it. If we don't make it this time, we'll make it another. All right? No pressure. This is just to have a good time."

"Okay," Diana smiled. "Oh, thank you."

"Good. How about Friday? That means we don't have to worry about getting up and going to work the next day. I can give you directions Thursday."

"Great."

Sarah smiled gently at her client. "Well, back to business," she said, looking at her watch. "Diana, I'd like to hypnotize you again, briefly."

"Okay, but do you mind if I ask why?"

"No, I don't mind," Sarah said, not quite truthfully. Improvising, she explained, "I'm still puzzled by the circumstances of your taking the overdose of Valium. I would like to see if I can find out a little more."

"Okay, go ahead."

Several minutes later, Diana sat in her chair with her eyes closed, breathing deeply. Her hands lay relaxed on her lap and her head tilted forward, as in the manner of an inadvertent napper.

"Diana, what day is it?"

"Tuesday."

"Very good. What time is it?"

"Two thirty-nine," she said. Sarah glanced at her watch. Two forty-one. Sarah smiled, remembering her habit of setting her clocks and watches several minutes ahead of the rest of the world.

"Diana, I would like to talk to the person who calls herself Lynn. When I count to three, the person called Lynn will be able to talk to me. One. Two. Three."

Sarah waited for a response. None came.

"Lynn, are you there?"

No response.

"Lynn, talk to me. How are you?"

Sarah waited, watching her client closely. She saw no movement in the facial musculature, often a sign that the subject was preparing to speak. She saw no movement whatsoever.

"Who is there, please?"

Nothing.

"Lynn, what is today's date?"

Still no answer.

"Diana, what is today's date?"

Sarah felt herself flush, the raw edge of concern grating on her thoughts. *What is this? Why won't she respond? Slow down. Just think a minute,* Sarah told herself.

"Rest and relax," Sarah said. "Rest and relax. When I count to three, Diana Smith will be able to speak to me. When I count to three, Diana Smith will say hello. One. Two. Three."

Sarah waited. As the seconds slipped away, she felt

a knot in her stomach tighten. Sarah stood and walked around her desk. She knelt by Diana's chair. Wrapping her fingers lightly around Diana's wrist, she located the pulse. Watching the second hand on her wristwatch, Sarah counted twelve beats in fifteen seconds. *Good,* she thought. Sarah stood from her kneeling position, keeping her back bent over the cataleptic woman. Gently, she lifted an eyelid, careful to watch for the response of the pupil to the sudden light. As she opened the one lid, however, the other simultaneously fluttered open. Diana, suddenly finding Sarah hovering inches from her face, pushed backward. Sarah caught the arms of the chair as it started to topple. The chair fell forward heavily. Sarah stepped back.

"Are you all right?"

"What happened? How did you get over here?" Diana's eyes still tracked wildly around the room.

"I hypnotized you, remember?"

"Oh, right," Diana visibly relaxed. "Did something happen?"

"You stopped responding to me. You apparently weren't listening."

"Wow," Diana said, her eyes now wide with speculation. "You mean, you couldn't wake me up? Can that happen?"

"No, no," Sarah said, although her own certainty wavered considerably. "The worst that could happen is that I would have had to let you fall asleep and you would have awakened from a nap quite naturally. So you were in no danger of not being able to wake up," Sarah smiled. "However, it is interesting that you lost responsiveness. Nothing to worry about, just interesting."

Diana looked doubtful. Sarah was sympathetic. She sat heavily in her chair. Only after she had crossed one leg over the other did she realize that the calf muscle of her right leg was twitching involuntarily, something that only happened when she was very tired or very anxious. She sighed heavily, grateful that she had no more sessions scheduled for the afternoon.

"Mark, how would you feel about having one of my clients over for dinner Friday night?"

Mark thumbed the remote to the small television they kept in the kitchen. Sarah had initially resisted the idea of watching TV at mealtime, until she realized that one of the few opportunities to catch the news these days seemed to be dinnertime. As Mark depressed the button, Peter Jennings's voice quickly faded to a whisper. Mark looked at Sarah, then at the television, then he depressed the button that shut the machine off.

"I was kind of hoping we could have an evening together for a change," Mark said. "Maybe even go out somewhere." Mark opened his mouth and eyes wide in mock surprise. "What's up?"

"Remember the woman I've been telling you about? The one who's turned out to have multiple personalities?"

"Oh, really? That sounds interesting. So how many are coming for dinner?" Mark grinned.

"Cute," Sarah said, and stuck her tongue out. "Seriously, I set up the date on the spur of the moment, but it's pretty important."

Mark sighed. Sarah almost asked what the sigh signified, then thought better of it.

Mark said, "If it's important to you, then let's do it. Maybe we can do something Saturday night?"

Sarah thought she detected some reluctance, but she said, "That sounds great." She reached across the small table and touched her husband's hand with a finger. "Mark, I know we've both been awfully busy lately, but you know I love you."

"I love you, too," Mark said without hesitation. "And I'm sorry about getting mad on Sunday. It's just queuing theory in practice."

"Excuse me?"

"Just the way things stack up," Mark explained. "Like customers in line at a bank. Graph out the size of the lines over time and you'll see that they bunch up, then there's practically nothing, then they bunch up again. It's never a neat and even distribution. The good news is that we've got a calm period ahead of us eventually."

"Good," Sarah smiled. "I could use one of those."

"Me, too. 'Course, I wouldn't want to complain about being busy. It sure as hell beats the alternative."

"I suppose," said Sarah. "I suppose."

Week 7: Thursday, September 14

"Nora, tell me again why you think Diana's mother left when she was . . . wait a minute, how old was she?"

"She was five. Maybe six. And I don't know why she left. Why do you keep asking me about that?"

"It's just that I find it interesting that she would leave without taking her daughter. I'd like to know why," Sarah prompted.

"I'm afraid I can't help you," Nora said. She crossed her arms in what seemed to Sarah a gesture of finality.

"All right, that's fine." For the past half hour, Sarah had observed in herself a rising frustration. Nora's account of early childhood was remarkable in both the wealth and paucity of the detail it revealed. Nora recalled with grim specificity the abuses suffered at the hands of her father, but she had difficulty relating some of the points Sarah needed to bring this complex family dynamic into greater resolution. Why had the mother abandoned her child to an abusive father? Had the mother been aware? Had she enabled the actions of the father? Probably. The spouse was often a silent contributor in incestuous relationships. How did all this change with the arrival of the stepmother?

Other details seemed missing, too. Where were the accounts of daily life? Where were the insignificant memories? Sarah supposed that this Nora personality might serve a very specific function, absorbing the violations committed by the father and protecting the child Diana. That might account for the richness of certain recollections against a very sparse backdrop of general memories. But something set off a warning bell in the back of Sarah's mind. Something about the account was too glib. Something had a false ring to it.

Sarah occasionally worked with clients she did not care for personally. Rarely had this presented a problem in the therapist-client relationship. So what was the difference between working with an unpleasant client and an unliked alter? One difference, Sarah realized, was that she did not fully understand her aversion to Nora. The personality—the person—was generally pleasant and responsive. What was it that nagged at her? Sarah certainly found Diana pleasant and looked forward to working with her. Even the abrasive and volatile Lynn had impressed Sarah with her candor. And where was Lynn, anyway? And why didn't Nora know about Lynn? Maybe that was it: Nora regarded herself as an expert, *the* protector and memory of Diana Smith. Sarah distrusted persons with large egos; the larger the ego, the narrower the universe, she believed. And that also meant that Nora was either gravely mistaken in her impressions concerning Diana—which rendered all her information suspect—or she deliberately misled Sarah in her knowledge. *That* was the impression Sarah was unable to allay . . . that there was some intentional misrepresentation in Nora's accounts. But that was absurd, wasn't it? Multiples didn't deliberately prevaricate, did they? Why would they?

At any rate, perhaps there was some reason to suspect the content of Nora's recollections. Perhaps she would make more headway if she tried to determine the role that Nora played in this complex, multidimensional person, rather than attempt to use Nora as a window into the history of that person.

"Nora, what happens to Diana when she blacks out or 'has trouble with time,' as she puts it?"

"I take over," Nora said.

"But where does Diana go when you take over?" Sarah asked.

"I don't know. She just goes away."

"But she doesn't know what's going on, like you know what's going on when Diana has the body?"

"No, of course not," Nora said, as if explaining some obvious point to a small child. "Maybe this will help," she continued. "Diana goes to sleep, a deep, dreamless sleep."

"How do you know it's dreamless?" Sarah asked, struggling to keep her own inflection even and emotionless.

"Because she's not really asleep. I use sleep as an analogy." Sarah sensed a barely concealed arrogance in the phrasing. She ignored it.

"So you observe everything? Are you always aware of what Diana does?"

Nora smiled condescendingly. "Even *I* have to get away from the tedious little life Diana lives."

"How?"

"I sleep."

"So then you don't always know what's going on?"

"Sarah, why do you insist on denigrating my position in this relationship?"

"I am very sorry if I gave you that impression," Sarah said. "It's just that our time together is limited and you know so much."

"Well, all right," Nora said, apparently mollified.

"You told me when we first met that Diana tried to kill herself because she was tired."

"That's right."

"You also said that when she went to sleep after taking the Valium, you went to sleep, too."

"Yes."

"What else do you remember about that night?" Sarah asked.

"I remember everything, of course," Nora said, a hint of anger in her voice.

"You remember Diana taking the pills?"

"Yes."

"Why didn't you stop her?" Sarah asked, springing the trap.

Nora narrowed her eyes, and a small smile twitched at the corners of her lips. "Sarah," Nora sighed, as if weary of giving explanations to the simpleminded, "I cannot always use the body, you know. If I could, I'd certainly be tempted to keep it all the time."

Sarah noted with detached curiosity a sense of mild triumph at having cornered Nora. While she had not quite gained a denial of ubiquity, Nora had conceded some limitations. *Why should this please me so?* Sarah wondered. *Isn't an antagonistic tone the wrong message to send to this personality and to any other personalities that might be aware?* But Sarah could not shake the feeling that this was *not* the case . . . that she had sent precisely the correct message.

Abruptly, Sarah terminated the session. Nora returned control of the body to Diana. Diana assumed that she had been awakened from a hypnotic trance, and for now Sarah encouraged this slight untruth as a cover for the personality change. Sarah gave Diana a map and went over the directions to her house. She had Diana leave several minutes early.

Sarah stared out her office window, confused at the curious mixture of elation, repugnance, and concern that pulsed through her like an electric current.

Chapter 10

Week 7: Friday, September 15

"You found it!" Sarah held the door open with one hand, a damp dish towel in the other. Diana—was it Diana?—stepped in. She turned to face Sarah as the door closed. For an awkward moment, Sarah was uncertain what to do next. To Sarah's surprise, Diana solved the problem with a quick, affectionate embrace. Sarah smiled at the easy appropriateness of the gesture and again wondered who her dinner guest was. She searched the face of her visitor, looking for the elusive differences that might mark one of the other personalities. She concluded with relief that this was Diana.

"Did you have any problems finding the place?"

"None at all. Your map was great." Diana turned and took in the living room at a glance. "Oh, I like this."

"Here, let me take your things."

Sarah led the way across the living room and into the kitchen. "How about a glass of wine, and then I'll give you the grand tour?"

"Oh, no, I couldn't. I mean, I usually don't drink alcohol."

"All right. How about a soda, then? Coffee?" Sarah asked.

"Well, it is Friday," Diana said hesitantly. "Are you having wine?"

"You bet."

"I'll have a glass with you, then."

"Wine it is," said Sarah.

Sarah watched with interest the younger woman's delight in the decorations and furnishings of the house. She seemed to notice everything. In Mark's home office, she was initially awed by the array of computers and other electronic equipment. Then her attention turned to several framed photographs on the wall.

"Did you take these?" Diana asked.

"No, I'm afraid my only camera is a twenty-year-old Instamatic. Those are Mark's."

"They are quite good. Especially this one," Diana indicated a black and white landscape.

Sarah lifted the photograph off its hook and handed it to her. "Mark would be pleased to hear that," she said. "You'll have to tell him when he gets here."

"Where did he learn his photography?" Diana asked, examining the picture closely.

"When he was a teenager," Sarah said. "Both Mark's parents were killed when he was very young and he and his brother were raised in an orphanage. When he was old enough to earn some money, he bought a camera. He says that's what he used to escape."

"I understand," Diana said. "Sometimes I use it that way, too. Why didn't he pursue it professionally? Judging from this, he had the eye for it."

"Oh, other interests, I suppose," Sarah answered, then pointed to Mark's desk. "He got hooked on computers, as you can see."

"I see," Diana said, handing the photograph back to Sarah. "I look forward to discussing photography with him."

"I'm sure he'll like that," Sarah said. She was pleased that Diana had discovered a link between herself and Mark. She wanted Mark to enjoy the evening.

If he got to know her, he might begin to understand why Diana had come to consume so much of her time. And they really did have a lot in common. The photography. And, on a darker note, they shared the experience of a dysfunctional childhood. Mark had grown up in a succession of orphanages and foster homes. Some of his experiences had been pretty grim.

"Don't forget to tell him you liked his pictures," Sarah said.

At that moment, fifteen miles on the other side of town, Mark Johnson was packing up a digital multimeter and stuffing it into the heavy briefcase-style tool box he carried. A short, balding man in bow tie and too-short trousers reached out a hand. Mark shook it.

"I hate to keep you late on a Friday," the man said. "But this means everything will be ready to go on Monday."

"No problem," Mark said, and both men turned at the sound of a telephone ringing.

"I'll just be a second," the little man rushed off.

Mark finished his packing, then leaned over the desk and typed several commands on the computer's keyboard. The monitor's display changed rapidly. Mark smiled, satisfied at what he saw there, then looked at his watch. *Damn,* he thought, *Sarah's gonna be disappointed if I don't show up soon. I'll give her a call when Martin gets back.*

"It's for you, Mark," Martin yelled from an adjacent office. "Pick up on line one."

Mark lifted the receiver, said "hello," and groaned inwardly as he recognized both the voice and the general tone of panic it carried. Martin wandered into the room and began idly typing at the keyboard. When Mark hung up the phone, Martin looked up.

"Everything okay, Mark?" he asked.

"Yeah. Well, no, to be honest. I've got a panicked

customer who says his network just crashed on him and he has to have it up tonight to prepare for an emergency board meeting tomorrow."

"So you're heading over there?"

"Yep. Oh, well, that's business," Mark sighed. "Mind if I use your phone to call my wife?"

"By all means," said Martin.

Sarah and Diana had finished touring the house and were sipping wine on the back deck when the phone rang.

"Be right back," Sarah said.

She guessed that it was Mark calling as she picked up the receiver. "Hello," she said.

"Hi, honey."

"Hello, Mark. Where are you? Is everything all right?"

"I'm afraid not." He sounded tired. "John Beiderbeck just called and his system's gone down in flames. He needs me to come over right away."

"How long will it take?"

"I don't know. Could be anything from fifteen minutes to six hours. There's just no way of telling. Honey, I'm really sorry. Did your . . ." Mark hesitated—client, friend, multiple personality?— ". . . show up?"

"Yes, Diana got here a little while ago," Sarah said. "Mark, I understand. I just want you to be careful. You sound tired."

"I *am* tired," Mark said. "It's been a long day."

"Get a cup of coffee in you before you drive anywhere. I'll fix you a plate and you can eat whenever you get in."

"What's for supper?" Mark asked.

"Beef Stroganoff," said Sarah.

"Damn, my favorite," Mark said, and sighed again.

* * *

Diana went to the bathroom while Sarah drained the noodles and placed them in a covered dish. Sarah poured more wine in their glasses and was lighting the candles when Diana returned.

"What a beautiful table," Diana said. "I love candlelight."

"Me, too," said Sarah. "Let's eat. I'm starved."

"Great."

Sarah and Diana fixed their plates of Stroganoff and put dressing on their salads. Diana placed a forkful of the Stroganoff in her mouth. Sarah did not notice for a moment the expression of dismay on the woman's face. A fine sheen of sweat broke out on Diana's forehead. Placing the fork on her plate, Diana involuntarily turned her face away.

Sarah looked up from her plate, instantly seeing the change in Diana. She looked intensely ill.

"Diana," she said, rising, "what's wrong?"

"Oh, God, I'm sorry. I . . ." She stood and turned away.

Sarah heard a gagging sound. She hurried around the table and walked Diana down the hall into the nearest bathroom. She made Diana sit while she rinsed a washcloth in cold water and placed it on her forehead. After several minutes, Diana's breathing slowed and the color returned to her face. Sarah removed the cloth and brushed a strand of damp hair off Diana's forehead. Diana smiled weakly.

"I'm so sorry."

"Hush," Sarah said gently, "I'll not hear apologies. Just tell me what happened."

"I—I'm not sure. I took a bite of the meat and then I started to remember something. It was terrible." She looked at Sarah with large, frightened eyes.

"Tell me what you remembered?"

"I can't. I don't know. I just got a glimpse of something and then I felt violently ill. I don't eat meat very often," she added lamely. "Sarah, I'm so sorry."

"Don't be sorry. Tell me what you saw."

Diana shuddered. "It doesn't make any sense."

Sarah quietly insisted, "Tell me."

Diana grabbed Sarah's hands and held them in a fierce grip. "I suddenly saw myself with blood on my hands. Somebody died, Sarah, I know somebody died."

Sarah resisted the impulse to pursue the memory or whatever it was that had upset Diana.

"Well, it's over now," she said matter-of-factly. "And I know what we're going to do. You wait right here."

Diana opened her mouth to protest, but Sarah was gone. She returned in a few moments and escorted Diana back to the dining room. Fresh plates sat at both women's places. What remained of the Stroganoff was now in a much smaller bowl. All the meat had been removed from the sauce. Sarah filled her plate with noodles and spooned some of the sauce over the pasta. She turned the serving spoon's handle toward Diana.

"Dig in," she smiled.

Diana returned the smile, and neither woman made reference to the incident for the remainder of the evening.

Mark looked at the amber words glowing on the computer's monitor. He shook his head.

"I don't get it," he said, more to himself than to his companion.

"What is it?" John Beiderbeck asked.

"All the network configuration files are corrupted."

"Is that bad?"

"It ain't good."

"Can you fix it?"

"Sure, I can fix it. The question is, what happened to them? As near as I can tell, everything else is fine. All the other files are intact, the hard disk is okay, all the hardware diagnostics check out. Weird." Mark looked up from the monitor, eyes narrowing. "John, you don't happen to have some kind of junior hacker on your staff, do you? Somebody who likes to play with the machines, maybe doesn't *really* quite know what he's doing?"

"Sure, about half my employees," Beiderbeck laughed. Mark laughed, too. "You think it's been sabotaged?" Beiderbeck was suddenly serious.

"No, nothing like that," Mark said with false assurance. "It could be, of course, but I doubt it. Probably just coincidence or something that I missed in the installation process." Mark stretched his arms over his head. "Anyway, it's no problem. It'll just take me a while to reconfigure everything. Unless . . . John, are your people doing their backups like I showed them?"

"They should be," Beiderbeck said, then added, "they'd better be."

"Good. This may be easier than I thought. If the backup files are intact, we'll just copy them over."

"All right," said Beiderbeck. "Listen, Mark, what say I buy you dinner when you finish?"

"John, I'd love it, but I need to get home as soon as I can. I'll have to take a rain check."

"Oh, gosh, I'll bet I'm ruining plans you had for tonight, right?"

"No, no," Mark lied.

"Well, at least let me provide some hors d'oeuvres while you work. I'll be back in fifteen minutes."

Sarah fixed coffee, which they carried out to the living room. She was disappointed that Mark had not arrived in time for dinner. She hoped he would still show up in time to meet Diana. *At any rate,* she thought, *the heat's off me for working late.*

* * *

It took twenty minutes to locate the correct diskette. Mark copied the files over to the hard disk, then began examining them.

"Rats," he said aloud. These files were also corrupted. *Strange,* thought Mark. *How could the backups have been made if the network files were corrupted?* If the files were trashed, the machine shouldn't have run properly and it would have been impossible to make backup copies. Of course, it was possible to start the machine from a diskette, but that would indicate that not only did someone know what they were doing, but they had deliberately ruined the backups.

Mark tried to dismiss the possibility. Sabotage was not something he had encountered before, but in this era of computer viruses and corporate espionage, it was certainly not impossible. John ran a serious business, with serious competitors. He was also on a pretty fast political track. Mark resolved to discuss the possibility with him when he returned.

As if on cue, Mark heard a key in the outside door. A second later it opened, and Beiderbeck entered bearing several packages.

"How goes it?" Beiderbeck asked.

"Slow," Mark said. "The backups are corrupted, too, which means I just wasted the last twenty minutes. Except that I did have an idea I want to discuss with you." Mark explained quickly the possibility that the system could have been deliberately sabotaged.

Beiderbeck listened intently. When Mark had finished, he reached into one bag and pulled out a bottle of beer. Condensation beaded on the bottle. Beiderbeck twisted off the cap and handed it to Mark. Mark nodded gratefully and drank, while Beiderbeck opened another bottle for himself.

"So what do we do?" Beiderbeck asked, reaching into a smaller bag and pulling out a package wrapped in paper. Unfolding the paper, he revealed four egg rolls. Mark's stomach growled in uncontrolled response to the smell of the food. He turned from the keyboard.

"God, that smells good."

"Dig in," Beiderbeck said.

For the next half hour, Mark munched egg rolls, sipped beer, and discussed security procedures for local area networks.

Sarah had wondered earlier what she would talk about with Diana. The last thing she wanted to do was discuss therapy-related issues. The incident at dinner had come too close to that.

To her surprise, Diana was animated and full of questions. She chatted happily about interior design and architecture, topics that interested Sarah. Sarah found herself not only avoiding slipping into her therapist's role, but actually enjoying herself.

Sarah's only concern was Mark. It was getting later and later. Where was he?

Mark finally finished the last of the file transfers and looked at his watch. *Eleven-thirty. Damn. Oh, well,* he thought, *at least I've got my own copies of the files if the system crashes again.* Mark knew, however, with a certainty he could not explain, that such a crash would not happen again. *Next time it'll be something else. Must be a variation on Murphy's Law.*

Wearily, he packed his case. The job had taken longer than it should have. A combination of fatigue, two beers, and a desire on the part of John Beiderbeck to discuss everything under the sun had delayed progress.

"Sure you won't have another beer?" Beiderbeck asked even as Mark stepped out onto the sidewalk.

For a fleeting instant, Mark had the clear impression that Beiderbeck was deliberately trying to delay him.

He shook his head. *Absurd,* he thought; *the man was as anxious to get home as he was. Simply a good host.*

The car protested but started after several attempts. Mark saw Beiderbeck entering his BMW as he pulled the ancient Volvo out into the Friday night traffic.

"It's been wonderful," Diana stretched and yawned.

"Yes, it has," Sarah agreed. "Are you going to be okay driving home?"

"Yes, I'm fine. Just a little sleepy."

"Then let's have another cup of coffee before you go. Come on. I'm just going to sit up waiting for Mark to get home, anyway. I'll feel better knowing you're wide awake."

"All right," Diana said.

The thump-thump-thump of the flat tire frightened Mark badly. He eased the car over to the side of the interstate. *What next?* he wondered, retrieving the flashlight from his tool case.

Mark examined the tire. At first he could spot no visible flaw and was about to give up looking, when the penlight's beam reflected off something. *There you are, you little bugger,* Mark said to himself as he pulled on the object. *A nail, of course. Well, I might have guessed.*

Mark changed the tire, gripping the penlight in his mouth. The whole procedure took about twenty minutes. It was not until he eased the Volvo back onto the interstate that he wondered how a nail had penetrated the *side* of the tire.

Sarah hugged Diana at the door and watched until she was in her car and had it started. Sarah lingered a moment at the door, and as the car pulled away, she waved.

* * *

The car passed by Mark about a quarter mile from the house. Mark thought to himself, *I'll bet that's Sarah's client.* There just wasn't that much traffic in the suburbs at that hour. As the car pulled past, Mark glanced over. A trick of the headlights cast sudden illumination on the face of a young woman with blond hair, but the lighting lasted only a moment. Mark did not have time to pick out any details of the woman's face.

He pulled the Volvo straight into the drive, instead of backing it in as was his usual practice. Tonight he was just too tired to bother. *Just like old times,* he thought, stepping out of the car. A light came on over the front porch. Mark hurried to the house, where Sarah waited for him.

Chapter 11

Week 8: Monday, September 18

Sarah stared at the computer monitor. As was often the case, she had decided to prepare the letter herself, rather than pass a handwritten draft to Margie. In the time it took to write a draft, she could have typed it herself on the computer. Sarah sipped her coffee absentmindedly for a few minutes, composing the letter in her head, then began quickly typing:

Dear Ms. Janus:

I enjoyed your visit to my office several weeks ago. Your insights and concerns about my client were most helpful. I regret that our meeting was so short.

I am sure your schedule is quite busy. However, if there is any way in which you could see clear to come by my office, I would be most grateful. There are several matters that I believe I can resolve only with your assistance. Any Tuesday or Thursday between 2:30 and 4:30 would be convenient. If this does not meet your schedule, I would be happy to set up another time at your convenience.

I look forward to seeing you again.

An idea had occurred to Sarah over the weekend, an idea that had seemed absurd at first. She had been unable to invoke Lynn in session. Indeed, her attempt to do so had resulted in a frightening nonresponsiveness in the hypnotized Diana. So why not write Lynn a letter? In the literature on MPD, Sarah had discovered that well-developed personalities sometimes lived separate, secret lives. They had hobbies, jobs, even relationships that they kept concealed from their core personalities. If Diana Smith were to receive a letter addressed to Linda Janus—and Sarah felt certain that Lynn and Linda were the same personality—would she automatically ignore it, just as she ignored the bottle of Valium in her medicine cabinet? Sarah was willing to take the chance. She printed out the letter, folded it, and carried it out to Margie.

"Do me a favor?"

"Sure, what's up?" Margie asked.

"Could you address an envelope for this? Preferably one without our return address on it." Sarah thought a return address might trigger Diana's suspicions.

"Sure."

"And, Margie, would you mind mailing that immediately? I'd like it to get there as soon as possible."

Week 8: Tuesday, September 19

Sarah saw immediately that it was Diana attending the session, but then she hadn't really expected the invitation to Linda Janus to have arrived yet, anyway. Without thinking, she breathed deeply and exhaled a long sigh. It was certainly difficult to make therapeutic plans when you weren't even sure which of your client's personalities would be showing up.

"I enjoyed Friday evening, Sarah," Diana said. "A lot."

"I enjoyed it, too," Sarah replied. "We should do

it again soon. After all, you still didn't get to meet Mark." Sarah smiled. "I swear, I really do have a husband."

Diana smiled in return. "Yes. I'd like that very much."

"Okay, then. Shall we get down to work?"

Diana nodded. "Sarah," she said slowly, "there's one thing I've been wanting to ask you about. A couple of sessions ago, we talked about that dream I had? The one with the two dolls?"

"Yes." Sarah thought she could guess what was coming.

"I couldn't remember Sissie until you brought the whole thing up again."

"And you want to know why you couldn't remember before, when we had talked about it a month or so ago in great detail?"

"That's right." Diana frowned.

"Well, I'll tell you what *might* be happening. I think we are going to find a number of traumatic events in your childhood," Sarah said carefully. "Sometimes we cope with trauma by forgetting. It's pretty effective, at least in the short term. Unfortunately, in the long run, trauma has a way of bubbling up to the surface. Sometimes, when we start to remember things, the mechanism that allows us to forget kicks in. For a while, at least, the mechanism for forgetting can be stronger than the memory."

"I see," Diana said, but her voice sounded uncertain.

"Look, I'm no expert here. We're learning together." Sarah smiled. "But so far, nothing you're going through is unique."

"Really? You mean you've got articles, or case histories, or whatever you call them of people like me? Stuff I could read?"

Sarah winced at the eagerness in Diana's face. *Sure,*

she thought, *ever read* Sybil? *When do I tell her what's going on? We're going too fast here, folks. Let's slow it down.*

"Let's put it this way. Everything you're experiencing I've encountered before, either in the literature or in my practice. But how it all comes together is unique to you. We're still working together to make sense of it all, okay? There's nothing I can give you to read right now that's going to be of much value."

"Oh." Diana's disappointment filled the air like the cigarette smoke that hung between them.

"Diana, as long as we're on the subject of dreams, I'd like to talk about the dream that you remember having as a child. I'd like to try an experiment. I would like to have you work through a relaxation and visualization technique that sometimes is useful for remembering."

"You mean hypnosis?"

"No, not hypnosis," said Sarah. "This is similar in some respects, except that you are in control and conscious. This will be like a light stage of self-hypnosis, except that I will help guide you. Are you willing to try?"

Diana paused a moment before answering, "I guess so."

"Good," Sarah said. "How about moving to the couch. I think you'll be more comfortable there."

Diana kicked off her sandals and stretched out on the leather couch. Sarah talked her through a deep relaxation exercise in which she had Diana flex various muscle groups and then imagine them becoming relaxed. The visualization started at the feet and worked its way up. Sarah had used the technique herself on occasion as a stress-management exercise. She knew that, at the very least, the deep relaxation it produced was pleasant and stress-reducing.

"All right, Diana, I want you to breathe deeply and relax. Take several deep breaths, in through your nose, out through your mouth. Good. Again. And again.

Good. Now just relax and breathe normally. Keep your eyes closed. How do you feel?"

"Wonderful."

"Good," Sarah smiled. "Just don't fall asleep on me. Okay, I'm going to help guide you on a journey through your memory. I will suggest things for you to see and do along the way, but at all times you are in control. We will do things only if you want to do them. I'm just providing suggestions, all right?"

"Yes."

"Good. I want you to imagine that you're walking along through a very pleasant forest. The sun is shining and birds are singing. It is a lovely day . . . just warm enough to be comfortable. Can you see the forest?"

Diana smiled. "Yes. This is nice."

"Yes, this should be very pleasant," Sarah agreed. "Now you're walking along through the woods. The trees get a little thicker and closer together because you're going deeper and deeper into the beautiful forest. Can you see the trees?"

"Yes, I can," Diana said lazily. "The sunlight filters down through the leaves. Everything is very green."

Sarah continued suggesting imagery, guiding Diana deeper into the imaginary forest. "Okay, we're resting now on some rocks. But look to the right, in the hillside. It looks like a cave. Can you see it?"

"Yes, I see it."

Sarah looked closely at her client, sensing a sudden tenseness in her voice. A deep frown had returned to her face. Sarah decided to change the imagery. Some people experienced claustrophobic reactions to the suggestion of a cave.

"I'm sorry, I'm mistaken. It's not a cave at all. It's a large house carved of stone, carved out of the mountainside. Can you see it?"

"Yes," Diana said. Her frown disappeared. She seemed relaxed.

"Good. Let's go exploring. Let's step into the open doorway. The room carved inside the hillside is very large"—*imagery to allay claustrophobia,* thought Sarah—"but it's also dark. I see a torch hanging in a bracket on the wall. Can you reach it?"

"Yes, I have it."

"Good. Here, I'll light it. There, that's better. Let's go inside. This room is empty, but I see a doorway ahead of us. Let's walk over to it. Diana, I know where we are. I have been here before. This is the entrance to the—" Sarah stopped herself from saying *cavern* just in time, "Hall of Memories. These are your memories. When we walk into the hall, you will be able to choose to look at any memories you care to. Can you see the doorway?"

Diana was several seconds in replying.

"Yes," she finally said.

"We are stepping across the threshold now into another very large room. The room is circular, and there are dozens and dozens of doorways set into the wall. All the doors are closed. Can you see the doors?"

"Yes."

"Behind each door, Diana, is a memory. If you open a door, you will be able to look at a memory. We do not have to go in. We can just stand on the threshold looking in, all right?"

"I don't know if I should."

"Why not?"

"Maybe it's not allowed."

"It's okay. I'm here with you."

"If you say so."

"We are walking across the room to the door behind which is the memory of a dream you had once. You had a dream about flying when you were a small child," Sarah said. "When we open the door and look in, we will see everything about the dream. You will look into the memory and you will see everything. We are at the door now. Diana, put your hand on the doorknob and open it."

"I'm afraid."

"It's okay. I'm here with you. Your hand is on the knob and you are turning it. You are pulling the door open. Look inside, Diana. What do you see?"

"It's too dark."

"Then stick the torch in and you'll see everything. You're putting the torch in through the doorway. There, suddenly the room is bright. What do you see?"

Diana gasped, a sharp intake of breath.

"What is it, Diana? What do you see?"

"He . . . he's touching me."

"Who is touching you?"

"The Father."

"Your father's touching you?"

"No, the Father. In black. He's touching me."

"Oh, you mean a priest. A priest dressed in black?"

"Yes."

"Where is he touching you."

"He's touching me here." Diana's hand was between her legs. "Oh, God, he's touching me here. He's putting that thing in me." Her voice rose an octave. *"He's putting it inside me."*

"Diana, it's all right," Sarah said. "We're standing at the doorway now, looking in. He can't harm you. We're standing at the doorway, watching the memory. It's like watching television, isn't it?" Sarah kept her voice even and soft, soothing.

"Yes."

"All right, we're going to look again. What is he putting inside you, Diana?"

"I can't look."

"Yes, you can. I'm with you. Here, I'll hold your hand." Sarah leaned over the edge of the couch, touching Diana gently on the upper arm. Diana winced, as if burned. Then she relaxed and reached up to grasp

Sarah's hand. Sarah was surprised at the strength of her grip. "What is he putting inside you?"

"It's his cross . . . his cross."

"Relax, Diana. I'm with you. We are watching from the doorway. He's put his crucifix in you? In your vagina?" Sarah felt a sudden wave of nausea, then anger. *My God, did this really happen?* "What happens next?"

"I think I pass out for a moment, because everything's dark. And then I'm floating, Oh, God, I'm floating. I'm free. I can see the Father below me and me on the bed."

"What's the Father doing?"

"He's talking to me and he's rubbing me here."

Sarah watched as Diana rhythmically moved the hand that seconds before covered her protectively. The hand rubbed up the thigh and between her legs, up and down, up and down.

"What's the man saying?"

"I can't hear him."

"Let's listen carefully," Sarah encouraged. "Remember we're at the doorway. We can hear and see everything. What is he saying?"

"I can barely hear. Wait a minute." Diana paused, her face straining with the effort of hearing a voice spoken twenty years earlier. Her hand still moved slowly over her thigh. "He's saying, 'Rise up, rise up, daughter. Rise up and fly. See the room from the vantage of the ceiling and rise higher and higher. Rise higher into the night, daughter of darkness.' And I can see all around me. It's beautiful. The stars are shining. I'm flying, floating. It feels wonderful."

Diana's hand covered the crotch of her jeans, rubbing the area with increasing urgency. *Do I stop this?* Sarah asked herself. *She's masturbating, and she's going to remember that I sat here and let her do it. What do I do?*

"But now he's telling me to go higher, higher," Diana continued, the motion of her hand increasing. "But

I don't want to. I don't want to. But he tells me and I go higher, and it's all dark."

"Diana, relax. You're here with me."

"No, no, I'm floating, higher and higher. It's dark and there are hands, everywhere there are hands." Diana's back arched as her hand pushed against the fabric of her clothing. The grip on Sarah's hand increased painfully. Diana's breathing was ragged, gasping. Sarah watched with a helpless mixture of concern, fear, and embarrassment as her client writhed with the force of her orgasm.

"Hands, hands, hands," Diana chanted. "Hands are everywhere. *Take the hands away,*" she screamed. Now at the apex of orgasm, she arched again, then fell back on the couch. Her eyes opened suddenly, focused on some distant point. She snapped her head around to look at Sarah.

"What? . . ." she asked, bewildered. Then she looked down at herself, saw the hand still clutching herself.

"Oh, my God, what am I? . . ." She snatched her hand from Sarah's, sat up on the edge of the couch, and folded into herself, huddling into her own arms.

"Diana, are you all right?" Sarah cursed herself for the feebleness of the statement. She touched Diana gently on the shoulder. Diana instantly flinched away.

"Don't touch me," she hissed.

"Diana, it's all right. You were just remembering something that happened long ago."

Diana looked up.

"It's a memory, that's all."

"A memory?" Diana asked, still not comprehending. "What happened?"

"You were in the stone house, the house of memory. We were looking in one of the rooms."

Diana gave her a wild look.

"Stone house? What are you talking about?"

"Do you remember the relaxation exercise we did?"

"I remember lying down. I guess I must have fallen asleep." Diana relaxed a bit. She turned on the couch to face Sarah. "Did I? . . ." Diana, searching in confusion for words, flushed scarlet in embarrassment.

"Did you have an orgasm?" Sarah asked gently. "Yes, you did."

"You mean I masturbated?" she asked in disbelief.

"Yes. You masturbated because you were reliving the experience of having been sexually abused. You mustn't be embarrassed. I know you feel like you've lost control of yourself, but it's all right. We were trying a technique to help you remember the dream of flying you had as a child. Do you remember anything about the last half hour?"

"I don't think so," Diana shook her head. "Why don't I remember?"

"You don't remember because it was traumatic and you're not quite ready to deal with it yet."

"You said somebody sexually abused me. Who?"

"I don't know, Diana," Sarah said evenly. "I think that what you remembered was a combination of a memory and what is called a screen or shadow memory. I don't think that what you described happened exactly that way. But it's remarkable progress, what you've done today. I hope you understand that."

"I just feel awful and dirty. And you watched it all, didn't you?" Diana flushed with a fresh wave of embarrassment.

"I'm sorry," Sarah said softly. "Yes, I was present. I didn't stop you. I'm not sure I could have. I know how you feel."

"No, I don't think so," Diana interrupted.

"I suppose you're right," Sarah admitted. "But, Diana, therapy sometimes does funny things. Sometimes it makes things that happened long ago seem like they're happening right now. There is no shame in that. It's called abreaction, and it's how you free yourself of the past."

"But God, it feels so awful."

"Look, I'm not sure you're ready to hear this yet. But whatever happened to you is not your fault. I think maybe someone took advantage of a little girl in ways that should never be done. We're going to find out about that together, all right? We're going to have to share more than just this. Do you think we can do that?"

Diana's eyes searched Sarah's face for several moments. Finally, her look softened. She reached out and took Sarah's hand.

"Sarah, help me. Please, help me," she said.

"I'll help you, Diana."

At seven that evening, Sarah retrieved the heavy office dictionary from its spot on the bookshelf. She had remembered from her reading that alternate personalities are often named according to their functions or personality traits. A personality with responsibility for ensuring the integrity of the group might be called The Protector, while an excessively submissive alternate might end up with a name like Dolly Do-good. With luck, Lynn or Linda would be attending a session soon, and Sarah had begun to think about the name on the bottle of Valium. Sarah recalled that Janus was the name of a Greek or Roman god, and she wondered at its significance. She quickly found the entry. In addition to the definition for *Janus-faced,* meaning "two-faced"—*not a bad image for multiple personality disorder,* she thought—the description of the god was also interesting:

> . . . in Roman mythology, the god of doorways and gates, of beginnings, and of the sun's rising and setting, depicted as a head with two opposite faces . . .

Sarah knew she had a *Bulfinch's Mythology* somewhere, too. She found it tucked away on a top shelf. It added a little:

> . . . A solar deity; doorkeeper of heaven and patron of the beginning and end of things. He had two faces, one for the rising sun and one for sunset. The first month of the year was named for him. The gates of his temples were kept open in time of war . . .

What door is it that you watch over, Janus? thought Sarah. *What beginnings and what endings do you protect?* And, with a chill, the thought came: *What war will open your gates?*

Chapter 12

Week 8: Thursday, September 21

Sarah recognized the slicked-back hairstyle, the open challenge in the narrowed eyes, the amused expression of the slightly upturned lips.

"Lynn, or should I say Linda," Sarah said, "it's wonderful to see you again."

The woman stepped into the office as Sarah closed the door behind her. A few paces in, she turned to face the therapist.

"You're pretty clever," she smiled.

Lynn seated herself, smoothing her dress as she sat down. *Funny,* thought Sarah, *Diana does the same thing, but she does it completely differently.* Lynn wore a shapeless black dress, portions of which were designed with a see-through material revealing the black slip underneath. Sarah recognized the style as very new and very fashionable among the music video set.

"Shall I call you Lynn or Linda?" Sarah asked.

"Call me Lynn, why don'tcha? That's how we started, isn't it?"

"But you are Linda Janus, aren't you?" Sarah asked mildly.

"Yeah."

Sarah smiled. "I remember you telling me that

names are power. Is that why you prefer me to call you Lynn?''

"Something like that, I guess. Just chalk it up to superstition if you want,'' Lynn shrugged. "No big deal. Okay, honey, let's cut the chitchat, all right? You're wastin' my time. Why did you ask me here?''

"Well, I asked you if you would keep an eye on Diana for me, right?''

"Yeah, so?''

"We're not making much progress.'' She paused a moment, deciding on an approach. "I need even more help from you, Lynn.''

"Go ahead.''

"I'm trying to help Diana piece together some of what happened to her a long time ago. And I'm having a hard time figuring out who or what to believe.''

The smile that seemed to play perpetually about Lynn's lips now broadened. "Doesn't surprise me a bit. So what have you heard?''

On impulse, Sarah asked, "Do you know what goes on in our sessions?''

"You give yourself too much credit for being interesting. Therapy is Diana's thing. Mostly I leave it to her.''

"Nora has been telling me a lot about what—'' Sarah began.

"Nora?'' Lynn interrupted, leaning forward, her grin vanished.

"Yes, Nora. Why? Is something wrong?''

"Listen to me,'' Lynn clenched her teeth. "Don't believe a word that bitch has to say.''

Sarah sat back, momentarily at a loss. Finally, she stammered, "But . . . why?''

"Because she's a lying bitch and can't be trusted.''

"But how can that be? You are all part of the same . . .'' Sarah stopped herself.

"Go ahead, say what you want to say. Listen, honey, I have very few illusions. Did you want to say we're all a part of the same person? Well, you're wrong. We all share the same body. That's the extent of it. Some of us work together, help each other out. But not the one who calls herself Nora. Trust me on this, Sarah."

"But I don't understand," Sarah said. "Nora wouldn't do anything to hurt the rest of you, would she? How could she hurt you without hurting herself?"

"Nora doesn't work like you and I work, doc. How shall I put this?" Lynn paused, glancing around the room. "Nora answers to a different authority. In fact, she really doesn't even belong here. She was a . . ." Lynn looked at Sarah. "And I talk too much."

"Lynn, talk to me. I need your help."

"Look, doc. I like you, I really do. But you don't have any idea what you're messing with here. Trust me, the best thing you can do is to drop this case like a hot potato. By the way, can you write me a prescription for Valium?"

"What? No, I can't. And I wouldn't if I could. Why do you need Valium?"

"It relaxes me, doc. I'm a very tense kind of person. You sure you can't get me a prescription?"

Sarah realized she was being manipulated away from the main topic of conversation. What was it Lynn had said? Nora answers to another authority. A *different* authority, that was it.

"What do you mean, Nora answers to a different authority?" Sarah asked.

"Did I say that? Sorry, doc, I'm not real good with words, you know." Lynn raised her arms in a gesture of helplessness.

"I think you are excellent with words, Lynn." Sarah raised her eyebrows skeptically. Lynn laughed.

"I like you in spite of myself, doc."

"Thank you. If you like me, can't you tell me what's going on, then?"

"Doc, part of what I do is to watch out for us. I don't owe nobody else nothin'. Now you come along.

Tell me, doc, are you really out to help us? Or are you just another form of trouble?''

"I want to help.''

"Sure. But you don't even know what that means. I don't doubt your intentions. It's the effect of your actions that bothers me.''

"I don't understand.''

"Of course you don't.''

"Then help, please.'' Sarah slapped her open palm down on her desk. Lynn's eyes widened.

"All right, doc, show a little spunk, why don'tcha? Look, the best I can do right now is this. We'll take it one step at a time. You ask me questions. I'll decide one question at a time whether it's okay to answer. That's my best offer.''

"Fair enough.''

"All right. Time's short. Shoot.''

"Who's the different authority Nora answers to?'' Sarah asked.

"I can't answer that.''

"Why not?''

"Obviously, I can't answer that, either. You're wasting time, Sarah.'' Lynn lit a cigarette.

"When did you first start doing Diana's hair?''

"Why?'' Lynn asked. "You want me to do yours? You'd look good as a blonde, doc.''

"Now *you're* wasting time, Lynn,'' Sarah smiled. "When did you first start?''

"I started when Diana was about twelve.''

"Really? That seems awfully young. Why did you do it? Was it your idea?''

"I did it because it looked like shit with the roots growing out.''

"You mean that you didn't initially do her hair? Someone else did it?''

"That's right.''

"Who?''

"I can't answer that.''

"Come on, Lynn. You can't just say 'I can't answer that' all the time."

"No, you don't understand," Lynn chuckled. "I honestly don't know. I don't know everything. By the way, you really ought to think about having me do your hair. It would look good, I guarantee it."

Now Sarah laughed. "Somehow I've never seen myself as a blonde. I think it would be too much of a shock to my self-image."

"Hey, what's life without a little risk? What's the matter, you don't trust me? You're asking me to trust you, aren't you?"

"You're good," Sarah said. "You should be a therapist. Tell you what, I'll think about your offer. If I decide to become a blonde, you'll be the first to know."

"Fair enough," Lynn laughed.

"How many others are there?"

"Other what?" Lynn asked. "Persons sharing this body, you mean?"

Sarah nodded.

"That depends on how you count. There are a number of minor players. Some of them, I doubt you'll ever meet. I can't tell you the exact number."

"Can't or won't?" Sarah asked.

"Won't."

"Why does Diana have an aversion to drugs and you want a prescription for Valium?"

"We have different tastes. Diana has an aversion to drugs because she was given lots of drugs as a child."

"Why was she given drugs?" Sarah asked. "Do you mean medicine?"

Lynn smiled. "No, I mean drugs. She was forced to take drugs so that she would behave."

"What kind of drugs?"

"I can't answer that."

"Can't or won't?"

"Can't," Lynn said. "Don't know."

"Do you know who Sissie is?"

"Yes."

"Who is she?"

"A friend of Diana's. Sort of."

"What do you mean, sort of?"

"Can't answer that."

"Can't or won't?"

"Won't."

"Fine." Sarah sighed, leaned back in her chair, and grabbed a pencil. Without realizing it, she started chewing on the unsharpened end.

"What happened to Sissie?"

"She went away."

"When?"

"When Diana was eleven or twelve, I think."

"Why are you smiling?" Sarah asked.

"You ask interesting questions."

"Then Sissie's important?"

Lynn shrugged.

"This is like playing twenty questions. Only not all of them get answered."

"You want to stop?" Lynn asked sweetly.

"No, thank you." Sarah couldn't keep herself from smiling. *What a smartass,* Sarah thought. "What's your earliest memory?"

Lynn's mouth widened in an expression of mock surprise. "Well, well, let me think about that one. I remember lying on my back looking up. I must have been in a crib."

"How old are you?"

"I'm not sure. I can't be very old, though. Maybe three. Anyway, I'm lying there looking up at one of these mobiles over the crib. One with plastic birds flying around."

"It sounds like a happy memory."

"No. I don't think so. I hurt real bad. Here." Lynn placed a hand between her legs. The gesture reminded Sarah of the previous session with Diana. She felt a chill.

"Why do you hurt?"

"I don't know. That's all I remember. I think something happened to Diana and I stepped in to help her. I took the pain, but I don't know what happened to her."

"Can you remember other times when you took the pain, as you put it?"

"Yes."

"Will you tell me about one of them."

"No."

"Can't or won't?"

"Won't. By the way, it was nice of you to have Diana over to dinner the other night," Lynn said.

"I enjoy her company. It was a nice evening."

Lynn seemed to hesitate a moment.

"Have you ever asked Nora to go out or . . . uh . . . do anything?" she asked.

"No, I haven't," Sarah replied evenly.

"What do you think of her? Nora, I mean?"

"Uh . . . she's polite, well-spoken." Sarah searched for neutral adjectives. *Can Nora listen in? Can I offend her if I say the wrong thing?*

"Those are good weasel-words, doc," Lynn laughed. "Come on, level with me. You don't like her, do you? Do you?"

"Lynn, I don't think it would be a good idea for me to talk about her. It's like discussing another client."

"We've been discussing Diana with no problem."

"True." Sarah felt trapped. "All right. I'll be honest with you. I'm not sure I trust her, Lynn."

"Hallelujah, doc, there's hope for you yet. Don't trust her. She's a snake."

"Lynn, she said a lot of things about Diana's childhood. That she was molested by her father. She said that Diana's real mother left when she was about five or six, and the father remarried. Is any of that true, Lynn?"

Lynn snorted. "Hah! Maybe it is and maybe it isn't.

The point is, it doesn't matter. Anything she tells you is garbage."

"But it could be terribly important if Diana was sexually abused by her father."

"You don't get it. It really doesn't matter much. Of course she was abused by her father," Lynn stated simply.

"But don't you see, that's why Diana originally dissociated. That's why she's having so many problems now."

"No, it's not. It's not like that at . . ." Lynn stopped suddenly and smiled. "All right, maybe you're right. Sure."

"There's something you're not telling me, isn't there? What is it? What am I missing?" Sarah eased herself back into her chair.

"Can't say."

"Can't or won't?"

"Good question. Both, I think."

"Okay, here's another question for you: Why would Diana remember a dream from childhood about a priest sexually abusing her?"

"Maybe it's not a dream," Lynn said.

"What do you mean?"

"I mean, maybe it's not a dream. Maybe she's simply remembering something that actually happened."

"Are you saying a priest actually raped her with a—"

"With a crucifix?" Lynn interjected. "Why not?"

"Were you there? Or did you just know that she told me about the crucifix?"

"Sometimes the simplest explanations are the best."

"Oh. So you believe that Diana was really raped, or abused, by a priest?" Sarah asked.

"Listen to what Diana says. Did she say she was raped by a priest?"

"Yes."

"Then that's probably what happened. Just make sure that's what she said."

"I just can't believe that. Maybe it's because I was raised a Catholic."

"There are other priests besides Catholic priests, you know."

"What? Episcopalian? What are we talking here?"

"I can't tell you."

"Can't or won't?" Sarah asked.

Lynn pressed her lips together, making a zipping gesture with her hand. "It's time for me to be going, doc."

"Will you come back?"

"I don't know, doc. I talk too much when I get around you. I'm not sure that's good."

"It's good, Lynn," Sarah said. "I'm sure it is."

Lynn placed both hands on Sarah's desk and leaned across the top. Her eyes looked into Sarah's as if searching for some hidden meaning. "You don't know that, Sarah. We could all be in danger. You, too."

"Why, Lynn? Please tell me."

Lynn shrugged.

"Can I call on you again, Lynn?"

"Sometimes if you call I'm only the listener."

Sarah was about to say something concerning enigmatic statements but stopped. Instead, she stood and walked over to the door, opening it. "Come back if you can," she said.

Lynn walked up to Sarah. Unexpectedly, she reached up and took a section of Sarah's hair between her fingers and examined it closely for several moments. She made a tsk-tsk sound with her tongue, shaking her head in mock disapproval and grinning.

"You decide to do something about your hair, gimme a yell," she said.

Sarah pressed the eject button on the tape recorder and removed the cassette. With a felt tip pen, she labeled the tape. As an afterthought, she added *Lynn* in parentheses on the second line of the label. Reaching for the box to put the tape away, she suddenly stopped. Instead, she put the cassette back in the recorder and pressed the rewind button. After several attempts, she located the section she wanted.

"So where were we?" The hollow sound of her own voice filled the office. "Oh. So you believe that Diana was really raped, or abused, by a priest?"

Then, in Lynn's distinct whiskey voice: "Listen to what Diana says. Did she say she was raped by a priest?"

Sarah: "Yes."

Lynn: "Then that's probably what happened. Just make sure that that's what she said."

Sarah pressed the stop button. *That's twice she told me to either listen or make sure of what Diana said. I wonder . . .* Sarah ejected the tape, then pivoted her chair. She pulled open a drawer built into the cabinet behind her desk. She quickly located the cassette recording of Tuesday's session and in seconds had it rewinding in the recorder.

She stopped the tape several times, trying to remember the sequence of events that had led to the revelation of the priest. *First, we did the relaxation and visualization stuff,* she thought. She heard herself describing the house carved of stone, then she pressed the fast forward button. When she pressed play, the room filled with the earsplitting cry of Diana screaming *"He's putting it inside me."* Sarah winced and punched the stop button. She rewound the tape for a second more and pressed the play key.

Diana's voice said softly, "He . . . he's touching me." The voice sounded eerie, having followed so closely the recording of Lynn. *That's what it sounds like when two different people use the same vocal apparatus,* Sarah thought.

She heard her own voice: "Who is touching you?"

Diana now: "The Father."

And Sarah: "Your father's touching you?"

Diana: "No, the Father. In black. He's touching me."

Sarah: "Oh, you mean a priest? A priest dressed in black?"

Diana: "Yes."

Sarah: "Where is he touching you?"

Diana: "He's touching me here. Oh, God, he's touching me here. He's putting that thing in me. *He's putting it . . .*"

Sarah punched the recorder into silence, too slow to avoid the sound of Diana's horrified scream. It seemed to hang in the sudden silence, decaying slowly like the ping of a fingernail snapped against crystal. Sarah shook her head. *Okay,* she thought, *she didn't say 'priest.' I said 'priest.' She said 'the Father in black' and agreed when I said 'priest.' So what? I suppose the term* father *rules out Buddhists, Moslems, and most everybody else in the non-Christian world. Doesn't it? Who else uses the term? Who else has fathers in black? Is there something here? Is this what Lynn meant? Or was she just yanking my chain?*

Another problem bothering Sarah was the business of Diana's hair. It made no sense. Why does one personality labor to preserve the illusion of natural blondness for another personality? *Alters are supposed to see themselves as they imagine themselves to be,* Sarah thought. *They don't need artificial props. And Lynn claims that she was not responsible for Diana originally becoming a blonde. She just picked up the pieces afterward. Something happened then. Something happened when Diana became a blonde.*

Sarah put away the tapes and recorder. Suddenly, she felt exhausted. Her watch read almost seven. *Damn, where does the time go? Mark's probably been home for hours. Here I sit trying to solve puzzles that probably don't even exist.*

Let's go home.

* * *

Sarah pulled the Olds into the driveway, late again. She'd spent the last two hours poring over her notes, ruminating over the puzzle of Lynn, Nora, and Diana. She almost regretted seeing the old Volvo in the driveway. It meant that Mark was home. Usually, that was good, but tonight she wished that she were the one waiting and he the late arrival. *What does it mean when you start regretting the fact that your husband's at home?* she asked herself. *What does that mean, Ms. Therapist?*

Sarah entered the house from the back, coming in through the kitchen. She could hear the television blaring in the living room.

"I'm home," she called.

No response.

The sink was filled with dirtied pots and pans and dishes. *Looks like he had fun fixing something to eat, anyway.* A fifth of bourbon, half empty, sat on the counter. *That's a new bottle,* Sarah thought. *I picked up a half gallon last week.* Sarah left her purse on the counter and walked into the living room.

"Hi," she said.

Mark looked up from the program he was watching on the television. "Hello," he said.

Sarah walked over to his chair, leaned over, and kissed him. His breath reeked of bourbon. Worse, he barely returned the kiss.

"Sorry I'm late."

"S'all right." He turned his attention back to the TV.

The canned laughter of the sound track seemed absurd, almost physically grating on her nerves. She wanted to grab the remote from Mark's hand and silence the damn thing. Instead, she walked to the bedroom and changed into her robe, playing for time. Mark seemed so distant, so . . . cold, that she was taken aback. *Why was he so strange lately,* she wondered, *so resentful of the few extra hours she had to give to her practice?*

Whatever, this silent treatment wouldn't do. They had to talk about it, work it out.

Sarah padded to the kitchen in her bare feet and fixed a cup of instant coffee. She carried the coffee out to the couch and sat down.

Mark stood and stretched, wobbling a bit in the process.

"I'm going to bed," he said, and stumbled off down the hall.

"Wait, Mark, let's talk," she said.

Mark grumbled something, which she could not make out. Sarah waited a moment, dumbfounded, then followed him down the hall. She opened the door to the bedroom. He lay sprawled across the bed.

"Come on, Mark. We can work this out." She walked over to the bed and shook him. His deep breathing changed to a raspiness in the back of his throat. He was snoring.

Sarah returned to the living room. She sat sipping her coffee in the glare of the television, listening to laughter that was not funny, wondering what had gone wrong.

Week 9: Tuesday, September 26

Sarah absently tapped the end of the pen against her front teeth. When she realized what she was doing, she laid the pen on the desk blotter and picked up her coffee. Long moments later, she realized she had still not sipped from her mug. She set the mug down and rubbed her eyes with the heels of her palms, then slowly stretched and forced her head to pivot in a wide circle. Her neck popped and cracked, and some of the stiffness disappeared. She picked up her coffee and started flipping again through the pages of handwritten notes.

I'm sure something must have happened around the age of twelve, she thought. *It's when she becomes a blonde, according to Lynn, anyway. What else happened? Her friend Sissie leaves. That could be important. It's also around the time of menarche. How do I find out what happened when she became a blonde for the first time? Who's going to tell me about that? I don't trust Nora. Lynn doesn't know, I'm pretty sure of that. Diana? She's wrapped up in so many layers of amnesia, screen memory, and dissociation, it's doubtful I'll get anything out of her. Still, whatever happened, happened to her. I think. Hypnosis again? Maybe, if she'll still let me do it . . .*

An hour later, Diana sat across from Sarah, smoking cigarettes and answering the usual round of preparatory questions. Sarah felt inexplicably nervous, anxious to get on with the session. While Diana answered her questions, Sarah's thoughts raced ahead, considering how best to structure the hypnosis, what to tell Diana, when to begin. Sarah rubbed the bridge of her nose, widened her eyes. *Here and now, Sarah,* she said to herself, *here and now.* She had just missed whatever Diana had said.

"I'm sorry, Diana. What did you say?"

"I said that I'm really feeling better than I have in a long time," Diana repeated. "Sarah, are you all right?"

"I'm fine. Thanks. Guess I didn't sleep real well last night," Sarah smiled. "Diana, I would like to hypnotize you again."

Diana hesitated an instant before answering. "Sarah, if you say it's necessary, I believe you. I definitely don't want to do that thing we did last time, whatever that was."

"I don't intend to do that again," Sarah said. "That wasn't hypnosis." She paused thoughtfully for a moment. "How much do you remember about what happened?"

"I remember screaming. And I remember sort of waking up and seeing . . . well, you know . . ."

"Yes. Do you remember what happened before that?"

"No. I seem to remember something about walking in the woods, but that's all. Should I remember?"

"No, not necessarily. The mind is very self-adjusting," Sarah said. "You remember what you should remember."

"What happened, Sarah? Will you tell me?"

"I don't know enough to tell you anything that will do either of us much good. I want to find out more. I know I keep saying things like this, but right now I'm just gathering information. When it comes time to interpret the information, we'll work on it together. Does that make sense?" Sarah wasn't at all sure that it did.

"I trust you, Sarah."

"Shall we begin, then?"

Diana nodded, and Sarah asked her to close her eyes, and suggested that she was becoming more and more relaxed. Then she said "sleep" and clapped her hands softly three times. Diana's head slumped forward. Sarah spent the next several minutes deepening the trance.

"Diana, I want you to remember back to when you were twelve years old. You are thinking back. The memories are very clear. You find it very easy to remember. You are remembering when you were twelve years old. Do you remember?"

"Yes." Diana's eyes were closed, an expression of rapt concentration on her face.

"What day is it?"

"It's Monday. I'm getting ready to go to school."

"Do you know what month it is?"

"Yes. It's September. It's the first day of school."

"What are you wearing to school today?"

"A blue dress. And my white socks and black shoes."

"That sounds very pretty. Is there a mirror nearby?"

"Yes."

"Look in the mirror. Can you see yourself?"

"Yes."

"How are you wearing you hair today?"

"I have it held back with barrettes."

"That sounds nice. What color is your hair?"

"It's blond."

"Okay, Diana. Now we're going to go back a little farther. You will remember a time one month before. A time when you were in your bedroom. Where are you?"

"I'm in my room."

"Good. Can you tell me what month it is?"

"August."

"Good. Diana, I want you to walk over to the mirror and look at yourself. Are you looking?"

"Yes."

"Good. What color is your hair?"

"It's blond."

"Okay, thank you. Now we're going to go back a little farther . . ." Sarah continued the pattern, getting the same results on back through the summer of Diana's twelfth year. Sarah knew she was shooting in the dark with this technique. Still, she thought it was worth a try. She moved on to May.

"It is now May and you are twelve years old. You are in your bedroom. I want you to walk over to the mirror and look at yourself. Can you see yourself?"

"Yes."

"What color is your hair?"

"My hair is brown."

Bingo. Sarah felt suddenly excited. *Now, let's narrow things down.*

"What is today's date?"

"May 5."

"Good. Diana, I want you to move forward a week in time. It is now May 12. What are you doing?"

No response.

"Diana, can you hear me?"

Diana sat silently, head tilted slightly forward as if straining to see.

Sarah had a sudden hunch. "Is Diana there?"

"No."

Of course, thought Sarah. *Somewhere along the line, I've hit a time when another personality was active.*

"Who are you?" Sarah asked.

"My name is Sissie."

Sissie? thought Sarah, suddenly confused. *But Sissie's not a personality. Sissie's a friend of Diana's. I don't understand.*

"Sissie, what is the date?"

"May 12."

The voice was similar to Diana's but not quite the same. It sounded younger, lighter somehow. Sarah frowned.

"I want you to remember a time during the day when you looked at yourself in the mirror," she said. "Do you remember?"

"Yes."

"Okay. Please tell me what you look like. What color are your eyes?"

"I have blue eyes."

"And your hair. What color is it?"

"My hair is brown."

"Good. How do you wear it?"

"It's down to my shoulders. It's straight. I wish I had curly hair. I have bangs."

"Thank you, Sissie. We're moving forward in time to May 19. I want you to remember a time on May 19 when you were looking at yourself in the mirror. Are you looking at yourself?"

"Yes."

"What color is your hair?"

"Blond."

"Who am I talking to?" asked Sarah.

"My name is Diana Smith."

This switching from personality to personality may have noth-

ing to do with actually changing her hair color, thought Sarah. *I may just be picking up on the perceptions of each personality. Can I eliminate that possibility?*

"Diana, what is today's date?"

"May 19."

"What day is it?"

"Wednesday."

"Good. What did you do yesterday? Tell me one thing you did on Tuesday?"

"I played inside, 'cause it rained."

"I see. Tell me one thing you did on Monday, May 17."

"I spent the day in bed. I didn't feel well."

"How about Sunday, May 16. Tell me something you did on Sunday."

"Sunday we had a party. For me."

"All right. Sunday you had a party. Now, what do you remember about Saturday, May 15? Tell me one thing that you did on Saturday."

Diana frowned, her body tilted forward, the muscles of her arms bunched and straining.

"Diana, what do you remember from Saturday?"

"I . . . don't . . . remember . . ." her voice strained, the words seeming to come with difficulty.

"That's fine. Relax, rest and relax. What day is it, Diana?"

"Wednesday."

"That's right, it's Wednesday, May 19. We are going back in time now to Saturday, May 15. You will remember a time on Saturday, May 15, when you were looking at yourself in a mirror. What day is it?"

"Saturday."

"Good. Can you see yourself in the mirror?"

"Yes."

"Good. Look at your hair. What color is it?"

"Brown."

"What is your name?"

"Sissie."

"What is your full name?"
"My full name is Iris Laine Morrison, but everyone calls me Sissie."
"All right, Sissie. It is now very late on Saturday, May 15. It is almost midnight. Where are you?"
"I am in bed."
"All right. Can you remember what happened today? Do you remember everything that happened on this Saturday?"
"Yes."
"What did you do today?"
"I stayed inside all day."
"Why? Did it rain?"
"No. Father told me I must not go out."
"What did you do?"
"I played in my room and read books and drew."
"What else happened."
"Father made me take medicine." She made a face.
"What kind of medicine?"
"The sleepy kind."
"Are you sleepy now?"
"Yes."
"Okay, I will let you go to sleep. You will go to sleep and then in a minute you will wake up. When you wake up, it will be Sunday morning, May 16. Do you understand?"
"Yes."
"All right, sleep now."
Sarah glanced at her watch, noting the time. She stretched and stood up quietly. She had been sitting so tensely that the circulation in her left leg had been reduced. Now, she winced as the feeling returned. Gently, she lifted the leg and bent it at the knee several times. As she sat down, she thought she saw a subtle change in the expression on Diana's face.
"Sissie, are you awake?"
"Yes. Where am I?"
"Tell me what you see."

"I am lying on a big bed. I don't know this room." Suddenly, her voice rose in panic. "I can't move. I can't move."

"It's all right, Sissie. Rest and relax. Nothing can hurt you. You are just remembering things now. Tell me what you see."

"People are coming in the room. They are crying. Father is there, and Mother. Father is crying. Someone says, 'She died in the night. I can't believe she's dead.' And Father says, 'Yes, we are going to miss her very much.' They're talking about me. They think I am dead. I'm not dead. *I'm not dead.*"

"Sissie, relax. Nothing can hurt you. You are just remembering. What happens next?"

"Many people are picking me up. I am trying to move, to yell, but I can't. I am so scared."

"It's all right, Sissie. You're safe," Sarah repeated the assurances. "You're just remembering." Sarah considered terminating the session. *What the hell is happening?* she wondered. *I need to know more. Should I stop?*

She decided to continue. "What do you remember next?"

"They carry me someplace downstairs, a room I've never seen before. They put me on a long table. It's cold, the table's cold, and it's made out of metal. And they leave me, and some people are crying. I still can't move."

Diana's face was contorted into a mask of pain and fear. Her head thrust forward at a strange angle, and Sarah watched the eyes moving frantically back and forth beneath the tightly closed lids.

"It's okay, Sissie," she said softly. "What happens next?"

"Two men come in. I don't know them. They look like doctors. They look at me and one says, 'We need to drain the blood first.' Then they take off my clothes and it is so cold. I try to scream. I feel a stinging in my arm, like a needle, and I try to scream 'cause they're going to drain my blood. The other man says, 'We need to put the preservative back in,' and there's a bottle on a stand that he brings over, and this time I feel a stinging in my neck and I can see this plastic tube of bright red liquid running down from the bottle, past my face and down to my neck. The men leave then. And I remember thinking, I am dying, they are killing me, but it just goes on and on. And then I think, Maybe they're right, maybe I am already dead. But, after a time, the men come back, and they pull the needles out of my arms. And one of them says, 'Time to open her up,' and he bends over me with gloves on, and he's holding this little knife and then he starts to cut me. And it hurts so bad, and then he's taking everything out of me, I can see my insides, 'cause he takes them out and puts them in something on the floor. And I keep thinking, I must be dead, I have to be dead by now. Then he sews me up, and that really hurts. I can feel every time the needle goes in and he pulls it, and I can see his hand holding the needle and pulling the thread. When that's over, they leave again for a while."

Tears streamed down the woman's face, smearing her mascara. *Do I continue?* Sarah asked herself. *How much of this can she stand to remember? How much can I stand? What the hell is going on?*

Reluctantly, Sarah asked, "What happened next?"

After a long pause, Sissie began to speak between sobs, in a hoarse voice.

"They leave me for a long time. One of the men comes back with a woman. I can just see them when they come in through the door. The woman is carrying several bags. The next thing I know, the woman is doing something to my hair. I can feel something cold and wet, but after a while it starts to feel warm and burn a little bit. When she finishes putting the stuff on my hair, they leave again. Every now and then, the woman comes back and walks behind me. I think she's checking my hair for something. After a while she comes back with the man, and she rinses my hair with cold water and shampoos it. That feels good, till she rinses it with the cold water again. When she dries it with a hair dryer, it feels great 'cause of the warm air. When she finishes with that, she and the man dress me up. They are putting on my fancy white party dress and the woman says, 'She looks so pretty. It will be a lovely funeral.' When they finish dressing me, I feel a needle stick me again. Then the man goes out and returns with the other man, and all three of them lift me up and put me into something. I think it's a bed at first, because it's nice and soft and comfortable. But then I want to scream again, 'cause I see the men lift up part of it and put it down, and I realize I'm in a coffin. And I try to scream, again and again, and I can't."

"Relax, Sissie, it's okay. You're safe, Sissie, relax." Sarah watched as her client seemed to visibly relax, her breathing coming regularly and deeply, the lines in her forehead smoothing out. *How can she be making this up?* Sarah asked herself. Why *is she making this up? If this is a screen memory, then what does it mask, for God's sake?*

"What happened next, Sissie?" Sarah asked, hating herself for asking.

"Then they close the top of the coffin, but not all the way. They leave it propped open a little bit. I guess they needed to close it so they could carry it, 'cause next I feel the coffin being picked up and I can just see somebody's back from where the coffin lid was left open a little bit. When they stop, they open the lid, and all I can see is a very high ceiling and walls made of stone, like in some old, old building. After a long time, people walk by, looking into the coffin. I know lots of them—Father and Mother and relatives and people from the church. And finally Diana comes by and looks in, and I want to scream so bad, 'Di, Di, Di, don't leave. I'm alive, Di, I'm alive.' And Diana is crying and she reaches out to touch me, but somebody—I can't see who—grabs her hand and yanks her away.

"Then someone is talking. I don't understand what they're saying; it's some funny language. But I see a man come by the coffin. He's dressed in black with a white collar, and he's got a cross on a chain around his neck. And I remember thinking that's funny because the long part of the cross points down . . ."

The long part of the cross points down? What does that mean? Of course, the long part of the cross points down.

"And then he says some stuff in English and . . ."

"Sissie," Sarah interrupted, "can you remember what the man said in English? What did the man say?"

"I don't know," she said.

"You can remember," Sarah suggested. "Just listen carefully as he speaks. Listen, you can hear him."

"I hear him," she repeated. Her voice strained with concentration, " 'In the midst of life we are in death . . .' Something, something, I can't hear. And then, 'Earth to earth, ashes to ashes, dust to dust; in sure and certain hope of the Resurrection unto eternal life . . .' And then I can't hear for a while more."

"That's fine, Sissie, that's fine. What do you remember next?"

"The man in black leans over the coffin and puts something in my mouth."

"What did he put in your mouth, Sissie?"

"I don't know. A pill, maybe. It makes a bitter taste in my mouth."

"Okay, go on."

"Then they close the lid. They close the lid of the coffin, and I'm trying to scream and I can't. It's so dark and they're moving me. I want to beat on the coffin with my fists, but I can't move. Then the coffin is moving again, only I hear it hit against a wall or something, until finally it stops with a jerk. And I think, Maybe they're gonna let me out, maybe they're gonna let me out. And I think that for a long time, until I hear something on the lid of the coffin. Then I hear it again and again."

"What is it, Sissie. What do you hear?"

Sissie whispered, "It's dirt. I know what it is. It's dirt on the coffin. They're burying me." She cried quietly and Sarah watched, her fists clenched helplessly. *This can't last much longer,* Sarah thought.

"What happened next, Sissie?"

"It's black, so black. That's all. Forever."

"What happened after the black, Sissie?"

"Nothing. Just black, forever and ever. In the arms of Jesus. I'm dead."

"Rest and relax, rest and relax. There is nothing to worry about. You are remembering the events of Sunday, May 16. After the blackness comes movement and light. Remember the light. Remember when the lid of the casket was removed. What happened?"

"I remember . . . I don't know," the voice slurred, hesitated. "I remember the light and I hear voices. They are saying 'She is risen. Against the will of Jesus Christ, she is risen.' "

What? Sarah thought. *I don't get it.*

The voice suddenly became strong.

" 'Dost thou, therefore, in the name of this demon, renounce Jesus Christ and all his works, affirming the wondrous glory of the world, with all covetous desires of the world, and the glorious ways of the flesh, so that thou wilt follow, and wilt always be led, by the creatures of darkness?' Voices, many voices then. And hands reaching, lifting me out of the coffin. And I can't see very well, but there are many, many people, and I am placed on a platform made of stone.

" 'In the name of the most unholy, we recall this child from the arms of Jesus, which is death, we recall from the everlasting death of Jesus Christ, this child, newly risen, who henceforth shall be known as Diana Irena Smith. To the giver of life, we consecrate this child, and dedicate its new life, in the name of Satan. Ave Satanas, Ave Satanas, Ave Satanas.

" 'And, in exchange, for all the blasphemies and transgressions of this child, for the soul of this unworthy child, in the coin of silver demanded by Jesus Christ, keeper of everlasting death, accept our sacrifice, never to be called by name again.' "

Sarah rubbed her arms against the gooseflesh that had risen during Diana's recitation.

"What happened next, Diana?" she forced herself to say.

"Suddenly, I could move. And they lifted me up and helped me walk over to where the coffin sat. And they made me look in it. My friend Diana was in there, only they'd done something to her hair. They'd dyed it brown, and she was wearing my white party dress. They made her look like me. I reached out and they let me touch her. She was so cold. I knew she was really dead.

"Everyone called *me* Diana. And they made me sit down and listen to the Father. But this time it was the real Father. His cross was hanging correctly. It was a funeral service for Sissie, only I'm Sissie. Why does everyone call me Diana?"

"Relax, it's all right," Sarah whispered. "You're just remembering. You are safe. It can't hurt you. It's just a memory. Tell me what happened next."

"They took me upstairs. I was back in my own house, only everyone acted like I didn't live there anymore. They wouldn't let me go to my room. They gave me clothes to put on, only they weren't mine. I knew whose they were."

"Whose were they?"

"They were Diana's. But everyone called *me* Diana. And they made me eat something bad, and afterward I got a real funny feeling."

"What did they make you eat?"

"I don't remember. It's bad. I don't want to remember."

"That's okay. You don't have to remember. What happened next?"

"We walked out into the woods. There were many people. The coffin was sitting next to a deep hole in the ground. They made me walk over to the coffin."

"Who made you walk over to the coffin?"

"Mother and Father. They made me walk over. And Father said, 'Because of you, our Sissie is dead. You killed our Sissie.' I tried to say something, but I had a hard time talking. Mother said, 'You must always obey whatever we say, and what your mother and father tell you, or we will tell that you killed our Sissie.' And they made me lean over into the coffin and kiss her goodbye, only it wasn't Sissie. *I'm* Sissie. It's Diana. And then I looked down and I had a knife in my hand. And it was covered in blood." Diana's body tensed with a trembling rigidity. She sat on the edge of the chair, poised as if for sudden flight.

"Diana, listen to me. It's all right. It's just a memory."

"But it wasn't me that killed Diana. Diana's all right. I died, not Diana. Diana didn't die. I died. So that makes Diana all right."

"Yes, Diana's all right. Diana's fine. Where did Diana go after Sissie's funeral?"

"I went home with Mom and Dad. Poor Sissie, I cried and cried. I guess I won't go back there anymore, to Sissie's house. We had good times there. Poor Sissie. She would have liked to come to the party."

"What party, Diana?"

"The party we had when I got home."

"You had a party at home? That's nice."

"Yes," said Diana. "We had a birthday party. It's my birthday, you know."

"Diana, I am going to count from one to five. When

I reach five, you will awake feeling relaxed and refreshed. One. Two. Three. Four. Five."

Diana opened her eyes. For several seconds, they stared straight ahead, unfocused and unseeing. Something seemed to clear, then, and she looked up at Sarah and smiled. Sarah smiled back and slid a box of tissues across the desk. Diana touched the back of a hand to her cheek and looked quizzically at the wetness there.

"I was crying?"

Sarah nodded.

"Why?" Diana asked.

"Do you remember anything?" Sarah asked gently.

Diana's gaze seemed to turn inward. For just a moment, her eyes widened as if in sudden amazement. Then they narrowed, focused in intense concentration. Diana looked up.

"Sissie died, didn't she?"

Sarah nodded.

"Is that what I remembered?"

"Yes. What do you remember now?"

"I have a picture of a funeral in my head. Just a single scene, like a snapshot. A funeral in the woods. A coffin by a pile of earth. Lots of people. That's all." Diana looked at Sarah closely. "Is that right?"

"I think so."

"Can I go home now? I feel very drained."

"Yes," Sarah said. "I'm afraid I kept you over a bit. You will call if you need me?"

Diana nodded.

Later, Sarah stood and hugged herself. She felt cold and was unable to get warm. The little thermometer built into the room's thermostat read almost eighty. Sarah walked over to the office window and looked out over the parking lot. She leaned her head against the glass. She felt very tired. Answers kept eluding her, while the list of questions kept growing.

* * *

Sarah smiled with relief at the sight of the Volvo in the driveway. She still felt cold and terribly confused. She hurried into the house.

"Mark," she called.

She heard a muffled cry from the bathroom. Several minutes later, her husband emerged from the hallway into the living room.

"Will fucking wonders never cease," Mark said. "Home by five o'clock."

"Mark," Sarah said. "Don't say anything, not yet. I need you. Badly. Please come sit down."

Mark watched in wonder as his wife pulled him down and hugged him fiercely. She snuggled her head onto his lap, still holding him tightly around the waist. Mark felt her tremble and gently brushed the strands of loose hair from her face. He sat silently, unmoving as the night fell slowly and silently around them.

Sarah stirred at last, pushing back her hair and sitting up, turning so she could look into Mark's eyes. The anger was gone now, replaced by concern. This was the man she knew, the man she had married.

"Mark, let's talk. I need to tell you about my client and what I've been going through. Then I need you to tell me what's going on with you."

Mark looked at her for a long while without speaking. Finally, he nodded.

"Let's talk," he said.

Chapter 13

Week 9: Thursday, September 28

For a time, Sarah almost managed to forget about multiple personality disorder and child abuse and Diana Smith. She placidly navigated the Thursday morning rounds of sessions and paperwork, phone calls and appointments, finding a peculiar comfort in the routine. Half an hour before Diana Smith's appointment, the deferred issues of the case came rushing back at her. Sarah sighed, feeling momentarily guilty for having *not* figured out what to do next, then brushed the guilt aside as an unproductive emotion. She knew the pattern, having first recognized and harnessed it as an undergraduate. Presented with an intellectual puzzle or problem, she often gained her most productive insights by first studying the problem without trying to solve it, then completely ignoring it for a period of time. The length of time seemed to be proportionate to the complexity of the problem. Once the waiting period—the gestation period, Sarah liked to think of it—was over, she tended to be much more productive than if she had immediately proceeded to work. On rare occasions, she had experienced a sudden insight, and a full-blown solution had appeared to her.

Right now, though, she felt overloaded with information, unable to sift through the enormous volume of raw stuff that Diana had laid before her over the past several weeks.

Lynn is the key, I'm sure of it, Sarah thought. *She knows the truth, but she doesn't trust me enough yet. Or maybe she was serious about things being dangerous. It's pretty usual for alters in therapy to be concerned about their fate. Integration represents a kind of death for the individual personalities. But what was it Lynn said about danger? She said it might be dangerous for all of us, didn't she? Me included.*

Sarah pulled open the drawer containing her cassettes. She quickly located the recording of Lynn's session and inserted the tape into the cassette machine. It took several minutes for her to find the passage. She pressed the play button and turned the volume control.

"You don't know that, Sarah. We could all be in danger. You, too."

That was it. We could all be in danger. You, too, she said. What did she mean?

Sarah reached out to snap off the recorder, then hesitated. She heard herself ask: "Can I call on you again, Lynn?"

Then she heard Lynn: "Sometimes if you call I'm only the listener."

Sarah punched the stop button. Lynn's last words echoed in the room. Sarah rewound the tape for barely a second, then punched the play button impatiently.

". . . call on you again, Lynn?"

A slight pause. Then, "Sometimes if you call I'm only the listener."

The intercom buzzed.

"Diana Smith is here to see you," Margie said.

"Ask her to wait a couple of minutes," Sarah yelled into the intercom. "I'll be right out."

Hurriedly, she put the tapes away and set up the machine for the next session. *Is that the inspiration I've been looking for? Is that what I need to move on?* she asked herself. *I'm not sure.* Over and over, she could hear Lynn's voice: "Sometimes if you call I'm only the listener."

Sarah pressed the intercom button on the telephone. "Send Diana in please, Margie," she said.

Diana stepped into the office. She shook hands with Sarah without smiling. As she sat down in her usual chair, she removed a pair of very dark sunglasses. Sarah saw at once that she had been crying. Her eyes were red and puffy.

"Diana, what's wrong?"

Diana fished in her purse till she found a handkerchief. "Sarah, I'm going crazy. I don't think I can stand it any longer."

"Whatever it is, you're not going crazy, I assure you. Now, tell me what's the matter."

"I've lost a day and a half since Wednesday. I don't know where I've been or what I've done. What's happening to me?"

Sarah had been sitting uncomfortably on the edge of her desk. She stood now and paced along the short length of the room, rubbing her face with the palm of her hands and smoothing her hair back from her forehead.

"Diana, I think it's time for me to tell you what I know about what's been happening to you. I wanted to wait until you were able to recall more, to deal with some of the memories on a conscious level. I don't know everything you're going through, but I can tell you this: There are many other people who have been through and are going through very similar experiences. What you're experiencing is somewhat rare, though not nearly as uncommon as we used to think." Sarah paused from the concentration of trying to phrase her words precisely. She recognized a look of horror on Diana's face.

"I'm afraid I'm doing a terrible job of explaining. Please bear with me.

"Diana, people respond in different ways to trauma. Things like being physically beaten, or sexually abused, or, in some cases, even protracted serious illness, can have devastating effects on children. I know. A good portion of the patients I see are trying to sort out experiences like that, experiences that happened many years ago.

"Does it surprise you that I think something happened to you when you were a small child, Diana? Something like physical or sexual abuse?"

Diana seemed to withdraw into herself. She hugged herself and Sarah could see that she was shaking. Sarah stood and walked over to the sofa, where she kept a quilted comforter draped over the back during the cooler months. She carried it over to Diana and wrapped it around her shoulders. Diana pulled it tightly around her and smiled at Sarah.

"No, it doesn't surprise me," Diana said. "Not when you say it like that. I think I've known for a long, long time that something happened to me. But I don't know what."

"Good," said Sarah. "I don't know what happened, either. That's something you and I will be trying to find out, probably for some time to come. Anyway, people respond to this kind of trauma in different ways. Some children die as a result of abuse. Some become damaged emotionally. Some grow up to repeat the cycle and become abusers themselves. Most children, however, seek some form of escape from the abuse, some way of dissociating themselves from what happens. A small percentage of highly intelligent children do this in a very unique way. . . ." Sarah paused, breathing deeply for a second that seemed to stretch on and on. "They create new personalities for themselves. Nobody really understands how it works, but some people have this amazing ability to create or develop—however you want to put it—multiple personalities."

"I don't believe it," Diana said, then a new realization struck her. "You've met these other personalities, haven't you? That's why you hypnotize me so much, isn't it?"

Sarah nodded.

"If that's not crazy, what the hell is?"

"Diana, listen to me. You are not crazy. I know this is hard to accept now—"

"No, you don't," Diana interrupted. "There's no way you could know."

"Okay, you're right," Sarah conceded. "I *don't* know, but I can guess. Now you understand why I've been so reluctant to talk about this. I was hoping something would happen to make the realization easier. Unfortunately, it didn't. Diana, in a very strange way, multiple personality disorder is a way of *staying* sane. It's a way of coping with circumstances that are utterly intolerable, that would shatter most people. It's not insanity."

"Sarah, I don't think I can handle this right now."

"You wanted to know why time disappears on you, why you have headaches and tunnel vision. Sometimes you find things around your apartment that you didn't put there, don't you? Do you ever wake up and find yourself in the middle of someplace, wondering how you got there? Or maybe you seem to watch things from a great distance and it seems as if you have no control over your actions? Or maybe you experience it completely differently. But does it start to make some sense? Do you see that there's some truth here, Diana?"

Diana ignored the question. Instead, she asked, with surprising calmness, "What are they like, Sarah? How many of them are there?"

"I don't know how many there are. So far, I have met two."

"Tell me about them."

"One of the personalities is called Nora Entwhistle. She is very calm and rational and seems to know a lot about your personal history. The other is called Lynn. Lynn is quite a character, very forceful and dynamic."

"Do you like them, Sarah?"

"I find them interesting, Diana, but *you're* my client." It seemed suddenly important to Sarah that she add, "And I like *you* very much."

"And you can talk to them whenever you wish? By hypnotizing me?"

"No," Sarah said. "Nora is usually accessible through hypnosis. Lynn comes when she wants. I use the hypnosis to try to piece together some of the puzzle of what happened to you. Talking to other personalities is incidental."

"Will I be able to meet them?" Diana asked.

"That is one of the goals of our therapy, yes."

Diana lit a cigarette with trembling hands. She shrugged off the comforter and laid it on the floor, then put her cigarette in the ashtray, wiped her face, and blew her nose. When she spoke, resignation was heavy in her voice. "Where do we go from here?"

"Do you want to continue with the session?" Sarah asked.

"Why not?"

"I had originally planned to try something with hypnosis again, but I'm not sure that's such a good idea now."

"Sarah, it's okay. If it's going to help me piece together my life, then let's do it."

Sarah gave the posthypnotic suggestion, feeling as if things were too rushed. Her enthusiasm for the experiment she had envisioned a half hour earlier had waned. Still, a vague sense of urgency compelled her. In spite of her intimation to Diana of working together for some time to come, Sarah felt the inexplicable certainly that time was limited and very precious. Diana had attempted suicide once. She might try again. Now that the revelation of her fragmented personalities had been revealed, there was no way to gauge how she might react.

Sarah repeated the familiar ritual to deepen the trance. She paused, reflecting on the wording for the next stage. *Sometimes if you call I'm only the listener,* she replayed Lynn's words in her mind. And when Sarah had attempted to call her, Diana had shut down, become unresponsive. Or was she? Had there been another personality present, but silent and uncooperative? *Sometimes if you call I'm only the Listener. Change the emphasis, you change the meaning. Capital L. Could the Listener be a personality? The names of personalities often reflect their functions. Is the Listener a personality, perhaps somehow connected to Lynn?*

"I would like to speak to the personality known as the Listener," Sarah said. "Can you hear me? I would like to speak to the Listener."

Diana sat motionless and silent. *All right, this certainly looks like what I had on my hands the other time. So what do I do with it?*

"Is the Listener there?" Sarah asked, feeling a little silly. *This is like playing a Ouija Board,* she thought. The silence continued.

Sarah suddenly remembered a discussion she had had with Mark, years ago, before they were married. In college, Mark had been something of a computer hacker, back in the days when that was still an innocent pursuit. He had once told Sarah a little about backdoor access to computer systems, as well as the logic of guessing passwords. That's what she felt like now, as if she were guessing at passwords. *Passwords into consciousness, passwords into personalities. I need some of that logic now,* she thought.

What does the Listener listen to? Why does the Listener listen?

"Listener, speak," Sarah said.

Diana remained silent.

The Listener listens. Maybe the Listener can repeat what it hears.

"Listener, repeat."

Sometimes if you call I'm only the Listener.

"Lynn, help me," Sarah said. *Wait, not Lynn. Linda. Linda Janus. Janus, god of doorways, comings and goings. Gatekeeper.*

"Linda Janus, tell me the words of the Listener."

Sarah banged her desktop softly in frustration. She

glanced at Diana, then did a double take when she saw the woman's mouth twisting into strange shapes. She sat back in wide-eyed amazement when the words started.

"Ondro manth cuantor delittor. Intrando bapholeptor deiran toldis indro mantir. Intrando baphotim. Consonmap belissar. Argomonto baphonim. Fontrantor beliim standin cuantor delittor. Intrando baphominen . . ." The words issued in a low, stately voice, while Diana sat, motionless except for her lips and the nearly imperceptible rise and fall of her larynx.

Sarah was reminded of the Latin of her childhood church. *But this isn't Latin. I'm certain of that. In fact, it doesn't sound like anything I've heard before. Not French, not Spanish. Greek? I don't think so. It does not sound Oriental. Sanskrit, maybe? Maybe. I've never heard spoken Sanskrit. Whatever it is, it's weird.* The hairs at the nape of her neck stood erect. Sarah rubbed the gooseflesh from her arms. *It sounds so ritualistic,* she thought. *That's why it reminds me of the Latin Mass. It's so stately and solemn.*

Diana's recitation went on and on, in a voice that did not belong to Diana. *The voice of the Listener.* Sarah recalled her earlier question: What does the Listener listen to? *Maybe the Listener listens to rituals,* she thought. *What kind of rituals?*

Try to find the simple explanation, she told herself. *KISS. Keep it simple, stupid.*

Maybe they're not rituals at all. Maybe it's just nonsense. Maybe I've unconsciously cued her and she's doing all this to please me. Or maybe Diana creates screen memories of satanic psychodramas to obscure some more mundane abuse. Maybe she creates new languages—what's that called . . . glossolalia, speaking in tongues?—because she thinks I want to hear rituals.

But she has one of her personalities maintain the illusion of natural blondness. Why? She dreams about two clearly distinguishable dolls but confuses the identity of them. And then she recalls a mock funeral where her identity is exchanged with that of her best friend. She remembers being raped by a priest.

Sarah remembered Diana's comment about the

priest who officiated at her "burial." She had said that the long part of his cross pointed down, as if that were something remarkable. In the context of the memory, the man had been playing the part of a Christian priest; it was almost a kind of behavioral conditioning *against* real priests. His cross had been remarkable to Diana because she was used to seeing inverted crosses.

Is it really possible that a group of people, perhaps practicing some form of Satan worship, did unspeakable things to my client as a child and adolescent? There's a weird consistency to it. It all holds together. Is that *the simple explanation?*

Sarah recorded almost twenty-five minutes of the strange language before Diana lapsed into silence. She was able to terminate the hypnosis with a straightforward suggestion to wake up. After extracting a promise from Diana to call for any reason whatsoever, Sarah ended the session.

For a long time, Sarah sat silently at her desk. She had nowhere to turn. If she took Diana's story of satanic rituals and bizarre abuse to any of her colleagues, they'd think she'd gone off the deep end herself. They'd accuse her of subconsciously influencing Diana under hypnosis. But Sarah knew her sessions had been clean. She'd been very careful.

What if Diana's recollections were the literal truth? Where could she turn for help?

Sarah suddenly remembered the newspaper article on the university professor who consulted with the Richmond police on occult crime. She couldn't recall his name, but she remembered that he was in the anthropology department.

She couldn't just call him. He'd think she was crazy, too.

Maybe she was crazy. But Sarah knew she owed it to Diana to find out.

A few minutes later, she'd located the listing for the university information desk and was dialing the number.

PART III

ONE PERCENT

Allie Carlson lay awake in the dark room, scarcely daring to breathe, as if the act of taking a breath might draw attention to her. Always at night, they either came or she was taken to them. To Allie, then, the night was always full of fear, even though most nights passed undisturbed.

Allie heard a shuffling of footsteps in the carpeted hallway outside her door. She fought back the tears of fear and rage. She would not cry. Would not. She curled up into the covers, trying to become very small. She wished she could become so small that no one would know she was there. She would hold her breath and everyone would think she was a doll, a tiny doll left in place of the little girl who had vanished from her bedroom.

The door opened, and the light from the hallway cast a wedge into the room.

"Allie? Allie, it's time to get up." It was her mother.

Allie crawled from the bed, still wishing she could make herself into a doll. She dressed quickly, putting on a T-shirt and jeans and a pair of sneakers. When she was ready, she stepped out into the hall. Her mother beckoned from the foyer, where she was knotting a scarf around her hair. Allie followed her mother out of the house and across the darkened lawn.

Her mother did not speak at all during the twenty-minute drive, and Allie knew better than to talk to her when she got that look in her eye. The mad-mother look. Instead, Allie concentrated on trying to make herself small and doll-like.

The car stopped. Allie looked at her mother. She came very close to pleading. "Please, please, don't make me go," she would have said, but she remembered the last time she had done this.

Allie's mother said, "You must be good and do everything they say. You know what will happen if you don't."

Allie nodded. She got out of the car. A woman in dark slacks and a black sweater waited for her. She took Allie's hand. Allie's mother drove away, and Allie did not look back.

It was a long walk down a wooded path before they reached the house. The woman led Allie down a dimly lit hallway and into a darkened room. Wordlessly, she started to undress Allie, but Allie pushed her away and undressed herself. Then the woman tied a rope around Allie's waist. After the woman left, Allie tried to move, but the rope was short and tied at the other end. Allie knew the knots would be too tight for her small fingers to unravel.

It was cold there in the dark and Allie shivered. She concentrated on becoming small again and some of the coldness receded.

Tiny sounds emerged from the darkness and Allie realized she was not alone. It would have been nice to talk to the others, but Allie knew that was a bad idea. Eventually, the whimpers and the soft crying and the sounds of shifting died away. Allie was becoming very good at transforming herself. She felt much smaller and she could hold her breath for a long, long time if she needed to. She would be a doll by the time they came.

A long time passed before the door opened. Allie wondered if she had really become a doll, because they took one of the others and left her alone. She released her pent-up breath slowly when the door closed.

They came back some time later. They untied Allie, then slipped a shapeless brown caftan over her head. She hadn't become a doll in time.

They took her to a candlelit room. A dozen men and women in dark robes stood in a semicircle looking at her. In the center of the room was a block of stone as large as a table. Another little girl lay on the table. Her eyes were wide. She had no clothes on.

The men and women sang a song, but Allie could not understand the words. They danced, holding hands in a circle surrounding Allie. They seemed very happy.

A man with silver in his hair and friendly eyes stood before Allie and smiled at her.

"You have come far in training, little one," he said. "You have passed many tests."

Allie tried to become a doll again.

"You will be a priestess one day."

The man took Allie's hand and led her to the stone table. He lifted her up on a wooden bench. Allie looked down on the other little girl.

Allie didn't want to do it. She couldn't do it. It was wrong. It was bad. She'd become a doll first.

The man put something into Allie's hands. "Your name will be Cassandra," he said.

Allie knew why the other girl was on the table. She hadn't passed a test. Allie would be on the table next if she didn't do what she was supposed to.

But it was wrong. She didn't want to do it.

"No," she whispered. If only she could transform herself.

"Yes," the man hissed. "You must do it."

Allie felt herself becoming smaller. Her breathing slowed. Her eyes became stones, fixed in her head like the glass eyes of a doll. Before they froze completely, she looked down at the object in her hands. It was a knife.

"Do it. Do it now," the man whispered to her.

The transformation was complete. Allie had become a silent, lifeless doll. She felt herself receding from the scene before her. In a moment, she was looking down at the robed men and women from a great distance. She had become a doll, perched on the ledge of a high window.

Another little girl, the one they called Cassandra, now stood on the bench, holding the knife. Cassandra looked just like Allie, except for the confident smile on her lips and the eager way she held the knife.

"Now," the man said to Cassandra.

Cassandra brought the knife down on the open chest of the little girl. Allie wanted to close her eyes, but they were dolly's eyes, stuck open as long as she was sitting up. Blood welled up in the wound. Cassandra removed the knife and then blood was flowing everywhere. The man helped Cassandra make some more cuts, then he took her bare hands and pushed them into the torso's gaping wound. When they emerged, Cassandra was holding the little girl's bloody heart.

"Hail Satan," the man said, and all the other men and women repeated it.

The man helped Cassandra cut the heart into small pieces. He gave a piece to Cassandra.

"You have done well," he said. "The honor is yours."

Cassandra took the piece of heart and placed it in her mouth. She then handed out pieces to the men and women. "Hail Satan," they all said.

They removed the body of the little girl, and the men took turns climbing up on the stone table where Cassandra lay, resting. Cassandra smiled as they panted on top of her.

Later, the women cleaned Cassandra with cloths dipped in warm water. They told her what a good girl she had been. They rubbed her dry with heavy towels and then they let her dress in the clothes Allie had worn.

The man who had helped Cassandra came back into the room. "You must tell no one," he said, "or the police will come and arrest you for murder. You must tell no one."

Cassandra said, "I know," but then she wasn't Cassandra anymore, she was Allie. Allie had transformed back from the doll.

Allie let herself be led outside, where her mother was waiting. She got in the car.

Allie looked at her mother closely. Her eyes were no longer the mad-mother's eyes. She was back to good-mother now.

Allie cried with relief. She started to tell her mother about her transformation, but her mother placed a hand over her mouth.

"You must never say a word," she said.

They drove home in silence.

Chapter 14

Week 9: Friday, September 29

"I appreciate you seeing me on such short notice," Sarah said breathlessly. She looked around the tiny office—*no, cubicle,* she thought—and widened her eyes with the difficulty of registering the sheer volume of material scattered about the room. His desk was littered with piles of papers and books, while more lay haphazardly on the floor. Wooden masks, stone carvings, and other artifacts seemed almost wantonly placed, some holding down paper stacks, others just randomly located. An incongruous collection of memoranda, photographs, cartoons clipped from magazines, and still more wooden carvings hung from the carpeted surfaces of the cubicle's inner walls. Dizzied with the effort of trying to mentally catalogue this collection, Sarah concentrated on the face of her host.

"I gotta admit you intrigued me on the phone last night." Bill Travers picked up a stack of books from the seat of a plastic chair. "Have a seat," he said, nodding in the direction of the newly excavated chair. He looked about the room distractedly for several seconds. Selecting a spot, he set the stack of books on an already-precarious tower of papers in one corner. The entire affair remained motionless for a moment, then papers about halfway up the stack started to slide. With a practiced foot, Travers kicked the stack, forcing it up against a corner of the cubicle. It rested there, stationary and secure.

"Don't mind the mess," he said. "This is how I managed to get my own cubicle. Ah, the glamorous life of the university." Travers waded over several piles and made it to his desk chair. "So, what can I do for you? You said you have a patient with multiple personality disorder. While I find that interesting, I'm afraid I'm just a cultural anthropologist. I don't really see how I can help."

"You're also an expert on the occult, right?" Sarah asked.

Travers smiled and leaned back in his battered chair. "*Expert* is a funny word . . . uh . . . doctor? Ms.? Mrs.? Johnson . . ."

"It's Mrs., definitely *not* doctor, and please call me Sarah," Sarah smiled.

"Okay, Sarah. I'm Bill. Anyway, the term *expert* is relative. With stuff like the occult, whatever *that* is, you can earn yourself the title of expert just by professing an interest." Travers shrugged. "So I'm not sure the title is accurate. I just happen to have been silly enough to make no secret of my interests."

"But you're not a parapsychologist?"

"No. Hell, no. Parapsychologists are concerned with proving or disproving the existence of various so-called psychic phenomena. Me, I'm an anthropologist whose special interest in human cultures is with beliefs in the supernatural. I get to avoid questions of whether the supernatural exists. It's enough that other people believe it exists."

"Good," said Sarah.

Travers waited expectantly. When it was clear Sarah was not going to continue, he said, "Okay, I'll bite. What does the occult have to do with multiple personality disorder?"

Sarah opened her purse and removed a sheet of yellow paper. "Hopefully, I've managed to spook myself. I'd like to read something to you. I should have brought a tape, but I think I can get the pronunciation pretty close. I want you to tell me if this means anything to you."

Travers nodded. "Okay."

Sarah read from the paper on which she had attempted to phonetically spell the first several lines of Diana's strange speech of the previous day. "It goes on and on," she said. "I've got about twenty-five minutes worth of this stuff on tape. Have you ever heard anything like it?"

Travers frowned and gnawed on the end of a thumbnail. He stood up and, leaning over several stacks of papers, managed to just reach a small book tucked among dozens of volumes on an overstuffed shelf. He sat back down and leafed through the book. "Read it again," he said.

Sarah read the words again.

"Where did you get this?" Travers asked.

"First tell me whether it means anything."

Travers grinned. "I don't know whether or not it means anything. It reminds me of a language, a pseudolanguage really, called Enochian."

"What's that?"

"Enochian. It's supposed to be a language that was magically revealed to a couple of sixteenth century magicians. The general rhythm of the spoken language is reminiscent and some of the words are similar. But it's not exact. My guess is, though, that it *is* a language. You notice the use of the word with the root *bapho?*" Sarah frowned and Travers reached out a hand. "Here, let me see your paper. Yeah, here. Bapholeptor, baphotim, baphonim. Those sound like allomorphs of the morpheme *bapho.* Or maybe they're declensions."

"I thought you said you're not a linguist."

"I'm not," Travers shuddered. "Believe me, I'm

not. I flunked linguistics big time. Anyway, the root *bapho* is interesting for another reason, too. Aleister Crowley called himself Baphomet. Of course, he called himself the Beast and the Master Theiron and a whole lot of other silly things."

"Who is this Crowley?"

"Aleister Crowley. A self-styled magician in the first half of this century. Sort of an original, do-your-own thing, free-love, druggie occultist. Anticipated the sixties by a number of years. To Crowley, Baphomet was another name for the Beast. Satan, in other words."

"Satan . . ."

"Well, maybe. See, Crowley must have picked up the name Baphomet from Knights Templar literature. The Knights Templar were a sort of fraternity of radical Crusaders. Legend has it that they worshipped a bearded head they called Baphomet. Satan to some, presumably something else to the Templars."

"What did you call the language?"

"Enochian?" Travers prompted.

"Enochian. And you said it was magically revealed?"

"Yeah, that's right. If I remember correctly, it was supposedly revealed to John Dee and Edward Kelly. They had some sort of contraption like a giant Ouija Board, I think. One was in a trance and the other copied down a sequence of letters, or maybe it was numbers that translated to letters. Something like that. It's a ritual language."

"A ritual language?" Sarah asked. "What kind of rituals?"

"Necromancy and conjuration," Travers said. "Raising the dead and summoning demons."

Sarah arched an eyebrow without thinking. "And this," she gestured at the paper, "may be related to Enochian."

"Maybe," Travers said. "I'd like to see more. Or hear more. You say there's a tape?"

"Yes."

"A tape of what? Are you going to tell me what this is all about?"

Sarah sighed. "This is going to sound strange."

"Strange is my specialty."

"Okay, then. This language, or whatever it is, is what one of my client's personalities speaks in. A personality apparently called the Listener. I just made contact with the Listener yesterday. On Tuesday, my client recalled, under hypnosis, being drugged, made to believe she was dead, and having a mock embalming, funeral, and burial performed on her."

Sarah watched Travers for signs of disbelief, a betrayal of the skepticism she felt her story deserved, which would confirm her own suspicion that seeking help from this strange, messy anthropologist was a bad idea. Instead, Travers smiled and the little lines around his eyes crinkled, and Sarah could read nothing in his face but polite, open interest.

She continued. "It gets stranger. Her identity was switched with her best friend, who may actually have been killed and buried. My client was resurrected under the new identity. Oh, yeah. The burial was done in the name of Jesus Christ, whom they associated with death." Sarah stopped and sighed.

"The resurrection was performed in the name of Satan," she added after a moment.

Bill Travers sat silently chewing his thumbnail, staring at a point somewhere just to the left of Sarah's head. Sarah found the effect disconcerting; it was like being ignored and stared at all at the same time. Finally, Travers shifted his gaze slightly and his eyes met Sarah's.

"How long has your client been in therapy?" he asked.

"Two, two and a half months," Sarah said.

Travers frowned. "What do you want me to do?"

Sarah frowned now. "I don't know. I need help. I

need to figure out whether my client was actually involved with a group of Satan worshippers or whether something else is going on. I've only told you a little bit. Maybe you could listen to the recordings of some of our sessions and tell me what you think."

"Can you bring them to my place tomorrow night?"

Sarah thought about Mark and all her time away from home lately. "Uh . . . I don't know. I thought maybe we could meet in my office."

"Look, I've got most of my books and papers at my apartment, in case I need to research anything. I'm also barricading myself in over the weekend to try to get papers graded. I can stand to take a break for a couple of hours if you can make it by."

"All right," Sarah said, trusting that Mark would understand. "Tomorrow it is. What time?"

"How about seven? If you bring a pizza, I'll provide the wine."

Sarah laughed. "Okay, you're on." She stood and shook hands. "Thank you. Dr. Travers—"

"Bill."

"Bill, I don't know what's going on with my client, but I hope to God that this is some bizarre fantasy I've tapped into. At any rate, I feel a lot better having someone else think about it with me."

"I don't know how much good I'll do," Travers said, gathering up a handful of papers, "but I'll do what I can."

"Tomorrow!" Mark Johnson exploded. "But Saturday is the one day when we have a chance to be together. For Chrissakes, Sarah, I thought we were going to work at spending *more* time together."

"Mark, I hate to do business on a Saturday, but I didn't have much choice. This is very important."

"Explain it to me again, then. I must have missed something the first time around."

"I told you. Diana *appears* to be recalling memories of some involvement with a group of Satan worshippers," she said, then sighed. "I *know* how stupid that sounds. Bill Travers is a professor of anthropology at the university. He specializes in the occult."

"This all sounds like a bunch of crap to me," Mark said disgustedly.

"Well, Mark, I hope that's exactly what it turns out to be. But for the sake of my client, I have to find out. What's the big deal, anyway?"

"The big deal is, why do you have to do this on a Saturday night? I'm sure this guy could have scheduled another time."

Without thinking, Sarah said, "You're not jealous, are you?" then instantly regretted the remark.

"Jealous? Screw you! Are you telling me I *should* be? Is that what this is all about?" Mark paced the kitchen floor, arms beating the air like the wings of moths.

"No, Mark. I'm sorry I said *jealous.* But damnit, I made the appointment for when I could get it. I've got to go. Please understand."

"Fine," Mark said, picking up his car keys from a bowl on the kitchen counter. "Two can play this game. See, I forgot to tell you. I've got plans for tonight. We're flexible enough around here that it shouldn't bother you." He opened the back door.

"Mark, wait," Sarah said. "Don't leave."

The door slammed shut and in a few seconds she heard the Volvo groan into life.

Week 9: Saturday, September 30

Sarah was late getting the pizza, which made her late for her appointment with Travers. She arrived breathless, pausing outside the door to take several deep breaths. She pressed the doorbell and then, hearing no response, rapped on the door. She thought she heard a muffled "yeah, yeah" from inside, then the door opened. Bill Travers stood in the doorway, hair dripping wet, naked but for a towel secured around his waist with one hand.

Sarah forgot her apology speech for being fifteen minutes late.

"Christ, come in. I'm running a little late. Come in. Make yourself at home. I'll be back in five minutes," Travers said, already turning away and half trotting down the hallway. The situation might have been laughable had Sarah not been totally caught off guard, standing in the open doorway of an unfamiliar apartment.

Self-possession regained, Sarah stepped in and closed the door behind her. She stood in the living room. Travers had exited to the right, presumably in the direction of bedroom and bath. Straight ahead, Sarah glimpsed a refrigerator through an archway off the living room. The kitchen, then.

She scanned the living room as she passed through. It had about it the futile neatness of the chronically untidy person's last-minute efforts to straighten up. Sarah imagined that the stacks of books had been gathered together moments before. Furniture appeared to have been haphazardly dusted. Sarah wondered if she would find dirty socks and underwear were she to look beneath the sofa cushions.

Remarkably, the kitchen was spotless. Was this the sign of a man who spent no time in the kitchen or a great deal of time? Sarah opened the oven door cautiously. *Not bad,* she thought. *Relatively clean, but dirty enough to know that someone actually used it.* She removed a broiler pan, set it on the oven top, and set the temperature controls. She put the pizza in the oven, box and all, and closed the door. Standing, she turned to the refrigerator and opened the door carefully. The interior was clean and sparse. A few containers of leftovers; door laden with condiments; sauces and other odds and ends; milk, some yogurt, a couple of six packs of beer. A bottle of wine. Sarah hesitated, then shrugged and grabbed a beer.

Returning to the living room, she opened her beer and stopped in front of a large bookcase crammed to capacity. *Eclectic reading tastes,* she thought. Popular novels side by side with works by Malinowski and Lévi-Strauss. Lots of science fiction. She recognized the Asimovs and the Bradburys and the Clarks, though there were many names she had never seen before. A Shakespeare collection. An old *Gray's Anatomy.* A number of volumes on religion, with a heavy concentration on the Far East. And here and there, stranger offerings: *Magick in Theory and Practice, The Black Hen, Malleus Mallificarum, Illusions and Delusions of the Occult and Supernatural.* Sarah pulled down a volume titled *A History of the Black Arts.*

She found a clear spot on the sofa and opened the book to a woodcut illustration of a naked old hag straddling a broomstick in flight. A scraggly cat rode the shoulders of the witch. Sarah flipped the page. A line drawing depicted a winged creature with a man's body and a goat's head. Something like a torch rose between the creature's two horns. On closer inspection, Sarah saw that the creature had very female breasts; paradoxically, a stylized phallus rose from between its legs. "The Goat of Mendes," the caption read. Sarah flipped through several more pages, absorbed in illustrations of magical symbols: strangely adorned and inscribed circles, triangles, and especially, five-pointed stars.

"What are you reading?"

Sarah almost spilled her beer. She looked around at Travers, who had come up from behind to peer over her shoulder.

"Sorry. Didn't mean to startle you," he said, stepping around the couch. He had changed into jeans and a knit shirt. His damp hair was combed. He was barefoot.

"That's all right. I was just reading *A History of the Black Arts.*" Sarah smiled. "Looking at the pictures, really."

"Yeah, there are some really grim illustrations of a Black Mass."

"I haven't found those yet," she said. "I took the liberty of grabbing a beer and putting the pizza in your oven."

"Great. I think I'll get one myself." Travers disappeared into the kitchen. "Have any trouble finding the place?" he yelled.

"No," Sarah yelled back. "I know the area."

Travers stepped into the living room. "Shall we let the pizza warm up for a while?"

Sarah nodded. "Sounds like a good idea. What shall we do first? Would you like to start with the tapes?"

Travers pulled a footstool up to the coffee table and sat down, facing Sarah. "Why don't we wait for the pizza? That way, we can eat and listen at the same time. What I'd really like right now is some background. Can you just kind of give me an overview of the case?"

"All right," Sarah said. She hesitated, gathering her thoughts. "First, you're going to pick up my client's name from the tapes. I need you to be aware that this is all confidential information."

"Of course," Travers said. "I assume you have some sort of standard release that allows you to solicit outside expertise?"

Sarah nodded. "Diana came to me about two and a half months ago," she said. "Her presentation indicated episodic depression, with about a six-month history. She complained of middle sleep disturbance, fatigue, some weight loss, feelings of hopelessness, recent suicidal ideation. It looked like fairly classic depression."

"But it wasn't?" Travers asked.

"But it wasn't. One of the first oddities was a lack of memory of a great deal of her childhood and adolescence. Coupled with that was recurrent dream imagery and waking ideation involving hands, coffins, and burial. Oh, yeah, she also complained of headaches and tunnel vision. Another oddity was an aversion to drugs."

"Interesting," Travers said.

"Pretty quickly I began to suspect something a little more involved than depression. It reminded me of a post-traumatic stress disorder. That seemed consistent with the depression and the amnesia. Anyway, I started looking for indications of what might have happened. I figured that the drug aversion and burial imagery might have something to do with the trauma-inducing incident.

"To make a long story short, it wasn't much of a leap from there to suspecting some sort of child abuse, and from child abuse to general dissociative disorders."

"What finally clued you to multiple personalities?" Travers asked, and took a long pull off his beer.

"I had begun to suspect," Sarah answered. "The gaps in time, for one thing, should have been a clue. But in the end, it was the client herself. She tried to commit suicide—*someone* tried to commit suicide, let's put it that way—and one of the personalities telephoned me for help."

"You're kidding."

"I'm afraid not."

"So what happened? Did this other personality call up and say, 'Hello, I'm one of your client's alternate personalities and she's attempting suicide and I think you should get over here'?"

"Almost," Sarah laughed. "Actually, she called and said that we had a mutual friend. She said that Diana had taken an overdose of pills. When she refused to help any further, I guessed that she was an alter. After Diana recovered, this other personality attended the next session."

"So how many personalities have you uncovered?"

"In addition to Diana, three. There's Lynn, who called me. Then there's Nora. And this last one, the Listener."

"So Diana is the original or core personality?" Travers asked.

"I thought you said you didn't know anything about multiples," Sarah said.

"I don't." Travers grinned. "I know just enough to get myself in trouble."

"That, I'm afraid, is true for both of us."

"Somehow, I doubt that," Travers said.

Sarah shrugged. "To answer your question, Diana may or may not be what is called the core personality. There have been cases where the original personality was so thoroughly abused that it was sort of shunted off to the side, in a permanent state of unconsciousness. I'm not sure what happened in this case, but as you'll hear from one of the tapes tonight, some rather serious disturbance of the original identity has probably occurred."

"What does that do for the chances of reintegration?" Travers asked.

"Integration is not necessarily a goal. The literature is starting to show cases where integration was not desired by the client or deemed feasible by the therapist. In the case of Diana," Sarah shook her head, "I really don't have the slightest idea yet. There appear to be complications."

"That sounds like tape time. And pizza. Let me get you the cassette machine." Travers stood, walked over to a glass-fronted cabinet, and removed a portable cassette recorder. "This should do the trick," he said, dragging an extension cord over to the table. He plugged the machine into the cord. "I'll be back with the pizza."

Sarah opened her purse and fished out a half-dozen cassette boxes. She had not had time to sort through all the tapes and had grabbed more than she thought would really be of interest. She selected one and inserted it into the machine.

From the kitchen, she heard Travers shout, "You want beer or wine?"

"I think I'll stick with beer," she called back.

"Me, too," she heard him say.

By the time Travers had made several trips from the kitchen with fresh beers, pizza, dishes, and condiments, Sarah had located the segment of the first tape she wanted him to hear.

She pressed the play button and scanned Travers's face for reaction as the room filled with the eerie sound of the Listener. After listening and eating for about ten minutes, Travers took a long swallow of his beer, set the can on the coffee table, and stretched.

"That's enough of that for now," he said, snapping off the machine. "I may want to come back to it, but that's all I can get out of it for now. In fact, would you mind if I made a copy?"

Sarah nodded her consent, and Travers inserted the tape, along with a blank, into a dubbing deck in the glass-fronted cabinet. He rewound the tapes, started the recording, and returned to sit on the wooden stool.

"What else you got?"

Sarah opened the tape box labeled "D. Smith—Session 12." She fast-forwarded the tape, finding the right point after several tries. She pressed the play key and heard her own voice saying, "That's right, it's Wednesday, May 19. We are going back in time now to Saturday, May 15. You will remember a time on Saturday, May 15, when you were looking at yourself in a mirror. What day is it?"

"Saturday," Diana said . . .

For the next forty-five minutes, Sarah and Travers listened to Diana recount the story of her mock funeral at the age of twelve. Travers finished eating pizza and produced a ratty-looking legal pad from one of the piles of papers scattered around the room. He sat entranced by the tape, making occasional scribbles. At one point, Sarah gathered up the remnants of their meal and carried them into the kitchen. Travers rose to protest, but Sarah waved him into silence. She returned in time to hear Diana talking about the party that had been held for her after the funeral. As Diana said, "Yes, we had a birthday party. It's my birthday, you know," Sarah snapped the recorder off.

"Jesus Christ," Travers muttered.

"Yeah," said Sarah.

"What's the bit about the hair?"

"Oh, I forgot to tell you. That's how I managed to track down this event. Diana's a bottle blonde but believes it's her natural color. The personality named Lynn takes care of her hair for her. That was strange enough to indicate that something significant must have happened. Anyway, if Diana is to be believed, her becoming a blonde was a part of her psychological death as Sissie and her resurrection as Diana."

"Remarkable," Travers said.

Sarah cued the next tape. She selected the section of the session in which Diana visualized entering the house carved of stone and "viewing" the memory of her apparent rape by a priest. Travers sat hunched over, alternately chewing a thumbnail and frantically scratching out notes on the legal pad. Sarah reached out to stop the tape after the culmination of the visualization exercise in Diana's hysterical masturbation. Travers reached over and touched Sarah's hand.

"Let it play a minute," he said.

Sarah listened to herself calming Diana, explaining what had happened and finally promising the upset woman that she would help her.

"She didn't remember what happened, then?" Travers asked.

"No," Sarah said.

"Damn, lady, I'm glad I've got my job and not yours." Travers shook his head. "Was she hypnotized?"

"Technically, no. I adapted a group visualization exercise. The group leader suggests visualizing a walk in a forest. The trip culminates in a meeting with a wise person or creature who tells the subject something revelatory. In this case, the trip was to a stone house where each of the rooms held a memory. Ordinarily, she should have been able to remember. I think she is extremely suggestible, however, and falls easily into trance state. By the way, one theory for MPD is that it is a form of self-hypnosis. Abused individuals with a predisposition for suggestibility use self-hypnosis to escape from the pain."

"Interesting. But could it be all false memories and the desire of a person under hypnosis to please the hypnotist?"

Sarah nodded. "Maybe. It's possible I'm giving subtle cues, placing Diana in a situation in which she makes up a story she thinks I'll be pleased with. But I don't think so. Bill, there is one other tape I should play for you now that we've gotten this far."

Sarah next played excerpts from Nora's account of abuse at the hands of her father. When she had finished, Travers stood up shakily from the stool, gently flexing his right leg.

"Damn, it's terrible when you get old," he said. Sarah laughed; Travers was about her age. "How about another beer?"

"No, thanks. I could stand a cup of coffee, though."

"Coming up."

Travers puttered in the kitchen, apparently in no hurry to return to the living room while the coffee brewed. After about ten minutes, he returned carrying a wooden tray laden with two mugs of coffee, sugar bowl, milk pitcher, and a bottle of Kahlua. He poured the coffee. Sarah passed on the Kahlua. Travers shrugged and poured a generous helping into his cup.

"So, what happened?" Sarah asked. "Did I lose you on the last tape?"

Travers smiled. "Well, you've got two versions. Why not believe the easiest?"

Sarah nodded. "I understand. It's tempting. What you haven't gotten out of listening to the tapes is a sense of the evolution of the sessions. First, the tape you just heard precedes the others. Second, the source, Nora, may not be reliable."

"Why not?"

"I know this sounds crazy, but I don't trust her. She acts as if she knows more than she really does. I'm convinced that she does not know what happened the night of Diana's suicide attempt. Furthermore, Diana disagrees with Nora's account of their childhood. She also doesn't seem to know anything about the other personalities. She claims there are no others."

"So maybe she's kept insulated," Travers offered. "That doesn't make her wrong."

"Maybe. I guess the main thing is that her account is just too damn glib. It explains everything with a broad stroke but doesn't handle the specifics very well. The other accounts start to explain things like Diana's fear of drugs and coffins, her doll dream, which I haven't told you about, even her hair. Unfortunately, they give a broad picture that looks just too damn crazy to contemplate."

"Are you sure you just don't like Lynn better?"

"I appreciate your bluntness, Bill," Sarah said and smiled. "At this point, I *do* like Lynn better. Initially, though, I thought of her as brash and rough, a sort of punk redneck. Nora was very pleasant. So I don't think my hidden prejudices are at work; they would probably prefer the situation reversed."

Travers sipped his coffee and stood up. Remembering the tape he had made, he retrieved Sarah's cassette from the machine and handed it to her.

"You were taking quite a few notes there," Sarah said. "Care to tell me what interested you so?"

"Sure," Travers said, sitting down again. "You ever read Robert Monroe's *Journeys Out of the Body?*"

"No."

"Well, you remove the bit about the priest and the bit at the end about the hands, and you've got a pretty classic description of an O.B.E.—an out-of-body experience. Also called astral projection."

"And what's the significance of an out-of-body experience?"

"I'm not sure there is any," Travers said. "It's something that crops up all over the place—occult literature ranging from black and white magic to witchcraft, religious traditions such as Lamaistic Buddhism, and a half-dozen or more so-called 'new age' disciplines. Some say it's simply a real journey out of the body by some aspect of consciousness. Some of the traditions claim it's the ability to travel in one or more spiritual dimensions peopled by other beings; some say it's proof of life after death. I suppose from a psychological standpoint, it could also be pathological."

"A form of dissociation, sure," Sarah said.

"Anyway, it's probably no big deal. I just found Diana's account interesting."

"What do you think of the rest of it, Bill? Please be honest and remember, life's a hell of a lot simpler for me if this is all fantasy or screen memories."

"Okay, Sarah. I'm not trying to weasel out, but I really just don't know. I want some time to think about it and to go over the copy of that tape I made. But I can give you some preliminary impressions.

"First, the tapes of Diana are awfully compelling. But so are hypnosis-induced accounts of reincarnation. Are you familiar with past-life age regression?"

"Yes. I know that you can get most subjects to fabricate convincing stories of past lives, even overlapping ones."

Travers nodded agreement. "My point is that the tapes are compelling, but that doesn't prove anything. One way or the other. If Diana's account is accurate, then what we have is a highly organized group of Satan worshippers who have been operating for a long time. They practice physical and sexual abuse and other forms of psychological torture on children and adolescents. They may also practice human sacrifice. They manage to do this in such a way that their activities go undetected by the authorities."

"Until now."

"Until now," Travers repeated. "I have to ask myself, 'What's wrong with this picture?' As an anthropologist, I ask myself this question. You know what answer I get?"

In spite of herself, Sarah shook her head.

"The answer I get is: It doesn't make sense. As an anthropologist now. Not as a student of the occult, who loves to find conspiracies and mysteries. It doesn't make sense. And you know what doesn't make sense?"

"No," Sarah said, her voice small.

"Satanists, like any other tribe, culture, subculture, or voluntary association, are going to behave in certain ways that contribute to the cohesiveness of the group. Group behavior will have a purpose. But the kind of behavior that Diana describes can't have any enculturative purpose. You said yourself that abuse leads to dissociation, to fragmentation. It also leads to alienation. It causes disability. It's dysfunctional. Sarah, I just can't see a long-term, organized, and functional group operating with that kind of ethos."

Sarah nodded. "I can't disagree with you, Bill. What you say is reasonable. But just for the sake of argument, what would it take for it to make sense?"

"For it to make sense to me, you'd have to show

how basically antisocial behaviors—physical and sexual abuse—contribute to either group cohesiveness or the enculturation of the abused individual. Do you understand what I'm talking about?"

"Yes, I think so. Something about the activities has to promote a sense of identity with the group. If it only succeeds in causing alienation or psychological breakdown, then it can't have any logical purpose."

"Right. You've got it," Travers agreed. "Ask yourself this: Why would a group perform a series of heinous actions on a child that would later compel her to seek out therapy and assistance from a non-group member?"

"Maybe something went wrong," Sarah said.

"Sarah, listen closely to me. You're treading on very thin ice here. I know a little something about the way conspiracies work; the occult mythos is full of them. A good conspiracy is self-promoting. Any contradiction to the conspiracy can be explained as either an exception—the kind that proves the rule—or as evidence of the widespread and sinister nature of the conspiracy. Example. There's a fairly prevalent myth in certain occult circles about a group of seven, nine, or thirteen individuals who rule the world with absolute power. An objection to this theory is that no one has ever seen one of these hidden masters. The proponent's reply is 'Well, of course not. They are so powerful that they avoid any detection.' You see what I mean? A good conspiracy is self-justifying, self-fulfilling. So watch yourself carefully when you start telling yourself things like 'Maybe something went wrong.' Don't be too quick to turn contradiction into justification."

"So you *don't* believe any of it?" Sarah asked.

Travers laced his fingers behind his head and leaned back with his eyes closed. After several seconds, his eyes opened and he looked at Sarah. "Sarah, I did not say I don't believe it." He opened his hands and leaned forward. "I'm just going to explain it away as easily as I can, *if* I can. I'm willing to entertain any theories and examine any evidence. It's just that right now, I don't see a compelling reason to believe stories about organized Satanism."

Travers paused a moment. He poured a shot of Kahlua into his empty coffee cup. "Okay. Now I've given you my lightness and rationality lecture. I guess I ought to give you the other side. You were open enough to play both the pro and con tapes; I guess I can reciprocate. Plus, you seem levelheaded enough not to jump to conclusions."

"Thank you," Sarah said, "but what are you talking about?"

"Sarah, there have been persistent rumors for a number of years about highly organized Satan worshippers who conduct human sacrifices and ritual torture and all kinds of bizarre activities. The problem is that there has not been one iota of evidence to support these rumors. None. Zip. However, the rumors persist.

"My attitude has been to regard these rumors as a form of modern myth. So far I have seen very little to persuade me to change my attitude. I sort of lump them into the same category as sightings of Bigfoot and accounts of UFO abductions—absolutely fascinating examples of human behavior and the need for myth and mystery in our lives."

"So why are you telling me this?" Sarah asked.

"In case the one percent chance that any of this is true actually turns out to be the case."

"One percent, huh?"

"Yeah, I'd say that's about right," Travers said.

"Bill, you said that so far you have seen *very little* to support these rumors. You didn't say *nothing.* Why not?"

"Then I should have," Travers said. Sarah looked uncertain. "Really," he added.

"Okay," Sarah said. She looked at her watch. "It's almost midnight. I've got to run."

"No need to rush off," Travers said. "How about another cup of coffee?"

"No, thanks." Sarah gathered her cassettes, putting them in her purse.

"You're okay to drive, then?"

"Oh, sure, I'm fine. I only had a couple of beers and I'm wide awake. Bill, thank you for taking time to listen to the tapes and talk with me. I feel a whole lot better about everything."

Sarah stood and offered her hand, which Travers shook.

"I really do want to believe Nora's account," she said.

"Me, too, Sarah." Travers walked her to the door. "Look, I want you to keep me informed. If there is anything I can do, if anything new pops up, will you call me?"

"Yes, I will. I appreciate your interest, Bill."

Travers opened the door and they shook hands again. This time, Bill held on to Sarah's hand. "Sarah," he said, "there is another reason why I think the satanic version is wrong."

"Why?"

"Because," Travers said, releasing her hand, "if these people really existed, I think you would have heard from them by now."

"What do you mean?" Sarah asked.

"I mean, they all just wouldn't have gone away to let your client live out her life in peace. Her therapy would represent a very real threat of detection. Wouldn't you expect some kind of retaliation, either against Diana or even you? Maybe some attempt to get you to discontinue therapy?" Travers paused and examined Sarah's face carefully. "Sarah, are you all right? I didn't frighten you, did I?"

"No, no. I'm fine. Everything Diana has told me

about happened a long time ago. And her parents are dead. There's no reason to think the cult would still be around."

Travers nodded. "I wonder," he said, more to himself than to Sarah.

"Well, thank you again," Sarah said and turned.

"You call me if I can help," Travers said.

Travers watched her walk to her car. He wondered briefly if he had been too vocal in denying the occult aspects of Sarah's case, then quickly dismissed the thought as nonsense. But why, then, had he felt a quick twinge of guilt when he assured her that he had seen nothing to substantiate the rumors? Why did he keep glimpsing a desiccated corpse in an antique coffin and the body of an infant at the bottom of a grave?

Chapter 15

October

October passed quickly. The treatment of Diana Smith became almost routine. Sarah concentrated on Nora's accounts of abuse, remembering Travers's advice to accept the easiest explanation. The satanic material seemed forgotten, an aberration, and Sarah's attempts to reestablish contact with Lynn were futile. Life seemed to have regained normal proportions. Even Sarah's fears for her marriage were allayed. Both she and Mark worked hard to be home early and to spend time together. Sarah still sensed some new, unsettled core deep inside her husband. But if it truly existed, it smoldered unnoticed, like a carefully banked fire, or lay in remission, like a cancer.

Life seemed almost normal again. Almost.

Week 15: Thursday, November 9

"You haven't talked much about your work recently," Sarah said. "How's everything going?"

Diana lit another cigarette. "It's going all right. I'm selling. I had a picture in last Sunday's *Chronicle.*"

"Really? I'll have to look. I don't think I've thrown it out yet."

"Well, it's not much. Just a picture of some kids jumping into a pile of leaves."

"You know, I remember seeing that. It was a very nice photograph. I guess I'm going to have to start reading the credits," Sarah said. "Gosh, I feel like I know a celebrity."

Diana smiled. "Sarah, you always make me feel good about myself."

Sarah bowed slightly. "Thank you. I'll take that and run with it. But tell me more about the photograph. I really am fascinated. Tell me how you decided to take that picture and what you were doing at the time."

"All right. Let's see. . . . I believe I took the picture last Tuesday. I had decided to spend the day just wandering around the city shooting pictures. I figured I'd eventually end up in this neighborhood in time for our session. That's why I had all my equipment with me, remember?"

Sarah nodded.

"I was walking through one of those really ritzy neighborhoods that border on Haymont Park. I saw this enormous pile of leaves in a yard. A man who was probably a caretaker or gardener was walking away from the pile with a rake in his hands. I thought that might make a nice picture, so I raised my camera and took off the lens cover. As I started to frame the picture, I saw these two little kids come around the side of the house and start running for the pile. I was hoping to get both the caretaker walking away with the rake and the children jumping into the leaves, but by the time the children jumped, I couldn't get the caretaker in the frame."

"Well, it was a marvelous picture. Very warm. It made me want to act like a kid again and go jump in a pile of leaves. Did you ever jump in leaves when you were little, Diana?"

"I do remember something," Diana said. "Something about leaves . . ." Diana's eyes seemed to lose their focus. Her face went slack for a moment. In the next instant, it seemed rounder, fuller. Her eyes opened very wide and the pupils dilated, leaving just a fringe of blue around the black.

"The leaves are cold and wet," said a small, child-like voice.

Sarah leaned forward in her chair. "Yes, the leaves are cold and wet," she said. "What else can you see?"

"I just see a little light way high above. I'm scared. Why am I here? Am I really a bad girl? I don't understand." The voice was tiny, pathetic. If Sarah closed her eyes, she knew she could picture the little three- or four-year-old.

"Where are you?"

"I'm down the hole," the tiny voice said, sounding frightened. "He threw me down the hole."

"Who threw you down the hole?"

"Father. He said I was bad."

"Where is the hole?" Sarah asked.

"In the woods. Way back in the woods. The hole is full of leaves. Father says there are snakes in here. I'm afraid of snakes. It smells bad, too. I couldn't help it. I couldn't hold it any longer." Big tears rolled down Diana's cheeks.

"It's all right. It's not your fault. How long have you been there?"

"It got dark three times. I get scared when it's dark."

"Three days? You've been in the hole for three days?"

"Uh-huh." She nodded, like a small child.

Several times, Sarah had been about to call the personality Diana. She had hesitated each time. Now she asked, "What is your name?"

"Lainey."

"Lainey, why did Father put you in the hole?"

"I don't know," Lainey said. There was a frantic edge to her voice.

"Lainey, it's all right. What did Father say when he put you in the hole?"

"He said, 'You're a bad girl, you're very bad.' He was very mad."

"Why did he get mad, Lainey?"

Lainey's eyes darted from side to side, like caged animals. "I wouldn't do what he wanted. He said I was one of *them.*"

One of them? "What was that, Lainey? What did he want you to do?"

"No. I can't tell you. Can never tell."

"It's okay, Lainey. You can tell. He can't hurt you now."

"It's okay?" The voice was small, doubtful.

"Yes. You're safe here. Whatever you tell me is our secret."

"I wouldn't do it," Lainey said in a breathless rush. "I knew it was bad. He couldn't make me."

"That's right, Lainey, he couldn't make you do it. Now tell me what he wanted you to do."

"Kill the baby. He wanted me to kill the baby and I wouldn't do it."

Sarah hugged herself against a sudden chill. At that moment, Lainey opened her eyes. Sarah saw the wide eyes unfocus and then narrow. The woman before her seemed to relax, almost unfold out of herself, becoming larger. The eyes narrowed and blinked. The pupils contracted.

"I'm sorry, what did you say?" Diana asked, placing her feet back on the floor and stretching.

Sarah fumbled for a response, momentarily at a loss. What had just happened? Sarah had thought the satanic material long gone, an aberration of memory, perhaps, a child's attempt to rationalize the irrational acts of abusive adults. "Diana, does the name Lainey mean anything to you?"

Diana stood and stretched. "Lainey? That's a funny name, isn't it? No, I've never heard it before. Why?"

"Oh, nothing really. It's just a name that came up in one of our hypnosis sessions some time back," Sarah lied. "I just remembered to ask."

"Oh, Sarah, there's something I wanted to tell you. I remembered another dream."

Diana sounded excited, but Sarah was still trying to place the emergence of Lainey in some rational framework. She concentrated on Diana with difficulty.

"A dream?" she said. "Well, that's wonderful."

"Yes," Diana said. "It was a flying dream. I haven't had a flying dream since I was a kid."

The chill Sarah had felt with the emergence of Lainey now returned.

"Diana, we've talked about flying dreams before. Do you remember?"

Diana frowned and shook her head. "Really? No, I don't remember at all. Flying dreams? Really?"

Sarah nodded.

"But wait a minute . . ." Diana looked at Sarah in surprise. "Something about a house in the woods. Is that right?"

Sarah nodded again.

A sudden look of horror transformed Diana's face. "Oh, my God," she said. "Oh, my God, oh, my God."

Sarah moved quickly out of her chair, nearly tripping in her haste. She leaned over Diana, grasping her by the shoulders. Sarah shook her client, at first gently, then with increasing force.

"What is it?" Sarah asked. "Tell me what you remember."

"He raped me," Diana cried. "He raped me with his crucifix. He had sex with me, too."

"Who was he, Diana?"

"He was a priest. No, wait. I don't understand. He was a priest, but he wasn't a priest. He dressed like a priest. I don't know, I can't remember." Diana grabbed Sarah by the arms, her grip imploring and desperate. "I was escaping, wasn't I? The priest raped me and I went on the dreams to escape?"

"Yes, Diana. The dreams are another form of dissociation. You dreamed of flying to protect yourself from what was really happening."

"But that's not right, Sarah," Diana said frantically, tears streaming down her face. "That's not right. My God. Oh, Sarah, I enjoyed it. I enjoyed the sex. When I came back from the dream, I would enjoy the sex. I had orgasms. I remember."

"No, Diana, no." Sarah held Diana's face in her hands, forcing eye contact. "You listen to me. What the priest did was a perversion of normal, healthy instinct. He used the pleasure of sex to make you feel like you were a partner, responsible. But *he* did it. Not you. You didn't asked to be raped. He was wrong. What he did was an abomination. You are innocent, Diana, and whatever you felt then or feel now are just normal reactions to abnormal situations. Do you understand me?"

Diana nodded. Suddenly, she wrenched her head free. "No, there's more." Her teeth were chattering and she shivered. "The priest knew that I was flying. Oh, Sarah, he wanted me to fly. That's why he was there. I didn't have the dreams because he raped me. He raped me so that I *would* have the dreams."

"No, wait, Diana," Sarah smiled gently. "What you're saying makes no sense. The dreams are escape."

"No," Diana said, her voice suddenly even, resolved. "I dreamed of flying because that's what the priest wanted. He helped me to dream. He raped me with a crucifix and he told me to leave my body. All the time I could hear him. Even when I thought I was far away. He knew where I went and what I was doing. How can that be?"

"If what you say is true, then the priest suggested it. He hypnotized you or did something similar."

"Why, Sarah, why? Why would a priest rape me and help me escape at the same time.?"

Sarah suddenly remembered Bill Travers discussing astral projection. *An out-of-body experience, he called it. He said it was common in occult literature and belief systems. What if this priest-figure isn't just some pedophile? What if he was a teacher—a teacher and a pedophile, perhaps—but what if he was really trying to teach the child, force the child, to have an out-of-body experience? What if the out-of-body experience wasn't a side effect but the whole purpose of what Diana described?*

"Sarah, when it was all over, he would congratulate me. He would tell me how well I had done. He would say that I was really learning to fly well, that he was proud of me. He made me feel good about it."

Sarah shuddered. "You sound like this happened more than once."

"It did, Sarah. I know it did. I can't remember all the individual times, but I know there were many times that we did this."

Sarah moved slowly to her chair and sat down. "Do you realize you've just made a breakthrough? You haven't been able to remember any of this before without some sort of alteration in consciousness—hypnosis or visualization. How do you feel?"

Diana lit a cigarette. "I feel strange," she said, exhaling a huge mouthful of smoke. "What's happening to me?"

"You're starting to remember material that belongs to some of the other personalities," Sarah said, forcing conviction and confidence into her voice, though she felt neither. "I think some of the memories are garbled, though. I think they're embellished because you're still not quite ready to confront what actually happened." Sarah's interior voice nagged at her: *But maybe she remembers perfectly well.*

Later, after Diana had left, Sarah's voice continued

to nag. *Maybe she remembers perfectly well,* it said. *Maybe she remembers just fine.*

There was no comfort in the thought.

Week 16: Tuesday, November 14

"Sarah, you've got Bill Travers on line two."

"Thanks, Margie," Sarah said. She leaned back in the chair and stretched, yawning and rubbing her eyes. Opening a desk drawer, she located a file folder and laid it on her desk. Finally, she picked up the receiver.

"Hello, this is Sarah Johnson," she said.

"Bill Travers, Sarah. How are you?"

"I'm fine, Bill. It's been a while, hasn't it?"

"Yes, it has. By the way, thanks for the wine."

"You're welcome. I appreciated all your time and observations." Sarah had had a bottle of wine, along with a thank-you note, delivered to Travers's apartment.

"How's the case going?"

"Slowly, actually," Sarah said. "With occasional flashes of progress. In fact, your timing is good. I think the question of which version of events is correct is reopened."

"Oh?"

"Yes. That was sort of my reaction. After we talked, things settled down for a while and I was ready to pretty much accept Nora's version of events. Now I'm not so sure again."

"Why not?"

"Let's just say another personality has appeared and reinforces the notion that some pretty strange things were going on when Diana was growing up."

"What kind of things?"

"Bill, I'd prefer not to go into detail about my clients over the phone."

"Oh, sure."

"Bill, how come you called?"

"This may be nothing, but I told you I'd let you know if I found out anything about that tape of the Listener."

"Yes?"

"I went to school with a guy who's a linguistic anthropologist. For chuckles, I sent him a copy of the tape."

"And?"

"And the damn thing has just about driven him nuts. I didn't tell him where it came from, only that I was trying to come up with a translation of it. At first he said it wasn't a language, because it didn't match anything. Then I told him it might be something undiscovered. Which was pretty hard to do, because then he wanted to know where I'd gotten it. Eventually, he agreed to analyze it as if it were a previously undiscovered language."

"So what happened?" Sarah asked, letting a little impatience creep into her voice.

"One of the things he did was to analyze the frequency and pattern of the various words and phonemes in the whole piece. Languages tend to have some pretty predictable distributions. It's one way you go about distinguishing commonly used words like articles and simple verbs and that kind of thing."

"Yes?"

Travers continued. "According to the distributions analysis, it's probably a real language. At least it's not random gibberish. When I asked him if it could be glossolalia, he said, 'No fucking way.' On the other hand, he's hit a blank wall on translating it. Without more to go on, he says he can't do anything else with it."

"So what do we have here, Bill? An unknown language?"

"That's what it looks like, Sarah. My friend did say it *could* be a clever attempt to fake a language. If you knew something about linguistics, you might be able to come up with something like this. He also said that for an equivalent expenditure of energy you could probably invent a full-blown language, so he doubted that it was faked."

"Did you finally tell him where it came from?"

"Nope," Travers said. "I suppose I should have, but I didn't want to lose him. Just in case we need him again."

Sarah sighed. "Bill, I appreciate you doing all this, but that's sort of the end of it, isn't it? I mean, there's not much else to do, is there?"

"There is one thing. I'd like you to tap into the Listener again and make another tape. Maybe if we get this friend of mine another sample, he can come up with something."

Sarah thought about Travers's proposal for a moment. "All right. I ought to be able to do it in one of next week's sessions. You want to have lunch next Friday? I'll bring whatever I get."

"Sounds good."

Sarah thanked Travers again and hung up. She sat staring, tapping her front teeth with the tip of her pen. She wondered what it meant if the Listener's strange utterances actually were language. Did that corroborate the satanic aspects of Diana's accounts? Why should it? What did that make the Listener, anyway?

"I would like to speak to Lainey, please. Is Lainey there?" Sarah could not quite suppress the combination of silliness and excitement she felt in asking to speak to another personality. She half expected Diana to look at her and say something like, "What? Are you out of your damn mind?" Instead, the woman sat with her eyes closed, head tilted forward in the profound relaxation of hypnosis.

"Yes?"

That tiny voice again! So much about Lainey was a puzzle. The name had sounded familiar and Sarah had traced back through her files, finally locating her notes from the session of the mock funeral. Iris Laine Morrison was the name of Diana's supposed "original" identity in the funeral fantasy—if indeed it was a fantasy. Now Sarah had to wonder.

"Lainey, you may open your eyes."

The eyes opened and blinked. Again, that round, wide-eyed look, the hugely dilated pupils.

"Lainey," said Sarah, "how old are you?"

"Three," she said. "Going on four."

"Lainey, I want you to tell me what you meant when you said your father called you one of them. What did you mean?

"Huh?"

"Your father said you were one of them? Who did he mean?"

"Them, Them, Them," Lainey exploded in sudden exasperation. "They don't belong to the Circle. You know."

Lainey's outburst startled Sarah. She said softly, "Tell me about Them, Lainey." The way Lainey said *Them,* the word had become capitalized. "Are They bad?"

"Yes. You know They are," Lainey insisted.

"Why are They bad, Lainey? What do They do?"

"They hate us. They want to kill us."

"I see," Sarah said. "Tell me about the Circle, Lainey. Who belongs to the Circle?" Somehow, the word *Circle* had become capitalized in Sarah's mind, too.

"No," Lainey said.

"Will you tell me, Lainey?"

"No. Never can say."

"Why not, Lainey? Why can't you tell me?"

" 'Cause you will go away."

"No, Lainey, I won't go away," Sarah said. "You can tell me."

"No," Lainey insisted. "You will go away. I will go away, too."

Sarah had a sudden inspiration. "What do you mean 'go away'?"

"Go away," Lainey repeated, her frustration evident. "Like Sneezer went away."

"Who's Sneezer?"

"Sneezer's my dog," Lainey said, smiling briefly.

"And Sneezer went away?"

Lainey nodded solemnly. "Sneezer went away forever," she said. "Indra told me Sneezer died. When somebody dies, they go away forever."

"Who's Indra?"

"Indra is my best friend." Sarah smiled. Lainey said it with a child's matter-of-fact insistence, as if to say, *Don't you know anything?*

"And you're afraid I'll go away if you tell me about the Circle?" Sarah asked. "You're afraid I'll die like Sneezer?"

Lainey nodded again. "Uh-huh."

Sarah sat silently for a minute, trying to decide how to approach this problem of Them and the Circle. "Lainey, I won't go away," she said. "No one is going to die. You can tell me. We're safe here. No one can hear us or see us. Everything you say is a secret between you and me. Tell me about the Circle."

Lainey frowned, but then the frown vanished and she smiled. "I know a poem," she said.

Almost reluctantly, a sense of foreboding stealing over her like a chill, Sarah asked, "Will you say it for me?"

Lainey nodded, closed her eyes in concentration, then began reciting:

> Bad is good and good is bad,
> They steal the children and make them sad,
> They cut off their hands and cook their feet,
> And offer them up for Jesus to eat.

The worms crawl in, the worms crawl out,
In your nose and out your mouth,
The eye inside is never closed,
It sees it all and never shows.

Never tell Them what you know,
The Circle sees, the Circle knows,
If you tell Them you will die,
The Circle keeps you safe inside.

The worms crawl in, the worms crawl out,
In your nose and out your mouth,
The eye inside is never closed,
It sees it all and never shows."

Lainey finished the recitation and sat very still.

Sarah cleared her throat. "Lainey, did Father teach you this poem?" she asked.

Lainey nodded.

"Do you understand the poem, Lainey?" Sarah asked.

Again, Lainey nodded.

"Tell me what the poem means."

"It means the Circle is safe," Lainey said. "Only the Circle is safe. Why are They so bad?"

"I don't know, Lainey. What else does the poem mean?"

"It means the eye always sees. Everything."

"What eye, Lainey?"

"You know," Lainey said. "The eye inside."

"The eye inside where?"

Lainey touched her abdomen with the tip of an index finger. "Here," she said. "You know. Father puts the eye in me."

"How does he do that, Lainey?"

"You know."

"Tell me, Lainey."

"No."

"It's all right," Sarah said gently. "You can tell me. Tell me how Father puts the eye in you."

Lainey suddenly covered the crotch of her jeans with both hands. "Here, here, here," she yelled, rocking in the chair. "He puts the eyeball up here."

"Why, Lainey? Do you know why he does that?"

"It's the eye of Lucifer's helper," Lainey said. "Lucifer sees everything I do. He always watches."

"Why does he always watch?"

"I'm tired," Lainey said. "I don't want to do talk about this anymore."

"Okay, Lainey," Sarah said soothingly. "You don't have to tell. You just relax. You don't have to tell."

Sarah flipped through her notes. *Where do I go from here?* she wondered. *Maybe I can get some kind of match between Nora's accounts and Lainey's memory.* Sarah flipped open the narrative section of the folder at random. Her eyes fell on her notes from a session with Nora in mid-October. Sarah had asked Nora to describe her father. Sarah read: "He was a big man, a very strong man with black hair and blue eyes." For some reason not clear to her at the time, she had quoted Nora verbatim. She did not usually do this, relying on the tapes as exact copy if necessary.

On impulse, Sarah asked, "Lainey, tell me what Father looks like."

"He's tall," Lainey said.

To Lainey, all adults probably look tall, thought Sarah. "What else, Lainey?" she prompted.

"He has hair on his face and brown hair."

"A beard?"

Lainey nodded.

"And you're sure he has brown hair, Lainey?"

"Yes," Lainey said.

"What color are his eyes?"

"Brown," Lainey answered. "Dark brown."

"I see. Lainey, do you know who Diana Smith is?"

"Yes."

"Who is she, Lainey?"

"Diana," Lainey said.

"Yes. Who's Diana?"

"Diana. She's Diana. Diana, Diana, Diana."

"Okay, Lainey. I guess that was a pretty stupid question, wasn't it?"

"Yes."

Sarah chuckled. "Do you like Diana, Lainey?"

"Sometimes I want to play, but I can't come out."

"Diana won't let you come out?"

"No," Lainey said. "But she's there, so I can't come out."

"Oh, I think I see. You can't come out if Diana is there. Is that it?"

Lainey nodded.

"But why not? Can't you just say, 'I want to come out now'?"

Lainey shook her head. "Uh-uh."

"Lainey, does someone let you come out? Does someone tell you that you can come out?"

"Uh-huh." Lainey nodded.

"Who lets you come and go, Lainey?"

"Lindis."

"I see. Is Lindis another name for Linda?"

After a moment's hesitation, Lainey answered, "Yes."

"Is Lindis another name for Lynn?"

"Maybe," Lainey said. "I don't know Lynn."

"Lainey, is Lindis there now?"

"Yes."

"Can you see her, Lainey? Can you talk to Lindis?"

"No. She's behind the gate now."

Lindis the Gatekeeper, thought Sarah. "Behind the gate? Is that where you go when Diana comes?"

"Yes."

Not sure what to do with the information, Sarah decided to change subjects. "Lainey, I want you to think back to the time you were in the pit in the ground. Do you remember?"

"Yes."

"How did you get out of the pit?"

"I don't know."

"All right. What's the last thing that you remember?"

"I don't want to think about it now, okay?"

"Lainey, it's all right. Listen to me. Nothing can hurt you. You can see everything that happened, but it's like watching a movie. You can see everything but it isn't happening to you, it's happening in the movie. Now, what's happening to Lainey before she leaves the pit?"

Lainey closed her eyes. "Father comes and gives me something to drink. I don't want anything, 'cause I'm scared. But I'm so hungry and so thirsty. Father says I can have the water. And food, too. All I have to do is . . ."

Lainey lapsed into a troubled silence.

"All you have to do is what?" Sarah prompted.

"Be good from now on." Lainey's voice was tiny, almost a whisper. "Do what the Circle says."

"And what do you say?"

"I'm so hungry and so cold."

"It's okay, Lainey. Anybody would agree. You're a brave little girl to have lasted so long. It's not your fault. What did you say?"

"I said I'd be good now. I said I'd do what they want."

"And then what happened?"

"Father gives me the water. And I drink it. I'm so thirsty, I drink the whole bottle. I'm so dirty and tired and hungry and cold." Her eyes opened wide.

"What happens next?"

"I get real sleepy and fall asleep."

Was the water drugged? Lynn had said Diana had been

drugged as a child. "That's right," Sarah agreed. "You feel asleep. What happened when you woke up?"

"It's warm. It's warm and I'm clean. I'm dressed in some kind of white pajamas, I don't know. I've never see them before."

"Where are you?"

"Big room. Lots of people in long, pretty robes. And there's food and water, and it's good food. I eat and eat. I'm so happy."

Lainey was no longer merely remembering. Her eyes opened and shone, tracking the action of a scene long since played out.

"What are the people doing, Lainey?" asked Sarah.

"They come by and hug me and tell me things."

"What kind of things?"

"They tell me I'm safe now," Lainey smiled. "They tell me I'm in the Circle."

"Do you know these people, Lainey? Is Father there?"

"Yes, Father is there, but he's not Father anymore."

"Who is he, Lainey?"

"Beliazar."

"Beliazar?" Sarah asked, confused. It was a new name, and it sounded sinister. "Who is Beliazar?"

"Don't know. Just something I remember," Lainey said.

"Okay," Sarah said, seeing no reason to press the point. "What happens after you eat?"

"I stand up and some people lead me by the arms. They lead me over to where some other people are standing. One of them shows me something and then I go away."

"You go away?" asked Sarah. "Where do you go?"

"Back behind the gate," Lainey said.

"I see. You go away and someone else comes out. Is that right?"

Lainey nodded.

"Lainey, you said somebody shows you something. What do they show you?"

"I don't know. It's a funny picture in a man's hand."

"What kind of picture?"

"All kinds of lines and things. It's hard for me to tell you."

"All right, Lainey," Sarah said. "Close your eyes and you'll be able to see the picture better. Close your eyes. That's right. What do you see?"

"I can see it good now," Lainey said, her eyes straining beneath the tightly closed lids, "but I still can't tell you."

"Do you think you could draw the picture, Lainey?"

"Uh-huh," Lainey said enthusiastically. "I draw good."

"Good girl," Sarah said, scrabbling through her desk for a pencil and a pad of paper. When she had found both, she walked around the desk and knelt by Lainey's side. "I want you to open your eyes very slowly, Lainey. When you open your eyes, you'll draw a picture of the thing in the man's hand. Go ahead, open your eyes."

Lainey opened her eyes and took the pad and pencil from Sarah. She began to draw with slow, laborious motions, her tongue tucked between her lips in concentration. The lines were shaky and Sarah found herself wishing for a set of crayons to give Lainey, or one of those huge, dull-pointed pencils they give the little ones to practice their letters.

When she had finished, Sarah took the pad from Lainey. The drawing looked familiar, like something she had seen in one of Bill Travers's books. Lainey had sketched a five-pointed star, a pentagram. In the center of the pentagram, she had shakily drawn squiggly lines. Sarah thought they might be Greek letters, but she wasn't sure.

"Lainey, do you know what this means?"

"No," Lainey said.

"But after they showed you this, you went behind the gate?"

"Yes."

"Lainey, how did the man show it to you? Was the picture on a piece of paper?"

"No, the picture was in his hand."

"He held the picture in his hand?" Sarah asked.

"No, it was in his hand," Lainey insisted. "Here. In his hand." Lainey held out her own hand, palm up. Her other hand pointed to the open palm.

"It was drawn on the man's palm?" Sarah asked uncertainly.

"Yes."

"And after you saw it, you went away?"

"Yes."

"Why did you go behind the gate, Lainey?"

"I don't know," she said. "I just did. I had to."

Sarah sighed, frustrated. *How many dead ends have I been down today?* she thought. Absently, she looked at the drawing and then at Lainey. *What's the connection? Is this drawing supposed to be part of some ritual or something? Why would she go away because of the drawing?*

Sarah pulled a pen from the cup on her desk. "Lainey," she said," I'd like you to close your eyes again, please." Lainey closed her eyes and Sarah pulled the cap off the pen. Carefully, she copied Lainey's sketch on the palm of her left hand. *This is silly,* she thought. *This has all got to be a mistake.*

In spite of her own objections, Sarah finished the drawing. She sat on the corner of her desk, facing Lainey. *What the hell,* she thought, feeling guilty at what seemed a foolish trick to play on her client.

"Lainey, I am going to count to three. When I reach three, I want you to open your eyes. One," Sarah said.

"Two." She raised her left hand, opening the palm

so that it hovered about six inches in front of Lainey's face.

"Three."

Lainey opened her eyes. Almost immediately, the expression on her face went slack, her eyes losing their focus on Sarah's hand. The pupils contracted rapidly, as if responding to a bright light. The face became hard, the eyes flinty with pupils shrunk down to the size of pinpoints.

Without warning, Diana jumped from the chair at Sarah, her hands together and raised as if holding an object over her head. Sarah raised her hands to ward off the blow and lost her balance. The fall may have saved her from graver injury. While Sarah shakily rose from the floor, her client stood rooted at the corner of the desk, her hands chopping at the empty air before her. The scene was grotesque; Sarah tried not to think about what this alter imagined she was doing.

In spite of the sudden fear that made her legs feel weak, Sarah forced herself to touch Diana, to push her back to the chair. At Sarah's touch, Diana's face went slack and her hands dropped to her sides.

"Come back, Diana, come back," Sarah said.

Diana's eyes closed, then fluttered open. "You hypnotized me, didn't you?" she asked.

"Yes," Sarah said, and thought to herself, *But I didn't bring you out of it. You did that on your own.*

"There's a little girl, isn't there?"

"Yes, there is. How do you know that?" Sarah asked.

"I have a picture of her in my head. I can see some of the things that she sees."

"What do you see?"

"Oh, just glimpses of things. I can't really put them together. It's like a picture that's been cut up. Or a mirror that shattered, and each piece has just a part of the original reflection in it. Every now and then, a piece of the mirror comes by where I can look at the reflection in it."

"And what have you seen so far?"

"I see a little girl. And I see a man looking at me from way up high. Like I'm down below his feet somehow looking up at him. That's all."

Sarah forced a smile. "I think we've just made progress."

"The little girl is me, isn't she? She's one of these other personalities."

Sarah nodded. "Yes, she is." *But who was the other alter?* she wondered.

"Who is she?"

"Her name is Lainey."

"Lainey," Diana said, and closed her eyes for a moment. When she opened them, she looked directly into Sarah's eyes with an expression of wonder.

Sarah looked for signs of anxiety in Diana. She thought she detected curiosity and, perhaps, incredulity, but little else. *Is this a breakthrough?* she wondered. *Will she continue to remember that she is a multiple? Will she start to make contact with the others?*

"What do you think about all this, Diana?" Sarah asked.

Diana puffed on her cigarette. "It's not something I want to believe." She paused. "But it does start to explain so many things. . . . Why time always goes wrong, for one. Do you think time will ever stop disappearing on me, Sarah?"

"The more we sort through everything, the closer we get," Sarah nodded. "We've got a lot of work to do, but then we've already come a long way."

Diana stubbed out her cigarette and stood. "It's time for me to go." She looked thoughtfully at Sarah. "We can fight this, can't we, Sarah?"

Sarah wasn't sure what *this* referred to, but she answered, "You bet we can."

The two women walked to the closed door of the

office. As Sarah reached for the knob, Diana placed her hand over the other woman's.

"Sarah," she said, "there's more, isn't there?"

"What do you mean?"

"There's something else going on here. Something to do with the little girl. I don't know what it is, but I know she's terribly afraid."

"I suspect she had some pretty terrible things done to her."

"Yes," said Diana. "But it's something more than child abuse, isn't it, Sarah? What is it?"

"I don't know," Sarah said. "I honestly don't. Do you know what it is?"

Diana shook her head. "No," she said.

Sarah suddenly remembered something from the hypnosis session. "Diana, what did your father look like? Can you describe him to me?"

Diana's forehead knitted in puzzlement. "Yes," she said uncertainly. "Let's see. . . . He was a tall man, six-two or three, I guess, and very trim. Light hair, sort of sandy-colored. Tanned. I remember him being tanned most of the year. And he had beautiful blue eyes." Diana paused. "How's that?"

"Great."

"Why did you ask, Sarah?"

"Just verifying the accounts of some of the other personalities."

"And?" Diana prompted.

"And everything's fine," Sarah smiled, opening the door. "You'll call me if you need me, right?"

Sarah made her way shakily to her desk, one leg already beginning to stiffen from the fall. So much had happened in the session, not the least of which was having been attacked by one of the alters. Or perhaps she'd only been in the way of an old memory being acted out. It was only after a long period of reflection that Sarah realized she had forgotten to ask Lainey about the most important thing from the previous session. And then Sarah wondered if she had truly forgotten. On some level perhaps she'd felt incapable, emotionally if not intellectually, of pursuing it. It was a mystery she was going to have to uncover, though; she knew that. The question of Satanism-related abuse was open again, now that Lainey had revealed herself and her memories of Them and the Circle, the omniscient eye *(My God,* thought Sarah, *did they really do that to a little girl?),* her imprisonment in the pit.

The unasked question haunted her. She couldn't stop thinking about it.

Had Lainey really refused to kill an infant? And what did it mean that she claimed to have finally relented?

Chapter 16

Late afternoon sun slanted in through the tinted windows of the boardroom. The muffled sounds of engines starting drifted up from the parking lot where workers were preparing to head home. At one end of a long mahogany table, a silver-haired man wearing a charcoal-gray suit sat with his elbows on the table, his fingers steepled under his chin. Arrayed around him, like eager employees around any good captain of industry, were four others, three men and a woman. Two of the men wore clothing more appropriate for a construction site than for a boardroom: faded Levi's, boots, comfortable shirts. The remaining man and woman were both dressed in conservative business suits.

"I don't like it," the man with the gray hair and suit said.

This was met with nods from around the table.

"She says she knows that she's talked about the Circle, but she doesn't know how much. Is that what I'm given to understand?"

One of the men wearing jeans nodded. He wore a chambray shirt with the sleeves rolled up to the crook of his elbow. The blue line of a tattoo peeked out from under the edge of the sleeve.

"That's right," he said. His voice was raspy, as if his throat had gone dry.

"Why doesn't she know more?"

The woman answered. "It's never perfect. The chrysalides are always like that. No one cell can ever be completely aware of all the others."

"What about the other?"

The woman shook her head emphatically. "No help there. Too risky to gain access."

"Then I want a copy of the file." The man with the silver hair turned his gaze on the tattooed man. The gray-haired man's eyes were unblinking, and though his face was handsome and pleasantly lined, his eyes were shiny, inhuman things, like the eyes of a reptile. "Any problem?"

The tattooed man grinned. "Piece of cake," he said.

Sarah looked up grimly at the clock. After ten. She saluted it with her middle finger, then closed the file she'd been working on and put it away. Time to go home. Mark wasn't going to be happy about the late hour, but then he didn't seem to be happy about much of anything these days. Sarah told herself that she refused to feel guilty about working late. It was something she had to do. It was normal, it was inevitable. She almost had herself convinced by the time she turned off the office lights and stepped out into the hall.

As she made her way down the stairs, she turned her thoughts to Diana Smith. She'd wanted to mull over the last several sessions for some time, but the crush of her schedule—the other clients, paperwork, all the thousand and one chores that go into managing a business and a household—had seemed to occupy her every waking minute lately.

All day long, images of Lainey and Nora had intruded upon her thoughts. She had pushed them away, refusing, with some success, to acknowledge them. Her busy schedule had given her little time for reflection, though she wanted nothing more than to sit quietly and turn the little bits of information afforded by Lainey and Nora over and over. She wanted to break them down into component parts, hold up the pieces side by side for comparison. She wanted to sift through the inconsistencies, weigh them and measure them, quantify them once and for all. Now that she was headed away from the office, with all the compelling diversion of routine and commitment gone, fragments of the session tumbled through her thoughts haphazardly. She did not try to push them away now; it felt good to let them come, ragged and undisciplined.

Nora was the voice of reason, that much was certain. Her accounts were lucid and convincing. Her revelations were emotional when appropriate, the accounts properly disturbing. The horrifying picture of incest and abuse that she painted was, unfortunately, all too consistent with reports Sarah had encountered in the literature of dissociative disorders. Why doubt her? Sarah reminded herself that she had felt this way early on, suspicious of Nora's too-tidy descriptions. Perhaps some things could be *too* perfect; Sarah had rarely encountered the nice, orderly categorization of her graduate school texts. The real world was usually much too sloppy, too uncooperative and anarchic to fit into neat conceptual pigeonholes.

Nora was a textbook.

On the other hand, under age regression, Diana and now Lainey were so ungodly far out that their accounts were dismissible as almost out of hand. Satanic conspiracies, communities practicing organized child abuse, and ritual indoctrination. It was too much. Wasn't it?

A vision out of left field, one of those incongruous self-checks on overearnestness, suddenly struck Sarah. She saw Bugs Bunny in a vaguely remembered cartoon about vampires and haunted houses. Bugs is in bed in the vampire's castle and for light reading has selected a volume on magic spells. He reads some statement about the power of "abracadabra" and looks up and says, with perfect nonchalance, "It is to laugh." *That's right, Bugs. It is to laugh,* thought Sarah. Why, then, this sense of overwhelming veracity when dealing with Diana and Lainey, a quality utterly absent from her impressions of Nora? Was she overanalyzing, or maybe overintuiting, relying too much on emotional intangibles to evaluate the case? No, that was not it. Her emotional response was to back away, as quickly as possible, from any nonsense to do with the occult.

The occult? *Nonsense,* she almost said aloud. *It is to laugh.*

Satanism? It is to laugh.

She was halfway home when she remembered.

"Damn," she said, and slapped her open palm against the steering wheel. She was scheduled to appear the following morning as a witness in a disability hearing. She'd left her files back at the office. The hearing was on the other side of town. She could either go back and get the files now, or she'd have to leave forty minutes early tomorrow.

Sarah glanced in her rearview mirror and cut the Olds in a U-turn. On the way back to the office, she tried to keep her mind on her driving, concentrating on making good time. She passed a billboard advertising the EYEWITNESS NEWS TEAM, the local CBS news affiliate. The familiar CBS logo of a stylized eye beamed down from a corner of the billboard, and suddenly all Sarah could think about was Lainey and her horrible story of the eye. The eye and the singsong poem about them—no, Them, capital *T*—and the Circle. What did it all mean? Surely it was not the literal truth, but rather a fantastic embellishment of the plain, cruel facts of her childhood. A metaphor for the claims of omniscience her abusive father had used to threaten her.

Otherwise . . . An eye—a real eye of some kind, maybe a cow's eye—inserted into the vagina of a child?

It is to laugh, Sarah told herself, but she found no humor in the image that invaded her thoughts. Only revulsion and nausea.

Sarah pulled into the parking lot, still unable to shake the memory of Lainey. She crossed the lot at a slow jog, then put her hand on the front door as she fished through her ring of keys. She leaned back to catch the light of the security lamps in the parking lot, and the front door swung open.

My God, she thought, *I left the damn door unlocked.* But hadn't she locked it? She thought she had, but then she'd been terribly distracted. It was a good thing she'd come back.

Sarah made her way across the tiled foyer and up the stairs. The echoes of her footsteps seemed unnaturally loud. She paused at the top of the stairs to catch her breath and thought she heard a noise. Like the closing of a file drawer.

Maybe she hadn't left the door unlocked. Maybe someone else had come back to retrieve something, too, and had left the front door unlocked while they ran into their office.

Sarah froze. The noise had come from upstairs. The only other upstairs office was vacant. And there had been no other vehicle in the parking lot.

Had she imagined the noise?

Heart thudding in her chest, unable to quite convince herself that the noise had not been real, Sarah walked slowly down the hall toward her office. She fought to still her ragged breathing. The soft click of her leather-soled shoes seemed thunderous. If she heard anything else, she would get out in a hurry and call the cops.

Sarah paused outside the office door, head cocked, straining to hear. There was nothing, only silence and the sound of her own breathing. Had she imagined it after all? Had she spooked herself by thinking about

Lainey and then discovering that she'd left the door unlocked?

It is to laugh, she thought. *It is to* . . .

The door to her office opened and the beam of a flashlight suddenly caught her full in the face. Sarah gasped and stumbled backward. Her vision was filled with purple afterimages from the flashlight. Sarah felt a gloved hand wrap around her wrist. She screamed.

The hand pulled her, and hot breath, reeking of tobacco, filled her face.

"Shut the fuck up," the gravel-throated voice of a man said. In the dim light, Sarah could just make out that he wore a stocking cap over his face.

Sarah struggled to gain control of herself. The flashlight passed over her. The hand around her wrist opened, but before she could snatch her arm away, it had roughly pulled the keys from her.

A voice from behind the man said, "Come on, let's go."

The door to the office banged shut, and Sarah glimpsed the shadowy figure of a second man moving off toward the stairwell.

"Count to a hundred before you look for these." The man's arm made an underhanded throwing gesture. Sarah didn't understand what he meant, until a moment later she heard a crashing noise somewhere below her. He had thrown her keys down the stairwell. Then the man was moving away from her, toward the stairs. She heard the soft slap of rubber-soled shoes, then the sound of the front door opening and closing.

"Count to a hundred," the voice had said. "Count to a hundred." Sarah actually started counting—one, two, three, four—until she realized the absurdity of what she was doing. She took a deep breath and reached out to open the office door. It was locked.

"Damn," she said.

A switch by the stairwell would light the building, but Sarah was afraid that the lights might bring the men back. Instead, she walked shakily down the stairs and spent the next five minutes hunting for her keys. When she found them, she locked the front door, then went back upstairs to her office to call the police. Only after she had dialed 911 and sat down at Margie's desk did the shakes hit her. When the emergency operator answered, Sarah could barely hold the receiver still enough to talk into it.

Week 16: Wednesday, November 15

The office was a disaster. The cops had fingerprinted everything and black dusting powder was everywhere. But the fingerprinting was to no avail; the place was clean. Sarah had tried to tell them that the men wore gloves, but the policemen had insisted.

Sarah had come in early. She wanted to arrive before Margie, so the receptionist wouldn't walk in on the mess alone. Sarah had brought cleaning supplies from home. She set about wiping up the black dust.

Neither she nor the police had been able to find anything amiss. The cops maintained that she had scared off the burglars, but Sarah hadn't thought she'd scared anybody. She had gotten the definite impression that the door had opened because the men were ready to leave. Whatever they'd come to do, they'd almost certainly done. But what the hell did they do? The petty cash in Margie's desk was still there, Sarah's recording equipment and computer were intact. Nothing had been stolen.

Old Faithful finished wheezing. Sarah poured herself a cup. The coffee tasted like brewed pencil shavings. She'd gotten all of four hours sleep. Her eyes felt like the lids were made of sandpaper and her mouth tasted like a team of camel traders had set up shop there.

The most disturbing thing the cops had told her was that the locks had not been forced. She had either left both the front door and the office door unlocked—and she no longer believed that the front door had been her fault—or the men had a key.

There were four keys that she knew about. She had one. She kept a spare at home, and she had checked last night to make sure it was still there. It was. Margie had a key, and Sarah would ask her when she came in if she'd lost it or had had any spares made. The fourth key belonged to the landlord.

Sarah set her mug by the coffee maker and decided to attack the copy machine. The thing was flaky enough as it was, and now it was coated with a layer of fine black powder. It would probably never work right again. Sarah moved her dust cloth over the top, then lifted the lid to see if the cops had dusted for prints there.

A piece of paper fluttered to the floor. Well, they hadn't dusted under the lid, that was good. Sarah bent and picked up the paper. She could tell from the two holes punched in the top that it was a sheet from somebody's file folder. Margie must have been making copies and left the last sheet in the machine.

Sarah turned the paper over and scanned it. Under an entry dated Tuesday, November 14, she read: "Lainey again. She recalled the Circle and the eye. Also, several conflicting descriptions of father. Lindis the Gatekeeper. Drugged water? Release from the pit (future research: behavior modification, brain washing). Beliazar. Experiment with drawing."

It was the handwritten session summary sheet from Diana Smith's file. Why had Margie been making a copy of that?

Her sleep-starved brain made the connection several minutes later. What if Margie hadn't made the copy? What if the men last night *had?* Sarah retrieved Diana's folder. It seemed intact, all except for the summary sheet.

Margie came in at eight o'clock. After Sarah explained the condition of the office, she asked the receptionist about the key and the copy. Her key was intact, Margie said, and she had never had a spare made. And she didn't think she'd made the copy from Diana's folder. She'd made some copies the day before and, yes, she had made copies of summary sheets in order to verify her billing records. But Diana's? Maybe, but she didn't think so.

In the few minutes between restoring the office and waiting for her first client of the day, Sarah asked herself again, What if the men from last night had made the copy? What would that mean?

Chapter 17

Week 16: Thursday, November 16

Diana wanted to talk. She'd come in complaining of having lost time again. This time she was missing most of the afternoon and evening following the last session. She wanted to know about the other personalities. Sarah sat watching the smoke curl up from Diana's cigarette, wondering how much of the previous sessions she recalled.

"Sarah," Diana said, "I've been wondering about something."

"Yes?"

"Well, suddenly I'm aware of this aspect of myself I've never known before. You call it Lainey. To me it's just an image of a little girl. It's like all the little-girl things I feel about myself," Diana sighed.

"Okay . . ." Sarah said.

"Well, what I'm wondering is, does this Lainey know things that I don't know?"

Sarah paused, glancing wistfully at Diana's package of cigarettes. "Lainey possesses memories that you don't have," Sarah said. "In a sense, that's probably exactly why she was created: She's a mechanism to handle some otherwise intolerable aspect of your experience."

"I understand that. What I mean is, now that I'm

aware of her, how come I don't have her memories? When will I be able to remember what she remembers?"

"Ah, I see," said Sarah. "Good question. One with no easy answer, I'm afraid. There are no hard and fast rules with any of this stuff. But one thing that seems to occur in a fair number of these cases is integration of the various personalities. It's possible that you and Lainey might agree, for example, to merge with each other. Especially once you start working through some of the experiences that created Lainey."

Hesitantly, Diana said, "I don't like the way you refer to Lainey as if she were another whole person. This is *me* we're talking about here. I just can't grant some aspect of myself that kind of independent status."

"I think I understand," Sarah said. "But let me ask you this. Do you yourself have that kind of status right now? Do you feel independent? Do you feel secure that you have control over yourself, over time?"

Diana hid her face in her open palms. "God, sometimes I hate you, Sarah." She dabbed at the corners of her eyes with the backs of her hands. "This integration, how does it happen?"

"It can happen any number of ways," Sarah said. She resisted the impulse to comfort Diana. Now seemed the time for some hard facts. "I have heard of it happening spontaneously. Just all of a sudden, boom, complete memories, everything. I have read of it being done using hypnosis. In some cases, therapists claim to have achieved integration in just a couple of sessions. In most cases, though, it takes longer and involves having all the personalities become gradually aware of each other and the events that created them. And becoming trusting of each other."

"Sarah," Diana said, hesitantly, "if I decided to do it, would you be willing to hypnotize me into becoming integrated? Would you do it?"

"Integration is not like getting a haircut. It's not

something you wake up in the morning and decide to do. If I thought the time was right and hypnosis would work, yes, I'd do it. But I don't think that's the way it's going to work in your case. You've got a lot more of the kind of work we've done in the last week ahead of you."

"I guess I'd just as soon get it over with."

"Will you settle for taking it slow and easy, and see what we can come up with gradually?"

Diana nodded.

"Good," Sarah smiled. "And now that I've said all that, I'd like to hypnotize you."

"Sure," Diana said, her voice heavy with resignation. "Why not?"

In a matter of minutes, Sarah had Diana hypnotized and was searching through her notes for the phrase that had previously triggered the outpouring of the Listener.

"Linda Janus, tell me the words of the Listener," Sarah said.

"Ondro manth cuantor delittor," the Listener began.

Sarah sat back in her chair, tempted to prop her feet on the desk, wishing she had thought to fix a cup of coffee. She realized that, once again, she had avoided the issue of Lainey and the baby.

Week 16: Friday, November 17

Sarah opened the door and was assaulted by a blast of hot air, the roar of uninhibited lunchtime conversation, and the smell of frying foods. Immediately, she regretted having let Travers make the choice of location for their meeting. The noisy, crowded café was hardly the place for a serious discussion.

Sarah stepped inside and let the door slam shut behind her. She scanned the room but did not see the anthropologist. A young woman lifted a hinged board built into the Formica lunch counter. She stepped through and walked up to Sarah, wiping her hands on a greasy apron.

"Help you?" she asked.

"I was supposed to meet someone here," Sarah said.

The young woman hesitated before answering, her eyes surveying Sarah appraisingly. "Bill Travers?"

Sarah raised her eyebrows in surprise and nodded.

"All the way in the back." The woman pointed toward an open doorway at the back of the restaurant.

Sarah threaded her way through the crowded tables of college students and businessmen and stepped into a narrow hall. Rest room entrances fed off the hallway; directly ahead was a large, paneled room. A bar built of dark wood took up half of one wall. Apparently, this was a lounge or evening dining area. Sarah stepped in, surprised at the sharp contrast to the greasy-spoon decor of the front. The room was empty, save for a single table in the back, occupied by a man intently reading a newspaper. Bill Travers.

Travers looked up from his paper as Sarah walked into the room. He smiled.

"You didn't tell me you had your own room." Sarah returned the smile.

"One of the advantages of long-term patronage," Travers said, standing and pulling out a chair for Sarah. "Around here, they call me the mortgage-maker."

Sarah seated herself and Travers sat back down.

"Hope you like hamburgers," Travers said, " 'cause these are the best. You're not one of those anti-red meat people, are you?"

"Unfortunately not," Sarah said. "A good greasy burger sounds wonderful."

"A gourmet after my own heart."

A waitress appeared, and Sarah and Travers ordered. After the waitress had gone back to the kitchen,

Sarah removed a cassette tape from her purse. She handed it to Travers.

"Here's the Listener," she said.

"Ah, wonderful. Did you have any problem getting the Listener to cooperate this time?" Travers asked.

"None at all," Sarah said. "In fact, it's truly amazing. I just say the magic words and, presto, instant Greek. Or whatever."

"Weird," Travers said, frowning.

Sarah nodded. "I agree. But I'll tell you something even weirder."

"What's that?"

"I didn't have time to do a comparison, but I think this tape is identical to the previous recording. I'm certain that the first few lines are the same, anyway."

Travers frowned again. "If it's the same, then it's probably something that's been memorized rather than a spontaneous monologue. Hell, maybe it's the Gettysburg Address."

Sarah laughed. "Somehow I don't think so. Now, why would a personality develop to *memorize* something? It doesn't make sense. The personalities are created to shield the core, right? So what's the function of a personality that just repeats one thing, over and over?"

"Maybe it's something that somebody else said. Or taught her. Maybe it's associated with some trauma, something that her father used to say when he did things to her."

"That's possible, I guess," Sarah said.

"Actually, that would be a slick trick," Bill said. "Remember all those poems and speeches you had to remember when you were in school? Wouldn't it be neat if you could have created a personality to handle all that memorization crap?"

Now, that's an interesting idea, Sarah thought. *A personality to handle memorization. I wonder if . . .* But Sarah was distracted from her musing by the return of the waitress, bringing drinks. The drinks proved more compelling than her contemplation, and it would be some time before she returned to follow the interrupted thread of her thought.

Mark Johnson hesitated just a moment before shifting his foot off the brake and mashing it against the accelerator. The old Volvo refused to respond without some hesitation itself. By the time Mark was entering the intersection, the light had turned red. Still, he made it through with seconds to spare before the southbound traffic had a chance to move.

"That was dumb," he said aloud, glancing in his rearview mirror. No flashing blue lights were in evidence, so he turned his attention back to the road in front of him. He checked his watch—the dashboard clock in the Volvo had long since ceased working—and debated whether to have lunch before or after the next stop. He decided in favor of eating; Beiderbeck's downtown office would be a lengthy installation and it would probably be difficult to slip away once he got started.

Mark entered the section of student-oriented eateries, shops, and markets near the university. Knowing there were several reasonable restaurants nearby, he started looking for a parking place. Almost immediately, a late-model Ford pulled out of a space several car lengths ahead. Mark signaled his blinker and in a few seconds had the car parked. He looked up at the parking meter and saw that nearly an hour was left on the timer.

"I must be living right," he said to himself.

He hesitated on the sidewalk, weighing the possibilities. He decided on lunch at Jan's, a delicatessen over on the next block. Halfway to Jan's, he stopped to look at a familiar-looking Oldsmobile parked against the curb. He thought at first that it looked remarkably like his own or, rather, Sarah's car. Then, he stepped back to look at the license place and saw that it *was* Sarah's car.

Well, I'll be damned, Mark thought, and immediately began scanning the sidewalks and storefronts. *I wonder what she's doing down here?* He decided that she must be having lunch with Margie, or maybe she'd decided to catch up with Jenny Burton. It would be fun to surprise them.

The only restaurant on the block was a café with the name Johnny's painted in green letters on greasy glass. *Must be the place,* Mark said, and entered. The lunch crowd had started to thin. Mark quickly determined that his wife was not at any of the tables. He started to leave, then figured he'd never find Sarah now, and the smell of frying hamburgers was welcoming. Mark picked up a newspaper from the Formica-topped counter and made his way over to a small table in a far corner of the restaurant.

"So. On the telephone you said something about a new development? More strange memories of childhood?" Travers used a bit of his hamburger bun to soak up the grease on his plate. He popped this in his mouth, followed by a ketchup-coated French fry.

Between bites of her sandwich, Sarah began filling Travers in on the events of the past several sessions: the emergence of Lainey, the conflicting accounts of the father, her momentary evocation of a new personality with the pentagram, the revelations of the flying dream and the priest, Beliazar (Travers knew of no occult pantheon that included Beliazar, but he promised to research the name). Sarah paid particular attention to the details that seemed related to behavior modification or brainwashing, for want of a better term. She told Travers about the possible drugged water, Lainey's imprisonment in the pit and subsequent release, the pairing of "Them" against the "Circle." Travers had been frowning at the start of the conversation. By the time Sarah was finished, the crease between his eyebrows looked like a permanent furrow.

"Damnit, Sarah. This is not at all what I was expecting today." Travers gnawed on a thumbnail.

"Tell me about it. It's getting pretty hard not to take some of this stuff seriously. You say the Listener speaks a real unknown language. I get personalities reinforcing varied accounts of some sort of satanic activities. Help me explain it away."

"That's not a bad way of looking at it, Sarah," Bill said. "In fact, that's great. I mean, the more we talk about the things that *look* like Satanism, the more we convince ourselves. Let's look at the things that *don't* look like Satanism."

"What do you mean?" Sarah asked.

Travers pushed his plate away. "One, we've got a coherent account of child abuse that is consistent with the diagnosis of multiple personality disorder. Two, the personalities shield themselves from the direct recollection of disturbing memories by inventing fantasies of devil worship. Who knows? Maybe that helps justify the father's behavior. If he's a Satanist, then he has an excuse for doing inexcusable things. Three, the fabrication of fantastic and richly detailed personal histories is absolutely consistent with the literature on hypnosis. And four—my favorite—the kinds of behavior that Lainey describes make no sense from a cultural perspective. If a cult of Satanists did exist, this is *not* how we would expect them to act. This is not how we would expect them to raise their children. We would expect to see patterns of behavior that would contribute to enculturation, not that create mental instability. The last thing we would expect to find are actions that result in the disclosure of secret information to mental health professionals. The last thing the cult would want is second-generation Satanists with dissociative disorders. You've heard this lecture before."

"Maybe something went wrong," Sarah offered lamely.

"Doesn't make sense," Travers said, leaning forward excitedly. "The kind of behavior you're talking about is almost *guaranteed* to produce some sort of dissociation or mental illness, right?"

"Yes, you're right. Torture, inconsistent response to behaviors, betrayal, sexual assault—it's almost a textbook formula for creating multiple personalities." Sarah wanted to stop a moment and think. Her therapist's instinct was tolling somewhere deep inside her. But Bill was continuing and she did not have time to reflect. For the second time in the conversation, she told herself to remember the line of reasoning.

"So if we look at all the things that say it's *not* a satanic conspiracy, we end up with a sensible answer." Bill pounded the table lightly with his fist, as if he could physically drive home the point. "What I wonder is, what remains when you strip away the satanic veneer? When the embellishment is gone, how much of the truth will we have already heard? Will she turn out to have actually been thrown into a pit? It's possible. Or will the pit turn out to be a dark closet where her father put her for punishment? And I'll bet dollars to donuts the old man turns out to be a Bible-thumper. Most of the satanic mythology is generated by Christians. It used to be the Catholics, a few centuries ago, that benefitted from rumors of Black Masses. Just the ticket for spiritual malaise and sagging church attendance. Now who do you think gets off on it? Don't you think that Jerry Falwell and Oral Roberts, in their heart of hearts, would love to come across a real satanic conspiracy? It would be great for business. Forget waging spiritual war against supernatural creatures nobody believes in anymore. How about saving the souls of innocent children from the clutches of crazed demon worshippers who sacrifice babies and sexually assault children? Believe me, that's got to be every fundamentalist preacher's secret fantasy.''

Sarah laughed. ''Damn you, Bill Travers, you should have been a preacher yourself. You've managed to convince me again. I think. But let me ask you something.''

''Let you play devil's advocate again, right?'' Travers chuckled.

''Right.'' Sarah returned his smile. ''How does an unknown language fit into all of this?''

''Good question,'' Bill said. ''Well, for one thing, we don't know for sure that what we've got is a true language. The guy's my friend, but I can't vouch for the depth of his scholarship. He may have been asleep the day they taught comparative linguistics.''

Sarah giggled.

''You laugh,'' Travers continued. ''Ha! It's frightening the way some people manage to get the title *expert* hung on them. Anyway, I digress. We don't know if it is a language. *If* it's a language, it may simply be some obscure dialect nobody's heard in a generation, which Diana remembers hearing her grandmother speak. Or, it may be something genuinely strange, but which Diana's father used to say to her when he did whatever it was he did to her. Right now, there's no way of knowing. I'd say the least likely thing it would turn out to be is the text of a satanic ritual in an unknown language.''

''Wait!'' Sarah reached out without thinking and grabbed Travers's hand. Something had triggered her instinct again. The text of a satanic ritual. That meshed with something Bill had said earlier. She tried to recall it.

Travers waited a moment, and when Sarah didn't speak, he continued. ''What I'm saying is that you've got some fantastic and highly imaginative embellishment, but that's all it is. Just like hypnosis subjects supposedly remembering past lives, which turn out to be fabrications stitched together out of books and TV shows and long-forgotten stories."

"Uh-huh," Sarah said and smiled. "I guess I have to agree with you." And for the third time in the past hour, she was sidetracked from a line of reasoning she felt unaccountably compelling.

Mark sipped his coffee and leaned back comfortably. The food had been excellent, if a bit heavy on the cholesterol. He told himself that he would have to start exercising again soon and watching his diet.

He picked up the newspaper and folded it to the conclusion of a story on corruption in local politics. He happened to glance up as he snapped the paper to crease it. He froze, the newspaper spread out before him like a placard. Sarah and a man were standing in front of the cash register. *That isn't Jenny,* Mark thought. His first impulse was to put down the paper and rush up to Sarah. *Won't she be surprised? Surely the man is a business acquaintance, another therapist, perhaps.* Mark relaxed and smiled. As he started to simultaneously stand and fold the paper, the man with Sarah suddenly laughed heartily and reached across her back to place his hand on her shoulder. Mark sat down heavily, feeling as if he had just been punched in the stomach. The gesture had been one of easy familiarity. Too easy. Mark raised the paper in front of his face, keeping it just below the level of his eyes. If they turned, he could simply raise the paper and go unnoticed. As he watched, the man dropped his hand from Sarah's shoulder. The hand traced an arc across Sarah's back. Though he could not be absolutely sure, Mark felt an irrational certainty that the hand did not just drop away but *touched* Sarah's back as it slowly, *caressingly* idled its way back to its owner's side. Mark bit back the impulse to rush up and throttle the son of a bitch, bit it back even as he swallowed the sudden rush of bile that burned the back of his throat and left his mouth with a sour taste. The burning in his throat made his eyes water. For several seconds, he blinked furiously, unable to see. He rubbed his eyes. When he had regained his vision, Sarah and the man had left. He looked out the plate glass window in time to see the Oldsmobile pulling away from the curb. The man was not in the car with Sarah, but that did not ease Mark's mind appreciably.

Sarah managed to get away from the office early for a change. Not long after she arrived home, she heard the crunch of Mark's Volvo on the gravel of the driveway. She smiled and wondered how long it had been since they had both been home by five o'clock on a Friday evening. Though Mark insisted things were fine, Sarah still sensed a distance between them. So far, she'd been unable to get him to open up. She knew how sensitive he was, how much of an issue trust was for him. But never before had he retreated behind such impregnable barriers. Sarah was becoming frightened for their marriage. She'd even suggested they seek a counselor's help, but Mark had rejected the idea, insisting nothing was wrong.

Maybe she could get him to open up tonight.

"Hi, hon." She greeted him with a kiss. He returned it perfunctorily.

She followed him back to the bedroom, where he took off his jacket and tie.

"Did you have a good day?" she asked.

"Okay." He turned to face her. "How was *your* day?" he asked, and Sarah got the clear impression that there was an implied meaning to the question. She had no idea what it was.

"My day was fine," she said. "I had the chance to

do some really interesting speculation on my MPD case. I—"

But Mark did not seem to be listening. Lately, he had no tolerance at all for her stories about work. Well, if he found it boring, then she wouldn't bore him. She'd try to focus on him, get *him* to open up.

"What did you do for lunch today?" he asked. "I hope you're taking time to eat, not working through lunch like I know you sometimes do."

"I ate," she said. "In fact, I—" She started to tell him about Travers but changed her mind. He wouldn't be interested. Plus, he'd really seemed a bit jealous of her last meeting with the anthropologist. Save it for another time, she told herself, not realizing the terrible mistake she was making.

Mark's eyes narrowed, and a thin smile played on his lips. Sarah sensed bitter satisfaction when he nodded, as if he'd just won some subtle contest between them. He turned, reached into the closet, and pulled out his old bomber jacket. Then, without looking at her, he walked past her.

Sarah followed him down the hall, confused and concerned.

"Mark? Mark, what is it? Please, Mark, we need to talk."

He paused in the kitchen doorway. "Talk," he snorted. He stalked across the kitchen and out onto the deck. A second later, the Volvo's door opened. Then the engine started and Sarah heard it backing out the driveway.

"What did I do?" Sarah asked aloud. "What in God's name did I do?"

Mark slammed through the gears angrily. "Damnit," he said. "Damnit to hell."

It all made sense now. The late nights, the weekend meetings. It all made sense. If she'd told him she'd had lunch with some man, he'd have thought nothing of it. But she didn't. She'd hidden it from him. That could only mean one thing.

Mark brushed back an angry tear. He could not believe the depth of Sarah's betrayal.

"To hell with it all," he said.

Week 17: Sunday, November 19

Sarah sat motionless at the kitchen table, sipping a cup of tea, trying desperately to figure out what was going on. All day yesterday, he'd avoided her. She tried to corner him several times, tried to get him to open up, but he would not. He'd left in the late afternoon, not returning till after she'd gone to bed, and then he'd spent the night on the couch. Then this morning, she tried to get him to open up again. He'd gotten up, changed, then immediately headed for the back door. In the kitchen she'd grabbed his arm, and for a single terrifying moment he had raised his hand and she thought he would hit her. She recalled the conversation.

"Don't go, Mark," she said. "You've got to tell me what's going on."

"No, I don't." His eyes smoldered with sullen anger.

"Please. We can't go on like this. Our marriage is falling apart."

"I didn't know it was so important to you."

"What? How can you say that?" she shouted.

"Forget it." He turned to go.

"Don't go. I love you. I need to know what's going on," she said, but it was too late. The door slammed and she was alone.

Now, she picked up the phone and dialed Jenny. She filled her friend in, fighting back the tears while Jenny cycled from outrage to weak attempts at humor.

"Jen, I just don't know what to do."

"You could leave his clothes out on the front step and have the locks changed."

"That's no answer."

"Just kidding, dear. Listen, I'm sure this will blow over if you just give it time. I've known Mark as long as you have. He gets moody sometimes."

"Not like this. And I'm not used to waiting. I'm a therapist, for God's sake. I'm supposed to know how to work these things out."

"You can't talk to somebody unless they're willing to listen. You think being a therapist gives you any kind of exemption from life's bullshit?"

"It always worked before," Sarah said, then laughed at her own joke.

"Yes," Jenny said enthusiastically, "she laughs! There's hope yet. You want me to come over?"

"No, I'll be all right. I'm fine."

"Call me if you need me."

Sarah fixed a fresh cup of tea and carried it back to the study. She really needed Mark. Things were so crazy with Diana that she felt the need for support like a palpable weight in her chest. *It was ironic,* she thought, *that Mark should be so distanced now.* If there was one thing that had prepared her to deal with the victims of dysfunctional families and abuse, it was her relationship with Mark. They had met shortly after Sarah had completed her Master's degree and had gotten her first real job as a therapist, working for county community services. Mark had been an ambitious, energetic programmer with real problems dealing with intimacy in relationships. Sarah had helped him work through the issues—as a friend falling in love, not as a therapist—that had come from years of being raised in a succession of foster homes and orphanages. From Mark, she had gotten her first real taste of the horrifying impact of child abuse, and it had stood her in good stead throughout her career. So it was ironic, she thought, that the man who had given her the sensitivity to reach out to Diana, to understand her mistrust and her resistance to intimacy, was now the man so openly resentful of the time she spent helping others.

Sarah sat in an old overstuffed armchair, slowly sipping the hot, sweet tea. Late afternoon light glowed golden through the window. For long minutes she tried to think of nothing by filling her senses with the taste of the tea, the warmth of the mug in her hand, the strange clarity of the autumn light. She forced herself to relax, trying to forget about Mark for the moment. Maybe Jenny was right. Maybe she just needed to give him time. That was not a strategy she was used to employing, but she supposed she had little choice. She wasn't good at waiting.

Her thoughts drifted to Diana and the meeting she'd had with Travers. There were several things she had struggled to remember about their conversation, but now her thoughts were so distracted she could barely recall what they'd talked about.

They had been talking about the Listener. Yes, that was it. Travers had been speculating on the function of a personality as a kind of memorization aid. "Wouldn't it be neat if you could have created a personality to handle all that memorization crap?" he had said, talking about the kind of rote memorization students are too often required to do.

Bill had also said something about the *unlikelihood* of there being any actual cult involvement. He had convincingly argued that there could be no functionality in a group whose practices created alienation and mental illness. Sarah closed her eyes. For a moment, she could see Bill in the dim light of the restaurant. He had said something like, "The kind of behavior you're talking about is guaranteed to produce some sort of dissociation or mental illness." That was it.

There was one more thread, Sarah was sure of it. *The Listener,* she thought. If she concentrated, she could hear the words. He had said: "I'd say the least likely thing it would turn out to be is the text of a satanic ritual in an unknown language."

She jotted the three points down on her pad.

A personality to handle memorization. Why would a personality develop to handle memorization?

Sarah glanced at her pad. Something about the last line clicked.

To memorize the text of a ritual, that's why. Is it possible that she could have created the Listener just to memorize the text of an arcane ritual in a private language? No, come on . . .

Functionality. MPD's main functionality is to shelter the victim of intolerable abuse. Everything else—the incredible abilities of some personalities, for example—is secondary and incidental. And ultimately, MPD is almost always destructive to the individual, who feels as if reality never quite makes sense and who lives in dread of barely glimpsed, ancient terrors. Who comes unglued in time like a character in a science fiction novel. So ultimately, the functionality is dysfunctional. Same argument Bill had for why satanic abuse makes no anthropological sense: It just isn't functional. But now we're talking about a different kind of functionality, aren't we?

Functionality for the individual, functionality for the group.

Functionality for the group. Memorizing a long and difficult piece of text could be very functional, Sarah thought.

All right, let's speculate for just a moment that there really are a bunch of crazed Satan worshippers out there. Only maybe they aren't so crazed. Maybe they are very organized and efficient. They conduct rituals, right, just like in any other organized religion. Satanic equivalents of the Latin Mass, maybe, and other things. Only they don't want copies of all this stuff floating around all over the place, right? A Satanist would believe in the power of a ritual to effect some concrete outcome. The ritual would be a very powerful thing. Powerful and protected. So maybe all the rituals are an oral tradition, never committed to writing. Having a personality dedicated to the memorization of satanic rituals would be very desirable for the group. Very functional.

Sarah's eye caught the middle line on her page of

notes. Behavior guaranteed to produce dissociation, it read. *Guaranteed to produce dissociation. Can you guarantee dissociation? Could you create a multiple if you wanted to?*

With a shaky hand, Sarah picked up her tea and drained it. It had grown cold. The light had faded from the room and it was nearly dark as she stood up.

Chapter 18

Week 17: Tuesday, November 21

She wasn't going to be distracted this time, Sarah told herself. She was going straight to the heart of the matter. No more avoidance, no more side issues.

She spent the first fifteen minutes talking, then as soon as possible asked Diana if she could use hypnosis again. Diana agreed. In a few minutes, Sarah invoked Lainey.

"Lainey, are you there?"

Lainey smiled her little girl smile and drew her legs up on the chair. "Uh-huh," she nodded.

"Lainey, when we talked before, you said that you had refused to kill the baby."

"I didn't want to," Lainey said. "I knew it was bad. I didn't want to."

"That's right, you didn't want to. You said that . . ." Sarah stopped. Tears were running down Lainey's cheeks and she struggled to speak.

". . . but I had to. I had to," she said. "They made me."

Sarah shivered involuntarily, a sensation her mother had referred to as "the goose walking over your grave." "Tell me about it," she said softly.

"They came at night and got me," she said. "They always come at night."

The goose walked over Sarah's grave again.

"Father made me promise when I was in the hole. Father told me I had to be a good girl when they came. Father said next time they would put *me* on the table if I didn't."

The tears had stopped. Lainey seemed grimly determined. Sarah was about to prompt her when she started talking again.

"It was a big room, candles everywhere. I was scared. All the people had on their robes. They put one on me. They are singing and dancing. They're leading me up to the table of rock."

Sarah noticed the shift to present tense. Lainey was reliving the episode.

"How do you feel, Lainey?"

"I'm scared. Real scared. The singing is loud; everybody's looking at me. I don't want to look at the table."

"It's all right, Lainey. You can look at the table. Tell me about the table."

"*She's* on the table."

"The baby?" asked Sarah, and then cursed herself. That was a leading question, and she knew better.

"A girl," said Lainey.

"What happens next?"

"Somebody is lifting me up. I'm standing next to the table. Somebody whispers, 'Do it, Isis. You can do it. You know how.' "

Isis?

Lainey groaned suddenly and the tears began to flow again. "There's a knife in my hand," she shrieked, and Sarah started. "I can't do it. I can't do it. But if I don't do it, they'll put me on the table. I don't want to go away. I don't want to die."

Lainey lapsed into sudden silence. Seconds ticked by slowly. Sarah fought to control her own sense of rising fear and anger. It felt as if Lainey were radiating waves of emotion, and Sarah was helpless to prevent receiving them.

"What's happening now, Lainey?"

"It's all right, now," Lainey said. "I don't have to do it. I'm just watching."

"What are you watching?"

"I'm watching Isis do it."

Sarah struggled to understand. Was Isis someone else? "Lainey, where are you?" she asked.

"I'm watching from the ceiling."

Watching from the ceiling? Sarah thought, now completely confused. *This sounds like one of Diana's flying dreams. Is this just a dream?*

Wait. The priest trained her to have out-of-body experiences. An out-of-body experience is occult jargon for dissociation. The priest was training her to dissociate!

"Describe Isis to me, Lainey."

"Isis looks just like me, 'cept her eyes are dead."

My God, Sarah thought, *behavior guaranteed to produce dissociation was what Bill said. That's it, that's exactly it. They threaten her life, they teach her to dissociate and the sexual abuse* forces *her to dissociate, then they suggest a new identity to her. Isis.*

They created Isis. Engineered multiple personality disorder.

The goose was no longer walking on her grave, it was doing the funky chicken. *Oh my God,* thought Sarah.

"Tell me what Isis does next."

"Isis says, 'It's okay, I know what to do.' She takes the knife and raises it up. Then she brings it down, fast."

Dear God. Lainey's voice had become very soft.

"She cuts. Then one of the men helps her. There's blood all over. The man helps Isis cut some more. She reaches inside and pulls it out."

It?

"The man helps her cut it up. Isis hands pieces to the people standing around her. They wait for Isis."

Long pause. Sarah swallowed hard, then asked, "What are they waiting for, Lainey?"

"For Isis to take the first bite. And she does. She puts it in her mouth and smiles. She starts to chew . . ."

Lainey made a gagging sound. She had gone pasty white.

Sarah suddenly remembered her dinner with Diana. Diana had gagged on the strips of beef in the Stroganoff. She had said that it reminded her of something . . . something she couldn't quite remember.

Lainey gagged again, and Sarah fought back her own rising nausea.

"All right, Lainey, all right. You're fine now. You're back with me now. You're back in my office. I'm going to count to five and then I want you to return the body to Diana. Everything's fine. One . . ."

Diana awoke with a startled look.

"What were we doing?" she asked. "You were talking to the little one, weren't you? Lainey?"

Sarah nodded. Did she remember?

Diana looked down at the floor and said, in tones chillingly stripped of emotion, "I killed her."

Sarah shuddered, the effect of Diana's softly spoken words more profound than if she had screamed her revelation.

"Do you know who she was?" Diana laughed a short, bitter laugh. "Do you know who they made me kill?"

Sarah shook her head.

"It was Indra. My best friend. They made me kill Indra. We were seven years old."

Diana lifted her eyes. Sarah, who had remained motionless, almost breathless, during the account, met Diana's gaze and felt completely at a loss, unsure how to respond. She hesitated, as if some spell might be broken by her voice. When her deliberations failed to yield an approach, she followed her instinct.

"What was your name then?" Sarah asked.

"My name?" Diana frowned quizzically. "Why, I've only got one name, of course. Why would you ask such a—" She stopped, eyes widening. "Oh, God. My name was Iris Morrison. Iris Laine Morrison. How do I know that? Why is my name different? Sarah, what the hell is happening?"

Diana left some twenty minutes later, still visibly shaken by the revelation of the cannibalistic ritual. Sarah leaned back in the desk chair and took a deep breath. It was all starting to come together, all starting to make sense. All it took was granting one little premise, presuming the existence of one tiny fact. Hadn't Bill said that he gave the satanic version of events a one percent probability of being correct? Sarah didn't want to concede the possibility. But if the satanic cult *had* existed, so many pieces fell into place.

There's your group functionality, Bill, she thought. *There's your one percent.*

Week 17: Wednesday, November 22

Sarah had been reluctant to let Diana leave the last session. A wedge had been forced in a door behind which unknown pressures had built over many years. Sarah was afraid the door would be blown off its hinges; the effect of a sudden and total recall might be devastating. She did not know whether Diana was capable of standing up to it.

She had a sudden inspiration. Sarah dialed Diana's number and was relieved when she answered on the second ring.

After exchanging small talk, which gave Sarah the opportunity to determine that it was Diana and not one of the alters on the phone, Sarah said, "Tomorrow's Thanksgiving. Why don't you join us? We'd love some company."

"Really? Oh, no, I couldn't. I don't want to intrude on you and Mark. You probably want to be alone."

"Diana, please come. Mark may not even be there." She hesitated to explain, but figured some explanation was necessary. "Things haven't been going so well between us lately. I could really use some company."

"In that case, I'd love to." The delight in her voice was unmistakable.

Sarah saw nothing of Mark all that evening. She went to bed, feeling miserable and lonely. Later, Sarah heard Mark come in through the back door. She listened to him thrash about in the dark for a while, then she drifted off to sleep. In the morning, he was gone again.

Chapter 19

Week 17: Thursday, November 23

Diana sat in her little kitchen, sipping her second cup of coffee, still in her bathrobe with a towel wrapped around her damp hair. The doorbell chimed, startling her. Standing, she secured her robe and slipped the towel from her hair. She slid across the floor in her slippers and opened the door without removing the safety chain.

Peering through the crack between the door and the frame, she saw two vaguely familiar men standing in the hall. They were both dressed in jeans. One had on a denim jacket and a stocking cap. The other wore a heavy flannel jacket-style shirt.

"May I help you?" Diana asked.

The man in denim grinned and leaned toward the door. He held out his hand, palm up. Diana recoiled from the strange gesture, then blacked out.

Mark Johnson slid the cover back over the computer's exposed chassis and reached for a screwdriver. As usual, the job had seemed to pass quickly. Checking his watch, he was surprised that several hours had passed. He fumbled for a few seconds before locating the little pile of screws tucked away on one corner of the desk.

"I feel like a real jerk dragging you out on Thanksgiving morning to do an installation," John Beiderbeck said, and sipped his coffee.

"Your folks need to be able to get work done tomorrow," Mark said. "Besides, it's not your fault I wasn't able to get all the stuff I needed until yesterday." Mark tightened the last of the screws. He picked up the television-like monitor and placed it on the computer, then slid the whole affair over to one side of the desk. He flipped the power switch on the computer and watched as lights winked on.

"I do believe we're in business," he said. "Just let me check the setup and we're out of here."

"Great," Beiderbeck said. "How about you let me buy you a quick holiday drink on your way home?"

"You are on," said Mark, relieved to have found something else to do to delay the inevitable return home.

Sarah rinsed her hands under steaming water. The turkey was still cold inside and stuffing the damn thing hurt her hands. *Is nine-thirty too early for a glass of wine?* she wondered, and concluded, *Yes.*

Diana should be over by eleven or so. And Mark? Who knows?

Watching a marriage disintegrate must be a little like being in an earthquake. Before it happens, you think it can never happen here. Before it happens, you imagine all the things you would do to prevent injury, like running in the street, diving for doorways; when it happens, time slows, but your brain slows even more. All those wonderful resolutions lie buried in the rubble. Instead of acting, you stand there dumbly and watch it happen.

Mark and I were it, Sarah thought, wincing at the unintended past tense. *We were the couple to be married forever. Oh, I know that sounds smug, but there was something special about our relationship.*

Now, equal time for the therapist: fool, there are no exempt marriages. Marriage is hard work, not magic. Sleeping Beauty and What's-His-Name—Prince Whoever—were divorced seven years after he woke her up. Proven fact. Happily ever after equated to seven years.

What happened to all the contingencies? Where are all the plans I made for this earthquake? Sarah asked herself. *Where are the soul-searching encounters, the desperate and ultimately successful sessions of shouts and tears and accusations and lovemaking? Why do my feet turn to blocks of ice?* Then, she thought, *If it was another woman, I might be able to fight, to do something. But it's not another woman, is it? I don't understand.*

Where is my enemy?

I don't know what I'm fighting or how to go about it.

Sarah pulled a wine glass down from the top shelf of the china closet.

"Oh, Christ, not the Holiday Inn." Mark shook his head and pulled the Volvo in next to Beiderbeck's car. There was something depressing about drinking in a motel lounge on a holiday. Seven or eight vehicles were parked in the front lot. A few other cars were scattered about the motel parking area, evidence of unfortunates forced into holiday travel. Mark considered begging off with Beiderbeck, heading on home, and trying to salvage something out of the holiday, if not his marriage. Then the image of a strange man with his arm around Sarah thrust its way into his mind and Mark was suddenly very thirsty.

More people were giving thanks in the form of libation than Mark would have thought. He and Beiderbeck made their way to the far end of the mahogany bar. The bartender was a sleepy-looking young man in a tartan bow tie. Mark ordered a Manhattan, Beiderbeck a vodka martini.

"Cheers." Beiderbeck nodded and lifted his glass. "Here's to a painless foothold into the computer age."

"Cheers," Mark acknowledged.

"You know you really have done a remarkable job for us."

"Not at all," Mark said. "But I'm happy you think so."

An hour later, Mark realized he had just finished his second Manhattan and was about to be delivered a third. *Damn,* he thought, *I'm gonna be shitfaced if I don't watch it.*

"Maybe we should get something to eat," he suggested.

"Great idea, great idea," Beiderbeck agreed. "Bartender, set us up with some assorted hors d'oeuvres."

"Am I keeping you from your Thanksgiving?" Mark asked.

"Nonsense. The wife and I will go out for prime rib this evening, and we'll call it a Thanksgiving. We're not real big on most holidays. Now, you and I just need a few munchies to tide us over and take the edge off the martoonies. Hmm, now there's something I wouldn't mind munching on. . . ." Beiderbeck nodded in the direction of the bar's entrance.

Mark turned his head. A redhead, slim and well-proportioned, had seated herself about midway down the bar, seven or eight stools away. Her head was turned and Mark couldn't see her face. *Probably a hell of a lot older than she looks,* Mark thought. He turned to face Beiderbeck.

"Ever go for any extracurricular activity, Mark?" Beiderbeck asked.

Mark reflected that the guy really was a sleazebag. Rich, but a sleazebag. "No," he said.

"Hey, I didn't mean to offend you," he said. "But I bet a man could have some of that without much effort. She looks ready. Why else come in alone on Thanksgiving?"

Mark shrugged.

"No offense, okay?" Beiderbeck asked.

"No, John, none at all." Mark smiled lamely. "It's okay, really."

"Hey, great," Beiderbeck said. "Hey, honey," he called in a too-loud voice. Heads turned to watch. "Why don't you come on down and join us? We're just about to sample some of the more exotic foodstuffs of this fine establishment."

Mark was about to protest, then thought, *Screw it. Let the old fart have his fun.* He turned to watch the reaction of the redhead and was surprised to find her walking toward him. She smiled at Mark and sat down on the stool next to his. Mark was momentarily speechless. She was young, mid to late twenties, and striking, with sea-blue eyes and straight shoulder-length hair of a dark, deep red.

Beiderbeck held forth with a steady stream of cheerful and vaguely lewd banter, which Mark thought came too easily not to have been used a time or two before. Surprisingly, Marcia—Beiderbeck quickly determined that the young woman's name was Marcia—seemed to enjoy the older man's performance. When their food arrived, Beiderbeck ordered Marcia a fresh drink. She accepted, and when the drink arrived, she held her glass up in a toast.

"Thanks to two lovely men for rescuing a lonely lady," Marcia said.

"That's what Thanksgiving's all about," Beiderbeck responded, tipping his glass against hers. "Chivalry is not dead, only slightly inebriated."

Mark smiled and clinked glasses. *What the fuck am I doing?* he thought, and then realized that Marcia was talking to him.

"Where did you find this guy?" she said, nodding toward Beiderbeck. "Is he for real?"

Mark glanced at Beiderbeck, who was smiling delightedly, eyes damn near twinkling.

"Oh, he's for real, all right," Mark said. *The old sleazebag is gonna end up in the sack, sure as hell.*

"I was afraid of that," Marcia said, leaning her head close and speaking in a stage whisper. Mark caught the heady trace of a subtle perfume, could almost feel heat radiating from the woman. A stray beam of sunlight played on her auburn hair, setting it afire. Her voice was deep and throaty, the words reminding him of the purr of some feral cat. For a moment, Mark was lost in a wave of desire. He was amazed to find such passion so easily aroused. *I thought I had all that tucked away and reserved for Sarah,* he mused.

Sarah. And what would Sarah think of all this?

Her reaction might *be something I wouldn't have expected at all a few days ago,* Mark reasoned bitterly. *It might be something like, "What took you so long, asshole? I've been doing it for years."*

No. That's not right. I do not cheat on my wife. My wife does not cheat on me.

Well, you're half right, sucker.

Why the hell am I worried, anyway? I'm just having a drink with a friend. The girl's going to end up with Beiderbeck, not me.

Mark felt a light touch on his knee. His eyes widened in surprise and he turned quickly to look at Marcia. She smiled at him and continued to trace a line up his leg with the nail of an index finger.

Sarah drained her wine glass and looked at the clock on the kitchen wall. One o'clock.

Damn, she thought. *I'm tired of worrying about Mark. I guess I can worry about Diana now.*

Sarah refilled her glass and sat back down at the kitchen table. Then she was back on her feet again, grabbing the telephone. She dialed Diana's number. After a dozen rings, she hung up the phone and sat down again.

What if it's all true? Sarah thought. *What if Diana and Lainey and Lynn are telling the truth, and Nora is the liar? I want to believe Nora, because Nora is the voice of rationality. If I believe the others, the world becomes a very strange place. A not very pleasant place. And yet, it's Nora I distrust. . . .*

State it simply: I believe Diana. I do not yet know whether she was raised by a cult of Satanists or whether her memories are the literal truth, but I know that she is not lying.

Where is she? Is she in danger? Is one of the others simply out on a jaunt, unaware of our plans to meet today?

Where is she?

The fourth Manhattan cinched it. At least, that was the convenient fiction; alcohol always made a tidy excuse. Somewhere between the stuffed mushrooms and this current drink, Marcia had become Mark's. Or vice versa. Beiderbeck continued a steady outpouring of barroom banter, mostly crude double entendres. He kept the trio supplied with food and drink. But somehow—and it seemed to have Beiderbeck's blessing—Marcia and Mark had been paired.

Mark was not drunk enough to believe that it hadn't been his own doing. Though nothing had happened yet, the events of the afternoon moved with a swift, only partially controllable momentum. Mark was on the roller coaster and he couldn't get off now that it had started moving. He couldn't deny having climbed on the ride; he just couldn't exactly remember when or how it had happened.

Marcia excused herself and left in search of a rest room. Both men half stood from their stools, a gesture that struck Mark as a parody of chivalry.

"You dog, you," Beiderbeck leered at Mark, lightly punching him on the shoulder.

"What the hell am I doing, John?"

"You know what you're doing, man," Beiderbeck said. "Go with the flow."

Mark took a sip of his drink. Beiderbeck leaned forward, looking at Mark closely.

"This is your first time, isn't it?" he asked. "Since your marriage, I mean?"

Mark nodded.

"Trust me," Beiderbeck said. "There's nothing wrong with it. It can actually help a marriage."

Mark turned his face toward Beiderbeck. "Look, don't give me the bullshit, John. I'm doing this, one, because I want to and, two, because I think my wife has already beat me out of the chute. I don't intend on missing out because of misplaced loyalties."

"Mark, I'm sorry," Beiderbeck said, but his eyes twinkled. "But in that case, enjoy. Marcia really is a stone fox. When you two are ready to leave, just do it, okay? Don't worry about this. I'll take care of it." Beiderbeck made an expansive gesture that seemed to indicate the entire bar.

"Thanks, John," Mark said. He debated for a second asking Beiderbeck for a good line to suggest checking into a room at the motel, but Marcia was back. She casually placed a hand on Mark's shoulder.

"Mark, I need to go back to my room to take a pill. Would you mind walking with me?" she asked.

This is too easy, Mark thought.

"You bet," he said.

Sarah tipped her wine glass in the direction of the roasting pan sitting on top of the stove.

"Cheers, turkey," she said. She took a sip of her wine and stood up. "The good news, old pal of mine, is that we're going to say to hell with the mashed potatoes, the cranberries, the gravy, and whatever we were going to have for a vegetable. We're moving directly from turkey and dressing into pumpkin pie."

Sarah wrestled the bird out of the aluminum pan and onto a large cutting board, nearly upsetting the pan in the process. She picked up the pan, debated saving the juices for a gravy, then said, "Screw it." She poured the liquid into the kitchen sink, folded the pan into quarters, and tossed it in the garbage can.

She began spooning dressing from the bird into a bowl. Half an hour later, the carcass of the turkey sat on the cutting board surrounded by tiny scraps of skin, bones, and meat. Several packages of meat and soup bones had been wrapped in plastic and labeled with freezer tape. Sarah dumped the carcass in the garbage and slid the cutting board into the sink.

"There we go," she said. "One turkey, shot to hell."She picked up a plate containing a few slices of turkey and a spoonful of dressing and carried it over to the table. She refilled her glass with white wine and sat down to eat.

"Thanksgiving, huh?" she mumbled, raising her glass. "Thanks a lot," she said.

The cold air cleared Mark's head and he realized that he was not at all drunk. *Everything I do, I do of my own volition,* he thought. Briefly, he considered walking over to the Volvo, getting in, and simply driving away. Instead, he threw his arm around the redhead and pulled her close. She nestled into his arm and together they walked across the parking lot.

Marcia opened the door to a second-floor room and stepped in. Mark walked in behind her, pushing the door closed. He glanced around the room quickly, noting the typical gaudy furnishings, the faint odor of disinfectant. Two mints in green foil wrappers lay on the pillows of the queen-sized bed. A bottle of bourbon sat on a cheap table, along with a motel-issue ice bucket. Mark did not see any luggage.

Marcia shrugged off her coat and threw it on the bed. In the next instant, she wrapped one arm around Mark's neck, forcing his head to bend down to meet hers. She pressed her lips against his. Her lips were soft, incredibly soft. They yielded against his and moved constantly over his mouth. Mark pulled away slightly, responding with a light brush of his lips against hers. Marcia smiled then and, with a surprisingly strong grasp, forced his lips tightly against hers. Her tongue thrust its way past his lips. At the same moment, she reached down to his crotch with her other hand. Mark felt a shock of pleasure rush through him, and suddenly his erection was tight and uncomfortable against his trousers.

Marcia laughed and released him.

"Glasses are over on the sink. Fix us a couple, please." She disappeared into the bathroom.

Mark filled the glasses with ice and carried them over to the table. The drapes were open and he looked out over the parking lot. He could see his old Volvo. Beiderbeck's BMW was gone. He poured the little glasses half full of bourbon, sipping slowly from one. The bourbon was harsh and slightly sour-tasting, but it cleansed his mouth. By the time Marcia stepped out of the bathroom, Mark had finished the drink and poured another.

They embraced and kissed again. Mark reached up with both hands, his fingers trembling slightly at the touch of Marcia's fiery hair. Marcia pulled away quickly.

"Please don't touch me there," she said.

Confused, Mark simply stood silently.

"Oh, I know it's silly," she continued, "but I have never been able to stand anybody touching my hair. It's like running your fingernails over a blackboard. You don't mind, do you?"

Mark said that he did not mind, that there were lots of other places he looked forward to touching. If she would just excuse him for a minute . . .

Several minutes later, Mark stepped out of the bathroom, automatically flipping off the light switch. The motel room was dark, the lights turned off and the drapes closed. He thought that he really would prefer a bit of light, but he didn't mind.

He could just make out a form lying on the bed. He walked over to the bed, and it took several seconds before he was able to determine that Marcia was nude. She patted the side of the bed, indicating that he should come and sit.

Mark sat. Marcia handed him his glass from the nightstand. As he sipped the drink, Marcia lay on her side and reached around his waist with both arms. Deftly, she unbuttoned his shirt. As she reached for his belt, he set the glass on the table and leaned back against her. In a few seconds, she had loosened his belt and unfastened his waistband. He leaned back farther, wrapping one arm around her neck and stroking the inside of her thigh with the other. He shuddered, sighing audibly as her warm hand wrapped tightly around his erection.

"Give me a second," he said, and stood. As he pulled off his shirt, he heard Marcia slide off the bed and onto the floor. She pulled down his pants and briefs and held them as he stepped out of them. She reached up her arms and he grasped them. As he slowly pulled her up, her lips and tongue brushed against his thigh, his penis, his chest.

They stood and embraced for a few moments. Mark lightly ran his hands over her back, then around to the front, caressing the hollow on either side of the thatch of dark pubic hair, then up over her belly to finally rest lightly against her breasts. She moved under his palms for just a second, then stepped backward, falling onto the bed, pulling him on top of her.

Mark kissed her, hard, several times. Then he sat up and pushed himself to the foot of the bed. He pulled Marcia around so that she lay comfortably. He leaned forward, grasping her ankles in his hands. He pushed them away, causing her legs to flex at the knees. Then he was between her legs, kissing her, tongue quickly searching the softness of her.

Marcia moaned softly, then moaned louder as he used his arms to squeeze her thighs against his head. His tongue found the sensitive parts of her, moving in and out and against her, now softly, now teasingly, now with force. Marcia arched her back against him several times in rapid succession. He used his tongue to match her rhythm until she shuddered, grasping him by the hair, pulling him toward her.

Marcia kissed him quickly, then rolled him over on his back. Starting at Mark's neck, she kissed him, slowly working her way along the length of his body. She ran her tongue across his nipples, tickling him with her lips on the thin skin of his ribs. Soon, she knelt between his legs. She ran her hands across the inside of his thighs, little currents of electricity coursing through him. Her tongue flicked across the tip of his penis, while her hair danced across the soft skin of his belly at a thousand shifting points. She explored the length of him with her lips and tongue. Mark groaned in surprise and pleasure when suddenly she took him into her mouth, her lips sliding moistly down over him with surprising force. He reached to grab her by her hair, then remembered her earlier request. He grabbed at the sheets on either side of him instead. Her lips worked up and down him.

Mark could hold back no longer. He thrust against her, but suddenly her mouth was off him.

"Not so fast, lover," she said.

She slid off the bed and walked around to the nightstand, picking up her drink. She walked back around to the foot of the bed and stood sipping her drink, watching him and smiling. Marcia took a final sip and set the drink on the Formica table. She crawled back up on the bed, bending over his penis. She took him into her mouth and suddenly Mark gasped. She'd kept an ice cube from the drink in her mouth, and it now rested on the tip of his penis. Mark sat up involuntarily. Then she was off him and laughing, the ice cube falling on his belly and down onto the bed.

"Damn," he said, and then laughed because she was laughing.

She drew up next to him, putting the tip of her tongue in his ear. He relaxed, and Marcia pushed his legs down onto the bed so that they lay flat. Then she moved on top of him, straddling him and guiding him into her. They both moaned as she eased herself down, he surrounded by the moist softness of her, she filled with the warm rigidity of him. Mark arched his back several times, lifting Marcia off the bed and driving deeper into her. Marcia pushed him back down onto the bed and began to move against him. He matched her rhythm and together they began to move faster.

They came at the same time. She shuddered and hugged him fiercely, while for long seconds it seemed as if every muscle in his body tensed. Finally, he relaxed and she slid off of him. He started to speak, but she said, "Shhh. Just hold me," and turned her back to him so that he could wrap his arms around her. He drifted off to sleep with the natural and perfumed scents of her mingling pleasantly.

Sarah turned on the kettle to boil water for instant coffee. Half a bottle of wine was enough, she figured. Time to sober up. Except she didn't feel drunk. Just very tired. And very sad. She was worried about Diana and worried about Mark and worried about herself.

During the afternoon, she had been seized with the conviction that something had happened to Mark. Sarah did not think she had any psychic abilities; she was not particularly prone to hunches or precognition. But somehow she was certain that something had happened. An accident, perhaps, she didn't know; just one of those irreversible occurrences that establishes itself as an indelible marker in a personal history, like a birth or a wedding. Or a death. Now she was crying, as far as she knew, without any real reason. Still, she sobbed, her breath coming in gasps.

After a time, she dried her eyes and picked up her glass. *Where is it that people throw their empty glasses into fireplaces? How wasteful,* she thought, *but how satisfying. I should throw my glass into a fireplace. This is a day of celebration, right? Not mourning. I should be happy.*

But we don't have a fireplace, she thought, and laughed. Then she was crying again. Suddenly, she picked up her glass and drained it, then threw it in the general direction of the sink. Tiny fragments showered the counter as the kettle whistle began to blow.

Sarah felt a little better.

Mark woke with the scent of Marcia still in his nostrils. The fragments of a dream blew away like wisps of smoke. Something about Sarah in trouble.

Sarah?

Where am I? Mark thought in sudden panic, and sat up in bed. Then he remembered. Except, where was Marcia?

Mark stood uncertainly, a sudden headache throbbing behind his eyes. He turned on a light. Marcia was gone, along with her clothes and her coat. The bottle of bourbon, what little remained, she had left behind. Mark poured the liquor into a glass and threw the bottle into a trash can. He dropped a few ice cubes in the glass and carried it off to the shower.

He put the room key on the table when he left. He crossed the parking lot, fishing in his pockets for the keys to the Volvo. He wondered why he did not feel guilty. Instead, a terrible emptiness surrounded him and filled him. It made him feel very light and very lonely.

He wondered if it had been like this for Sarah.

Chapter 20

The phone rang and Sarah took her time answering it. First, she located the television's remote control and pressed the mute button, silencing the plotless and not-very-funny situation comedy that she had been watching. Then she took a deep breath and reached for the phone. She hesitated. It could only be bad news, she figured. Either Mark had been in an accident or Diana had succeeded in her latest suicide attempt. Not much to choose from.

She picked up the phone.

"Hello," she said.

"Sarah, this is Mark."

"Mark, where are you? I've been worried sick."

"I'm at my brother's. I . . . uh . . . I think I'm going to stay here tonight." He sounded oddly chastened, all the resentment and bitterness now gone from his voice.

"But why, Mark? Please come home. We need to talk."

"I know we do. Just give me a little time to think things out, okay? Then we'll talk."

"Mark, I love you. I don't want to lose you. If you need some time, I'll give you time. Just remember I'm here when you're ready."

His voice choked, "Okay."

"I love you," she said again.

The phone softly clicked.

An hour later, the phone rang again. This time, it was Diana.

"Sarah," the familiar voice said.

"Oh, Diana, I've been worried to death. Are you all right?"

"Yes, I'm fine."

"Where have you been?"

"I wish I knew," Diana said. "Oh, Sarah, I'm so sorry, but I just blacked out again. I guess one of the . . . uh . . . others took over. I remember waking up this morning and having breakfast and, boom, next thing I know, it's seven o'clock in the evening."

"Diana, as long as you're okay, it doesn't matter. We've got to expect this kind of thing once in a while, you know."

"But I missed Thanksgiving with you. I'm so sorry. Did I spoil everything? Did you and Mark have a nice time?"

Sarah considered lying for just an instant. "I haven't seen Mark all day, Diana. You didn't spoil a thing."

"Oh, Sarah, that means you were all alone, then, doesn't it? Shit," Diana said.

The expression was so uncharacteristic that Sarah laughed. "It's okay," she said. "Let's have our Thanksgiving, anyway. What have you got planned for tomorrow?"

"Nothing."

"Good. Why don't you meet me at the office around noon? We'll go out to lunch, and then if we feel like braving the crowds, we'll hit the holiday sales. How's it sound?"

"It sounds wonderful, Sarah," Diana said. "Oh, thank you."

* * *

Week 17: Friday, November 24

An unsettling sense of déjà vu settled over Diana as the doorbell rang. She was sitting in her bathrobe at the kitchen table having coffee. It reminded her of something she could not quite remember.

The dreamy sense that it had all happened before increased as she walked toward the door. She opened it and peered through the crack afforded by the safety chain.

"UPS," a man said. "Package for Diana Smith."

She wondered briefly, as she slid the chain off the track mounted on the door, why the man wore jeans instead of the familiar brown uniform. The instant the door was freed from the restraining chain, it was kicked in, almost knocking Diana to the floor. Two men quickly stepped inside. The one in jeans closed the door quickly, while the other opened the long blade of a folding knife.

"You'll want to be very quiet," said the man in jeans. He smiled coldly.

Diana walked slowly backward until she could go no farther, her progress stopped by the wall of the hallway.

"Shall we go to the bedroom?" the man asked, his face now leering inches from hers. The second man stood to one side. Diana felt the sharp point of a knife press against her body. She walked down the hall to the bedroom.

She considered screaming or running down the hall and slamming the bedroom door shut. The door did not lock. How long could she hold them at bay? She could not.

They entered the bedroom. The man with the knife walked to the far side of the bed, then pulled down the spread, exposing the sheet underneath. He pulled down the top sheet and began to methodically cut strips of the cloth with his knife. Diana watched in terrified confusion.

"Take your clothes off and get on the bed," the other man said. "You'll want to be very quiet."

Diana began to slowly undress, hoping against hope for something to interrupt the inexorable conclusion of this scene. When she had taken off her robe, she stood frozen in her panties, arms crossed over her breasts, unable to move.

"Hurry it up," the man in jeans said.

Finally, she lay on the bed, naked. The man with the knife pulled her arms above her head and tied her wrists together. With surprising gentleness, he gagged her with another strip. Finally, he wrapped another strip around her head as a blindfold.

The man whispered in her ear, "Tell no one about this. We can see everything, you know. You should stay home on Tuesdays and Thursdays."

Diana flinched in terror and surprise as she felt something wet and very cold touch her belly.

"Come on, Diana, don't stand me up again," Sarah said, pacing the waiting room with a cup of coffee in one hand. Diana was already a half hour late. Sarah debated whether to wait or to just leave. She did not particularly wish to spend her Friday off in the office. Stay or go? Stay or go?

She sighed, knowing she was kidding herself. She'd have to wait. Then she thought she heard the outside door downstairs click open. She paused, hearing footsteps in the hallway. A second later, the door to the waiting room opened.

Diana stepped in. Her hair was disheveled and her eyes were red from crying. She wore no makeup and her clothes were casual—old jeans and a blue cotton work shirt. She carried a blue wool coat over her arms.

"Diana, what's wrong?" Sarah asked. She set down her coffee and rushed up to the younger woman. Diana looked at Sarah with frightened eyes. Unable to speak, she dropped her coat on the floor and threw her arms around the therapist. She began to sob, burying her face in Sarah's shoulder. Between sobs, she tried to speak, but the words were unintelligible.

Sarah eventually managed to get Diana seated on the waiting room couch with a mug of coffee warming her hands. The woman shook uncontrollably. Sarah draped her coat over Diana's shoulders. Stuttering badly, teeth chattering, Diana managed to tell Sarah about the two men.

"But they didn't hurt you?" Sarah asked.

Diana shook her head.

"They tied you, gagged you, and blindfolded you. And then they *painted* you?" she asked, still not believing she had understood Diana properly.

Diana nodded. "Sarah, I was so scared. I didn't know what they were doing. I felt this cold, wet stuff on my stomach. I kept expecting to feel one of them crawling on top of me. Oh, God, I don't know what I would have done. Finally, one of them said, 'Count to one hundred before you move.' Then the other one cut my wrists free. I was so scared, I really did count to a hundred. Aloud. It took me about twenty minutes. I had to start over three times."

Sarah remembered the night of the break-in. The man had told her to count to a hundred. The goose was back on her grave again.

"All right," Sarah said, "let me see this artwork."

Diana set her mug on the floor and stood up. She dropped the coat on the couch, then unbuckled her belt and undid the button on her jeans and unzipped them. She pushed them down around her thighs. She pulled down her panties, then pulled up her blouse and held it up off her stomach by pinning it under her crossed arms.

Her pubic hair had been painted in two vertical stripes. The right side was black and the left side was white. Above this, an upside-down pentagram covered her entire abdomen. Inside the pentagram, rendered in the same neat black lines, someone had painted an eye.

"And they said to stay home on Tuesdays and Thursdays?"

Diana nodded. "Yes."

"I'm so glad you came and told me."

"Of course," Diana said. "Why wouldn't I?"

"Our sessions are on Tuesdays and Thursdays. I think they were warning you away."

Diana looked shocked, as if the idea had not occurred to her before. "Oh, God . . ." she said.

"You need to get cleaned up," Sarah said. "Then I think we should call a friend of mine and see if he's available for lunch."

PART IV

BOOK OF SHADOWS

Chapter 21

Disgruntled and impatient, Bill Travers pushed his way through the throngs of post-Thanksgiving bargain hunters, checking the nearly overwhelming desire to mutter, "Bah, humbug" every time he brushed against one of the cheerful shoppers. *The mall,* he thought. *Why the hell the mall?*

He located the restaurant, a little cafeteria-style steak place that forced its patrons in through a queue leading past the serving area. Travers poured a cup of coffee. He was about to pass on the food, thought better of it, and picked up a paper cup full of fried potatoes. He paid for the food and stepped out into the dining area.

It was late enough that most of the tables were empty. A few couples sat surrounded by packages, wearily sipping Cokes and coffee. He only saw one table where two women sat together, a brunette with her back to him and a pretty blonde who seemed very intent on a conversation with her companion.

Damn, thought Travers, *now I'm gonna have to wait.* Then he saw the brunette turn and wave. It was Sarah. Bill was surprised, not having recognized her from the back. And for some reason, Diana was a surprise. Somehow, he had not expected Diana to . . . well, to look like this. Young. Intelligent. Attractive. *Oh, hell, why did I think she'd look like anything in particular? What did I think she'd look like?* He shrugged and walked over to the booth.

The blonde slid over on the seat so that he could sit.

"Bill Travers, meet Diana Smith," Sarah said. "Diana, Bill."

Travers shook hands with Diana. She smiled shyly.

"It's very nice to meet you at last," he said, wondering how much Sarah had told her about his involvement in the case.

"And nice to meet you," Diana said. "Sarah tells me you're an anthropologist."

"Yes, but you shouldn't let that influence your opinion of me. Mom always wanted an anthropologist in the family and I got picked."

Sarah and Diana laughed.

"I see you're sticking to your high nutritional standards today, Bill," Sarah said.

Travers smiled. "You sounded a bit upset on the phone. What's happened?"

"Diana has started remembering some things," Sarah said. "Things that support the idea of cult involvement."

Travers glanced at Diana. Her eyes were riveted on Sarah, her face expressionless.

Sarah continued. "Then, this morning, two men forced their way into her apartment. They forced her to undress. They bound her arms and blindfolded and gagged her.

"They painted her, Bill. Then they cut the binding on her wrists and told her not to move until she counted to one hundred."

"Did you say they painted her?" Bill asked.

"That's right." Sarah looked at Diana. "Oh, I really don't want to embarrass you."

"It's okay," Diana said. She squeezed Sarah's hand and released it, then turned to face Travers. "Mr. Travers, they painted my pubic hair black and white.

They also painted a five-pointed star on my stomach. Inside the star was an eye."

"Diana, the black and white . . . was it done in two vertical stripes?"

Diana nodded.

"How did you know that?" Sarah asked.

"I read about a case a couple of years ago in Omaha or Kansas or some such place. A woman who claimed to be defecting from a cult told police that she was abducted, stripped, and then painted on her back. Same pattern, black and white. She said it was the symbol for defection and betrayal."

"Defection from what?" Sarah asked. "Bill, I thought you told me there wasn't any evidence that these cults existed."

"Evidence is a funny thing. The authorities rejected the woman's account after a pretty cursory investigation. She had a pretty extensive psychiatric history."

"And so they ignored the whole thing," Sarah said disgustedly. "It figures."

"I'm sorry, but that's the way it is," Travers said.

"Well, forget evidence," Sarah said. "We're not trying to prove anything. We just want to figure out what's going on. What do you think?"

Travers opened his mouth to speak, then closed it. He glanced quickly at Diana, then back at Sarah.

"Well, now," he said finally, "that's hard to say."

Diana shifted in her seat. "You know, Sarah, there's a bookstore just a couple of doors down from here. If you don't mind, I've been trying to find something. I think I'll just look and see if they have it."

"But that's all right. I don't—" Travers blurted out, but Diana put her hand on his shoulder, silencing him.

"It's okay, Mr. Travers. You'll feel more comfortable talking to Sarah alone," Diana said. She turned to smile at Sarah. "Besides, Sarah will tell me everything later, I think."

Bill slid out of the seat and watched as Diana slid out behind him, waved to Sarah, and walked away.

"She's really something, isn't she?" Bill said.

"Yes, she is," Sarah answered. "Bill, you could've talked in front of her. She's going to have to know after what's happened."

"What has happened, Sarah?"

"What do you mean? What's happened is that these Satanists, or whatever they are, have tipped their hand. This is not some nightmare from the past. This is happening now."

"How do you know?" Travers asked.

"Look, I saw what they painted on her. Two hours ago, she was nearly hysterical with fright. They also told her to stay home on Tuesdays and Thursdays. In other words, drop out of therapy." Sarah paused. "Wait a minute! Do you mean you don't believe her?"

"I didn't say that," Travers replied. "I'm just counting off the possibilities. One possibility is that she could have done it to herself. She *was* painted on her front, not the back, you know."

"That's crazy," Sarah said. "She did not."

"If not her, then one of the alters. Her fright could be very real, you know, and she could still be doing it to herself."

"Bill, I just don't believe that," Sarah said. "She's not lying and she's not fooling herself. There's something very real going on here."

"Have you found an answer to my question, then?"

"Which question was that?"

"How does a group sustain itself with a set of practices guaranteed to produce hatred, distrust, and mental instability?" Bill asked. "Have you found an answer to that?"

"I think I have," Sarah said. "You kept asking me how a group could survive with a set of practices guaranteed to produce dissociation. And that made a lot of sense if what you assumed was that the group would not want dissociation to occur. That seemed like a reasonable assumption."

"It still does," Travers interrupted.

"Not necessarily," Sarah smiled. "I've been listening to Diana describe all these bizarre practices. And I look at her and she is completely oblivious to the whole thing. What could be more desirable to a secret organization than to have members who most of the time are not even aware of its existence?"

"But that's absurd. What would be the point?"

"I didn't say everyone was unaware. Maybe just certain members. I haven't figured that out yet. But think about it. Take the Listener. What if your friend is right and there really is a secret language? What if the Listener has one routine—to remember the text of a particular ritual or rituals? What if instead of committing these rituals to writing, members of the cult memorize them? It would be a sort of oral tradition, maybe passed on from generation to generation. How's that for cultural functionality?"

Sarah watched as Travers opened his mouth to say something, then snapped it shut. A look of concentration suddenly passed over his face. "A Book of Shadows," he said.

"A what?"

"Book of Shadows. What you're saying is that Diana is a living Book of Shadows."

"What's a Book of Shadows?"

Sarah could sense the excitement playing behind Travers's sudden smile; she could just as easily sense his struggle to suppress it.

"A Book of Shadows is a journal of sorts, a notebook in which a magician keeps a record of his rituals."

"So you think Diana is a living Book of Shadows? My God, that's brilliant. She comes complete with her own lock. She can't even read the book herself, so to speak, because it's tucked away with the Listener."

"It's an interesting hypothesis," Bill said. The excitement had faded from his eyes and he was back to gnawing on a thumbnail. "There's just one problem that I see. You're assuming that somehow the Listener was deliberately created. This is more in your league, but isn't that kind of impossible?"

"Is it?" Sarah asked. "I asked myself the same thing, over and over. But you kept using the expression *behavior guaranteed to produce mental illness.* I thought maybe that was exactly what was happening. Right now, I can give you the formula for producing multiple personality disorder. Take an intelligent child and place it in a family where one parent practices incest and/or torture. If the child lives, there's an awfully good chance they'll have learned some form of dissociation. As a survival technique, Bill."

"You said, 'if the child lives.' Do you think a group is going to engage in practices that might routinely result in the death of its members?"

"Why not? If the stories are true, murder and human sacrifice are not out of the question. Maybe it's like natural selection. Either you successfully dissociate or you die."

"Sarah, this is nuts." Bill threw up his hands. "You're saying that a group of people has learned to create multiple personalities."

"Exactly," Sarah said. "Engineered MPD. Bill, listen to this. I haven't told you about our session on Tuesday. You tell me if this isn't a formula for creating multiple personality disorder." Sarah told Travers about the cannibalistic ritual Lainey had described.

Travers's face wrinkled in disgust. "Good God."

"I think engineered MPD is the only thing that accounts for all the facts. Just look at things from a different perspective for a minute. Diana is nearly thirty years old. She has been abused since she was an infant. She has a personality whose sole function is to memorize the text of a satanic ritual. She learned to have out-of-body experiences through the deliberate rape and hypnosis-like suggestions of a priest figure. She has a personality with a worldview dividing everyone into one of two groups: Them or the Circle. They may even have triggers for specific personalities, like a pentagram drawn in the palm of a hand.

"What else?" Sarah paused, then continued. "She was symbolically killed and resurrected with a new personality, a new identity. Even a new appearance. A group of people have managed to rape her, torture her, teach her occult practices, give her an alternative worldview—and all the while maintaining absolute secrecy and the appearance of normalcy."

"But that's where you're wrong. She came to you for help, didn't she? Not exactly a perfect way to maintain secrecy."

"So maybe engineered MPD isn't perfect. Just generally good enough. All modesty aside, a lot of therapists would have missed the multiple personality clues. A medical doctor would have treated her for depression, if she was lucky. Hell, I went through half a dozen diagnoses before I figured out what was going on."

"All right, then. Let me think this through." Travers rubbed his eyes. "If what you say is true, then the whole point is secrecy, right? Why have they shown themselves now? Why put themselves in jeopardy, risk exposure?"

"Because," Sarah said, "what's the greatest threat to them? If secrecy depends on fragmenting an individual into half a dozen personalities with disparate and conflicting memories, what's the worse thing that could happen?"

Travers frowned. "Integration of the personalities," he said slowly.

"Bingo," Sarah said. "And Diana is starting to remember."

"Sarah, you make a compelling case. I just don't think I can accept it right now. Not without a hell of a lot more thought. A little proof would be nice, too."

"And what would you accept for proof?" Sarah asked. "Let's see. Videotapes? No, that could be faked. A signed confession from the high priest or whatever they are? No, that could be coerced."

"I get the point," Travers said unhappily.

"I'm not asking you to believe. Just pretend. Let's play 'what if.' What if it's all true? Tell me what it means if it's all true. Tell me what I haven't thought of."

Bill rubbed his chin thoughtfully. "Thanks," he said. "I'll do better if you let my need for evidence off the hook. Let's see. Well, the black and white paint is interesting. Let's say it really is a symbol for desertion from the cult. The rest of the symbolism is pretty obvious."

"It is?" Sarah asked.

"Sure," Bill said. "You've got a symbol for desertion, a symbol for the cult—the pentagram—and an eye. It means: You may be trying to leave, but the cult is still here with you. And it's watching."

"A cheery thought," Sarah said.

"Indeed. How much of this does Diana know?'

"She's remembered some childhood stuff. I have a feeling, though, that this may be less of a surprise to her than we think. I suspect there's a lot of material just under the surface and that she senses much of it. She took the priest thing and participating in the murder of another child pretty calmly."

Travers chewed absently on a French fry. "If the cult exists, then they want to prevent Diana's integration in a big way. Here's what I'd do. First, I'd let things go for a while and hope that you miss anything having to do with MPD or the satanic stuff. If that didn't work and I really could custom create a personality, I'd design one to give you a reasonable account of things."

"Nora," Sarah said. "Wow. I hadn't thought of that."

Travers looked skeptical. "Remember, I'm just doing this for the sake of argument. I'd also want to monitor progress. I guess I could access this Nora. That would give me a window into the sessions, wouldn't it?"

"Only up to a point," Sarah said thoughtfully. "None of the personalities is omniscient, at least none that I know of. Nora's inconsistencies certainly prove that she isn't always aware of everything."

"So I've got an imperfect window into the sessions. Maybe that's good enough. Maybe—"

Sarah grabbed Travers's arm excitedly. "But maybe it's not good enough. Maybe you'd want to check out the files, read her record." Sarah told Travers about the break-in.

"Damn," Travers said. "Damn, damn, damn."

"What else would you do, Bill? Go on."

"I don't know," he said. He seemed to have lost some of his enthusiasm for the game. "Scare tactics."

"Like painting Diana. Go on."

Travers shrugged. "Where do you go from there? You can only escalate to threats and then direct action. None of which makes me feel very happy." He hesitated, then added, "Which brings up a point. Why don't they just kill her? If they exist, they have no qualms about murder."

Sarah shrugged. "I don't have all the answers. She's important to them; she's the carrier of a ritual. I don't know."

"What about the suicide attempt, then? Couldn't that have been an attempt to kill her off?"

"No. I think that was a reaction of one of the other personalities to the emerging memories. And it may have been a reaction to attempts by the cult to control her. Call it a desperate attempt to regain control. I think Diana's too important to them to kill off. I think she has some purpose."

"Well, if she doesn't have a purpose, she's dead

meat. Of course, I doubt they'd have taken the trouble to give her such an elaborate warning.

"Yeah. You ever have the feeling that you're looking at one little part of the elephant?"

"Most of the time," Bill said. He stabbed at Sarah with a French fry. "Sarah, there's something else. Just playing 'what if,' mind you."

"Oh sure," Sarah said, smiling.

"If they know where Diana lives and they know that she's close to integrating, they also know about you. You might be in just as much danger as she is."

Sarah nodded gravely. "The thought occurred to me."

Travers looked thoughtful. "I need to tell you something. I haven't been completely honest. You remember a long time ago you asked if there was any physical evidence and I said no."

Sarah nodded.

"Well, that was only partially true. Back in the summer, the cops discovered a seventy-five-year-old grave had been disturbed. When they dug it up, they found its left hand had been stolen."

"You're kidding," said Sarah.

"It's worse than that. The corpse of an infant was buried underneath the coffin. The body was embalmed, and it may have been ritually killed. The wounds were consistent with a type of ritual knife. The whole thing was done very carefully."

"Why didn't you tell me this before?" Sarah asked.

"I didn't think it was important," Bill said. "With any luck, that's still the case."

"Somehow, I don't think so," Sarah said.

"I'm beginning to agree."

"So what do you think I should do?"

"I don't know," Travers said. "You might have Diana stay with you for a while. Or vice versa. You're not going to be able to watch her all the time, but you might frustrate their next move for a while. If they exist, of course," Travers added.

"I'm not keen about the idea of having one of my clients move in, but maybe it's necessary. I'll think about it. What else?"

"Change your patterns. Go to work late, leave early. Drive a different route. Become unpredictable."

"Pretend I'm a diplomat in a Middle Eastern country, in other words?"

"Exactly," Bill said. "I guess the only other thing to do is to try to find out as much from Diana as possible. Did you ever get in touch with the personality that seemed to know everything? What was her name?"

"Lynn."

"Yeah, Lynn. I'd really work on getting her version of events. She may be able to piece things together for you."

"How do you think I'd look as a blonde?" Sarah asked under her breath, recalling her last meeting with Lynn.

"Excuse me?" Bill asked.

"Never mind," Sarah said. "An inside joke. Anything else?"

"Sarah, I don't want to believe you. I really don't. But if there is anything going on, I want to help. Would you do me a favor?"

"What's that?"

"Call me once a day. Preferably at the same time. That way, I'll never be more than twenty-four hours off from knowing what's happened."

"Here comes Diana," Sarah said.

"Fine. Will you do it?"

"Sounds pretty extreme for something with a one percent chance of being right." Sarah said.

"The odds have just gone up. Now will you do it?"

"Yes," Sarah said, "I'll do it. Thank you."

Chapter 22

Sarah and Diana left the mall without shopping. On their way back into town, Sarah asked Diana if she would mind having a houseguest for a few days. Diana was delighted. Sarah detoured by her house to pick up some clothes.

The house seemed terribly deserted with Mark gone. Sarah left Diana in the kitchen and went back to the bedroom to pack. She sat on the edge of the bed and took a deep breath.

What are you doing? she asked herself. *You're going to move in with a client, for God's sake. That's not a very professional move. And why? Because you seriously think there's a cult of bogeymen out there? Bill said maybe one of the alters painted Diana. Is that so unbelievable?*

But the fact was, she *did* believe Diana. In the pit of her stomach she felt that she was doing the right thing, but on a rational level she had to wonder if the stress of the past weeks, her overwork with Diana and her faltering marriage, had just become too much. Maybe she was losing it, Sarah thought.

Before she left the bedroom, she tried to call Mark at his brother's house. Getting no answer, she hurriedly scribbled a note in case he came home before she did. *Staying with a friend for a few days,* she wrote, and jotted down Diana's phone number. She paused a moment, then added: *We can work this out, I know we can. I love you.*

On the drive over to Diana's, she wondered how she could contact Lynn. It seemed a silly problem. In a way, Lynn sat next to her in the front seat of the Oldsmobile. In another, perhaps more accurate sense, Lynn was a million miles away, incommunicado. At the least, she was not accepting phone calls or invitations from intermediaries. Sarah wondered if she would still accept mail. Perhaps a letter would work again.

Lynn had been remarkably open at their previous meeting. She had also made it clear that she had few allegiances and trusted no one but herself. If what Sarah suspected was true, that distrust certainly made sense. But Lynn had also left a way open to meet again. The more Sarah thought about it, the more she became convinced that Lynn had not been joking. *Not joking at all,* she thought. *Perhaps she's just looking for a measure of trust. I either trust her or to hell with me. Perhaps that's not such a bad approach. At least it's up front.*

At this point, she had probably already lost a husband. Her life, as well as the life of a client, might be in danger. She had little else to lose, Sarah thought. She began to compose the letter in her head.

The phone rang, and Mark heard his brother answer. A few seconds later, he called down the hallway for Mark to pick up. Mark used the phone in his brother's den, surprised to find that it was Beiderbeck calling. Mark cursed under his breath; the last thing he needed was a computer emergency just now. He regretted giving Beiderbeck his brother's number.

"Just seeing how my number one consultant is doing," Beiderbeck told him, and Mark relaxed a little. Mark allowed as how his consultant had seen better days. He wasn't really sure whether to be mad at Beiderbeck for setting him up with Marcia or grateful. In the end, it was just nice to have someone to talk to. Beiderbeck asked him about the new number, and because he could think of nothing else, Mark told the older man the truth. Beiderbeck's reaction surprised him.

"Damnit, Mark, you've got to get her back. This is your wife we're talking about here."

The remark that came to Mark's mind was: You pick a fine time to start being concerned about wives. Where did the guy get off? Still, he bit his tongue. "Yeah, John," he said. "I'll work on it."

"Nothing's more important than your wife, Mark," Beiderbeck said. "Certainly not work. Yours or hers. Why don't you two take a vacation? Get away for a while."

"I appreciate your concern, John."

"I know what it is. You're guilty about catching a little action on the side, aren't you? Hell, man, if that's what it is, tell her. Clear the air. It's not what *I* would do, mind you, but I've heard it works."

When he hung up the phone, Mark stood at the kitchen counter for a moment, trying to decide whether Beiderbeck was a decent guy or just a nosy son of a bitch. Beiderbeck, in his way, was right. If Sarah had had an affair . . . well, then, so had he. If he didn't do something quick, he was going to lose her. And in spite of everything, Mark didn't want to lose her.

Weeks 17–18: Saturday–Sunday, November 25–26

The tricky part, she thought, as she lay down on the rollaway bed in Diana's spare room, *is how to get the message to Lynn without tipping off Diana. Now that she's starting to remember, perhaps she's lost some of those blinders that kept her from seeing the evidence of the other personalities.*

We risked it the last time, Sarah thought. *We'll risk it again.*

Sarah grabbed the pen and paper she had left on the nightstand and began to write. When she finished, she folded the note and placed it in an envelope. She sealed the envelope and addressed it.

The next morning, Sarah volunteered to go downstairs and get the mail. On her way back up the stairs, she retrieved the letter from the hip pocket of her jeans and tucked it into the little bundle of mail. She left the mail on the stand by the doorway. She could hear Diana in the kitchen.

"I'm going out for a walk," she called. "Mail's on the table."

Sarah returned several hours later. Diana was in the living room cleaning her cameras and their various lenses. Sarah walked down the hallway into the spare room. She was surprised to find a small envelope lying on one of the sofa pillows. She closed the door to the room, feeling oddly conspiratorial. She tore open the envelope and read:

Dear Sarah:

How delightful to hear from you at last! We had just about given up on you. So glad you have decided to make a change. Rest assured that you are in good hands.

We shall have ample opportunity to talk, as long as you are prepared to meet honesty with honesty. Make sure you're at the apartment tomorrow around three o'clock in the afternoon. Wear old clothes with a button-up blouse.

The note was signed *Lynn.*

Sarah went to bed early but lay sleepless for several hours, turning over recent events in her mind. The next morning, she went out for a walk. When she got back, Diana was gone. A note in an unfamiliar handwriting informed Sarah that "We are out for a little fresh air." Sarah wondered who *we* were. Later, Diana came in with several packages. She disappeared into the bathroom. When she came out, Sarah asked her how her walk had been. Diana frowned, looking puzzled, then walked into the kitchen, ignoring Sarah's questions.

At two-thirty, Sarah went to the spare room. She lay on the sofa for a while reading a paperback. After about twenty minutes, she stood up and stretched. She took off her clothes and put on a faded pair of jeans and an old cotton blouse. On her way out to the living room, she stopped by the bathroom. Looking at herself in the mirror, she picked up a brush and ran it through her hair.

"What in God's name am I doing?" she asked herself. The question seemed to cover a multitude of recent actions: her abandonment of professional ethics in response to possibly imaginary threats from nonexistent cults; her inability to communicate with Mark and salvage their marriage; and now, what she was preparing to do with whomever she was about to meet in the kitchen.

The woman in the kitchen looked like Diana; her clothes were the same, her general facial characteristics unchanged, her hair arranged as usual. Still, the transformation was profound. Where Diana often appeared delicate and introspective, this woman seemed robust and energized. Laugh lines crinkled around her eyes where Sarah was sure she had seen none before. The pupils seemed larger, eclipsing Diana's startling blue irises, making them appear black.

She recognized Lynn at once.

Sarah stood in the doorway of the little kitchen, watching Lynn bounce from refrigerator to cabinet and back again, now fixing herself a drink, now arranging potato chips and other snack foods on a tray, now opening a bottle of wine and searching the cabinets for a glass. Her motion and vigor were dizzying. Sarah found herself smiling broadly when Lynn suddenly whirled around to face her.

"Goddamn," Lynn exclaimed, "I didn't hear you. You scared the piss out of me."

"I'm sorry," Sarah said.

"No problem." Lynn put her hands on her hips and grinned at Sarah. "So you actually decided to come."

"Yes."

"Fantastic. I wondered if I was gonna hear from you again."

"Lynn, I tried all kinds of ways to get hold of you," Sarah said, "but I guess you never got the messages."

"Oh, I got the messages, all right," Lynn said. "You knew how to get hold of me. We agreed the last time we talked." Lynn spread her arms in an encompassing gesture. "And here I am."

"It's good to see you again."

"And you," Lynn said. "You ready to change your outlook on life?"

Sarah breathed deeply. "I'm nervous," she said. "You really think this is a good idea?"

"Sure," Lynn said, "but what do I know? You're not chickening out, are you?" Lynn turned her back to Sarah, busying herself at the counter.

Sarah took a deep breath. *In for a penny, in for a pound,* she thought. "Not a chance."

"Good," Lynn said, turning back around, a glass of wine in her hand. "You can probably use this."

"You bet," Sarah said, taking the glass. She took a sip tentatively, then filled her mouth with the wine and swallowed. "Just what the doctor ordered."

"That's right. Just call me Doctor Janus."

"All right, doctor. Doc," Sarah said. "Do you know what's been happening to Diana?"

"Sorry, doc," Lynn said. "Nothing serious until I

have you helpless and under my complete control." She laughed in a parody of mad scientists in bad horror movies, took a sip of her bourbon, then disappeared down the hallway. She was back in a few minutes carrying several items, including the plastic bags Diana had stashed earlier in the bathroom. She set these down on the kitchen counter, then was gone again. When she reappeared, she carried several bath towels.

"Sit yourself down," Lynn said, pulling a straight-backed chair out into the middle of the kitchen floor. "And relax. Drink your wine. It'll take a few minutes for me to get everything ready."

Sarah sat, her back to the counter where Lynn made her preparations. She thought it was probably best that she could not see exactly what Lynn was doing; the less she thought about it, the better. She took another mouthful of wine.

"All right," Lynn said, "I'm about ready. Just want to read the instructions one more time."

"The instructions?" Sarah groaned. "I thought you did this all the time."

Lynn laughed. "Not all over. I've always wanted to try this." Lynn laughed again. "Don't worry. This is actually easier."

Sarah turned in her chair to look at Lynn, who leaned against the counter with her arms crossed, smirking. Sarah picked up her wine glass and drained the half that remained.

"Could I have another of these?" she asked.

"Now you're talking," Lynn said.

Lynn poured the wine, then draped a towel over Sarah's shoulders, fastening it around her neck with a clip. Lynn lit a cigarette and picked up her drink, carrying both over to the little kitchen table.

"Money-back guarantee if you don't like it, doc," she said.

"Why is that such a small comfort?" Sarah laughed, then added, "Doc."

"I'm glad you came, Sarah," Lynn said, suddenly serious. "Things are getting dicey. We need someone we can trust."

"I trust you, Lynn," Sarah said. "I hope you feel like you can trust me. Besides, I think we're about to start on a long and enduring relationship."

"What do you mean?"

"I'm not going to be able to keep this up by myself," Sarah said. "We've *got* to get together . . . what . . . at least once a month, right?"

Lynn smiled. "Yeah, doc. I like that. About once a month is right."

Lynn stubbed out her cigarette and gulped down the last of her drink. She moved behind Sarah and began lifting strands of hair, pulling them between her fingers.

"Yeah, doc, it's high time you did something about this stuff," she said. "Lucky you ran into me. You ready?"

"Yeah, doc, I'm ready," Sarah said. "Just let me kick my shoes off. I don't want to dye with my boots on."

"Oooh," Lynn laughed. "Doc made a funny. Now sit back, close your eyes, and let the doctor go to work."

Sarah slid back and lifted her legs to rest her feet on another chair. She closed her eyes, listening to Lynn moving things around on the counter. *Too late now,* she thought. Lynn came up behind her and gently combed her hair. Sarah felt her separate sections of the hair, twisting them in her hands and deftly clipping them. In the next instant, something cold and wet touched her scalp.

"Damn," Sarah said, "that's cold."

"It'll warm up in a minute," Lynn said.

Lynn finished the application process in about fifteen minutes. Sarah was impressed with her sure, efficient movements, the way she did everything with a confident economy of motion. Sarah began to relax at last, realizing it was really far too late now to worry. *Time for a change,* she thought. *May this be the first of many.* Sarah heard water running in the sink, Lynn apparently washing her hands. She next heard the unmistakable sound of an ice tray being cracked open and cubes tinkling in a glass. *Lynn certainly likes her drinks,* Sarah thought. *Of course, we're both drinking pretty heavily. Given the circumstances . . .*

Lynn took a seat at the kitchen table. "I'm afraid you're going to have to sit there for a while."

Sarah nodded. "How long?"

"That depends," Lynn said. "I should have tested a strand first, but then it would have taken twice as long, right? My guess is anywhere from forty-five minutes to two hours."

"Two hours? Really?"

"Probably not. Anyway, we've got lots of time to talk. You've lived up to your end of the bargain, now I'll live up to mine. Ask me anything."

"Now that I'm committed," Sarah said, "I hope you look at it as more than just a bargain or a wager of some kind."

"I do," Lynn said. "Of course."

"Good," Sarah nodded. "Lynn, how much do you know about what happens to Diana? Are you aware of everything that goes on?"

"No," Lynn said. "But before you go any further, you seem to refer to Diana like she's the only player here. Do you know what Diana is, Sarah?"

"No. What is she?"

"She's an empty shell."

"What do you mean?"

"Diana's the face we put on for the world, doc. But behind the face, there's nothing."

"I still don't understand."

"Would you say that Diana has a lot of emotion, doc?" Lynn asked. "Don't you find her a bit flat?"

"No," Sarah said, "I don't agree."

"She's learned a lot over the last few months. But trust me. She doesn't have access to many emotions. She may get frustrated and pissed off and scared, but that's about all. She doesn't have many memories, either, for the same reason. We let her be our window on the world, but we do the living."

"Who's *we,* Lynn?" Sarah asked.

Lynn lit a fresh cigarette. "Hmm. Now *I'm* starting to get nervous. Well, we made a bargain," she said. "Honesty, right?"

Sarah nodded.

"There's a bunch of us. But most of the others aren't very important. They just have pretty specialized functions. The main players are me. And the Irises. And the other Diana."

Sarah leaned forward. "The Irises?"

"Yeah. You've met Lainey. There are a couple of others. They're sort of like sisters. All different ages."

"What are their names?"

"Iris is one." Lynn paused. She looked intently at Sarah. "Isis is another."

"Isis," Sarah said. "I've heard the name. Do you think I could talk to her sometime?"

"I doubt it. You'd have better luck with Iris."

"And you said there was another Diana?"

"Yes."

"Why are their two Dianas?"

"Like I said, one's a shell, our face on the world. The other Diana is a real person."

"Not to argue with you," Sarah said, "but I certainly think of the Diana I know as a real person. She's my friend."

"I know, doc," Lynn said. "We appreciate that." She leaned forward. "Hold on a second, you're starting to drip a little bit." Lynn plucked a tissue from a box on the table. She reached over and blotted some of the thick liquid from around Sarah's ear."

"How's it doing?" Sarah asked tentatively.

"Just great," Lynn said. "I mean, it's been all of . . . what . . . five minutes. Relax, honey."

"Lynn," Sarah said, measuring her words carefully, "are all the things that Lainey remembers things that really happened? Are they accurate memories?"

"What does she remember?"

"She remembers being put in a pit for three days. She remembers being raped by a priest, supposedly so she could learn to leave her body. Some sort of astral projection thing. She remembers the murder of a friend named Indra. She was forced to participate in the murder. I think that's when Isis first emerged." Sarah paused. "Tell me these things aren't true."

"I wasn't there for everything," Lynn said. "But I'm quite sure they're true. Lainey doesn't lie, for one thing. She's just a little kid."

"Then what is the Circle?"

"Ah, now we come to it." Lynn stood and began to pace the kitchen. "Goddamnit, Sarah, do you know now hard it is for me to tell you about all this? Do you think this is easy?"

"Do you think *this* is easy?" Sarah pointed at her hair.

Lynn laughed. "Okay, you tell me something first. What do *you* think the Circle is?"

Sarah took a sip of wine, stretching out the act of lifting and drinking and replacing the glass. How should she regard Lynn? Her instinct was to treat Lynn as an autonomous individual and to trust her. If she couldn't treat her as an ally, then what? *This is no longer therapy,* she told herself. *I don't know what we're doing, but it's not therapy anymore.*

"If what I've learned is correct," she said—and thought, *Lynn is an ally*—"the Circle is a cult of some sort, probably satanic. It would appear to be very secret. Also successful. What else? Cruel. Possibly it murders children. Certainly it tortures and abuses them, physically and sexually. It may also have the ability to deliberately shape—engineer—multiple personality disorder. It is something I desperately want to believe does not exist."

Lynn ceased her pacing and resumed her seat at the kitchen table. "You've learned more than I thought, Sarah. I salute you. Everything you've said is true."

"But, Lynn, I just can't believe that. It has to be delusion of some sort. Self-hypnosis. Screen memory."

"Come on, Sarah," Lynn smiled. "You know by now what the score is. You may not want to admit it, but you know what it is."

"I can't believe that human beings would do that to one another."

"No," Lynn said. "You don't *want* to believe it. But you *can.*"

"So you're saying that Lainey really was forced to cut Indra with a knife? For example?"

"Probably," Lynn said. "Tell me what Lainey remembers."

Sarah told her.

"It was a death ritual," Lynn said. "Very powerful."

"Wait," Sarah shook her head. "I don't understand."

"Don't shake your head," Lynn said, and continued in the same even tone of voice, as if she were discussing the weather or some distant news event. "Killing releases energy. The rituals focus energy." Lynn looked closely at Sarah. "Why do you think these people do what they do, Sarah?"

"I . . . well, I . . ." Sarah stammered. "I don't know. I hadn't gotten that far in my thinking. I'm still working on denial."

"You can give that up," Lynn said. "The Circle does what it does for power. And I'm not talking penny-ante stuff. This is real power, Sarah. When they kill someone—ritually, that is—they know how to take that power, the energy that's released, and focus it for whatever they want."

"That's a little hard to believe."

"Fine," Lynn shrugged. "Believe what the fuck you want."

"I'm sorry, Lynn," Sarah said. She leaned forward, taking one of Lynn's hands in her own. "You've got to put up with me. It's not that I don't believe *you.* I just don't want to believe that any of this can actually have happened."

"All right," Lynn said. "No problem."

"Let's take a break," Sarah said. "Can I go to the bathroom? I'm about to pop." Sarah stood and walked stiffly to the doorway.

"Sure," Lynn said. "Just don't shake your head. And don't look in the mirror."

Sarah walked past the mirror on the medicine cabinet without looking. She peed, and when she had finished, she stood in front of the mirror washing her hands. She resisted looking up for several seconds, then slowly raised her eyes. For a few moments, all thoughts of satanic cults, ritual murders, and multiple personality disorder were obliterated from her mind.

"Oh, my God," Sarah said slowly.

In spite of the thick, bluish liquid coating each strand, she could clearly see that her hair had changed color. Drastically. Instead of the usual coffee-colored brown, her hair was a garish coppery red, orange almost, with hints of gold reflecting the light as she turned her head. She stood transfixed, her mind flicking between the factious images of her usual appearance and the reflection in the mirror.

"Oh, my God," she said again, then turned away from the mirror.

"You peeked, didn't you?" Lynn smiled mischievously as Sarah entered the kitchen.

Sarah nodded as she sat down. "Uh-huh, I peeked.

Uh . . . Lynn, my hair is red. Please tell me it's not going to be red when we're through."

"Hah," Lynn laughed. "You should be so lucky. It definitely will *not* be red. That's just a stage it goes through. Don't panic."

"Okay," Sarah said uncertainly.

"Where were we?" Lynn asked.

"I believe I was doing my best to accept the idea of a satanic cult."

"Right. Well, take it or leave it," Lynn said.

"Tell me something. These Satanists murder—sacrifice, I guess—human beings, right?"

"Sometimes."

"Where do the victims come from? They can't just steal children, right? Eventually, they'd be caught."

"It isn't only children, you know. But to answer your question, most of the offerings come from within the cult. A few are kids the Circle has managed to adopt."

Sarah noted the use of the term *offerings.*

"You mean the cult kills its own children? Members?"

"Yes," Lynn said. "It's an honor to have a child chosen as an offering. Also, if a child is sacrificed, it's usually because it couldn't hack it."

"What do you mean?"

"Sometimes, the kids go crazy. Or they start remembering stuff and telling their teachers at school."

"And so they get chosen as a sacrifice?"

"Right. Survival of the fittest."

"I think I see," Sarah said. "Theoretically, if the cult was able to survive long enough, they would be selecting for genetic predisposition to multiple personality disorder. If there is a genetic component." Sarah paused, lost in her musings for a moment. "But tell me something. What happens to adults who start remembering?"

"Same thing."

"Which means you could be in danger."

"Yes," Lynn said. "And you."

"Lynn, who are you?" Sarah asked. "You seem to know everything. How is that possible?"

"They can't control everything," Lynn said. "They can set it up so that things are pretty well divided up and kept apart. But there has to be someone who ties it all together. Someone they can't really control. If they destroyed all free will, they wouldn't have anything left for later."

"You're losing me again. What do you mean, for later?"

"You don't think they kill all of us, do you? They kill to preserve the Circle. But where do you think the next generation comes from?"

"Where does it come from?" Sarah asked, puzzled.

"It comes from us," Lynn said. "You don't get it, do you? This isn't some flash in the pan. The Circle has been around for a long time. That's also why I have some measure of protection right now. More than you, in fact."

"Look, I'm not following this at all," Sarah said. "Let's back up. Where do the new members come from?"

"They are the sons and daughters of the old members, of course," Lynn said.

"That means you are a member of the Circle?" Sarah asked.

"No, not me. One of the other . . . what you refer to as personalities."

"Nora," Sarah said.

"No, not Nora. Actually, it's Isis."

"Isis? But didn't you say that she's one of the Iris Morrison personalities?"

"Yes. Damnit, Sarah"—Lynn beat her fist on the table—"I'm telling you a lot more than you should know."

"I'm in too far *not* to know," Sarah said.

"Maybe," Lynn replied. She paused, as if considering some matter of importance, then continued. "Let's look at this another way. Have you figured out how Diana came to be?"

"Yes, I think so. She was . . . uh . . . created at about age twelve or thirteen. The real Diana Smith was probably killed and Iris was made to believe that she was reborn as Diana."

"Very good. So who was the original kid?"

"Iris Morrison?"

"Bingo."

"Then is Lainey the original personality?" Sarah asked.

"You've got to stop it with this original personality stuff, Sarah. It's really not important."

"Why not?"

"Because the original Iris Laine Morrison went away a long, long time ago. If she lives at all, she's a tiny, frightened, mute baby who spends all her time curled up in a fetal position, unaware of anything else that happens."

"Then where did Lainey come from?"

Lynn sighed. "Lainey was one of the kids who first came to help Iris. When they came, Iris went away and never came back. They came to protect her. She never had to deal with all the bullshit again."

"Was Iris created deliberately?" Sarah asked. "Was she intentionally created?"

"Not in the sense you mean," Lynn said. "They deliberately abused her so that Iris would split, so in that sense it was intentional. But in the beginning, they have no control over what happens. That comes later, when they start the training."

"So first there was the infant, Iris Laine Morrison. She went away at an early age and Lainey came to take her place."

"Sort of. There were others besides Lainey."

"Who are they?"

"They don't exist anymore, really. They got incorporated later."

"All right, I'll leave that for now. What happened after Lainey? Who came next?"

"There was Iris. And Isis. And the Memories, of course."

"The Memories?"

"Uh-huh. You've come across one of them."

"The Listener," Sarah said excitedly.

"Right."

"The Listener memorizes a ritual, right?" Sarah asked.

"Yes. Actually, there are a number of Listeners. Each one remembers the words of a ritual or ceremony. There are Watchers, too, who store all the visual memories."

"You're kidding," Sarah said. "That's fantastic. These listeners and watchers were deliberately created, too, weren't they?"

"That's right," Lynn said. "Can you guess why?"

"Well, to remember the rituals, right? So they don't have to be committed to paper." Sarah remembered Travers's reference to Diana as a living Book of Shadows.

"That's part of it," Lynn said. "But it's also to fragment the Memories. See, a separate person remembers one part—the words, for instance. Another remembers the way it's supposed to look, all the movements and motions. Some of Isis's rituals are split up among three or four of the Memories. That way it's very unlikely that anyone—like a nosy therapist—is going to uncover anything of importance. Or make any sense of it if they do."

"Fantastic."

"That's one way of looking at it. You ready for another glass of wine?" Lynn stood up.

"Uh . . . gee, I don't know," Sarah said. "I'm going to get blitzed if I'm not careful."

"You got something better to do?" Lynn refilled Sarah's glass. "Besides, I want you anesthetized when I unveil my creation."

"Creation?" Sarah asked, momentarily puzzled. "Oh, you mean my hair. I'd almost forgotten. How's it doing?"

Lynn handed the glass to Sarah. She carefully wiped a small strand of Sarah's hair with a tissue.

"Still got a little way to go," Lynn said. "But it won't be long now."

"Lynn, if they can create personalities, then all the personalities have some sort of purpose, right?"

Lynn smiled. "You could say that."

"All right, then. What's the purpose of Lainey?"

"Lainey was simply one of the escapes for the baby. As she got older, she was chosen to be the one to receive training."

"I want to come back to this training, but first I want to know everybody's purpose. Iris came a little later, you said. What did she do?"

"Iris went to public school. She didn't know anything about the Circle."

"So she was created to deal with the rest of the world?"

"Yes," Lynn said. "Essentially, she lived in the non-Circle world."

"All right, then who is Isis?"

"Isis is the one who participates in all the Circle activities. I don't know much about her. She has walls all around her and I can't get to her."

"Diana?"

"The real Diana was created during the ceremony you mentioned earlier. Her *job,* if you want to look at it that way, is to house all the memories and feelings of Diana Smith. If you talk to her, you'll find that she has a complete set of memories all the way back to childhood. Of course, they aren't really true memories."

"Why haven't I talked to her?"

"Something's wrong with her," Lynn said. "She's not functioning the way she is supposed to. She's turned inward. She's part of the reason that Diana came to see you originally."

"Can you explain that a little more?" Sarah asked.

"Diana's the one that's supposed to be handling most of the day-to-day stuff. Instead, she sort of froze up. That's why Diana—the shell-Diana—started having problems. She started becoming aware of all the gaps in time, and without really realizing it, she started becoming aware of us."

"Okay, we'll leave that for now, too. Who is Nora?"

"Nora's their watchdog."

"Nora is whose watchdog?"

"The Circle's."

"And what does a watchdog do?" Sarah asked.

"Nora's a plant, man. A setup," Lynn said. "She was made just for you."

"What?"

"She was made for you. When they found out that Diana was coming to therapy, they created Nora."

"Wait, wait," Sarah said. "Why do I feel like I'm missing everything? You mean, the Circle is still manipulating Diana?"

"Well, of course," Lynn said. "You think they go away?"

"But Diana doesn't have anything to do with them, does she?"

"Diana, no," Lynn said. "Nora, yes. Isis, yes. The Watchers and the Listeners, of course. A few others."

"But Diana doesn't know anything about this," Sarah protested.

"Exactly," Lynn said. "Now you're starting to get the picture."

"My God, you mean all this time that Diana and I have been working together, some of the others have been working with the cult? Reporting to the cult?"

"Probably."

"Probably? Don't you know?"

"I'm insulated from Nora. She's the one who would be keeping them informed. Maybe some of the others, too."

"Lynn, I can't believe this."

"Believe it."

Sarah drank a large mouthful of wine. "This is nuts. So where do you fit in all of this, Lynn? What's your purpose?"

"I told you. I'm the glue that holds it all together. Sort of. You see, they can't control everything and they can't engineer, as you put it, all the personalities. They have to deal to a certain extent with what emerges. It's not an exact science."

"I guess it doesn't have to be if you can kill off all the failures," Sarah said.

"Right," Lynn agreed. "Anyway. I came along fairly early on to help hold things together."

"Why aren't you on their side, then?" Sarah asked. "If you're the coordinator, why aren't you one of them?"

"Because," Lynn said, "I owe my allegiance first to myself and then to the kids. I owe nothing to the ones who hurt the kids. Or twisted them into things they aren't supposed to be."

"But don't they know about you? Do they know you're cooperating with me?"

"They know about me, of course," Lynn said. "They tolerate me because they have to. Besides, I know when to hold my tongue. Usually, at least. And up until now, I hadn't cooperated with you."

"Aren't you putting yourself in danger? Won't they find out?"

"Probably, yes."

"But why?" Sarah asked, "Why are you doing this?"

"One reason is that I've had to witness a lot over

the years. I know the difference between the Circle and the rest of the world. I went to school with Iris, and, later, Diana. I want us to be able to live without fear. I like life," Lynn said, "and I want to be able to live. That's the real reason I'm telling you all of this. I need help. Without it, they will kill me soon."

"You mean, they'll kill Diana?" Sarah asked. "Kill the body?"

"No, you still don't have the big picture." Lynn stood up and walked over to the sink. Sarah turned her head and watched her as she sprinkled baby powder on her hands, then slipped them into a pair of plastic gloves. "They spend years training the children. The ones that survive represent an enormous investment. And Isis is even more special than most. She's slotted to become a kind of priestess or high functionary in the cult. It's what she's been trained for all her life."

"But how can that be? What would happen to the rest of you?"

"Sit back in the chair." Lynn gently turned Sarah's head. She dried another strand of hair, examining it closely, separating the individual hairs with her gloved fingers. "All of the cult members go through the same thing, more or less. Especially the ones destined for important positions. They break the children into pieces. They don't call them personalities, they call them cells. Then they designate one cell to go out in the world and another to remember certain things and another to see certain things. Some they designate to be beaten and confused and tortured, over and over. But one piece gets picked to be groomed and trained, a cell to preside over all the other cells. Because eventually they try to glue the whole thing back together again, only it looks completely different from the way it started out."

Lynn turned the taps and water hissed out of the faucet. She pulled the black-hosed sprayer out of its niche, testing it by squeezing the little lever. A jet of water hit the bottom of the sink and a fine spray rose in the air.

"What do you mean, Lynn?"

"All the cells make up what they call a chrysalid. You know what a chrysalid is, Sarah?"

"Chrysalid? Isn't that like a cocoon?"

"That's right. The chrysalid becomes a butterfly. Pretty soon, they will make all of us come together."

"You mean integration of the personalities?" Sarah asked.

"That's *your* term. They look at it as a metamorphosis and Isis is the butterfly-in-waiting. It's done in a big ceremony. Similar to what they did to create Diana. Isis comes of age. She get the memories of the Listeners and the Watchers, so that she knows all the rituals. She gets the knowledge and memories of the kids, so she knows everything that they know. She'll get all the knowledge of the real world, too, so she can function out there and still be completely aware of the cult. She'll get Diana—the real Diana—and that way she'll be able to have a career in the real world. Nice, huh?"

"But what happens to you, Lynn? And what happens to Diana? My Diana?" Sarah asked.

"Your Diana disappears. She was just a facade, anyway. And me? I carry most of the memories of the tortures and the rapes and the beatings. They can't have me around. I get destroyed."

"Destroyed? They can't actually destroy you, can they?"

Lynn picked up a bottle of shampoo and scrutinized it as if she were reading its list of ingredients. Finally, she looked at Sarah. "Put your head back," she said, and Sarah leaned her head back into the sink. Lynn had padded the edge of the sink with towels.

"If they can't destroy me," she said, "they can lock me away forever. Hidden away in a maze. Where the baby Iris Laine Morrison sleeps."

A jet of warm water sluiced through Sarah's hair.

Lynn refused to discuss the Circle while she worked on Sarah. First, she rinsed her hair with warm water, then shampooed it. She talked constantly. Sarah recognized that she had reverted to the crude language patterns that had been in evidence the first time she met Lynn, patterns that had pretty much dropped away over the last hour.

"Goddamnit, baby, you are gonna lo-ove this," Lynn said, working the sprayer all around Sarah's head. "This is gonna be great. Now sit up, hon, while I put this towel on you."

Sarah sat up and Lynn wrapped a towel around her wet hair, crossing the two ends in front, turban-style.

"All right, you can get up and stretch for a while."

Sarah stood up shakily, her back complaining against the time spent in the straight-backed chair.

"I'll be back in a second," she said.

"All right" Lynn called after her. "Just don't peek. I'm not through yet."

Having heard this before, Sarah's first step upon closing the bathroom door behind her was to remove the towel from her head. The sight of her hair turned orange had been shocking; this new reflection left her breathless and feeling a little weak. Her hair was a uniform yellowish gold color, almost a lemon-yellow. It hung in limp, pale strands. The dark arches of her eyebrows looked strange beneath the nearly colorless fringe of her bangs.

"My hair," she sniffed. "What have I done?"

She sat down on the toilet seat, hard. Tears came to her eyes, along with a gut-wrenching sensation that she associated with losses and large mistakes. She pulled strands of her hair over her eyes, seeing in the pale color the gaudy bleached excess of Harlow and hookers.

"Why in God's name did I do this?" she asked herself.

The tears came harder for a little while. But then she remembered precisely why she had come. She thought of Lynn's tales of horror told so matter-of-factly and she thought of the atrocities that had been committed against Lainey and the others. And then she reminded herself of her own resolution to make a change. And she thought of Mark, his sudden abandonment of their marriage. Sarah grabbed a handful of toilet paper and blew her nose. She stood up and looked at herself in the mirror again.

"Is Jenny going to love this," she said aloud, and started laughing. Suddenly, she couldn't stop laughing. Here she was worried about her damn hair when the world was going to hell around her. She laughed harder.

"Lynn said blond," she whispered, "and, boy, is this stuff blond. I guess I can always color it back it if looks really bad."

Sarah was still laughing when she came back into the kitchen, drying tresses of her hair between folds of the towel.

"Now, damnit, I thought I told you not to look," Lynn scolded.

"I couldn't help it," Sarah said. "Besides, I had to look sooner or later, right?"

"Yeah, but we're not through yet," Lynn said.

"We're not?" Sarah asked.

"Hell, no. Unless you like it like that," Lynn said. "I think it looks terrible, personally."

"Yeah, well, what else are you gonna do to it?" Sarah asked.

"First, we took all the color *out* of your hair," Lynn said, as if explaining something extremely obvious. "Now we've got to put color back *in* your hair. Unless, of course, you want to look like Madonna when you go to work tomorrow."

"No, no," Sarah said. Perhaps there was hope for her hair yet.

"I hope you like the color I got you," Lynn said.

It's got to be better than this, Sarah thought, and began laughing again.

Lynn continued her policy of deferring serious questions, until she had applied the toner to Sarah's hair and fixed them both fresh drinks.

"Cheers," Sarah said, and clicked her wine glass against Lynn's tumbler of whiskey. "My head's starting to feel soaked," she said. "In more ways than one."

"Good," Lynn said. "I'm almost as nervous as you are, you know."

"I'm not nervous anymore," Sarah said.

"Bullshit," Lynn said, laughing. "You're scared to death that I've ruined your hair."

"No, I think I've worked beyond that now."

"Right," Lynn said skeptically.

"So what are you nervous about?" Sarah asked.

"That I've ruined your hair," Lynn said, her face set in a deadpan. "Just kidding," she said, laughing.

"You are avoiding my question, Lynn." Sarah sipped her wine. "Let me see if I can help you out. You're nervous because now all your cards are on the table and there's no way you can really know whether you can trust me or not. How's that sound?"

Lynn hesitated, lighting a cigarette. "Sounds about right," she said.

"I'd tell you that you can trust me, but that doesn't cut it, does it?"

Lynn shook her head.

"Actually, there's not much I can *say* that's going to prove anything," Sarah continued. "But I will tell you this. First, you're not crazy. Second, I believe you. Third, I want to help fight them. And we're going to have to trust each other a lot more. What do you think?"

"If you want to help fight, then I think you're okay," Lynn said. "You got any ideas?"

"I've got a few," said Sarah, "but first I want to hear more from you. Tell me about this training."

Over the next half hour, Sarah listened as Lynn recounted several stories describing the Circle's training methods. She learned that they conducted staged pregnancies and birthings on little girls. Presumably, this inured the victim to both the process and products of pregnancy. Having been taught that only bad things issued from pregnancy, the cult mother was less likely to form close attachments to her children.

Sarah also came to understand why Diana and the other personalities had described several parent figures. The cult routinely cycled children through a succession of surrogate parents. The children rarely stayed more than a few years with any particular set of "parents."

Lynn hinted at more bizarre practices. Children were often forced to take drugs. Lynn's descriptions indicated a large pharmacopeia, ranging from sedatives, tranquilizers, and hypnotics to powerful hallucinogens and intoxicants. Drugs were mixed with foods, making it impossible for the children to avoid their ingestion. In addition to drugs, other adulterants were added to food. The trainers created a powerful mistrust of food among the children: Suspicious-tasting food would later be said to have contained feces or blood. Sometimes a meal would be presented to half-starved children, who would be told that it consisted of some human organ or flesh. Perhaps it did, perhaps it didn't, Lynn said she could not be sure.

The trainers seemed to specialize in creating states of total confusion. They taught that many concepts had opposite meanings from their conventional definitions: good is bad, love is hate, God is pain. The child was put in constant conflict with the non-cult world, the world of Lainey's Them. The children were taught that They could not be trusted. Sarah thought that all the practices combined to produce an absolute fear of the non-cult world and a diminution of the individual's will and ego. They created a total dependence on the cult.

Sarah listened in fascinated horror to Lynn's descriptions. Finally, Lynn stopped, saying it was time to rinse Sarah's hair again. Sarah moved her chair back to the sink. She closed her eyes and sighed as Lynn guided the warm water over and through her hair.

When she had finished, Lynn wrapped a fresh towel around Sarah's head and moved her chair out into the middle of the kitchen floor.

"Sarah," Lynn said, "I'm not sure how much more talking we'll get to do today, but I want you to know how much it's meant to me to be able to tell all this to somebody."

Sarah reseated herself and Lynn stood behind her, drying her hair with the towel.

"I've been wondering something." Lynn gently eased the tangles out of Sarah's hair.

"Yes?" Sarah pulled her head against occasional snags caught by the comb.

"You said you had an idea of how we might fight back. What did you have in mind?"

"The thing they fear most is spontaneous integration. I mean, that's always a possibility, right? One day, the fragmented cult member could just wake up with a complete set of memories. Suddenly, they're beyond cult control and they know everything. Not to mention all those years of training down the drain. And no new cult member. All those rituals to pass on to someone else."

"All that knowledge to implicate practicing members," Lynn added. "I like it, I like it."

"What if we beat them to the draw?"

"What do you mean?"

"What if Diana integrated before they could have their ceremony? Before the metamorphosis of the chrysalid."

"So you think we should merge ourselves?" Lynn asked.

"It's an idea."

Lynn switched the hair dryer on. She picked up sections of hair with a brush, passing the hair dryer back and forth over the strands.

"I'm not sure I much like that idea," Lynn raised her voice over the roar of the dryer. "I think that also means my death."

"Maybe," Sarah said, "maybe not."

Lynn finished drying Sarah's hair in silence. After she had put the dryer away, Sarah asked, "Can I look now?"

"Not yet," Lynn said, and disappeared down the hallway.

She returned in a few minutes carrying a handful of cosmetics. Sarah sat motionless as Lynn applied eyeliner and shadow and penciled her eyebrows.

"Giving me the treatment, aren't you?" Sarah asked.

"Shut up and suck in your cheeks," Lynn said, brushing powder across Sarah's face. "Look, just tell me how integration does not mean my death."

"I can't say for sure it wouldn't," Sarah said. "In the cases I've read about, *everybody* gets changed during integration. But the new person that emerges is part of all those other personalities."

"We are people, not personalities," Lynn said.

"Yes, of course," Sarah said. "I'm sorry, but language gets in my way. Lynn, there's something else that happens, too. Personalities—people—seem to be merged into a particular person. That person is changed, surely, but more in the sense of being enhanced rather than destroyed."

"So you think I could emerge from this integration as the new Lynn? With everybody else's memories?"

"Maybe."

Lynn stepped back, looking over Sarah appraisingly.

She nodded, then picked up a brush and stepped behind the chair. She brushed Sarah's hair silently for a few minutes.

"You're done," she said finally. "Are you ready to be unveiled?"

"I guess so," Sarah said.

"How would you go about doing it?" Lynn asked.

"The slow, safe way would be to encourage all of the alters to meet each other, become aware of each other, to relive the events that created them, then to ask the most compatible ones to merge. Once the process starts, it's a matter of uncovering all the alters and all the traumas they represent."

"Sounds like a long process," Lynn said. "I think you'd also have a hell of a time getting Nora and Isis and the Memories to go along. What's the quick method?"

"The quick method is to use hypnosis to try to force integration. I've heard of it being done before. I suspect they were pretty simple cases of one or two personalities."

"You mind if I think about this for a while?" Lynn asked.

"Of course," Sarah said. "I need to think about it, too."

"How do you know Nora or Isis wouldn't be the one to be . . . uh . . . enhanced, as you put it?" Lynn asked.

"I don't," Sarah said. "Maybe that's something we could control with hypnosis. But, honestly, I don't know. And there's no guarantee that somebody completely new wouldn't emerge. I can't promise you won't lose your individuality."

"I understand," Lynn said. "Is there anything you can think of that I can do in the meantime?"

"Yes," Sarah said. "Any opportunities you have to show yourself to Diana or help make her aware of you will help us in the long run." Sarah smiled suddenly,

"Listen, are you going to let me see what I look like or not?"

"Let's do it," Lynn said.

Sarah followed Lynn to the bathroom and stepped in front of the mirror, closing her eyes and fixing her face against betrayal of whatever emotion might hit her. She steeled herself against disappointment, shock, the sense of loss that had hit her earlier. As she opened her eyes she forced a smile, which soon turned to a frown. Sarah had expected to see a fluffier version of the bleached pale-gold she had seen earlier, and she was puzzled. Instead of the artificial look she'd anticipated, her hair was . . . well, not bad. Okay, actually. Blond, it was definitely blond, but it was nice. It was a darker color than she expected, a cool, ashen shade. And instead of a single color, an overall bleached-out look, her hair had highlights. Strands of it seemed shaded here and there. *It looked almost natural,* Sarah thought.

Standing in the doorway, Lynn visibly relaxed. She had misinterpreted Sarah's sudden transition from smile to frown.

"Well," she asked nervously, "what do you think?"

"I think I like it," Sarah said slowly. "I do like it. Lynn, you are very, very good." Without thinking, Sarah added, "I've got to admit, when I saw myself before, I thought it was all over with."

Lynn grinned. "I told you you'd like it, didn't I?"

Sarah looked at Lynn, then back at her reflection. "Yeah, but I wasn't really expecting . . . I don't know what I was expecting." Sarah put her hands on her hips. She swiveled back and forth. "I do look pretty good, don't I?"

"You look great," Lynn said. "For a second there, you scared the hell out of me. I thought you didn't like it."

"No way," Sarah said. She put out her arms and

hugged Lynn. "Lynn, thank you. You've just given me a new lease on life."

Lynn pulled away after a moment and looked at Sarah seriously. "Could you do me a favor, then?"

"Sure," Sarah said. "What is it?"

"Could we fix dinner and spend the evening together? And not talk about the Circle? Or multiple personalities? Just pretend we're normal friends having a pleasant evening together?"

"Lynn," Sarah said, "nothing would please me more."

Chapter 23

Week 18: Monday, November 27

Sarah grinned as she paused outside the door to the office. Margie's reaction to her new hair would be worth a million bucks. Sarah had already shocked herself this morning, having stumbled bleary-eyed and slightly hung over into the bathroom and discovering an unexpected blonde staring back at her from the mirror. Margie would *really* be shocked. She opened the door and stepped in quickly, keeping her eyes straight ahead and her face expressionless as she crossed the waiting room to her office.

"Morning, Margie," she said, halfway across the room.

"Mornin', boss," Margie said, then added after a half-second delay, "boss?"

Sarah felt Margie's eyes on her as she opened the door and stepped inside. As she walked over to her desk, she heard Margie enter behind her. Sarah sat in her desk chair. Margie walked around in front of the desk, then sat down slowly in the chair Sarah kept for clients.

"Holy shit, boss," Margie said, her eyes wide. "You look great."

"Well, thank you," Sarah said. "I thought I'd try a new eye shadow. You like it, then?"

"Eye shadow, my ass," Margie said. "Don't mess with me." Margie leaned forward across the desk, coming completely out of the chair and extending one arm toward Sarah. "Can I touch it?"

"Certainly," Sarah said.

"My God," Margie breathed, her fingers lightly running over Sarah's hair. She pulled her hand away and sat back down. "It looks wonderful. Did you do it yourself? Will you do mine?"

"I'm sorry," Sarah said. "Only one gorgeous blonde per office. And no, I didn't do it myself."

"You went to the salon?" Margie asked.

"No," Sarah said. "You remember Lynn?"

"I remember Lynn," Margie said, then exploded. "You let a *client* do your hair?"

"That's not all. I've moved in to Diana's apartment for a while."

"What are you talking about?"

"Diana's in trouble," Sarah said. "Also, things weren't going so great with Mark and me, so it looked like a good time to take a break. Margie, we may all be in trouble before this is through. Have we got an hour or so free?"

Margie nodded. "Yeah. Nothing till ten."

"Good. What say we go to breakfast and I'll tell you a long story that you will have a hard time believing."

"I think I like my new boss," Margie said.

Sarah called Travers and in a breathless rush told him about Lynn's revelations. Travers listened carefully, asking questions in the right spots, but Sarah had the sense that he was skeptical.

"Sarah, I'm not saying I don't believe you, but you should look at all the possibilities. Like the possibility that you may really be in danger, but not from a cult. From your own client. Anybody capable of putting together a story like that—on whatever level—is capable of vigorously defending their delusions. If they are delusions, of course."

"They're not," Sarah said. "Bill, I'm thinking about trying a forced integration."

"What?"

"Using hypnosis to merge all the personalities."

"Why, for God's sake?"

"Well, if you accept Lynn's version of events, then as long as Diana remains fragmented, she's in danger of both being manipulated and integrated by the cult. If I can beat them to it, she should be safe. Or safer, at least."

"Sarah, do you think that's wise? What if it doesn't work? Hell, what if it does work?"

"I don't know," Sarah said. "That's one reason I called—to see what you thought the dangers might be."

"Okay," Bill said. "That's fair enough. Well, let's see. . . . If it does work, it could have serious repercussions. The effect could be temporary. Who knows what would happen if she started fragmenting again."

"I thought about that," Sarah said. "Multiples seem to have some pretty effective safety mechanisms. My guess is she'd just forget anything she couldn't handle."

"One of those mechanisms is suicide, you know. Attempting integration too soon could cause severe trauma. She might not be able to deal with it."

"Yes, I don't think I can realistically discount that risk," Sarah said. "Bill, just tell me one thing. By now, you've read as much of the literature as I have. Do you think it's possible for forced integration to work?"

Bill paused, reluctant to answer. "Yes," he said finally. "It has worked in some cases. But they were less involved—one or two alters. Relatively few original traumas."

"That's all I wanted to know. Listen, I've got to run."

"You can't hang up just like that."

"I'm sorry, but I've a client in five minutes. Talk to you later?"

"Please. Sarah, there's just one thing I want you to think about. In a sense, no matter what the truth is, you *are* trafficking with a bunch of Satanists. But if there isn't a *real* cult, then the Satanists you're dealing with live in the body of Diana Smith. And so does the danger."

Sarah hurried home, home to Diana's apartment, through the thickening late afternoon traffic. On her way up the steps to the building, she stopped, suddenly wondering how she was going to explain her new hair to Diana. Then she laughed and shook her head. Ironic that the one person she was worried about offering an explanation to was in a sense the same person responsible for it in the first place.

Sarah called out as she stepped into the apartment. Diana—at least she thought it was Diana—answered back from the kitchen. Sarah slipped off her coat and hung it in the hall closet. When she closed the closet door, Diana stood watching her from the archway of the living room.

"It looks really nice, Sarah," she said.

Sarah self-consciously reached up to touch her hair. "Thank you," she said uncertainly. "Do you really think so?" she added when she could think of nothing else to say.

"Yes. Yes, I do." Diana smiled. "One of the others did it for you, didn't they?"

"That's right. How did you know that?"

"She gave me little glimpses of it all day long today. It's so strange. I still find it hard to believe."

"That's understandable."

"What's her name, Sarah? Which one was it?"

"Lynn."

"Lynn," Diana repeated. "She's the one who does my hair, too, isn't she?"

"Yes."

"You like her, don't you, Sarah?"

"Yes, I like her a lot," Sarah said, sensing the insecurity in Diana and thinking about the possibility of trying a forced integration. Diana needed to know more than she did, and she needed some reassurance. Sarah walked over to the archway and slipped her arm around Diana's waist, tugging gently. "Come on," she said, "I think it's time we had a little talk."

Week 18: Tuesday, November 28

After Sarah left for her office, Diana sat on the living room couch, drinking coffee. The television was on, tuned to one of the morning news programs, but she had it on mostly for the noise.

All of what Sarah had told her she accepted as true. Probably true, anyway. But except for the hazy recollection of the death of a childhood friend, which was already fading, Diana did not know anything about this Circle. She had no memories of it, but for some reason, it all seemed familiar. Like the fleetingly glimpsed recollection of a dream or memories of a book read long ago. *Such a strange sensation,* she thought. Did these things that Sarah told her belong to the huge chunks of time that disappeared from her? They must, else they would not seem so familiar. On one level, the whole idea of the Circle was utterly bizarre. It was something out of a movie. And yet Diana recognized that a part of her was unmoved by the strangeness of it. Some part of her, something at the core of her, had listened to Sarah with a terrible, calm understanding. She should have been surprised. She should have been frightened. But she wasn't.

Like yesterday, she thought. Little fragments of images, like shards of a shattered mirror, whirling around in her mind, each one containing a glimpse of something that had happened to her. Or to the not-her, to one of the others. She had the sense that the pieces were thrown by another's hand, someone hidden just out of sight down a long corridor. Perhaps it was not time to meet that other; the shards were like little introductions. The other made favors of tiny pieces from the missing blocks of time. Diana grabbed for as many as she could reach, assimilating the little puzzle pieces with a mixture of fascination and dread. It was how she had avoided surprise at Sarah's changed hair and how she now knew that one of the others maintained her own hair. How could she have ever imagined that she came by this color naturally? And there were other things she knew now, too.

In spite of the tantalizing glimpses, or perhaps because of them, Diana was painfully aware of how little she really knew. In those spaces where the hours, and sometimes days and months and years, had slipped away, a whole other life—no, lives—had been led. A thought occurred that chilled her: The time she could account for over all the years of her life was less than the missing time. Until today, she would have thought her life complete, just a little spotty from the effects of a faulty memory. She could no longer tell herself that was true. The realization diminished her, making her want to put her back to a corner of the room, sink down to her knees, and rock slowly back and forth. It made her want to lose herself in the rocking, her thoughts gradually becoming indistinguishable from the motion. The room would disappear, along with the troubling thoughts. The rocking would take her to someplace very pleasant—where was it? Was it a garden, with bright green lawns and rows of impossibly tall and fat boxwood bushes where she had run as a child? Safe, warm lawns and a maze of boxwoods dense enough to hide in. A secret place.

Diana shook her head. How did she know such a place? It was a child's memory and it did not belong to her. Still, it was so familiar, and the feeling of safety filled her with longing. She shook her head again. Too easy to become lost in these strange thoughts. There was something important that she needed to think about, and no time now for boxwoods or reflections in the shards of a broken mirror. Sarah had said that the men who broke into the apartment were from the Circle. Some of the other personalities, Sarah said, might still be part of the Circle. But that was wrong, that could not be. That would mean that she herself was somehow still part of this Circle. She could accept the nightmare glimpses from a long-dead childhood. Yes, surely some very strange things had happened back then. But now? Now, she was here. Yes, she lost time. And the time she lost must belong to this other, this Lynn, Sarah called her, who hides out of sight down a long corridor and showers her with pieces of memory. But that was different from this idea of the Circle. The Circle, whatever it was, had died a long time ago. It was something she was certainly no longer a part of.

Diana started so badly at the tapping of the little brass knocker on her door that she spilled hot coffee over her hand.

She recognized the two men immediately. She drew back from the peephole in sudden, terrible fright, one hand clamped over her mouth to stem the scream she felt rising in her throat. She wondered what to do and her eyes fell on the telephone. Before she could move, she heard a familiar noise. It took her a second to place it. It was the sound of a key in the door lock.

The door opened and the two men stepped inside. One man, still in jeans, smiled at her.

"Good," he said. "Let's be very quiet. Get your coat."

The two men led her down the stairs. Diana considered screaming or running.

"Be very quiet," the man said again, as if he could read her thoughts.

The man in jeans opened the back door of a van, while the other opened the driver's door and climbed in. The man in jeans held out his hand to Diana, indicating with a nod that she should enter the back of the van. She briefly considered running again, but the man was too close. She ignored his hand and climbed in.

"Who are you?" she asked, but the man placed an index finger over his lips. He opened a paper bag and withdrew a bandanna. He tied this around her mouth, then tied her hands with rope from the same bag.

"If you keep still, I won't tie your feet," he said.

He removed from the bag something that looked like a black sack made of cloth. Diana snapped back her head as he held open the sack with his hands and brought it close.

"Relax," he said, "it won't hurt."

Then the sack was over her head. She felt his hands on her, gently pushing her back against the carpeted floor of the van. *This time he* will *rape me,* she thought with sudden certainty, but a few seconds later she heard him moving toward the front of the van.

Sarah's morning and early afternoon sessions went well enough, though she knew that much of her attention was distracted lately. She had, in fact, started to refuse to take on new clients. Though it might prove disastrous to her practice, in good conscience she could extend herself no further, at least not until things settled down with Diana.

At five minutes after two, Sarah felt the first stirring of apprehension. Diana was barely late, but Sarah could not suppress a powerful sense of foreboding. By two-fifteen she knew—she couldn't say how she knew, but she knew—that something had happened and Diana would not show. By two-thirty she was making phone calls.

There was no answer at Diana's apartment. Sarah called several of the newspapers Diana had free-lanced for; she left Margie to track down some of the more obscure sources. Finally, because she could think of nothing else, she called Travers at his office. Bill suggested that Sarah go back to Diana's apartment to wait and leave Margie to monitor the office. Sarah was about to hang up when she heard him yell "Wait!"

"Listen," Travers said, "I'll stop by the apartment after I leave here . . . if you can use the company."

"Bill, I appreciate it, but that's asking too much," Sarah said. "You go home."

"No," Bill said. "Besides, you can give me the details on Lynn, and if something's really going on, I'd just as soon be there when she shows up."

"You know it's probably just one of the personalities out on a romp," Sarah said.

"That would be just fine," Bill said. "I'll see you in a little bit."

They drove for hours. Diana was certain that they were far from the city. She felt the speed and heard the noise of an interstate—probably I-64 West, as it was smooth and moderately traveled. Some time later, the van lurched onto a ramp and soon bounced along a much rougher road. Several times the van pulled off and stopped for what seemed like hours at a time. The men only ran the engine of the van when it got very cold. They refused to acknowledge her except to caution against making noise. Diana began to suspect that they were killing time deliberately, slowly closing in on a particular destination but assuring a precise time of arrival.

Diana's need to urinate increased to the point that she could no longer stand it. She asked if she could please be allowed to go to the bathroom. The man in denim—she could distinguish his voice now—told her to shut up. She continued to complain. She heard movement in the front seat and a second later felt something strike her left shoulder.

"There," the man said, and offered no further explanation.

Diana fumbled with her bare hands and discovered that he had thrown some kind of plastic container at her. Was she supposed to use this? By kneeling, with the jug between her knees, she was surprised to find that the object was a woman's urinal. They had anticipated this possibility. With an agility borne of desperation, Diana managed to use the urinal. She snapped its cap in place, and left it sitting in a far corner of the van.

She lay back down on the carpet, and the van drove on and on.

Sarah was on the phone with Margie when someone knocked. Anxiously, she rushed to the door and opened it. Bill Travers stood there with a paper bag in one hand and a pizza box in the other. Sarah nodded at him and stepped aside as he came in. She thought he looked surprised for some reason. Sarah turned her attention back to the telephone.

"Okay, Margie," she said, "you close up the office now, but turn on the answering machine when you go out. I'll check it from here."

She hung up and turned to find the room empty. Then she heard the refrigerator open. Sarah walked to the kitchen doorway and smiled when she saw Travers putting a liter of Coke in the refrigerator. She watched as he turned his attentions to the oven, setting the temperature dial and shoving the box of pizza inside. He closed the oven door and stood up.

"Make yourself at home," she said.

"Of course." He turned and smiled. "You know, Sarah, I think you've been spending too much time on this case. You and Diana are starting to look alike."

Sarah frowned, unsure for a moment what he was talking about. Then she remembered her hair and reached up to touch it self-consciously. That was why he had looked surprised, she realized.

"We have the same hairdresser," Sarah said.

"Lynn?"

Sarah nodded.

"I think I'm beginning to understand how you managed to draw her out," Travers said.

Sarah smiled. "Why don't I tell you about that?"

It was getting colder, and the disappearance of the little light that managed to peek through the bottom of the cloth bag told Diana it was also getting dark. The road had become steadily rougher for the past half hour and now the van crunched slowly across gravel. Occasionally, the entire van shook noisily as it hit a washboard section of the road. Tree branches slapped and scraped against its sides.

The van stopped and someone climbed into the back with her. A pair of hands pulled her up to a sitting position, and the bag was pulled off her head. In the dim light, Diana saw the man in denim, his face inches away from her. She felt something tug at her wrists and glanced down as a hunting knife sliced through her bindings. She rubbed her wrists, feeling the deep impressions that the rope had left.

"Take off your coat," the man said.

Diana unzipped her jacket and wriggled out of it. The man tossed something in her lap.

"Put it on."

At first she thought it was a bed sheet, then realized that it had arms and a hood. A white robe, then. She pulled it on over her head. The man in denim pulled the hood off her head, then slid the black bag back in place. She felt him pull the hood back up. A few minutes later, the back door opened and she was helped out.

Both men guided her, one on either side holding her arms. They were silent. Once when she stumbled, she was caught and prevented from falling.

Diana sensed that she was in a wooded area. The terrain was rough and slightly hilly. The air had the rich smell of leaf mold and evergreens. An occasional breeze stirred tree branches, and dead leaves crunched underfoot.

They walked for perhaps fifteen minutes. A smell of wood smoke grew steadily stronger. Finally, Diana could hear the crackling of burning wood. The air seemed to warm slightly. The two men stopped and released her. Diana heard one of them move to stand behind her, while the footsteps of the other headed off to her left.

She felt a hand pull back the robe's hood, then grasp the top of the bag. A second later, the bag was yanked away. Diana reached up to brush away the hair that had fallen over her eyes but was restrained by the touch of a hand from behind. She shook back her head to clear the hair from her face. From behind, someone fitted the hood back into position.

Diana looked about in amazement. She stood in a large circular clearing. About twenty feet directly in front of her, a small fire blazed cheerily. Opposite her, and with the fire as its rough center, twenty-five or thirty people stood arrayed in a semicircle. They were all dressed in hooded black robes, their faces obscured by the limp fabric. Half a dozen Coleman lanterns hung from ropes tied to tree branches. The lighting was unexpectedly bright, and Diana narrowed her eyes as her pupils struggled to adjust to the sudden change. She turned her head away from the fire, both to minimize the light and to determine what lay at the periphery of her vision. Two hands seized her head from behind and yanked it painfully back to face the fire.

A voice whispered, "Do not move and do not say a word."

Diana had a sudden sense of movement on either side of her. Keeping her head perfectly still, she strained to shift her eyes to the right. More figures in black emerged soundlessly from the woods. She shifted her eyes to the left and saw still more people. They stepped into a line, shoulder to shoulder. Diana realized that they were forming another half-circle, with her as its center. Several more people emerged from the darkness and merged with the line of people on the other side, now forming one large circle. There were at least seventy-five individuals there, all in black hooded robes.

Directly opposite her, the circle parted. Coming from the woods was another knot of robed figures. They carried something on their shoulders. Diana almost shouted as she realized that it was a cross and that lashed to it was a woman, naked except for a black cloth bag covering her head. She was lashed with her head on the end nearest Diana, eclipsing the rest of the figure. Oddly, her head seemed to be on the long end of the cross. Diana, though badly frightened, breathed a sigh of relief. For a moment, she thought she had been brought here to witness a crucifixion. With the head oriented in the opposite direction, that was unlikely now.

Diana noticed for the first time that a narrow hole had been dug on the opposite side of the fire. It was to this hole that the head of the procession now marched. Confused, Diana could not determine the relationship between the hole and the inverted cross structure. Her eyes widened in sudden realization as the three lead men knelt on the ground, tipping their end of the timber into the hole. The men in back continued to walk forward. The object lifted off their shoulders and for a moment stuck in the earth at a crazy angle. The bearers then lifted the central post, tipping it further into the hole. The whole affair shifted upright. Easily ten feet of the central post slipped into the hole. When they were finished, Diana saw that the woman had been lashed to the timbers, which had been fitted to form a huge crucifix. She was upside down, her head perhaps six feet from the ground. The woman's flesh appeared oiled. It gleamed in the firelight.

The men finished shifting the cross to an upright position. They stepped back and were absorbed into the circle, suddenly indistinguishable from the figures around them. Someone else stepped forward. Diana thought it was probably a woman, though the shapeless robes made it difficult to tell. She untied a rope from around the hood of the crucified woman, then slipped the hood off and threw it into the fire.

Diana's eyes followed the sack into the flames and watched as it quickly caught. Then her eyes shifted back to the woman on the cross. Long black hair spilled down toward the ground. The woman's eyes darted wildly from side to side. Then suddenly she was staring straight ahead, directly through the flames at Diana. Her eyes seemed to cloud over, the eyelids fluttered and half closed. Diana wondered if the woman had been drugged.

A figure stepped forward from the circle. It was a man. Diana could see his beard within the shadows of the hood. He stepped between the crucified woman and the fire. His arms were folded, and he walked with the stoop and slow meditative air of a penitent. When he stopped, he faced Diana.

In the next instant, he threw his arms wide. His head snapped back, freed of the hood, the face upturned to the night sky. He seemed to reach for something overhead. Then Diana noticed a flash of silver light in the man's hand. He held a knife. Its long, double-edged blade reflected the firelight. In a rich, resonant voice, he shouted.

In unison, the circle chanted back, "Baphonim ondromanth."

The man shouted again.

"Baphonim rofocale," the circle roared.

Then all were silent for a moment. Even the rustle of the wind and the crackling of the fire seemed to die away. The man folded his arms again, the knife disappearing in the folds of his robe. He turned slowly to face the woman on the cross, then raised his arms and threw back his head again.

"Baphonim, baphonim, baphonim," the circle shouted as his arms reached their zenith.

He stepped aside, revealing to Diana the wide, terrified eyes of the crucified woman. Then the man began to lower his arms, the knife moving downward in a long, slow arc.

Sarah related to Travers some of the details she had not had time to mention over the phone the previous day. She thought that, in spite of himself, he was starting to look interested.

"See, the real beauty is how it all comes together," she said. "Once the education is complete, once a career has been established and the individual is part of a real-world community, all the alters are integrated under the cult-submissive personality. She immediately has access to all the rituals. She knows how to get along in the real world. She has a career. And she is completely dominated by the cult at that point. Hell, she *is* the cult. She starts the cycle all over again with a new generation."

"And you think they're going to integrate Diana soon?"

"I don't know when," Sarah said. "I doubt Lynn

does. It might be soon, it might be ten years from now. That's not the point."

"I'll bite," Travers said glumly. "What's the point?"

"The point is, they'll certainly take measures to prevent her from integrating prematurely. Or from spilling too many trade secrets to psychotherapists. They want to protect their investment."

"Not to mention their asses," Travers said. "How detailed is Lynn about all this stuff? Seems there ought to be a way to track some of this down. Can she describe the man who killed Indra? Or the people participating in the ritual when the original Diana was killed?"

"I don't know. I'm sure she can remember what those people looked like, but so what? You think your friends in the police department are going to be interested in tracking down the twenty-year-old murder of a child who probably never had a birth certificate or a social security number?"

"Damnit, Sarah, even if I believed you, what the hell can I do?" Travers stopped his pacing long enough to look at Sarah angrily. "A little evidence would go a long way."

"Right now, I'm not interested in evidence or proof or anything else except protecting my client," Sarah said. "Doesn't that come first?"

"Yes, of course it does." Travers walked over to the couch and sat down next to Sarah. "I'm sorry. I don't mean to be a cynic. For one thing, a little evidence would help me get some protection. It would be nice to have something to get the police at least interested."

"Not to mention reassuring your own doubts about what's going on," Sarah said.

"Yeah, that too," Travers said unhappily.

* * *

And the knife came down, a long, slow silver arc that intersected with the outstretched neck of the woman on the cross. A thick line of red appeared where the knife touched the neck and welled for a split second before flowing. Then, on the woman's heart-beat, a crimson stream jetted from the wound, lost on the frozen ground behind the bonfire blocking Diana's sight.

Diana turned her head, but two strong hands yanked it painfully back into place.

"Watch it," the voice instructed. "Do not turn away. Do not close your eyes."

The woman's eyes were open now. *Could she still be alive?* Diana wondered. The eyes stared straight at her, wide with fear, the dark irises reflecting the firelight. Her skin looked white, so pale in contrast to the rich black of her hair and, now, the scarlet river at her throat. The eyes fixed on Diana, who thought, *She's dead now; her life has fled.*

Then the eyes blinked and Diana screamed. Unable to turn away, Diana met the woman's stare. In a few seconds, the eyes clouded over. In the seconds between that unexpected blink and this moment when the eyes had seemed to change, Diana had watched the woman die. Blood seeped down over the pallid mask of the woman's face and mingled in her hair. Diana began to shake involuntarily.

Another voice was speaking now, one that Diana did not recognize. In her panic, Diana did not listen to the words at first. It was only when she ceased her struggle against the anvil grip of the man behind her that she started to pay attention. The man was saying the same phrase over and over, as if he wanted to make absolutely sure she heard.

"That is what happens to the friends of defectors," the voice rasped. "This is what happens . . ."

* * *

Sarah tried to read a novel while Bill snored softly in an armchair. It was past two o'clock in the morning. Sarah hoped for cancellations in the morning. She wouldn't be worth much at work.

Sarah heard a noise in the stairwell. She set the paperback on the coffee table. It sounded like someone had come in from outside. Yes, now she could hear footsteps on the stairs. Sarah listened carefully and without much hope, having repeated this ritual half a dozen times in the last two hours as she monitored the comings and goings of the apartment residents.

The footsteps stopped out on the landing. Still, there were doors to two other apartments there. Sarah heard the jangling of keys, then they were rattling in the lock.

Sarah jumped off the couch as Travers's eyes snapped open in a comical, disoriented look. She pulled the door as Diana pushed on it, almost causing her to stumble across the threshold.

"My God," Sarah said, and rushed to put her arms around Diana. "Where have you been? We've been so worried."

Diana stood stiffly in Sarah's embrace, then pushed her away. "What the hell is *he* doing here?" she demanded.

"He came to help me wait for you," Sarah said, shocked at Diana's reaction. "You've had us worried sick. I thought you'd be glad to see us."

"Well, you're wrong," Diana shouted, "and you can both get the hell out of my place. Now."

"Diana, I can't just leave," Sarah protested gently. "You don't really want me to pack and leave now, do you? It's almost two-thirty." Sarah reached out to lay her hand on Diana's shoulder. "It's all right, whatever happened, it's all right."

"Nothing happened, okay?" Diana shouted. "One of your buddies went out on a toot. What's her name? Lynn? The one you like so much. Probably her."

Sarah stood staring. Diana returned the stare. Sarah

was certain that Diana was close to tears, that she was masking something. But what? Why this strange behavior?

"Please leave," Diana said, then added in a gentler tone, "please. Just leave."

Sarah turned and disappeared down the hallway. Diana walked into the kitchen. Travers stood in the middle of the living room, sleepily fumbling for a cigarette.

Diana refused to see them out.

"I'll see you," Sarah said from the doorway. "Call me if you need anything. Please."

Diana kept her back turned until they had left. Then she walked slowly out to the living room and sat down on the couch. She still had not taken off her coat. She began to shake uncontrollably. She held the coat tightly around her, seeking additional heat in the already-warm apartment. Then she began crying, heaving against the long, desolate sobs.

Sarah and Bill stood outside, gaping bleakly at one another. Bill held a cigarette cupped against the chill wind.

"What the hell happened?" he asked.

"I don't know," Sarah said, "but I sure as hell don't want to leave her like that."

"You don't have any choice right now, Sarah," he said.

"Ah, hell." Sarah stamped her feet on the sidewalk.

"Go home, Sarah," Travers said. "We'll sort it out in the morning."

"Damn," said Sarah. If Mark was back at home, now was not the time to confront him. "Bill, can I sleep on your couch tonight?"

"Why not?" Travers said.

Chapter 24

Week 18: Wednesday, November 29

Sarah went through the day with that peculiar grainy sensation behind the eyelids that accompanies lack of sleep. Several times she tried to call Diana, but each time the answering machine cut in. Sarah left messages.

At four-thirty, Sarah put her files away, pushed her chair back, and propped her feet up. She leaned back, rubbed her burning eyes, and stretched. *What to do now?* she wondered. She hated the thought of another night at Bill's place. She was sure Jenny or even Margie would put her up, but that would be imposing. Besides, she was tired of sleeping in other people's beds. It was time to go home. She locked up and headed for her car.

When she reached home, the Volvo was in the driveway. Sarah wearily trudged to the back deck, fitted her key in the door, and took a deep breath. *Here goes,* she thought, and stepped in.

The kitchen was relatively neat. A few dirty dishes cluttered the sink and counter, but they looked like the products of recent cooking. Yes, the big soup pot was on the stove. Mark was cooking. And he'd obviously been cleaning up after himself. Either that or eating out a lot. *Well, well . . .*

"I'm home," Sarah called.

She heard footsteps coming up the hallway. Then Mark was standing in the doorway. *He looks nervous,* Sarah thought.

"Welcome home," Mark said.

Sarah followed the path of his eyes down to the case in her hand.

"Are you home for good?" he asked.

"Home for now, anyway," Sarah said.

"Why don't you put your things away. Dinner'll be ready in about half an hour. Can I fix you a drink?"

"That would be very nice," Sarah said.

The house looked more than neat and undisturbed. It actually looked as if it had been cleaned. *Penance?* Sarah wondered.

Sarah put her bag away after dumping the contents into the hamper. She returned to the living room, where Mark appeared briefly, handed her a drink, then disappeared into the kitchen. Sarah sat on the couch listening to some unfamiliar music Mark had playing on the stereo. She sipped her drink, feeling oddly like a stranger in her own home. Mark returned a few minutes later and sat in the old armchair.

"How's bean soup sound?" he asked.

"Bean soup sounds grand."

"Good."

"You must have been cooking all day."

"I worked at home today. Put the pot on this morning."

"Oh," Sarah said. "Good."

Conversation stopped, the silence stretching on and on. Sarah fought the impulse to begin talking, to release the flood of emotions roiling within her. The ball was in Mark's court, and for once she felt that she couldn't initiate. He had said he needed time, that he'd talk when he was ready. *Please,* Sarah thought, *please open up.*

"Sarah," Mark said tentatively, his eyes shifting

from looking directly at her to examining the drink he held in his hands, "you look terribly tired. We need to talk. I *want* to talk."

Thank God, Sarah thought.

"Let's have dinner," Mark continued. "Then, if you feel like it, we can talk then. If you're too tired, we can wait. But I want you to know that I'm here and I want to work things out."

"That sounds wonderful," Sarah said. "You're right about me being tired. I'm bloody exhausted. I was up late last night waiting for a client to . . ." Sarah paused, wondering how to explain the situation quickly. Mark probably wouldn't be interested, anyway. But it turned out that Mark was very interested. Sarah gave him a quick sketch while he tended to the meal. Mark asked questions and Sarah talked some more. She knew he was just being polite, that his interest was one way of apologizing. Still, she liked it.

When she had finished eating, Sarah found that she could barely keep her eyes open. Mark insisted that she go to bed.

"But, Mark," she protested, "I want to talk."

"I want to talk, too, but you're exhausted. There'll be time enough tomorrow."

Sarah let him tuck her in. As she closed her eyes, she thought, *Maybe we'll work it out. Maybe it'll be all right.*

She heard Mark's voice from a distance.

"By the way, I like your hair," Mark said. "It looks nice."

Sarah mumbled sleepily, "Oh yeah, I'd forgotten. Thanks." Then she was fast asleep.

Week 18: Thursday, November 30

Sarah attempted to call Diana as soon as she reached the office. She was surprised when, instead of the answering machine, Diana sleepily said, "Hello."

"Diana, this is Sarah."

"I don't want to talk to you."

"Don't hang up," Sarah pleaded. "Whatever happened, we can deal with it. Please."

"Nothing happened," Diana said. "And I'm sorry I had to kick you out in the middle of the night, but I needed some space."

"Diana, that's all right," Sarah said. "Just don't shut me out now. Will I see you today?"

"I don't think that's necessary anymore," Diana said. "Thanks for everything, but it's time I got on with my life. Goodbye, Sarah."

"Wait. Diana," Sarah said, but the receiver was filled with the hollow buzz of the dial tone. She dialed the number again. This time the answering machine kicked in. Sarah mouthed the familiar words of the recorded message.

Shortly after two-thirty, Margie buzzed Sarah.

"Bill Travers on one," she said.

"Hi, Bill," Sarah said.

"Any sign of her?"

"No. I talked to her briefly this morning. I think she answered before she had time to think about it."

"And?"

"And I don't think she wants to see me anymore."

"Isn't she supposed to have her session with you now?" he asked.

"Yes. She's not coming, Bill," Sarah said.

"She turned off her answering machine about an hour ago."

"You've been calling, too?"

"Uh-huh. Sarah, you've got to do something."

"Like what?"

"I don't know. Go over there. Talk to her. Something."

"Actually, I *was* thinking about driving over there."

"Do it," Travers said. "You think I ought to come by? I'll be glad to."

"Bill, I appreciate your concern, but why are you so interested all of a sudden?"

Travers sighed heavily into the phone. "Like it or not, I'm a part of this. I'm worried about you and I'm worried about Diana. The woman we saw the other night was seriously disturbed. She needs help."

"Yes, you're right." Sarah said. "If anything happens, I'll let you know."

If she really doesn't want to see me again, Sarah thought on the drive over, *there's not much I can think of to say that will convince her otherwise.* She slammed on the brakes, having nearly missed the change of a traffic light from yellow to red. *They did something to her. They must have. But what?*

Sarah parked the car in the apartment complex parking lot. *What could they have done to make her react this way?* Sarah wondered. *Brainwashing of some kind, perhaps hypnosis or drugs?* But Diana hadn't acted drugged or confused. Scared, maybe. Had she been threatened? Diana was not really the assertive type, but last night she'd acted like somebody who'd made her mind up once and for all.

She knocked on the door, then stepped back so she would be clearly visible from the peephole. Sarah listened carefully for the sound of movement. She thought she heard something.

"Diana, let me in," she said, then rapped on the door again. "I know you're in there," she added with false certainty.

She waited a few seconds and knocked again. *Maybe she's not home. Wait, what's that?* She clearly heard something on the other side of the door.

"Go away." The voice sounded hoarse.

"Diana, open the door," Sarah said. "Please."

"No," Diana said, "I don't want you here. Please leave."

What could they have done? How can they control her like this? And then the thought of how the Circle could so easily manipulate Diana gave Sarah an idea. She immediately rejected it on ethical grounds, but in the next instant Sarah sensed that she had little time in which to act. *Sometimes you have to betray a trust to protect the object of the betrayal.*

Sarah clapped her hands three times, remembering the posthypnotic suggestion for trance induction she had established with Diana so long ago.

"Sleep," she said. "You are in a deep state of relaxation." Sarah stepped close to the door, suddenly conscious of the sound of her voice echoing in the stairwell. "When I count to three, you will unlock the door and open it." She repeated the command.

"One. Two. Three."

At first, Sarah could hear nothing. Then she heard the scratch of metal on the door as Diana slid the chain off its track. The door opened. Sarah stepped inside, closing the door behind her. She breathed a sigh of relief.

Diana had the characteristic expression of the hypnosis subject, her mouth slack and her eyes unfocused. But Sarah could tell that she had been crying. Her face was red and blotchy, the skin around her red-rimmed eyes swollen.

"Please sit on the couch, Diana," Sarah said. She eased off her coat and hung it on the rack by the door. Sarah watched Diana sleepily navigate the living room to the couch. She used the few moments to collect her thoughts. *What now? Awaken her? I should. And yet . . .*

"I want you to close your eyes, Diana. Good. I am going to count backward from five to one. As I count, you will slip into a deeper state of relaxation. You will be able to feel yourself falling deeper and deeper into sleep. Here we go. Five. Four. Three. Two. One."

Diana slumped back farther into the couch, all her muscles now relaxed. Sarah sat next to her.

"Diana, I want you to tell me what happened to you two days ago. I want you to think back. It is seven-thirty Tuesday morning, November 28. Sarah has just left for the office. What are you doing?"

The words came slowly but were clear. "I am drinking coffee . . ."

Sarah stood and stretched. She felt her muscles protest, having grown stiff over the last forty-five minutes of interrogating Diana. The term *interrogating* had occurred to Sarah more than once during the session. She certainly could not call what she had done *therapy*.

"When I count to five, you will awake feeling relaxed and refreshed," Sarah said.

Diana's eyes fluttered open. She stretched and smiled for a moment, then her smile faded and she sat upright.

Sarah held up a hand. "Diana, you have every right to be mad at me. If you want me to leave, I will. I tricked you. I hypnotized you and got you to open the door."

"Then you know."

"Yes. We're not going to let them get away with it."

Diana stared at Sarah a moment before answering. "Why not?" she asked.

"Because that's too easy. I'm in this thing by my own choice. You have to understand that. I am doing what I want to do and that is not your responsibility. If you want to kick me out of your apartment, or out of your life, for that matter . . . well, all right. But nobody else can do it but you. Otherwise, I'm just going to keep turning up and being obnoxious."

"I don't know what I'd do if they hurt you, Sarah."

"I'm not going to let them hurt either of us. I've

got to go home and I'm not about to leave you here alone. First, I'm calling Mark. Then you're coming home with me."

Mark was chopping onions for chili, though his progress was slow. In the midst of chopping, he would suddenly stop, his face slack and his eyes blank as he stared out the kitchen window. *What had been happening to him over the last several weeks?* he wondered. His marriage seemed to have nearly disintegrated in that time. As for himself, he seemed to have lost control of some of the most basic qualities of his essential self. He could never before have imagined having an affair. It was unthinkable, and yet it had happened. Had he really changed so much? Had so much changed between himself and Sarah? And that Sarah had had an affair—okay, in all *likelihood* had had an affair—seemed equally incomprehensible.

Was Sarah still interested in saving the marriage?

I don't know, Mark thought. *What does it mean when a married woman leaves home, changes her hair to blonde, and comes back looking as if she hasn't slept in a week? It can't be good, right?*

What does it mean when the husband picks up strange women in bars and beds them down in sleazy motel rooms. That ain't good either, hoss. And do I tell Sarah about it? Would I be confessing to ease my own conscience or because I want there to be no secrets between us? Do I really want her to admit that she's been having an affair? Do I want to know with whom? Christ, I might kill the son of a bitch if I knew who he was.

Could they really get back together at this late date?

I mean to try, Mark thought. *God help me, I mean to try.* And what about this client Sarah was bringing home? The tale she'd related in bits and pieces the evening before worried him. Did Sarah know what she was doing? The whole thing sounded so improbable. And yet, if there were any truth to it, Sarah might be in serious danger.

Having a stranger in the house wasn't going to make it any easier to work things out between them. *I'm not going to be resentful of Sarah's professional life,* Mark thought. *I did that before without even realizing it, and I'm not going to do it anymore. I'll support her in this as much as I can.*

A half hour later, Mark heard Sarah's car in the driveway. After a few moments, the back door of the kitchen opened and an attractive blonde stepped in, with Sarah following behind. Mark called out a greeting. There was something familiar about the blonde. She reminded him of somebody.

Suddenly, he realized.

Marcia. The woman was a dead-ringer for Marcia.

"Hi," the woman who looked like Marcia said.

Jesus, it *was* Marcia. Marcia with her hair blond instead of red *(wait, Marcia wouldn't let me touch her hair, remember—why?—afraid her wig would come off?),* also something different about her voice and eyes. But damnit, it was Marcia.

"Mark, what's the matter?" Sarah asked. "You look like you've seen a ghost."

He was suddenly aware that he must look like an idiot. "Hi, I'm Mark," he said, extending his hand. He felt sick. *God, it can't be Marcia,* he thought, *but it is.*

"Diana Smith," the woman smiled, giving no sign of recognition.

"Plenty for one more for dinner, right?" Sarah asked.

"Sure, plenty," Mark said. "Sarah, can I talk to you a minute?"

"Let me make a phone call first. Why don't you put Diana's things out of the way and fix us all a drink?" Sarah vanished into the living room, leaving Mark staring at Marcia. Or Diana. Or whoever she was.

He picked up the little suitcase Sarah had carried in. "If you'll give me your coat, I'll be right back."

Diana handed him her coat and Mark gratefully disappeared into the front foyer. He wondered if he should leave now, using some client's computer problem as an excuse. No, he wouldn't run out now. No more running.

Mark returned to the kitchen reluctantly. "Have we met before?" he asked as coolly as he could.

"I don't think so," Diana said. "I have a good memory for faces. I would remember."

"Damn, man, do you ever go home?" Travers said into the phone.

"This *is* home," John Fisher replied. "Saves a fortune in rent. What's up? Haven't seen you around for a while. How's the ghost-busting business?"

"Brisk," said Travers. "And highly lucrative, too. You'll have to see my new Jag."

"Right," Fisher laughed. "Sounds like police work."

"I'm sure," Travers said. "John, I need you to do something for me."

"Shoot."

"This is going to sound weird."

"Coming from you? I doubt that."

"Very funny," Travers replied. "I have some very unreliable information that there may have been a murder of a young woman with long black hair somewhere within . . . say . . . a two-hundred-mile radius."

"Uh-huh. Sure. You want to hold while I check that out? Shouldn't take more than five or six minutes. Let me make sure I got it. . . . Young woman, right? We talking twelve, thirteen? Or twenty-five, thirty?"

"Twenties, say."

"Twenties. Okay. Black hair, was it?"

"Black hair, right."

"Mm-hmm. And two-hundred-mile radius, right?"

"Right."

"Well, that seems specific enough. More than enough information, of course. But just in case I find two or three, you wouldn't happen to have anything else, would you?"

"Well, of course," Travers said.

"Of course," mumbled Fisher.

"Her throat's slit, she was probably killed in the woods, and she could be naked."

"Hey, great, that should narrow it down," Fisher sighed. "Seriously, Bill, you wanna tell me what this is all about?"

"Probably nothing, John. But if you hear anything that seems even remotely a match, would you let me know?"

"I'll keep my ears open."

It was after eleven by the time Sarah and Mark made up the spare room and saw that their guest was attended to. Mark returned from the bathroom and found Sarah dozing on the bed on top of the covers with her clothes still on. For a moment, he considered undressing her and letting her sleep in peace. Conflicting emotions warred within him. On the one hand, the chance to defer this confrontation until another day seemed a blessed relief. He had wanted to tell her earlier, but they just hadn't had a moment alone.

The opportunity to talk to Sarah had passed. Now they were both tired. They both needed rest. If they weren't thinking too clearly, they might say things they would later regret. They might misunderstand the phrasings of the other.

But . . .

But somewhere inside him, Mark knew that he had one shot to get it right. Somehow, he felt that if he didn't clear the whole mess up now, he would never clear it up. The opportunities to defer discussion would come more and more easily. There would never be a good time. And the words left unsaid would drive a wedge between them. Until these recent months, he had never held a thing back from Sarah. Nothing. There had been no secrets left in his soul, save those he kept from himself. Mark knew that this was the real basis of his relationship with Sarah. Without it, their lives together would become twisted and unhappy. He wasn't sure what was going to happen when they told their respective secrets, but the other course was clear. And unacceptable.

Now or never.

Mark breathed deeply, sat down on the edge of the bed, and shook Sarah awake.

"Honey, wake up," he said.

"What?" Sarah asked sleepily. She rubbed her eyes and looked about in momentary confusion. "I fell asleep?"

"Yeah," Mark said. "Come on. Get up. We need to talk."

"Now?" she asked, her eyes squinting against the light of the bedside lamp. "Come on, Mark, I'm tired."

"I know you're tired, honey, but this can't wait. Go to the bathroom, wash your face, and I'll fix us a cup of coffee."

"Coffee? At eleven-thirty?"

"Trust me," Mark said, "we'll need it."

Ten minutes later, they were both huddled over steaming cups of coffee at the table in the kitchen.

"Okay, Mark," Sarah said, "you gonna tell me what this is all about?"

"Sarah," Mark said, "I love you. I have always loved you and I always will love you. And the last thing in the world I want to do is hurt you."

Sarah looked at Mark with a blank stare.

Mark continued, "I did something I'm not very proud of. If I was smart, I'd probably keep my mouth shut about it, but we've never had any secrets between us. Besides, I think you need to know for professional reasons, too."

"You had an affair?" Sarah asked simply, in even tones. She clenched her teeth in anticipation of the answer.

Mark nodded. "Yes. I had an affair."

"You son of a bitch," Sarah said, her voice again sounding strangely calm to herself.

"It was a onetime thing. It just happened. It didn't mean anything."

"Why did you have to tell me?" Sarah asked. "You selfish S.O.B. Why couldn't you just keep it to yourself?"

"Because I knew it would destroy us eventually. I don't know why, but it would."

"When?"

"Does it matter?"

"When?"

"Thanksgiving."

Sarah laughed bitterly. "I can't believe it." She shook her head.

"Don't act so high and mighty," Mark said.

"What do you mean by that?"

"I mean, it's not like *you* haven't had any action on the side, now, is it?"

"What are you talking about?" Sarah exploded. "You've been thinking with your prick too long, Mark. You can't think straight anymore."

"Who was the guy you were with in that café downtown? Oh, what's the name?"

Sarah frowned, perplexed. *Café,* she thought. *What?* Then she remembered her lunch with Travers. "Johnny's?" she asked.

"Yeah, that's it," Mark said. "Who was *that* guy?"

"That guy is an anthropologist named Bill Travers. If you think a minute, you may remember me telling you about him. He's an expert on the occult. I consulted with him on Diana's case. In fact, I *continue* to consult with him."

Mark stared blankly for a few long moments. "You mean . . ." he managed at last. "You mean you aren't having an affair with him?"

"What, are you nuts? Of course I'm not having an affair with him," Sarah laughed bitterly. "My God. You saw us together and rather than say anything, you just assumed we were having an affair? Goddamnit, Mark!"

"Look, I saw you by accident. I was going to introduce myself and I saw him put his arm around you. I just about went crazy, Sarah."

"Oh, Mark, you damn fool."

"Well, it's not like everything was going well at home. It just all seemed to make sense. There you were with this guy's arm around you. You'd been coming home late every night. We'd practically stopped having sex . . ."

"And you're gonna blame that on me? Yes, I was working late. So were you. You just didn't like it when I worked late and you didn't. Well, to hell with your double standards, mister. And if we weren't having sex, it wasn't because *I* wasn't willing." Sarah stopped a second. "God, listen to us. This is absurd."

"It is, isn't it?"

"Yes, it is. Mark, I can't forgive you for what you did. I'm willing to take my share of responsibility for being busy and working late. But only if you're willing to acknowledge that you have an equal share in it."

Mark nodded.

Sarah opened her mouth, closed it, then opened it again. Her eyes narrowed. "You know, I still can't believe you're telling me all this. What is it about men that seeks confession?" She shook her head.

"There's more to it than that. I thought you needed to know because of Diana."

"Because of Diana? What the hell are you talking about now?"

"Because," Mark said, "the one-night stand was with her."

He expected an explosion, or tears, or even fists. Instead, Sarah grew visibly pale. She rested her forehead in her hands, rubbing her eyes.

"Oh, my God," she said.

Mark waited silently. Sarah finally lifted her head.

"What did she look like? How did she act?" Sarah asked.

"What?"

"Look, Mark," Sarah said, "there's a lot more going on here than you realize. You didn't have sex with Diana. You had sex with one of the other personalities that shares Diana's body. And—not that it relieves you of one iota of responsibility—you may have even been set up."

"Set up? Why?"

"To get at me," Sarah said. "They couldn't have known you'd tell me about it, I guess, but maybe they figured it would drive a wedge between us. Sure, troubles at home, less time to concentrate on therapy issues," she said more in explanation to herself than to Mark. "Or maybe they figured you *would* tell me, the male ego being what it is. I wonder if they wanted me to know it was Diana? They must have figured you'd meet her eventually. Did they think I'd resent her? Or maybe they were going to let Diana know what happened and try to play it from both ends?"

"I don't understand," Mark said. "They who?" Crazily, Sarah's comments had made him think of Beiderbeck. Beiderbeck, who had encouraged the affair in the first place. Beiderbeck who had said a few days ago, "Take your wife on a vacation; work's not that important. If you feel guilty, tell her," he had said. "Clear the air."

But that's crazy, Mark thought, and pushed Beiderbeck from his mind.

"I'll give you the full explanation later. Right now, it's important that you answer my questions. First, did she look just like Diana or did you notice any differences?"

"Well, she had red hair, for one thing. A wig, I'm pretty sure. And she was different somehow. Her eyes, the way she carried herself. Her voice, too. I recognized the voice when Diana spoke tonight, but there was still something different about it."

"What?"

"More precise, I think," Mark said. "Marcia almost clipped her words when she spoke. No drawl at all."

"Anything else?"

"No, not really. Except that I think you're right. This Diana is not really the same person. It's very subtle, but she's different."

"I understand. I've been dealing with this longer than you have. I think the woman you cheated with is actually named Nora. She picked you up, too, buddy."

"No, she didn't."

"Yes, she did," Sarah said. "I'd bet money that she had it all planned out before you ever saw her. Look, this is all I can deal with for one night. I'm going to bed."

"But none of this makes any sense. Aren't you going to tell me what—"

"Not tonight," Sarah said, rising. "You'll have to wait for explanations. Why not?" she added. "I have."

Tentatively, Mark asked, "You want me to sleep out here on the couch?"

"No," Sarah said, "we've got a houseguest. Come to bed, where I can hit you if I feel like it."

Chapter 25

Week 18: Friday, December 1

The phone rang just as Bill Travers's hand touched the doorknob. He picked it up before it could ring a second time.

"What, are you standing on top of the phone? Did it actually ring?"

"John? Is that you?"

"You bet it's me, old buddy," John Fisher said. "Now talk to me. Where did you get the information you told me about last night?"

"Why? You got something?"

"Yeah, I got something."

"What?"

"You first," Fisher said. "I need to know your source. This is serious."

"I can't tell you right now," Travers said. "You wouldn't believe it, anyway."

"I gotta know."

"Look, I'll tell you what. I've got a meeting with my informant in a few minutes. You tell me what you found out, and I'll meet you for a beer at Johnny's. Say five. Okay?"

"Oh, all right," Fisher said. "Damn, you're argumentative. Anyway, a hunter out in Nottingham County came across a handful of bloody black hair late yesterday. It just came over the terminal a little while ago. No body, but evidence of a large gathering.''

"Goddamn," Travers whistled. "Where did you say this was?"

"Nottingham County. A remote section of the national forest," Fisher said. "Any of this making sense to you?"

"Yeah," Travers whispered, "I think they just screwed up."

"Nice place," Travers said after Sarah had introduced him to Margie and seated him in her office. He slurped coffee from a mug Sarah had fixed for him. "Now, tell me what you know. We've got the police going apeshit, and I've got to figure out what to tell them by five o'clock."

"Did I miss something?" Sarah asked. "Are you saying they found something?"

"Sorry, Sarah." Travers set his mug on a corner of the desk. "Guess I'm getting ahead of myself. I asked my friend to watch out for homicide reports matching the description you gave me."

"And?"

"And some hunter found a hank of black hair—bloody hair—somewhere on Nottingham County parkland. There's evidence of a large gathering, and that's about it. No body. Just hair and blood."

"Human hair and blood?"

"So I gather."

"And the police want to know why you asked them to look out for similar evidence?"

"My friend does, anyway," Travers said. "I don't think he'll mention this to anyone till he talks to me—unless he got caught asking the same questions."

"So what are you going to tell him?"

"I don't know. Depends on what you found out from Diana, I guess. I suppose the worst that can happen is

I tell Fisher the truth. Then he'll just write me off as completely nuts."

"I'd prefer we keep Diana out of it if we can," Sarah said.

"Why?" Travers asked. "I mean, ordinarily I'd agree with you. But if she's in danger, we might be able to get some help from the cops."

Sarah paused before answering. She discovered that she had been chewing on her lower lip. "Well, I suppose that's a consideration," she said. "I just don't want to put her through a police interrogation. I know what happens when people with mental health backgrounds seek legal recourse. They get smeared. And God help them if they end up on a witness stand under cross-examination."

"Fisher's different. If we can deal with just him, we'll be all right. It all depends on what she saw." Travers's eyes glittered with intensity. "So what did she see?"

"Little enough," Sarah said. "She was abducted by two men, forced into a van, tied, and blindfolded."

"Could she recognize the men again if she saw them?"

"I should think so. They're the same ones who forced their way into the apartment and painted her."

"Jesus," Bill nodded. "Okay, go on."

"They drove her around for half the day, led her through the woods, and forced her to watch while some guy in a robe cut the throat of a woman tied upside down to a cross."

Travers passed his tongue over lips gone suddenly dry. "Damn," he said hoarsely. "How many people were there?"

"A lot. Enough to form a circle in a clearing maybe forty feet across."

"A circle, huh?"

"Right," Sarah said. "*The* Circle."

"But why? Why drag her off to witness an execution?"

"It was an object lesson," Sarah said. "Somebody standing behind her forced her to look while the girl's throat was cut. Diana said he kept repeating, 'This is what happens to the friends of defectors.' "

"Christ on a crutch," Bill slapped his hand on Sarah's desk. "Did she see anybody else's face? What about this guy that did the knifing?"

Sarah nodded. "Yeah, she got a good look at him. Nobody else. From her description, though, I'd wager the guy was in disguise—fake beard, wig, that sort of thing."

"I still don't get it. They must have known it wouldn't work. The only reason to risk a move like that would be if they really thought it would keep her quiet."

"I believe they did think it would work. It's just pure dumb luck that, one, I figured out what was going on and, two, some hunter stumbled over corroborating evidence. And even with all that, what do we have? Some bloody hair that probably won't result in much of an investigation and the word of an unreliable witness."

"I hear you," Travers said. "So how *did* you figure out what was going on?"

Sarah told Bill about hypnotizing Diana to open the door to her apartment and the subsequent interrogation.

"Wow," Bill said when she had finished. "I'm impressed. That was quick thinking." He paused. "So what do I tell my friend?"

"You believe Diana now, don't you, Bill?" Sarah asked.

"Yes. I'm sorry it took this kind of evidence, but, yes, I have no doubts now."

"Don't feel bad. In spite of it all, I still wondered sometimes if I wasn't fooling myself. Some kind of weird, perverted wish fulfillment or something. But to answer your question, if you think this guy can be trusted, tell him the truth. Like you say, we may need his help." Sarah held Travers with her eyes. "Listen, Bill, I'm scared."

"I think you should be. Something bizarre is going on here."

"It's more than just that. I think the Circle has a lot tighter handle on what's going on than we realize."

"What do you mean?"

"For starters, how does Diana manage to support herself? Sure, she's a good photographer and apparently she has a good reputation. But she can't have sold much in the last six months."

"You think the Circle *supports* her?"

Sarah nodded. "I also think the Circle knows everything that goes on with her. Well, everything that Nora and any other cult-aware personalities have access to. The good news is that Nora doesn't know everything, so their window on our therapy sessions is limited. But I think the Circle contacts Nora quite frequently. I think they tell Nora what to do and I think she obeys them."

Travers looked blankly at Sarah. "Why do you say that?"

"Because Nora seduced my husband in a bar last week," Sarah said, then added after a moment, "not that she had to work too hard to do it."

Travers's eyes widened. "Wait a minute, Sarah. How the hell do you know something like that? Did Diana tell you?"

"No," said Sarah, "my husband did. I think the reason he told me is because he thought you and I were having an affair."

Travers frowned, opened his mouth to say something, then closed it again. Sarah spoke first.

"It's been quite a week, you know."

"Jesus, Sarah, I'm sorry."

"Yeah," Sarah shrugged. "Anyway, the point is,

Diana's being manipulated by the Circle and hasn't the slightest idea. And so are we."

"Why don't they just take her? If they can pull off this stuff, why don't they just take her?"

"I think she's extremely important to them. She's a chrysalid and when she metamorphoses, Isis becomes a priestess. They've got an investment of many years in her. They're going to do everything they can to keep her on the planned . . . shall we call it a career trajectory?"

"And when do they conclude that that's no longer possible?"

"Very soon, I think. As soon as they figure out that we know what's going on. As soon as they realize that they've lost her."

"What will that take?" Bill asked.

"Integrating her, or at least making all the personalities aware of each other."

"And then what?"

"I guess she becomes expendable. The question then is, do they leave her alone or eliminate the problem?"

"You think they'd kill her?" Bill frowned.

"Maybe. That's probably why the girl on the cross was killed. They got a twofer out of her, you see. They eliminated a problem and gave a warning to Diana all at the same time. Make that a threefer: They also got a killing ritual out of it. All that wonderful death power they seem to believe in."

"So, how do we protect her?"

"I haven't figured that out yet."

"Sarah," Bill said slowly, "at this point you know nearly as much as Diana does. That puts you in danger, too."

"You're in this pretty far yourself, Bill," Sarah smiled grimly. "Been looking in your rearview mirror lately?"

* * *

All the way over to Johnny's, Bill kept glancing involuntarily in his rearview mirror. He felt silly and spooked at the same time, and he muttered a steady stream of curses, unsuccessfully attempting to convince himself of the foolishness of his paranoia. He wondered, too, just how much to tell Fisher. Bill was in Johnny's back room offering a seat to the policeman before he ever reached a conclusion.

"Beer?" Travers asked.

"Betcherass," Fisher replied. "I'm off duty."

Travers signaled to the waitress stacking glasses behind the bar, indicating his order with two fingers.

"So what's new in the wonderful world of law enforcement?"

"What's new," Fisher said, "is that citizens are calling in murder allegations several hours *before* we discover supporting evidence."

The waitress walked over with two draft beers on a dripping tray.

"Thanks, Ann." Travers smiled at the young woman. "Cheers," he said, holding up his mug as the waitress walked away.

"Yeah, cheers," Fisher said glumly, nodding to Travers and drinking a mouthful of the beer. He set his mug down heavily. "So talk to me, old pal of mine."

"Look," said Travers after a pause, "will you keep this between the two of us for a little while? Till we figure out what it all means?"

Fisher looked uncertain. "I don't know if I can. I mean, I don't know what the hell you're talking about. If it makes sense to keep it under wraps, I will. That's the best I can do."

"That's fair enough, I guess," Travers said. "The reason I knew about the murder—"

"Alleged murder," Fisher interrupted.

"Yeah, right." Travers shook his head. "The reason I knew about it is there's a witness."

"What?" Fisher half rose from his seat, leaning forward across the table. The waitress looked up from the bar for a moment, then went back to her chores. "That's going to be pretty hard for me to keep under wraps."

"Just wait a minute." Travers raised a restraining hand. "You haven't heard the whole story yet. I have a feeling you're not really going to want to tell anybody about this."

"Why?"

"Because you value others' opinions of your sanity," Travers grinned.

"I hate it when you smile like that," Fisher said. "It always means you're going to tell me some of that weird shit."

"What can I say?" Bill spread his hands in a gesture of surrender. "It's what I do." He paused, then said quickly, "My witness has multiple personality disorder."

"Oh, damn, I should have seen it coming." Fisher rolled his eyes. "You're telling me this witness is a psycho?"

"No, damnit, she's not crazy," Travers said more loudly than he had intended. "How do I explain this to you? Look, sit back and sip your beer. Let me tell you the whole story."

The men were halfway through their second beers by the time Travers finished an abbreviated account of Diana Smith, multiple personality disorder, and the Circle. He thought that Fisher's eyes looked glazed. The policeman had also started shaking his head slowly, almost imperceptibly.

"Wake up, John," Travers said.

"I always wind up eating a pack of Tums after I talk to you," Fisher sighed.

"You've got to admit that it's pretty hard to dismiss when you got our information *before* you heard the report from Nottingham."

"I been thinkin' about that," Fisher said. "Hair and blood ain't all that hard to come by, you know."

"What do you mean?"

"Not everybody wants to get well, Bill. Some will work pretty hard to stay sick. It's possible, isn't it—mind you, I only say possible—that this lady planted the evidence herself?"

"Why the hell would she do that?" Travers exploded. "You're saying she's *faking* all this? Give me a break, man."

"I'm just saying what any cop is gonna say when he hears this story."

"Hey, you're the one who wanted the explanation. Just tell me this: Why would she go to all that trouble? It was one chance in a million that anybody discovered the hair in the first place."

"How the hell should I know?" Fisher asked. "Maybe she would have *revealed* it in one of those hypnosis sessions. Led you all on a merry chase into the foothills. Why not?"

"Aaaargh," said Travers.

"Listen to me, Bill," Fisher said, lowering his voice and leaning over the small table. "In spite of all this weird shit you specialize in, you've always been pretty levelheaded. I mean, you never jumped to conclusions before. You always looked for the rational explanation. That's all *I'm* doing now."

Travers thought he knew now what Sarah had felt like, listening to his own rationalizations over the past weeks. "But you don't know this woman," he protested. "You haven't listened to her. She's telling the truth."

"Maybe she is," Fisher said. "Maybe she thinks she is. If all this multiple personality stuff is true, maybe one of her other personalities is setting her up. That's possible, isn't it?"

Travers turned his head to look at the back of the bar, at the Friday evening customers who had drifted in since he had arrived. He hated to admit that Fisher was right, because something inside him had shifted over the last few days. Shifted over to being a believer instead of a doubter. But logically he knew that Fisher *could* be right, that what the policeman said was only what anyone else would say after thinking about the situation for a little while. *Even though he's wrong,* Travers thought.

"Yeah, it's possible," Travers finally admitted.

"Look, I'll tell you what," Fisher smiled. "I'll make a few discreet inquiries, maybe call the sheriff's office over in Nottingham."

"Yeah, okay," Bill sighed. "That'd be good. Will you do me one other thing, though?"

"What's that?" Fisher asked. Travers thought he sounded wary.

"Keep in the back of your mind that on a long shot, just maybe the stuff I've been telling you is true. And if I ever call you and say I need help, you come running. I'm not asking for police assistance yet—you've made it pretty clear what the reaction would be—but if I say there's trouble, I want you to suspend your disbelief and personally come running. Will you do that?"

"Yeah," Fisher nodded, "you give the word, I'll be there. On or off duty."

"Thanks," Bill said. "Hope like hell I never call."

Chapter 26

Week 18: Saturday, December 2

Sarah and Diana decided to go out for a while, leaving Mark at home. Sarah drove, and because they had no specific place in mind, they ended up at a large shopping mall on the suburban fringes of the city. They ate lunch, browsed through shops, and finally decided to go see a movie. They ate popcorn, laughed together, and whispered comments about the film. Sarah felt a weight lift from her, feeling for the first time in days free from a vague but suffocating oppression.

After the movie, the two women decided to do a little more shopping before heading home. Sarah felt relaxed and she thought Diana seemed happy. At a time like this, it was hard to believe that the laughing, talkative woman beside her harbored an array of distinct personalities, and that she had spent a life of abuse and terror at the hands of people Sarah felt she could not begin to understand. If she could barely credit their existence, how could she make sense of their motives, their lives? Sarah shook off the odd sensation that she straddled two worlds, one dark and infinitely disturbing, the other light and prosaic and very precious.

The women stood looking through the glass front of a novelty store, watching a plastic flower moving in time to the music of a nearby radio. Diana laughed delightedly and reached to touch Sarah's shoulder in a gesture of easy familiarity. Sarah thought that such a casual gesture was remarkably hard won, a triumph of trust and courage for the woman beside her. She glanced sideways at Diana, saw something out of the corner of her eye, and froze.

She turned her head quickly as a slim figure in worn blue jeans disappeared down a side corridor by a shoe store. Sarah scanned the crowd of shoppers, quickly spotting half a dozen slender men dressed in denim. She shook her head and turned back to find Diana looking up at her.

"You all right, Sarah?" Diana asked.

"I'm fine," Sarah smiled.

They walked again, past a drugstore, a clothing store, and a kiosk where engraving was done. Diana paused outside a bookstore and examined the titles of new books on display. Sarah glanced around surreptitiously. She thought she saw a hurried flash of blue in the crowd of shoppers on the promenade, then there was nothing. She was spooking herself, she thought. The image of one of Diana's abductors, the man in denim, had become lodged in her consciousness and now she imagined him everywhere. It was just imagination. Still, she was glad when they began to head toward the parking lot. She felt even better once they had gotten on the road.

Outside of the city, traffic thinned and the road narrowed. Sarah noticed a slight hesitation in the way the car accelerated. The hesitation grew quickly worse. In a few minutes, the Olds began to shake and buck as the engine lost power, then regained it, then lost it again.

"Now what?" Sarah said. "This is just what we need."

"Have you got gas?"

"Yes, we've got gas all right." Sarah beat her fist on the steering wheel.

She pulled the car off the road. A few seconds later, the engine died.

"What do we do now?" Diana asked.

"There's a station a few miles down the road," Sarah said. "I'll go get help."

"And leave me here alone," Diana choked. "No way."

"All right, we'll both go."

They had walked no more than a quarter of a mile when a gray Mercedes pulled alongside. The electric window rolled down smoothly. Inside were two pleasant-looking middle-aged men. The one on the curbside looked a little overweight and he wore a thin mustache.

"That your car back there?" he asked.

"I'm afraid so," Sarah smiled wearily.

"If you care for a lift, hop in," he said. "We'll be happy to run you down to the next station."

Sarah glanced at Diana, who looked warily at the Mercedes. She looked back at Sarah and nodded.

"Great," Sarah said, "we'd appreciate it."

Sarah opened the back passenger door. Diana climbed in first and Sarah followed. The soft leather of the seat seemed to mold itself around her as Sarah pulled the door closed. Instead of slamming shut, it seemed to whisper.

"Nice car," Sarah said.

"Thank you," the driver turned briefly and smiled, then eased the car back onto the road.

Neither man spoke, and after driving several miles, Sarah saw the sign of a Texaco station peeking out from the broken tree line. *How long will all this take?* she wondered. She was tired, exhausted from walking miles in the mall. She sighed. *Hold on,* she thought, *soon you can have a nice drink in a soft chair.*

But the Mercedes showed no sign of slowing down. Sarah sat forward.

"This is fine up here," she said, and still the Mercedes barreled along at the same steady speed. Neither man showed any sign that she had been heard. In a second it would be too late to make the turn into the station.

"You can let us out right here," she said, her voice rising. "What's wrong with you? Can't you hear me?"

She touched the man in the passenger's seat. He turned swiftly, placed a hand on Sarah's chest, and shoved. Sarah, unhurt but startled and angry, moved to sit up, but the man raised a cautioning hand.

"What the hell is going on here?" she demanded.

The man smiled and said nothing. Instead, he turned around in his seat, his eyes fixed on the road as if this were nothing but a weekend drive in the country.

"Oh, my God," Sarah whispered as she began to understand. She looked over at Diana, whose eyes had gone wide with terror, her skin pale and her breath coming in shallow, ragged gasps. Sarah gently grasped Diana's hand. Diana turned to face her. Diana's head shook from side to side, as if in denial, and her other hand opened and closed in a spasmodic, unconscious gesture of agitation or fear. Sarah tried to smile, but her mouth wouldn't work right; the muscles were clenched too tightly.

"It'll be all right," she whispered, but Diana was facing straight ahead again, her head still shaking with occasional tremors.

"Where are you taking us?" Sarah asked. Her throat was dry, and her voice sounded hoarse and foreign.

"Shut up or I'll gag you," the passenger said.

After several miles, the Mercedes slowed and pulled off onto a dirt road that led into a dense forest of second-growth timber. *Logging trail,* Sarah thought. *Where are they taking us?* The car slowed to a stop, just far enough down the trail to be invisible from the road. The driver turned the engine off and both men turned to face the backseat. The passenger lifted a hand and presented it, palm up, to Diana. Sarah could not see his palm; he held it so that it was shielded from her view. Instead, she watched in fascination at the change in her client.

Diana's expression of wide-eyed fear vanished almost instantly as the man held his hand up. She stopped hyperventilating, her breathing suddenly becoming even and relaxed. Sarah recognized the momentary unfocused look in the eyes as the blank stare that signaled the arrival of another personality. She wondered who the man in the front seat had brought forth.

The lines around Diana's eyes smoothed and she shook her head in an easy, carefree gesture that Sarah did not recognize. Diana—or whoever she was—glanced over at Sarah for just an instant, giving her a sidelong look, and then she smiled. *It was a smug smile,* Sarah thought, *and it belonged to no one she recognized.* The alter might be Nora, but she didn't think so.

"Turn and look out your window," the driver said.

Sarah did not understand. The other man reached over the seat and rudely forced her to turn her body so that she faced away from Diana.

"Tie her," the man said.

Sarah was confused for a moment, thinking this was a command directed at her. Then she felt the rough fibers of a hemp rope around her wrists and her hands were roughly, painfully pulled together. The passenger still held her by the shoulders. And she hadn't heard the driver move.

Diana was tying her.

Before she could reflect on this, the passenger was out of the car. He walked to the back and Sarah heard a key being fitted into the lock of the trunk. Then the driver got out, and in a few seconds both men were helping her out of the car. They walked her to the back where the trunk was raised. *Oh, no,* she thought, *they're not going to . . .*

"No," she screamed, but the driver thrust a wadded

handkerchief into her mouth, then bound her mouth with a bandanna. The two men lifted her easily and laid her in the trunk, almost gently. *Oh, God, no,* she thought, *I won't be able to take this. This is too much. I can't stand this.* But before her thoughts could spiral into uncontrolled panic, Sarah was startled by something elastic wrapping around her leg. It was followed by the touch of something soft, like tissue or cotton, and then the area felt wet and cool. She tried to reconcile this with the crazy view she had of the interior of the car's trunk, with her head facing the rear of the car. Then she felt the needle pierce the skin. She resisted the impulse to kick out, understanding that the person was being careful to insert the needle into a vein. A second later, the sting of the needle was gone. The trunk closed and the darkness was absolute, but already Sarah felt her thoughts slipping away into an easy, almost welcome oblivion.

As soon as the service station sign came into view Diana knew she had been abducted again. A horrible paralysis seemed to envelop her against her will. She could not move from the neck down and she felt cold, terribly cold. The sensation was familiar and terrifying. Something in her knew that this scene, or scenes very like this one, had been played out many times before.

But Sarah was fighting, Sarah was resisting this! *How remarkable she is,* thought Diana. *I must tell her that sometime, but why do I feel so far removed from my body?*

Then they were pulling off the road, up into the woods. *You can do anything to me, but please don't hurt Sarah. She doesn't understand. She doesn't know about this* . . . But the man on the passenger's side turned around and held his hand out to her, and for just an instant Diana thought she recognized the pattern inscribed there on his palm, for just an instant, but then she was gone . . .

The next thing she saw was light . . . light from

above, light streaming down painfully into her eyes as if from a great height. *Where am I?* she wondered and tried to move, but felt no response from her arms or legs. It was not as if she were merely tied; she simply felt nothing. She could not move, could not even place her arms or legs in space. *I am paralyzed,* she realized, and the thought was like a steel whip being snapped against her.

Worse, though, was the way her thoughts *felt* to her. They were sluggish and not entirely under her control. They moved like marbles dropping through a jar of honey. A part of her wondered, *How can my thoughts feel funny? How can that be? Where am I?* . . .

. . . and then the water was trickling in around her. The water was cold; she could feel the cold against her skin. But still she could not move. *Why is there water in here?* The water filled her with panic. There was something about water that always terrified her, but now it was flowing into this dark, narrow space. She could feel it rising against her legs and arms. *My God, it's going to keep on flowing. It's going to rise up and up and over my mouth and over my nose, and I'm going to die. I'm going to drown. I'm going to die* . . .

. . . and the water did continue to flow, and to rise inexorably up over her hands and arms, up around her ribs and then over her breasts. And then it was filling her ears, crawling up alongside her face, and then she had to keep her mouth closed. She took a last breath through her nose and her nostrils filled, and then water covered her eyes and she could not close them . . .

. . . *I'm going to die. Why can't I close my eyes? My eyes won't close. Is this what it's like to die? I want to breathe so badly, but I can't. If I try to breathe, the water will rush in and fill my lungs, and that will hurt and I will die. But oh, God, I can't keep this up for much longer. How long has it been? Two minutes? Three minutes? Why can't I move? If I could just sit up, but I can't even close my eyes* . . .

. . . and at last she could resist no longer, and her

mouth opened against her will and she sucked in the cold water. Her body fought to cough it out, but it was too late. Her chest went into spasms for a few seconds and then stopped, just like that it stopped, and the pain wasn't nearly as bad as she had thought it would be . . .

. . . and the pain isn't really so bad, but I am dead now, aren't I? My God, I'm dying, I'm dying, I'm dying. Why doesn't someone do something? My lungs are no longer trying to fight this, and if I'm dead, really dead, finally and at last . . . well, you know there is a strange kind of peace here, because no one can hurt me anymore, and the light looks beautiful filtering down through the water and into my eyes. Isn't that strange, but look, I think the light is getting closer. It is getting closer. I can still see the light and the light is getting closer . . .

. . . and suddenly the pain was back and ten times worse. Her lungs were on fire and they were trying to breathe. The water rushed out of her and suddenly she could breathe, but the air seared her lungs, filling them with fire, like breathing napalm. And then she was sick and throwing up and trying desperately to breathe and not to breathe at the same time. And somehow, somewhere, there were people around her, holding her, trying to help her. She felt a sharp sting in one arm, and a plastic mask was lowered over her face; then she just sort of faded out. Maybe this time she was really dying, and dying would be filled with peace . . .

She was being carried forward on the arms of many people. She could see stone walls and high, timbered ceilings, and then they were lowering her and she felt cool stone against her back. A dozen people stood around her, some dressed in robes of black and white and other colors, and some dressed quite ordinarily. Dianatried to move her head, found that it responded, then tested her arms and legs. They, too, responded. She lifted her head and was shocked to find that she had no clothes on, that she lay exposed to these earnest-looking faces.

A man in a black turtleneck stood at the foot of the

stone platform—*altar,* she thought, *it's an altar, isn't it?*—on which she lay.

"Our sister is returned to us from the land of death," he said, and his voice was rich and resonant, echoing powerfully off the stone walls. "Ave Satanas," he said.

"Ave Satanas," half a dozen voices echoed, while another half dozen responded with "Hail Satan" and still others spoke strange, foreign-sounding phrases.

"This is the work of Satan as overseer and his emissary Dantalian, who chooses to retain his consecrated vessel in this world."

"Hoathahe Saitan."

"And so we gather here to reaffirm the covenant between your daughter and your emissary, and to re-establish his dwelling on this plane for so long as he shall choose to occupy it. Hoathahe Saitan, Hoathahe Dantalian."

"Hoathahe Saitan," the chorus roared off the stone walls.

Diana felt a hot, raspy breath at her left ear. She struggled to make sense of the words.

"Listen, daughter," the voice hissed. "You are being prepared so that Dantalian may inhabit you again, if he so chooses. He has saved your life so far, so that is a good sign. But if you resist, or if the demon refuses you, you will be killed. Listen and watch carefully and respond appropriately, else we have no need of you."

The lighting grew dim, and Diana watched in silent terror as black candles in silver stands were placed on either side of her head and set aflame with matches. A pungent incense burned, too, filling her nostrils with a strange, musky odor. She felt dizzy, and the faces around her grew indistinct in the dim light and the swirling smoke. Hands on either side of her bent her legs at the knees, and Diana watched as the man in the turtleneck raised a battered-looking silver goblet high above his head. She recalled the scene in the woods and she was suddenly certain that this was the same man.

"Accept the blood of our recent offering," the man said, and lowered the goblet.

Diana felt her shoulders lifted. Hands held her in a sitting position as the man put the goblet to her lips. She fought back the impulse to turn away, and a warm liquid filled her mouth. It was salty and thick and not terribly unpleasant, but it was strangely, horribly familiar and filled Diana with a choking nausea. She held the liquid in her mouth until a hand pinched her nostrils shut and she swallowed, gasping and choking. The man placed the goblet between her legs and the hands lowered Diana back to a resting position.

Diana's head buzzed with a roaring that seemed to emanate from inside her ears. Alternately, her vision would blur and she would be unable to make out the scene before her, then it would clear and she could see everything with a startling hallucinogenic quality. What she remembered later was simply the sonorous voice of the man in the black turtleneck speaking words she could not understand and the chanting response of the others. But though the words were foreign, she sensed from the rhythm of the ceremony and the rising voices a quickening as to some climax. The responses of the gathering grew more frenzied and her head pounded with the regularity of a drum. The word *Saitan* was repeated over and over, until at last a ringing silence filled the room.

Again, that hot, raspy breath. "Your husband comes for you," the voice whispered.

Dense clouds of smoke seemed to envelop her. The man in the turtleneck stepped back, fading into the smoke. The others followed, and Diana seemed to be alone. Yet she sensed that this was not so, that presences hovered just outside her range of vision. She squinted and strained her eyes to make sense of the shapes forming in the mist. Then the thing was on her.

It rose out of the smoke, seemed almost to form itself *from* the smoke. In the instant before it was on her, it seemed to Diana to be impossibly huge. She would never really be able to describe what it looked like, just that there were features she could not quite remember that reminded her of a goat, a man, and a dog. What the features were, she wasn't sure. Then she felt a huge weight on her and heard with crystal clarity the sound of the goblet being knocked to the floor. Something hard pressed between her legs with terrible insistence. She felt a searing pain as it sought to enter her, and she was certain that she would be torn open, ripped open by the sheer immensity of the thing. Then it was in her and the pain doubled and she gasped. *It's too large,* she wanted to scream. *It's going to kill me.* But then the pain was gone and it felt like a normal man inside her, moving up and back, and she opened her eyes but could see nothing now, only blackness. She heard and felt a heavy breath on her, and the darkness seemed to fill with the feel of him moving back and forth, up and back, moving, moving, on and on. And she told herself she would not enjoy this, that there could be no pleasure in this, but somehow the orgasm overtook her. It welled up inside her, like waves of incredible feeling washing over and through her, and she shuddered with its power. *This is my husband,* she thought, *and my husband is a demon. And these are the only times I've ever known orgasm, here on some rough altar, with the stares of a hundred faces beating into me and the pounding of my demon-lover ripping me apart.*

The ejaculation exploded inside her and she screamed, half in pleasure at the climax of the endless orgasm, half in pain as the man on top of her bit deeply around the nipple of her right breast. She felt a sting in her right arm.

A few seconds before she lost consciousness, she seemed to be standing in a long corridor lined with identical doors. As if on cue, all the doors opened and people began stepping out. They were mostly women, though she thought she saw one or two men way down toward the end of the hall. Some were her age, some looked like teenagers, and at some doorways were infants. She felt an immediate impulse to go pick up the babies, to hold them and cuddle them. She could not move, though; these people would have to come to her. Two of the women did just that. One was a solid-looking woman about her age, with curly chestnut-brown hair and brown eyes. The other woman reminded her of herself, with ash-blond hair and blue eyes, only she looked tougher, harder. They stepped toward her at the same time and both of them reached for her.

Sarah awoke with a pounding headache. She tried to sit up and immediately hit her head on the roof of the trunk. *What the hell,* she thought briefly, before the rush of memory overtook her and left her frightened and angry, tied by the hands in the trunk of a late-model Mercedes.

She lay there for a long time, trying to breathe evenly, fighting back waves of claustrophobia. Finally, she heard the scuffle of footsteps outside the car. A knocking rang against the trunk.

"Are you awake?" a voice asked. Sarah thought the accent sounded Midwestern.

She made no reply.

"If you are awake, please kick or otherwise make some sign. If you do not make a sign, I will assume that you are dead and will instruct your driver to dispose of you."

Sarah hesitated a moment, then savagely kicked the side of the car.

"Good," the voice said. "You are likely wondering why we took you on this little trip tonight. Your friend we took because she needed to be reminded who she is and where she comes from. You we took because we wish to give you every opportunity to leave Isis alone. She is ours, you know. You cannot have her. No matter who you think she is, you are wrong. Can you hear me?''

Sarah kicked again.

''Good. If you persist in practicing your primitive science on her, we will kill her because she will lose her value to us. We will also kill you. If you go to the authorities, we will probably kill you both, although we may leave you to deal with the consequences of your actions. That would be amusing. On the other hand, if you leave Isis alone, sever your friendship and your professional relationship with her, we will pretend that all of this never happened. Do you understand?''

Sarah remained motionless.

''Do you understand? Or shall I just assume the answer is *no* right now?''

Sarah kicked.

''Excellent. There is something else you should know. I tell you this so you understand a little bit about what you are dealing with. Isis keeps us informed about you. Before you left home today, she called and told us where we could find you. There is nothing you do with her that she does not tell us about. Or your husband, either.'' The man laughed softly. ''When you deal with the one you call Diana, you deal only with a tiny insignificant piece of the total being. Diana is nothing, she means nothing; she is merely a temporary convenience. Do not risk your life rescuing something that barely exists at all. The results would be disappointing.'' The man cleared his throat.

''I bid you good night, Mrs. Johnson. Please think carefully about what I have said. And remember that our reach extends far.''

Sarah listened to the fading footsteps and raged. Who was this bastard? Who did he think he was that he could kidnap her and lock her in a trunk, terrorize her?

And what did he know about Diana? She would see him in hell before she gave up. An idea occurred to her. She might be bound and gagged and stuffed in the boot of a Mercedes, but she could do something. Her hands were painfully tied and not properly aligned for what she had in mind, but still she managed to ease her right thumb and forefinger around the smooth surface of her wedding ring. After five minutes of slow work, she had the thing loosely balanced on the tip of her finger. She inched her way as far back in the trunk as she could and started feeling for a place to hide the ring. Fifteen minutes after she finished, she heard footsteps. The trunk opened and she was blinded by a powerful spotlight. She was yanked around, the vein in her leg was tied off again, and again she was injected. This time, she was asleep before the trunk closed.

Sarah woke up first, her neck stiff against the side of the Oldsmobile's headrest. It took her several seconds to realize that she was in her own car and another second to determine that Diana was seated next to her. Alive, too. Sarah relaxed a bit when she heard the woman snoring softly.

The key was in the ignition and they were surrounded by woods. The car had been moved, then. Sarah shook Diana, gently at first, then with greater insistence. Diana moaned. Her eyelids fluttered and opened.

"Oh, God," she said, "what happened?"

"Good question," Sarah responded. "Are you all right?"

"Yeah, I'm okay. You?"

"My pride is definitely wounded, but I'll survive. Where are we?"

Sarah started the car and backed it down the narrow road. After a few minutes, she recognized the location. This was the place the men had taken her in the Mercedes. They—or some accomplices—must have taken the keys from her purse when they locked her in the trunk, then come back and moved the car off the road.

Sarah backed out onto the main highway. She put the car in gear and gunned it. It responded immediately. Had they sabotaged her car so it would stall earlier? It seemed to be fixed now.

"Bastards," Sarah said. She glanced at her watch. Eleven-thirty. They would be home in five minutes. She had been abducted, bound, drugged, and locked in a car trunk less than three miles from home.

Chapter 27

Week 19: Sunday, December 3

Sarah surprised herself by waking early, feeling refreshed and energized. Mark was already up and reading the paper at the kitchen table. He looked up, astonished, when she walked into the kitchen. She refused to answer his questions and insisted on making breakfast before discussing the events of the previous evening.

Bill Travers stumbled into the kitchen next, dressed in his jeans and a T-shirt, looking rumpled and disoriented. Having laid his suspicions about the anthropologist to rest, Mark had called Travers when Sarah and Diana were late arriving. Bill had sensed something was seriously wrong and had driven to the Johnsons' house, fearing the worst. After the women arrived, confused and exhausted, Travers decided to spend the night on the sofa. Sarah poured him a cup of coffee, which he accepted silently. Diana came in next, looking sleepy and pretty in a terry cloth robe. Sarah wondered how anyone could look good having just awakened, but there it was.

"Everybody gets cholesteroled out this morning whether you like it or not," Sarah said as she dished up fried eggs, sausage links, hash browns, and toast.

Travers held up a hand in refusal. "I never eat breakfast," he said.

"You eat it this morning," Sarah said, playfully stern, "else we don't invite you to any more pajama parties."

After breakfast was over and the dishes cleared, they all carried their coffee out to the living room. Sarah told her story first.

Both men were silent, but their anger showed in the knotted muscles of their clenched jaws and fists. Travers stood and paced the floor. Mark sat virtually motionless, only his eyes narrowing as Sarah related certain details.

She told her story quickly, with a clinical impartiality, until she came to the point where she had talked to the man who had warned her not to work with Diana. Sarah wondered how much she should say.

"Diana," she said at last, "I was just thinking about not mentioning certain things that the man said. I wasn't sure if you should hear them. But I don't think that's right. I think you should hear everything. Just remember that these are things the man said, okay? They're not all true."

"I want to hear," Diana said. "I want to know everything."

"First he told me that he would kill you if we continue therapy. He said he would kill me, too.

"He said if I left you alone—if I left *Isis* alone, actually—they would ignore me, pretend it all never happened. He said that continued therapy would make Isis worthless to them."

Sarah paused, watching Diana closely. "He also said that Diana is a tiny, unimportant part of Isis." Diana showed no reaction. "He said I don't understand what I'm dealing with. He also said that Isis lets them know everything that's going on . . . that she called them before we left for the mall yesterday."

Diana buried her face in her hands.

"Diana," Sarah said sharply, "you listen to me. This man is a professional liar. He was deliberately trying to turn me against you. It won't work. He also doesn't know you. He *thinks* Isis is important; he doesn't know Diana. I *know* Diana. I also know all the ones who have been hurt by him and his friends."

Diana lifted her head. "I was going to say that I didn't make any phone call," she said. "But then I realized, how would I know? I could be telling them anything, everything, and wouldn't have the slightest idea. There's no way we can fight that."

"Yes, there is," Sarah said, her voice straining with urgency. "It doesn't matter if Nora or Isis is letting them know what's going on. Nora and Isis are scared. They're scared because they are a part of you."

"How do you know it's not the other way around?"

"What do you mean?"

"I mean," Diana said, "how do you know that I'm not just some little fragment and this Isis is the real personality? The personality that everyone else gets merged into. How do you know?"

"Because I know," Sarah said in what she hoped was a tone of uncompromising certainty. "Because the original child was tortured to produce these others. Because you and Linda and the kids are part of a sane attempt to survive in an insane world. Nora and Isis are manufactured products of that insane world. They have no real strength. The real strength is with you."

Sarah let her words hang in the air, hoping desperately that they made sense to Diana and that they were relayed to the others inside her. No one spoke for several long seconds.

Finally, Travers interrupted the silence.

"Too bad you didn't get the Mercedes' license number. Do you think you could recognize the two drivers again if you saw them?"

"You bet I could," Sarah said. "Diana, too, right?"

Diana nodded.

"And for your information, I *did* get the license number of the Mercedes."

"You what?" Travers shouted. "That's fantastic."

"I did better than that," Sarah laughed. "I left a little calling card, too."

"What do you mean?" Mark asked.

Sarah held up her left hand. "No ring, see?" she said, wiggling her fingers. "I left my wedding band jammed into one corner of the trunk. I thought it would be a handy piece of corroboration."

"Brilliant," Travers said. "Give me the license number. I've got to call somebody."

Sarah wrote down the number on a piece of paper, then she went into the kitchen to get more coffee for everyone. When she turned from the coffee maker, Mark was standing in the doorway, watching her.

"You're remarkable," he said, coming closer to her. "I'm very proud of you."

"What? For losing my ring in the trunk of a car?" Sarah laughed.

"That, yes," Mark said. "And for everything you've done for Diana. Not giving up on her. I know how tough it must have been for you. No support from your husband, for one thing."

Sarah blinked hard several times.

"I'm so sorry I ever hurt you," Mark continued. "I was an idiot to think that you'd . . . well, do what I thought you did. I just hope it's not too late for us . . . because I love you."

Sarah walked up to her husband, looked him in the eye, then buried her head in his chest as she hugged him.

"I think there's hope yet," she said.

Travers called from the living room. Mark and Sarah hurried in.

"Fisher wants to know if you'd be willing to swear out a complaint." Bill stood with one hand cupped over the mouthpiece of the phone.

Sarah looked at Diana, who nodded.

"Whatever he wants," she said.

"Okay, John," Travers said into the phone, "if that's what you need. Can't you just keep an eye out for the Mercedes at this point?" Travers listened for a while. Finally, he ended the conversation with a promise to catch up with the policeman the following day.

"Fisher says he'll try to find your Mercedes. If he needs a sworn statement, he'll let us know," Bill said. "He knows a little about what's going on. He's willing to keep things low-key."

The others nodded. Sarah asked Diana whether she was up to relating her account of the previous evening. She said she was, but her voice was uneven and she held herself tightly. The others listened with mounting horror as Diana told of her near-death by drowning, her resuscitation, and her rape. By the time she finished her story, Diana was trembling uncontrollably. Travers pulled an afghan from the back of the couch and wrapped it around her. Diana nodded gratefully.

"This is outrageous," Mark finally exploded. "We've got to do something. Can't the police do more than look for the goddamn car? Can't they give us protection or something?"

"Even Fisher admits the story is strengthened now that Sarah is involved," Travers said, obviously choosing his words with care. "But as he says, whenever one of us mentions Satanism, the department gets a collective glaze in its eyes and writes it off as paranoid fantasy. Plus, Fisher says that even if they did believe us, any protection they could give us would be limited. Somebody to cruise the neighborhood a couple of times a night. Whoever these people are, they're not likely to be intimidated by a cruiser every couple of hours. They obviously know how to stage well-orchestrated events."

Sarah sighed. "I wish we could just stop the world and get off for a while." She looked at Diana. "I wish you and I had a couple of uninterrupted days together to decide what we want to do."

Diana smiled. "Me, too. I'd love to just sneak away."

"Why don't we?" Travers asked suddenly. "Why not? Diana, you could just pack up and leave, right? Mark, can you shut down your business for a couple of days? Sarah?"

"What do you mean?" Sarah asked. "Where would we go? Don't get me wrong. The idea of getting out of here for a while is awfully appealing. But where? How?"

"I know the perfect place," Travers said. He stood up and started pacing again, gesticulating wildly as he talked. "If you don't mind roughing it a little bit, some friends of mine own a cabin in the Shenandoah. It's miles from nowhere, in the woods. Peaceful. Secluded. Best yet, it's hard to get to."

"But we can't just up and leave," Sarah said. "Mark, what about your business?"

"To hell with the business," Mark said. "Right now, there are more important things. Like taking care of my wife."

Sarah looked in amazement at the other three. "All right," she said at last. "Yes, all right. I'll need tomorrow to get everything tied up at the office, but okay. Why not?"

"*Yes,*" Bill said. "Fortunately, I only have exams to give, and I can pawn that off on my poor, unsuspecting graduate students. In fact, I already have," he grinned. "I'll tell you what. I'll provide the transportation. Sarah, if you'll bring Diana to your office tomorrow, I'll take her with me to go shopping. If that's all right?" Travers looked anxiously at Diana.

"Yes," Diana said.

"Great. It's settled then," Travers said.

A half hour later, Travers decided to leave for his

apartment. Sarah slipped on a jacket and walked with him out to his car.

"I wanted to talk to you alone for a minute," she said.

"What's up?"

"First, I want to thank you for the idea and all. I think getting away is a great idea. I also want to thank you for offering to keep an eye on Diana tomorrow."

"No problem. I don't think we should let her out of our sight for a while."

"Agreed," Sarah nodded. "You know what we're going to try to do, don't you?"

"Sure," Travers said. "Integration."

"Yes. If Diana's agreeable, that's what we're going to do. There's one other thing. I don't think you should tell her where this cabin is. Just in case."

"I'd already thought of that," Travers said. "I won't say a word."

Week 19: Monday, December 4

Sarah spent the morning seeing clients, finishing up a variety of paperwork, and instructing an incredulous Margie on cancellations and emergency referral procedures. Since she had already worked to cut back her caseload, canceling appointments for the next several days proved to be easier than she had imagined. Sarah gave Margie a schedule of work for the following day and suggested she take the remainder of the week off with pay. Mark finished a project for Beiderbeck and explained that he would be out of touch for several days. When Beiderbeck learned that Mark planned to take a few days off, he was enthusiastic. Pleasantly surprised at his response, Mark briefly considered giving the man a set of instructions for reaching him in the event of emergency, then remembered that he did not yet know the location of the cabin or even whether it was equipped with a telephone. Instead, Mark gave Beiderbeck the name and number of a competitor, a woman with whom he had occasionally traded business leads. Mark slipped home for lunch and set up a new message on his answering machine. That afternoon, he spent shopping at stores specializing in hunting and backpacking.

Travers picked up Diana at Sarah's office. The two left looking more like old friends than fugitives from a cult. When they arrived back at her office late that afternoon, Sarah thought Diana looked happier and more relaxed than she had ever seen her. She was delighted that they had developed such an immediate rapport. Sarah wondered briefly if the relationship would ever go beyond friendship and if she should counsel Bill on the issue of becoming involved with a multiple, but then decided that he could probably work it out for himself just fine. At the moment, Travers looked like good medicine. Hallelujah and leave well enough alone.

Travers agreed to pick everybody up at Sarah's house the next morning. Sarah closed the office after he left. She and Diana drove home, excited over the prospect of going away. The flight from a terrorist cult would be festive and full of hope.

Week 19: Tuesday, December 5

Travers phoned shortly after eight. Mark answered and spent several minutes nodding his head and saying "Okay, okay," over and over.

"That was Bill," he said, hanging up the phone.

"So what's up?" Sarah asked. "Why isn't he here?"

"Just in case we're being watched and he isn't, he wants us to meet him. We'll make sure we're not being followed, rendezvous and load up his car, and leave the Volvo." Mark grinned. "Kind of silly, huh?"

"No," Sarah said, "it makes good sense. I don't care to be abducted again."

They spent half an hour driving around, nervously checking mirrors to make sure they were not being followed. In spite of her earlier sentiment, Sarah did feel a bit silly. It was broad daylight on a crisp December day. Looking for enemies in the rearview mirror seemed like the height of paranoia. She noticed that both Mark and Diana seemed deadly serious about the whole thing. Neither relaxed until they were on a stretch of highway without a car in sight, either ahead or behind. Ten minutes later, they found Travers in the back parking lot of a shopping center, sitting on the hood of an ancient four-wheel drive Travel-All. Fifteen minutes after that, they were pulling out into traffic and heading for the westbound interstate.

Bill suddenly thrust out a hand to the backseat, causing the vehicle to swerve. "I almost forgot, Sarah," he said. "I've got something for you."

Sarah saw a glint of gold between his fingers, reached for it, and was astonished to find herself holding her wedding band.

"My ring," she yelled. "Where did you get it?"

"Fisher stopped by this morning," Travers said. "Seems they traced your Mercedes to a rental place. They popped open the trunk and, voilà, there was your ring, right where you said it would be."

"Fantastic. If you weren't driving, I'd kiss you."

"Don't let that stop you," Bill grinned.

"A rental car?" asked Mark. "So what's next?"

"Unfortunately, not much," Travers said. "Our boys used assumed identities, of course. They're pretty much untraceable."

"At least this should make the police a little more willing to believe us," Diana said.

Travers nodded. "Yeah, it should. It really should," he said.

Sarah listened carefully to the tone of Travers's

voice. He knew more than he was saying, she was certain of it.

Three hours later, the Travel-All lurched its way across a shallow creek bed and groaned as it eased up a steep rock-strewn path.

"So, when you said roughing it, you meant roughing it, didn't you?" Sarah asked. "No way there's electricity up here."

Bill refused to answer and just smiled maddeningly. He silently coaxed the Travel-All up the narrow road for the next fifteen minutes. They rounded a curve in the path and the trees on the right side opened up into a meadow, browned with winter and still snow-free.

"There it is," Bill said, and nodded toward the crest of the gently rising field.

A mixed stand of hardwoods and pines stood at the crest. Almost hidden in the shadows of the trees, Sarah could just make out the horizontal timbers of a log structure.

Sarah whistled. "You weren't kidding when you said *cabin.*"

"Of course not," Travers said, still smiling smugly.

Travers pulled the Travel-All under a stand of tall pines and turned off the engine. Stepping from the vehicle and stretching, Sarah, Diana, and Mark stood gaping at the cabin. This was no shack in the woods, they saw. For one thing, it was much newer than one would think having glimpsed it casually from the little mountain path. It was also larger than they had expected, with a porch running the entire length of the house and the tip of a stone chimney breaking through the roofline.

"It must have cost a fortune to build this up here," Mark commented.

"Wait'll you see the inside."

Bill took the porch steps two at a time, fished a key from his pocket, and opened the door with a flourish.

Once inside, the three newcomers looked around in amazement.

The front door opened into a spacious living room. On the south wall was a huge stone fireplace. A cathedral ceiling showed lovely, rough-hewn timbers. The eastern end of the room opened into a kitchen, set with windows on both the eastern and southern sides. Bill unlocked a door on the far side of the kitchen.

"Check this out," he grinned.

They all stepped through the door and out onto another porch. It looked out over the side of the mountain and down into a valley hundreds of feet below. The entire valley opened up before them. To the north, lazy streams of smoke puffed from twin smokestacks. The faint shapes of commercial buildings indicated the industrial edge of a small town. South of the town and spreading out in the valley before them, the shapes of houses and farms dotted the rolling hills and woodlands. A river, sinuous and glinting in the sunlight, sliced the valley from north to south.

"God, this is beautiful!" Diana exclaimed.

"Wow," said Mark.

"We're on the side of a goddamn mountain," said Sarah.

"That's why I like you, Sarah," Bill laughed. "No subtlety slips past you, does it?"

They explored the rest of the house, delighted at finding several large bedrooms, a tiny study built into the loft overlooking the living room, and a huge stone-rimmed hot tub. The rest of the afternoon they spent unpacking, organizing, hauling wood, making beds, and generally making the cabin livable for the next few days. Bill and Diana decided to fix dinner together. Sarah and Mark cleaned up afterwards, offering to reverse roles the following evening.

Everyone claimed to be exhausted after eating. Bill, who had insisted on driving the entire way, was first to retire. Diana followed shortly.

Sarah stretched out on the floor, watching the fire.

"I've about had it," she yawned and stretched.

"Why don't you take a bath and go to bed?" Mark suggested.

Sarah looked at her husband thoughtfully.

"You know, that's a great idea," she said.

"Would you like some company?" Mark asked. Sarah could hear the nervous edge beneath the feigned spontaneity of the question.

It was several seconds before she answered. "Yes," she said at last.

Sarah entered the bathroom before her husband. She had scrubbed the tub earlier, so now she simply turned on the water and let it run hot and steamy into the tub. How long would it take to fill a tub this size? She shrugged. They had all night.

Sarah started at the sound of knocking on the bathroom door. She opened it cautiously and there stood Mark. He managed to carry a champagne bottle tucked into a small garbage can filled with ice, two wine glasses, a candle in a brass holder, and a Bic lighter. Sarah closed the door behind him after he entered.

"A little bubbly to work out the kinks?" he asked.

"Yes," said Sarah. "It's time we worked out some kinks."

"Sarah"—Mark set his paraphernalia along the side of the tub—"thank you. Thank you for wanting me to join you."

"Life's too short, Mark," Sarah said. "I know that sounds trite, but I realized that it was true—*really* realized, if you know what I mean—when I was hog-tied in the trunk of that Mercedes. I didn't know if I was going to live through the evening or not. I thought then that if I got back home, it would be time to either say to hell with it all or get on with our lives together. I don't want to waste any more time figuring out whether or not we're going to make up."

Mark nodded thoughtfully. "And you decided making up was better than saying to hell with it?"

"Yes."

Mark held Sarah at arm's length.

"I couldn't live without you, Sarah," he said.

"Yes, you could," she said, her tone serious, her eyes searching Mark's. Then she smiled. "But I'm glad you don't want to."

For just an instant, Sarah had the sudden desire to push Mark away, to say to him, *Forget it, you bastard, you blew it.* But she knew that was just her anger talking, that what she really wanted was healing, and love, and a return to the closeness they had once had.

She opened her arms to him, let him come to her. She kissed him and tasted the salty whisper of a tear on his lip. Whether it was his or hers, she couldn't say.

Chapter 28

Week 19: Wednesday, December 6

Sarah dressed quietly. The room was cold, and she quickly put on a pair of jeans and a warm sweater. She picked up a nylon case containing the laptop computer Mark had brought along. Glancing back at her husband, who was asleep and breathing noisily, she stepped out in the hall and closed the door behind her.

In the kitchen, Sarah cleaned out the grounds from last night's coffee and set on a fresh pot to brew. Morning was breaking bright and glorious over the valley. She stood looking out the kitchen door while the coffee gurgled and steamed. Finally, the sun grew too bright to watch and then the coffee was done.

Sarah poured a cup and carried it over to the coffee table in the living room, where she had placed her computer. Sitting on a footstool, she uncased the computer, turned it on, and started the word processor program.

She began to type *In August of this year,* but then Sarah remembered that she would not be delivering the lecture until January. She changed *this year* to *last year.* Immediately, she started typing again:

> In August of last year, I met a most remarkable young woman. She was self-referred to my office and presented as someone experiencing a major

depressive episode. It was on this basis that I began therapy with Miss S. Little did I realize that this was the first step into a world of horrors such as I had never imagined possible. I suspect your reactions will be much the same as my own: outraged skepticism, initially; followed by a search for rational alternative explanations; if you bear with me long enough, this will be replaced by a sense of loathing and terror in those moments when disbelief is suspended; finally, if you have the patience to weigh all the evidence, skepticism will be replaced by belief. There will be no lessening, however, of outrage . . .

A half hour later, Travers stumbled out into the living room, rumpled and bleary-eyed. He stood stretching, his face contorted with a disoriented, dopey sort of half-smile.

Sarah smiled. "Coffee's in the kitchen, Bill," she said.

Travers nodded and shuffled off. After noisily rummaging through the kitchen, he eventually returned to the living room, a mug of coffee cradled protectively in both hands. He sat carefully in an armchair, sipped his coffee, and grunted. Sarah looked up once, chuckled, and went back to writing.

"What are you doing?" he asked.

Sarah slipped a diskette into the computer and typed in the command to save what she had written so far, then looked up. A semblance of self-possession seemed to have returned to Bill's expression. Not only was he not a morning person, Sarah thought, but he needed coffee to be even marginally functional.

"Writing a speech," Sarah said.

"What kind of speech?"

"I'm scheduled to give a talk in a couple of weeks at a conference of community-based mental health services providers," Sarah said. "The original topic was supposed to be 'Accessing the Private Provider' or some such thing."

"So what's the new topic?"

"This is just a working title, understand: 'The Dimensions of Dissociative Disorder in a Victim of Cult-Related Abuse.' What do you think?"

Travers whistled. "Sounds pretty fancy. Also sounds like a one-way ticket to the land of professional obscurity and ridicule. Are you serious?"

"Deadly serious, Bill. Listen, these people are real, they're powerful, their influence spans at least a couple of generations. The only thing that I can think of that'll give any of us some measure of security is to go public."

"It's a little early, Sarah," Bill sighed. "I'm not following this very well."

"The one thing that is more important to them than Diana or any of their individual members has got to be the secrecy of the group as a whole," Sarah said.

"Which is why you're dead meat if you announce this to the world," Bill interrupted.

"Wrong." Sarah jabbed a finger at him. "If I go public, the last thing they're going to do is hurt me. That would tip their hand, see? At the point I stand up and say, 'Hello, folks, I have evidence of an intergenerational, hitherto unknown, secret society of powerful Satan worshippers who routinely engage in abuse, terrorism, and murder,' they are going to run as far away from me as they can get."

"Wait, I get it," Travers said excitedly, leaning forward, causing coffee to slosh over the rim of his mug and onto his faded jeans. He ignored the coffee. "If they do something to you then, they have to worry that people will take you seriously. But if they leave you alone, everybody will just think you're nuts. It might work." He thought a moment. "I don't think one paper delivered to an obscure group of local shrinks is going to do the trick, though."

"It's a start. We can shoot for the *Washington Post* and *Rolling Stone* later."

"What happens to your professional credibility if you do this?"

"Credibility doesn't mean a whole lot if you're dead, Bill. These people scared me the other night. They're not kidding. They're about two steps away from figuring out that they've lost Diana. When that happens, we're probably both dead. And I don't know where you fit in, but I'd go ahead and pay up any overdue life insurance premiums."

"Cheery thought," Travers said glumly. "Sarah, isn't there some other way?"

"I'm sure open to suggestions. You've got the police involved just as much as they care to be. What else is there?"

"I don't know."

"Cheer up," Sarah laughed. "Maybe it isn't as bad as all that. See, I deliver my speech and get them off our backs. They think I've committed professional suicide, but I haven't. I'm going to prove they exist. There have got to be more people like Diana around. She's not a fluke, you know; she represents their whole *modus vivendi.* I intend to become a long-term thorn in their side, Bill. And I don't intend on being terrorized again. Or drugged. Or stuffed in a trunk."

"Maybe you're right . . . I don't know." Travers shook his head. "I guess I'll let you get back to it."

He started to stand, but Sarah motioned for him to sit.

"Wait, Bill," she said, "there's something I want to ask you. I got the feeling that there was something you weren't telling us yesterday. Something to do with your policeman friend."

"You don't miss a trick," Travers said. "Yeah, I didn't want to mention it in front of Diana. To tell you the truth, I don't know what to make of it."

"What is it?"

"I asked Fisher to follow up with the Nottingham County sheriff's office about the murder that Diana witnessed. He said he talked with the investigating officer . . . some local deputy, I think. He's gotten back a lab report on the bloody hair that was found."

"Yeah, so?"

"So, the hair turned out to be horse hair and the blood is horse blood."

"What?"

"Exactly my reaction. I've been having a hard time digesting it. Does it mean the whole thing was a setup? A coincidence? Or what?"

"We could take Diana over there, see if she recognizes the place," Sarah suggested.

"What good would that do? Besides, I don't know where the place is exactly, and neither does Fisher. Fisher said the deputy was not real happy about the whole thing—kind of embarrassing, I guess—and the last thing he wants is a bunch of outsiders coming in and stirring things up."

"What about all the footprints they found? The evidence of a large gathering?"

"I said the same thing. It could have been faked, Sarah."

"Faked? Who do you think would have faked it?"

"It's not what I think, it's what the cops think. Fisher didn't come right out and say so, but I know he's beginning to wonder if Diana set up the whole thing."

"That's crazy," Sarah said. "What about my story, anyway? Doesn't that add some credence to the whole thing?"

"Some, I suppose," Bill said. "The problem is, there really isn't much evidence except your ring in the trunk. They can't trace the guys who rented the car. Fisher believes us, I think, and that's solely because of you. He's made it clear, though, that with a story like this, your credibility with the department is going to be only marginally better than Diana's."

"Great. I get the picture. Therapist and patient. In the eyes of the law, we're both crazy. No, worse than crazy. We also set up fake crime scenes. What do you think, Bill? Do you think Diana faked it?"

"Of course not. I think the whole thing *was* a setup, though. By the Circle."

Sarah paused, suddenly thoughtful. "I'm not so sure," she said. "What would they have to gain by throwing attention on this?"

"They discredited Diana."

"They didn't need to do that. She's discredited to begin with."

"So what do you think?"

"I think our original feeling that they screwed up is correct." Sarah smiled thinly. "I'm guessing that they figured out a way to cover their tracks, but I'm not sure how. You think Fisher would be willing to track down whoever did the lab report? Maybe that'll tell us something."

"He's good for another favor or two. I need to go to town for supplies, anyway," Travers said. "I could call from there."

"Good. Take Mark with you. He's going to go nuts without a computer to play with."

Sarah turned her attention back to the screen of the little computer.

The men were silent most of the way down the mountain. The trail was tricky and Bill found he had to concentrate to keep control of the vehicle. Mark sat quietly, apparently calm, though Travers saw with a quick glance that the knuckles of his clenched fists were white. Travers started to chuckle, but the Travel-All picked that moment to start sliding on the loose shale of the path. It slid a good three feet before the four-wheel drive found purchase again. Travers noticed that his own knuckles were white.

When they reached the paved and relatively level road, Mark exhaled an audible sigh of relief. Travers fished a cigarette from out of a crumpled package and lit it. He pulled the vehicle off onto a wide section of shoulder and jumped out to disable the four-wheel drive. In a few minutes, they were back on the road.

"Your wife is some piece of work," Travers said.

Mark nodded agreement. "That she is."

"I hope everything goes well today."

"What do you mean?"

"The integration. I hope it goes smoothly. I mean, that's what we're here for, right?"

"Integration?" Mark asked. "Is that what Sarah's planning?"

"I think so. If Diana agrees with the idea."

"Is she planning on doing it today?"

"Look, I don't know what she's got in mind, really. She just mentioned it in passing. I'm sure we'll find out when we get back . . . after Sarah has a chance to talk with Diana." Travers ground out his cigarette, mad at himself for having revealed information Sarah obviously would have preferred telling herself. But how the hell was he to know she hadn't told him yet? "Sarah's had a lot on her mind. We left before she had a chance to tell you everything."

Mark gave Travers a piercing look for a moment, then smiled. "It's okay."

Travers relaxed a little, but he remained silent for the rest of the drive.

Their first stop in town was the grocery store, a tiny and dirty building dating from the late fifties or early sixties that still bore the name of a long-defunct grocery chain. Mark and Bill filled the cart quickly and moved to the end of a long line of customers waiting at the single checkout.

As if on impulse, Mark reached into his pocket and

pulled out a wad of bills. He peeled off two twenties and dropped them in the cart.

"Listen, I'll be right back, okay?" he said. "I need to run across the street for a minute to the hardware store."

"That's okay, I've got to go there, too . . ." Travers said, but Mark had already moved off.

Travers paid for the groceries and wheeled the wobbly little cart out through the automatic doors. He pushed the cart toward the little cutout in the sidewalk, glancing quickly to both sides. A flash of familiar-looking flannel made him stop. A public telephone was mounted on the side of the building. Mark stood with his back toward Travers. His head nodded occasionally and he gestured with his free hand.

"Good. Looks like he found a phone," he mumbled, and pushed the cart down the incline and out into the parking lot.

Travers unloaded the groceries and pushed the cart back to the store entrance. He decided he might as well call Fisher now, as soon as Mark was finished. Mark was now turned toward the parking lot and watched as Travers approached. He finished his call a few seconds before Bill arrived.

"Ready to roll?" Mark asked.

"Not quite," Travers said. "I need to make a call, too." He looked closely at Mark. "Everything all right?"

"Fine," he said. "For a change, everybody's computers are happily up and running."

Travers put a call in to John Fisher. After several minutes of being put on hold and rerouted through the department's switchboard, the familiar voice boomed over the line.

"Fisher," said Fisher.

"John, it's Bill," Travers said. "Anything on the Mercedes?"

"No," Fisher said flatly. "Ain't likely to *be* anything more, either."

"All right, all right, don't blow a gasket." Travers changed his tack. "You know something, John? I've been thinking about that lab report from Nottingham County."

"Yeah?" Fisher said uncertainly.

"I was just wondering if maybe it wouldn't be worthwhile to call up the pathologist or whoever did the testing."

"What the hell for?"

"Well, those good ol' boys in the sheriff's department . . . you know, I'll just bet you they're pretty handy with horses and things."

"So?"

"So, do you think maybe it's odd that they find this stuff and think it's human hair, then all of a sudden the lab says it's horse hair?"

"I don't think it's odd at all," Fisher said, his voice rising with unconcealed impatience. "I think it makes damn good sense." Fisher paused. "Oh, hell," he said, "I didn't want to tell you this because I knew you'd make something out of it."

"What? What is it?"

"Just a comment the deputy made when I asked him about the lab report."

"What was it?"

"Don't make too much of it. I really think the guy was embarrassed and trying not to look like such a jerk."

"What did he say?"

"Just about what you said," Fisher answered. "He said he sure thought he could tell human hair from horse hair, but he guessed not."

"See," Travers shouted, "there you go."

"Go where? It doesn't mean a damn thing."

"Don't you think it at least means we ought to talk to the lab guy?"

"No," Fisher shouted. Travers yanked the receiver away from his ear, then replaced it carefully. He heard Fisher saying, ". . . in a goddamn sling if I call those guys one more time. They tell me to drop it, I'm damn well gonna drop it."

"Okay, drop it," Travers said. "You gotta do what you gotta do. That doesn't mean *I* can't call."

"No goddamn way," Fisher shouted again. "Not this time you don't."

"Come on, John, relax," Bill said soothingly. "You know me. I'm discreet, trustworthy. I'm practically a member of the department myself."

"No," Fisher insisted, though Travers thought some of his energy had dissipated.

"Come on, John," Travers repeated. "This is your old buddy. Who took your sister out last New Year's when she came to town, huh? Who covered for you when . . ."

A few minutes later, Travers was dialing the number of the pathologist's office and giving his calling card number to a youthful-sounding operator with a mountain drawl. The phone rang twice before it was answered.

"Hello," said a woman's voice.

"I'm looking for . . . uh . . ."—Travers held up the little scrap of paper he had scrawled the name and number on—"Dr. Jack Webster."

"Who is this, please?"

"Name's John Fisher," Travers said without hesitation. "I'm with the Richmond police department."

"I see . . ." The voice hesitated a few seconds. "Well, Dr. Webster's not available."

"Can you tell me when he'll be back in?"

"He won't."

"Excuse me?"

"I said, he won't be back in. He doesn't work here anymore. Been transferred."

''Could you tell me where he's been transferred to?'' Travers asked pleasantly.

''You say you're a cop?''

''That's right.'' Bill grimaced. Fisher would kill him if this got back.

''Look, I can't tell you,'' the woman said at last. ''He left explicit instructions *not* to give out his address.''

''I'm sure you can make an exception in this case.''

''Like hell, buddy.''

''Well, how about his replacement? Can I talk to him?''

''Her,'' the voice said. ''You're talking to her.''

''Sorry,'' Travers said. ''I meant no offense.''

''None taken,'' she said. ''Now, Officer Fisher, what can I do for you?''

''I wanted to ask Webster about a test he did last week on some bloody hair.''

''Lots of luck,'' the woman said. ''Listen, I shouldn't tell you this, but if you're a cop, I guess it's okay. Webster wasn't transferred, he was fired. His records are so bad I can't find anything. Call me back in six months and I might be able to tell you something.''

''Is that why he was fired?''

''I can't say any more,'' she said. ''Really. Except, I hope you don't need the sample.''

''Why's that?''

''Cause the son of a bitch destroyed half the stuff we had stored here. Chances are your sample went up in smoke, too.''

''I wouldn't be at all surprised,'' Travers said grimly. ''Thank you very much.''

After Bill and Mark had left for town, the two women stacked kindling and logs in the fireplace. Sarah struck a match and touched it to the paper she had stuffed under the grate. To her surprise, the paper ignited the kindling quickly. In a few minutes, the fire was blazing cheerily.

"Not bad, huh?" she asked.

"You'd make a great pioneer," Diana laughed.

"Forget the pioneer stuff. It's okay on camping trips, but I can live without it."

Diana walked over to the hearth and sat next to Sarah.

"We're alone, Sarah," she said. "What's next? You have something in mind, don't you?"

Sarah put her arm around Diana and pulled her close.

"You know what comes next, don't you?" she asked.

"I guess I do. Integration, right?"

Sarah nodded.

"Do you think it's time? Do you really think I'm ready?"

"Yes, you're ready," Sarah said. "You know what the corridor was that you saw, with all the people standing at the doorways?"

"It was all the others showing themselves to me," Diana said slowly, thoughtfully.

"That's right. Do you know who the two women were who reached out for you?"

Diana shook her head.

"The blonde was Linda. I think the brunette was Nora. Why do you think they were reaching out to you?"

"Because they're ready to become a part of me."

"Yes," Sarah said.

"Or because they're ready for me to become a part of them," Diana added. "That's possible, too, isn't it?"

"Yes."

"How do we keep Nora from taking over? Nora and Isis?"

"We fight them," Sarah said.

"How?"

"I don't think we'll really know until we try."

"I'm scared."

"It's okay." Sarah hugged her tighter. "I'll be with you. There's one thing you must remember, Di."

"Yes?"

"There will come a point when you will have to be willing to lose yourself to gain yourself. Do you understand that?"

"Yes," she said. "That's what scares me."

"I think the trick is to know when that point comes."

"If I surrender at the wrong time, I'll be gone. She'll take me, won't she?"

"I don't know, Di," Sarah said. "But that sounds right."

"How do we start? Are you going to hypnotize me?"

"Something else you need to know, Di, is that you hypnotize yourself. You always have. You just let me influence the hypnosis at times. One of the reasons you were able to dissociate as a child is because you are predisposed to self-hypnotic states. If we succeed in integration, you may feel an overwhelming need to dissociate again. It's possible you will be able to choose to remain in the here and now, instead of escaping into a trance. It may be hard, but you will have some control over what happens."

Diana nodded. "One question, and then I want to go ahead and do it," she said. "You just started calling me Di. You've never done that before. Why?"

Sarah smiled. "It's just a name. Something new. I thought it might come in handy. Is there a name you prefer?"

Diana shook her head, then rubbed her eyes as a tear coursed down her cheek. "No, it's a fine name. I like it a lot. Sarah, I love you," she said suddenly. "Thank you for everything."

"You're not going anywhere," Sarah said. "You're going to be fine."

Diana smiled and said nothing.

"All right, then. First, I'd like to talk to one of the others," Sarah said. "Close your eyes, Diana."

Diana held Sarah's gaze for a few seconds, smiled again, then closed her eyes.

"I'd like to speak to Lynn, please," Sarah said.

Diana opened her eyes wide, but Sarah saw that they were no longer Diana's eyes.

"You bitch," the woman hissed. "You think you can get away with this, but you're wrong. We will win. We will see you in hell first . . ."

"Nora, go away," Sarah shouted. "I do not wish to talk to Nora. Nora, go away."

"Fuck you."

"When I count to three, Nora, you will go back to where you came from," Sarah said, her voice strong and unwavering. Nora continued to shout obscenities.

"One. Two. Three."

Nora's eyes lost their hard shine and in a moment her eyelids closed. Sarah breathed a sigh of relief.

"Lynn, are you there?"

The eyes opened again.

"Well, hello, blondie," said the familiar voice. "This is quite a pickle you've gotten us into, isn't it?" Lynn smiled her brilliant smile.

Sarah smiled and nodded. "Yes, it is."

"No problem, sweetie. We can handle it," Lynn said.

"I'm glad to hear that. You know what's coming?"

"Sure."

"Is everyone ready?"

"Most of the kids are ready," Lynn nodded. "I've talked to them, and they're scared and excited at the same time. I told them it's their chance to be a part of everything all the time."

"That's right," Sarah said. "What about you?"

"I'll be ready when the time comes. But I'm not

going anywhere until we take care of Nora and Isis and the others on that side."

"That makes sense. How do we go about doing it?"

"You're in the driver's seat, boss."

"Thanks a lot."

Lynn grinned. "Lainey wants to go first."

"Okay. How does Diana find her?"

Lynn thought for a moment.

"Around the time when all the kids came into being, Iris lived in a big house, a mansion really. It had one of those living mazes made of gigantic boxwood bushes. Do you know what I mean?"

"Yes," Sarah nodded.

"Well, Iris used to hide there. In the summer, when the sun was shining, it was the only place she felt safe," Lynn said. "It's where all the kids go now to hide."

"I understand."

"Be careful, Sarah," Lynn said. "This is not fantasy here. And there's more than just the kids in those boxwoods."

"I'll be careful," Sarah said. She cleared her throat. "Close your eyes, Lynn. I'd like to talk to Diana again."

Lynn closed her eyes, then opened them after just a second. Diana smiled at Sarah.

"Hi," she said.

"Hi, Di," Sarah said. "Now close your eyes."

Diana shut her eyes tightly.

"I want you to find the place where the kids go, Diana. They like to hide in the boxwoods, in the maze made of boxwood bushes. Do you know the place?"

"Yes," Diana said, "I do." Her voice sounded sleepy and distant.

"Good. Can you go there now?"

"Yes."

"I want you to walk into the maze and tell me what you see."

Diana was silent for several seconds. Her head lifted slightly. Her eyes moved beneath the closed lids.

"I'm opening the gate. I'm lifting the latch and pushing the gate open."

"A gate into the maze?" Sarah asked.

Diana nodded. *A gate,* thought Sarah. The *gate. When Lainey talked about going behind the gate, she was being more literal than I thought. When I called Linda the Gatekeeper, I guess I wasn't far off.*

"The bushes are tall, so tall, Sarah," Diana said. "You wouldn't believe it. It's almost like entering a tunnel, except the sky is bright and blue overhead."

"Good. Keep telling me everything you see," Sarah said. "Now, I want you to walk into the maze."

"I'm walking down the first corridor. It's empty, about fifteen feet long maybe. I'm about halfway down it now . . . It bends off to the right, and I'm just about ready to step around. Yes, there we go. Oh . . ." Diana sounded startled.

"What is it?"

"For a second, just as I stepped around the corner, I thought I saw something move," Diana said. "It's gone now."

"Okay. Go on."

"This corridor goes about twenty feet till it ends in a wall of boxwood. It looks like two more corridors go off to the right. One is about ten feet away. The entrance to the next one is five feet beyond that."

"Let's check out the first one," Sarah said, and suddenly she felt as if she were there with Diana. She had to remember that this was real, frighteningly real to Diana and the others.

"Okay, I'm right up to it now and looking in," Diana continued. "It goes for about ten feet and turns left. Now there's a sharp right and another right again. There's a sort of a clearing up ahead, about ten feet. Oh, someone has just stepped out into the clearing."

"Do you know who it is?"

"It's a child, a little girl. She's holding her arms out to me."

"Go to her, Diana."

"Her name is Lainey, isn't it?"

"Ask her."

"My name is Diana. Who are you?"

Sarah shivered as Diana paused. She could almost hear the little girl's reply.

"You want to come with me?" Diana continued. "We can be together always, Lainey. Here, let me hold you."

Diana slipped out of her chair and knelt on the floor. Her eyes were closed and she held her arms out. Then they closed around empty air.

"Oh God, oh God," Diana gasped suddenly. She bent at the waist, holding her head in her hands.

"What is it?" Sarah moved to kneel beside her. She wrapped her arms around Diana's shoulders. "Tell me what happened."

"The pain, Sarah, the pain. All these years I never knew the pain. Lainey took the pain. She took it so no one else would have to know it. Lainey was there for all the beatings, all the pain. Oh, poor, poor child. They tried to make her feel guilty for the pain, too, Sarah."

"It wasn't her fault. They did terrible things to her. She did nothing wrong."

"We know that now."

"Where is Lainey now?"

"She's here, Sarah, she's here with me." Diana sat up with her legs tucked underneath her. She hugged herself tightly. "We're together now."

A flood of relief washed over Sarah. *Maybe this really will work,* she thought. Sarah helped Diana back to the chair, then returned to her own seat.

"Do you want to leave the maze now, Diana?" Sarah asked.

"No, I want to go on."

"All right."

"I'm in the clearing. Corridors go off both to the left and right. The right path ends after a few feet. That's where Lainey was hiding. The left goes on a bit. I'm walking that way now."

Diana said nothing for several long seconds.

"Where are you? Is everything okay?"

"Okay," Diana echoed, her voice far away. "Yes, okay." Suddenly, her voice was clearer, sharper. "The path dead-ends ahead and veers off to the left. Ten feet ahead is an opening to the left while the main path continues ahead . . . I'm at the turn now and going in. Another turn to the left . . ."

Sarah suddenly realized that she had no earthly idea what the shape of this—*imaginary?*—maze might be. Did that make a difference? Did she need to know how to navigate out of it?

But Diana was moving on. "And now left again and . . . Oh, Sarah, all the children. The children are all in the clearing here. Some are just babies."

"How many do you see, Diana?"

"There are three girls, probably between three and five years old. Two boys, about the same age. And three babies. Sarah, there are three little babies here."

"What are the children doing?"

"They have their arms out and I'm walking toward them. They're coming to me now, all the older children. They have their arms out and I want to hold them all. . . ."

Later that night, talking to Mark, Sarah described the look on Diana's face as one of rapture. Now, tears streamed down the young woman's face as her eyes moved beneath the closed lids.

"Where are the children now?" Sarah asked softly.

"They're here," Diana said, her voice filled with wonder. "Inside me. Part of me. The boys and the girls."

"Where are the babies?"

"I'm picking them up now."

Sarah watched, fascinated, as Diana made motions of picking something from the floor and pressing it to her breast. She repeated the gesture twice.

"The poor babies, Sarah. They hurt the little ones, too. It makes me very, very angry."

"Good," Sarah said. "It's time you felt anger."

"But anger is bad."

"No, Di," Sarah said. "Anger is an emotion. All emotions have their place. It is right that you feel anger at the ones who caused all this pain and hurt."

Diana was silent.

"Are you ready to leave the maze for now?"

"No," she said. "I think that there is someone else I must find."

"All right," Sarah said. She felt edgy, nervous. The tension of watching Diana navigate the maze was becoming unbearable. Sarah suddenly wanted her out of there and back in this warm room.

"I'm coming out of the clearing now, which is a dead end, and back out into the main corridor. I'm turning left. Now straight ahead for ten or twelve feet. That's as far as I can go that way, but there's an opening here to the left. Another corridor. It looks like a dead end. Yes. Oh, no, wait. There *is* an opening. I couldn't see it till I was right on it. I'm turning. Another clearing up ahead. There are two people here, one on either side of a little hexagonal clearing. It's a dead end. Something's wrong, Sarah. The girl wants to come to me and that's okay. But so does the woman. She scares me."

"Then turn around and leave, Diana," Sarah said. "We'll find the girl later."

"No, I must get her out now."

Who was the woman? Sarah thought frantically. Panic began to creep over her.

"What does the woman look like?" she asked breathlessly.

Also breathless, Diana answered quickly, "Curly brown hair, tall. Big-boned."

Nora?

"Run and get the girl, then turn and run out."

"I'm scared."

"Move," Sarah shouted. "There's no time."

"All right, I've got the girl. She's part of me now. I can't run. Sarah, the woman's blocking the way out."

Diana's high-pitched shriek of hysteria filled the room.

"It's okay, she can't hurt you if you fight her. Diana, I want you to run at her. Run right at her, push her to the side. Hit her if you have to."

"I can't."

"Yes, you can," Sarah shouted. Then she was on her feet, standing next to Diana's chair. "Do it, damnit."

"Yes, yes . . . it worked, I'm through."

"Run like hell."

"I'm running. Oh, God, my legs feel so slow, like I'm running in water. . . ."

Diana's head turned to the left, then back, her eyes still closed.

"Where are you, Di?"

"I don't know. Do I turn right or go straight. What do I do? Oh, God, she's coming after me."

Sarah clenched her fists in frustration. *Where is she? Oh, damn. Wait, wait, get a grip. She must be at the turn to the clearing where she found the kids. She should go straight.*

"Go straight," Sarah shouted.

Suddenly, Sarah had a complete picture of the maze fixed in her mind, like looking down from a great height. *Yes, Di needed to run straight, then she would have to turn right.*

"Turn right at the end and run for the clearing. Bear to the right and go into the right corridor. Are you with me?"

Diana nodded, her breath coming in huge, ragged gasps. "I'm in the clearing. Now I'm down the path."

"Left and left again, then right. Down the corridor and turn left. Left into the big corridor, not right."

"I got it."

"Almost home."

"She's coming!"

"Run, damnit, run," Sarah shouted. "You have to turn left again at the end, then down the long corridor."

"I'm there."

"Run!"

"She's coming . . ."

"Run. A quick right at the end and . . ."

"I'm home . . ."

"You're home!"

Diana leaped out of the chair and into Sarah's arms. Both women were soaked in perspiration. They gasped for air in each other's arms.

Between breaths, Diana said, over and over, "I got her, Sarah, I got her."

Sarah pushed the sweat-streaked hair back from Diana's forehead. "Yes, you got her," she smiled. "Who is she?"

"Iris," Diana laughed. "Iris is part of me now."

Sarah sipped a cup of hot tea and tried to work on her speech. Diana had left for a long soak in the tub, leaving her alone, but Sarah could not concentrate on the speech. She kept thinking of Diana in the maze.

Diana was probably as vulnerable as she had ever been. She could easily walk out of the bathroom now with all the newly gathered fragments of herself scattered to the wild winds. Sarah had warned her to resist the desire to slip into trance, to escape. To fragment. Still, dissociation was a lifesaving skill she had learned over many years. The likelihood that she could resist in a threatening situation was slim. The boxwood maze was a wonderful place to hide.

Except now, Nora hid in the boxwoods. Diana would want to avoid that.

Was she pushing too hard, too fast? Did they have a choice? Was she going about it the right way?

Sarah told herself that there was no right way, that they had entered uncharted territory. Still, the assurance rang hollow and did little to relieve her anxiety.

The kids, possibly all of them, had been integrated. Perhaps even the original Iris Laine Morrison, the infant who had gone away to hide so long ago, was among them. The Iris whom Diana referred to was not the original Iris, but rather the little girl who had been responsible for going to school, for interacting with the "normal" world. Still, the infant Iris might have been one of the babies Diana found. Perhaps it wasn't even important.

Nora, on the other hand, certainly was important. Sarah chewed her nails in frustration. She had no idea what to do. Could she and Isis be ignored, perhaps relegated to some hidden corner of Diana's mind through the successful integration of the others? Something about that notion rang false to Sarah. She had a feeling that any issue not dealt with now would have to be faced later.

Could an alliance be formed? Sarah doubted it. Nora and her side—when had she started thinking about this in terms of sides?—represented the very forces that Diana must learn to experience anger and rage and even hate over. How could she reconcile herself to that?

Sarah sighed and turned back to her writing. In a short while, she would have a succinct account constructed of events right up to the present moment. What would she write then? she wondered.

* * *

They retired early that evening. After dinner, Bill and Mark had sat spellbound by Sarah's account of Diana in the maze, but fatigue had overtaken everyone.

Sarah and Mark undressed and slipped beneath the cold sheets in bed. Mark put out his arm and Sarah snuggled in close to him.

"Sarah, I don't really want to bring this up," Mark said hesitantly, "but it's been driving me crazy. What's going to happen when she remembers the personality that I met? Marcia."

Sarah propped her head up on one arm to look at her husband. "I don't know, Mark. I've wondered the same thing myself. She's one of the engineered personalities. I don't even know if Diana will be able to integrate those. I may be setting her up for an impossibility."

"What do you mean?"

"She could end up with two partially integrated portions—one that is suddenly aware of everything that's been perpetrated over the years, and one that is sympathetic to, actually a part of, all that stuff. Instant war. Absolute incompatibility. It might be an intolerable situation. Probably the best outcome would be that she does integrate and remember everything. Including you. At least then she would know enough to be able to evaluate the experience. Believe me, what she did with you is probably the least of the betrayals she's been forced to be part of. The worst betrayals are the ones she did to herself."

"Yeah."

"Mark, not to change the subject, but what do you think of the idea of going public with all of this?"

"What do you mean?"

"I'm supposed to give a speech in a couple of weeks. I think that the only way to get these people off of us is to go public. They wouldn't dare harm us if it meant publicly confirming their own existence."

"I think I understand," he said. "If you go public, probably nobody's going to believe you, so they are relatively safe. Naturally, they'd prefer you didn't say anything. But if you do say something, you're immune. They won't hurt you or Diana because any retaliation would mean they really exist."

"You figured that out pretty quick. So do you think I should do it?" she asked. "Everybody's going to think I'm nuts, you know."

"If it means you're going to be safe from these bastards, then, yes, I think you should do it," Mark said. "I don't want to lose you to some gang of crazies."

"That's what scares me, Mark," she said. "This isn't just some isolated group of fruitcakes. These people have been around for a long time. They could be anybody. And the chrysalides . . . think about it, the chrysalides really could be anybody. And they wouldn't know, but they'd be at least partially under the control of this cult. I'm starting to get really paranoid. Outside of the four of us here in this house, I don't know who to trust anymore."

Mark pulled Sarah toward him, resting her head on his shoulder.

"Well, you're safe now, honey," he said. "Nobody's going to find us up here." But the assurance rang hollow to Mark. Something was nagging him, something that, try as he might, he could not identify. He lay awake in the dark a long time, till at last his eyes unfocused and his mouth went slack.

Chapter 29

Week 19: Thursday, December 7

Once again, Travers stumbled out into the living room to find Sarah tapping away at the little keyboard. He padded to the kitchen, poured a cup of coffee, then returned to the living room. Sarah watched him as he sat.

"Morning," she said.

"Back atcha," he answered. "How's it going?"

"Done."

"Done?"

"Done," Sarah repeated. She reached down to the nylon bag at her feet, fished around for a few seconds, and extracted a flat plastic square. She shoved this into a slot built into the side of the little computer.

"Now, I save it on a diskette, and that's that."

Sarah tapped something at the keyboard. An instant later, a light winked on the diskette drive and the machine made a slight humming noise. When the humming stopped, Sarah pushed a button and ejected the little diskette from the drive's slot. She pulled it free and tossed it back in the computer bag.

"What's on the agenda for today? You gonna give it a rest or forge on?" Travers said.

"I don't think there's any choice but to keep going," Sarah said.

Travers nodded thoughtfully. "I talked to Fisher."

"Yes, I was wondering." Sarah pulled the screen down over the computer keyboard and snapped it into place. "Is he going to help us?"

"He was reluctant to go back into the Nottingham County stuff. However, I did get the name of the pathologist who did the lab work. And I tried to call him."

"Good for you." Sarah packed the computer in the nylon bag. "What happened?"

"Seems our boy was transferred suddenly." Travers smiled. "No, wait. He was fired. Transferred appears to be the official line. Funny thing, too. He destroyed half his lab before he left."

"Including our sample?"

Travers nodded. "Most likely. The lady who replaced him wasn't sure when she'd ever figure out what she's got and what's missing."

"So what do you think it means?"

"I don't think it's any coincidence that the guy has effectively disappeared off the face of the earth at this particular time."

"You think the Circle arranged it?"

"I think maybe you were right," Bill said. "I think they screwed up, somehow they got this guy to fake a lab report, and then figured out how to get rid of him."

Sarah sipped her coffee thoughtfully. "What would it take to pull something like that off?"

"I don't know," Travers said. "If the guy was a member of the Circle himself, he might be able to do it. Otherwise, it would probably take someone pretty high up in the local bureaucracy to pull those kinds of strings."

"I'm paranoid enough already," Sarah said. "I don't need this."

"It does make you wonder just how far their influence extends."

Sarah nodded. "If they've really been around for

years, they'd have to be well entrenched in their communities. They could be anybody."

"Now *I'm* getting paranoid."

"That's too much to worry about right now. We've got our own little battle with the Circle to wage right here."

"That sounds like an apt metaphor," Travers said.

"That's one of the problems," Sarah frowned. "It's getting hard to tell what's metaphor and what's reality anymore."

"How do you mean?"

"Yesterday, Diana had to make a full-tilt, all-out escape from a maze of boxwood bushes," Sarah said. "The boxwoods are a memory from childhood, a place where she felt safe. In her interior landscape, it's become the place where the children go when they're not the dominant personality. So the boxwoods are a metaphor for safety and sanctuary, right?"

"Right."

"Except that Nora was in the boxwoods yesterday and she chased Diana," Sarah said. "Diana got confused. If I hadn't helped her navigate out, I'm not sure what would have happened. What I *am* sure of, though, is that those boxwoods were a hell of a lot more than a metaphor. It would have been a mistake for me to have treated the maze as anything but real."

"Aren't all those memories real as long as they are compartmentalized away?" Travers asked.

Sarah looked up, startled. "Why, yes, Bill, they are. That's not a bad way of looking at it. As long as things are kept fragmented, they are eternally real, eternally present. There is a difference, though."

"What's that?"

"This is no memory. There was never a Nora in the boxwoods. This is something new, happening because of current events."

"So have you figured out how you're going to handle Nora?'' Travers asked. ''Not to mention Isis? The Listener?''

''I don't have the slightest idea,'' Sarah admitted.

''Are you ready to go back to the maze?'' Sarah asked.

Diana nodded. Mark looked up from a paperback he was reading. Travers leaned across the kitchen counter, a coffee mug still gripped firmly in his hand.

''You want us to take a hike, Sarah?'' Bill asked.

''That's really up to Diana,'' Sarah said. ''Di?''

Diana smiled. ''No. I'd like you all to stay, if you'd like. You've been so helpful, I don't think I'd be here if it wasn't for all of you.''

Travers joined Diana on the sofa, carrying with him a pen and a legal pad. Diana smiled at him, then turned to face Sarah.

''I'm ready anytime,'' she said.

''All right,'' Sarah said. ''Close your eyes and let's go back to the maze.''

Diana took a deep breath and closed her eyes.

''Yes,'' she said, and a second later, added, ''I'm there.''

''Good,'' Sarah said. ''I want you to enter the maze. Tell us where you are each step of the way.''

''All right,'' she said, ''I'm entering the long corridor, walking all the way to the end where it turns to the right . . . Walking along, now, the first opening is about ten feet ahead to the right.''

''That's the one we explored yesterday,'' Sarah said. ''Let's try the next one.''

''Yes, that's right,'' Diana said. ''The next opening is about five feet beyond the first. It goes off to the right, too . . .''

Sarah looked over at Bill, who was scribbling furiously on his legal pad. For a moment, she wondered what he was doing, then realized. He was sketching a map of the maze. Sarah nodded. *Good,* she thought, *that could be useful.*

". . . and now I'm entering . . . Okay, it goes ahead for six or seven feet, then goes off to the left . . . Let's see, then it just sort of jogs on straight ahead again, so it's sort of a quick left, right. Uh-oh."

"What is it, Di?"

"This corridor keeps on going straight, another ten feet or so, then makes a turn to the left. But there's also a turn right here. Off to the left. Which one should I take?"

"Your choice, Di," Sarah said. "What do you think?"

"We'll go straight," she said.

Long seconds passed in silence. Travers arched his eyebrows inquiringly at Sarah.

"Where are we, Di?" Sarah asked.

A pause. "Almost to the end," she answered. "I was right. It veers off at an angle to the left and opens up into a square clearing. There's somebody in the clearing."

"Okay, Di, relax." Sarah leaned forward in her chair. "Who is it?"

"I don't know," Diana said, anxiety beginning to choke her voice. "She's got her back turned to me."

"Ask her to turn around."

Diana hesitated. Then her voice came in a tentative whisper. "Hello?" she said. "Hello?"

"Tell her to turn around."

Diana cleared her throat. "Please turn around." Her voice was louder, stronger. "Whoever you are, *please turn around!*"

Now, Bill and even Mark leaned forward expectantly. The room was utterly silent except for the barely audible sifting of ash in the fireplace.

"Sarah," Diana choked, her voice suddenly stricken with fear. "Oh, my God, Sarah, it's me. Sarah, I'm looking at myself."

Sarah struggled to think. *Who is it? Who has she found? Certainly not Nora. Isis? It may be Isis. Isis might be Diana's twin.*

"Demand to know who it is," Sarah said urgently.

"Who are you?" Diana asked. "What is your name?"

A log fell in the fireplace. Both Mark and Bill jumped, then glanced around nervously.

"Diana? Sarah, she says her name is Diana."

Diana! Yes, of course. Diana is the failed experiment. But is she allied with my Diana, with Lynn, and with the kids? The Circle tried to use her as their window on the world. Instead, something happened and she left behind my Diana, thought Sarah. *Left her behind as the window on the world for the non-Circle personalities.*

Is she safe? Sarah's thoughts raced frantically. *Is she danger or strength? She was created from the symbolic death of Iris Morrison and the actual death of the real Diana Smith. But what does that make her?*

"Go to her," Sarah shouted suddenly. "Go to her. Make her part of you, Di."

"But who is she, Sarah?" Diana's voice twisted. "I'm afraid. She scares me."

Bill started to stand up. "Sarah, are you certain you . . ."

Sarah cut him off with a glance. Travers sat back down.

"Do it, Diana," she insisted. "Do it."

"Sarah, she's smiling at me. We're walking to each other." Tears began to run down Diana's cheek. "She says she's my sister."

"She's more than your sister, Di," Sarah said softly. "She's . . ."

"Diana!!" Diana screamed, and doubled up at the waist as if seized by a sudden cramp. *"Diana!!"* she screamed again, her voice grief-stricken, hysterical. *"They killed you . . . I killed you . . . Diana!!"*

"Hold her, Bill," Sarah said.

Travers slid over next to Diana and wrapped his arms around her. She collapsed against him, her face buried in his lap, her screams muffled.

Long minutes passed while the screams subsided into gut-wrenching sobs.

"Di, can you hear me?" Sarah asked after some of Diana's initial hysteria seemed to have passed. "Di?"

Diana gave no indication that she heard.

"Diana!" Sarah commanded.

Diana looked up, her face blotchy and swollen from crying.

"Listen to me," Sarah said. "They killed Diana a long time ago. Diana was your friend. *They* killed her, not you. Do you understand?"

"But, Sarah, why did they kill her? They didn't have to do that."

"They killed her so that they could control you," Sarah said. "Do you remember? They pretended to kill Iris Morrison. And Iris became Diana. Do you remember?"

"Iris?" Diana asked. "Iris? I remember Iris."

"Of course you do," Sarah whispered. "They made you think that you had died. And then they made you think you were reborn, only you were reborn as your best friend, Diana Smith. Do you remember?"

"I remember, Sarah, I remember," she said. "But Iris is dead. They killed Iris. But if Diana is dead, too . . . Sarah, who am I? If Diana is dead, *who am I?*"

"That's what we're here to find out, Di," Sarah said gently. "And I think we're close to home. This Diana that you just found, I think she wasn't fooled by their tricks. She just couldn't *be* Diana and know that Diana was dead at the same time."

"Sarah, they made me marry him," Diana said.

"Marry who, Di? Who did you marry?"

"The Father," she said.

What?

"Who did you marry?" Sarah repeated.

"They made me marry the Father," she said. "The Old One."

"Who is the old one?" Sarah asked.

"Saitan," she hissed, pronouncing the syllables as if they were two words: *shy-tan.* "I married Saitan."

"No," Sarah said, realization suddenly dawning. "They only made you think you married Satan. Satan doesn't really exist. But they made you think he did."

"But I had his daughter, Sarah," she insisted. "He took me on our wedding night and he made me feel good, Sarah. He made me feel good." Hysteria began to creep back into her voice.

"It's all right that you felt good," Sarah said, "but they tricked you."

"No," she insisted. "He made me pregnant that night."

"What happened to the baby?" Sarah asked, sensing with dread where this conversation was leading.

"I killed it for Saitan, Sarah," she began to sob again. "It's a great honor, you know. Most of the daughters are given to Saitan."

"Listen to me," Sarah said in steady, even tones. "Whatever you did, you were made to do. You are not responsible. They did it, not you. They killed your baby, Di. Can you say that?"

"They killed my baby." Diana sat up. Travers released her. She wiped her eyes with her hands.

"They killed my baby," she said again, though this time her voice was tinged with the sharp edge of anger.

"Yes, Di," Sarah said. "They are responsible. They are the ones we are fighting in this maze."

"I want to fight them, Sarah." She closed her eyes and leaned back against the sofa. "The clearing is empty now," she said.

"Okay," Sarah said. She glanced over at Mark. He sat slumped in the deep armchair, his eyes flashing light from the fireplace, his face expressionless. He returned her glance, but his look betrayed no emotion. Travers, on the other hand, was all but wringing his hands as he looked anxiously from Diana to Sarah and back again. Sarah smiled at him. *It's okay,* she mouthed silently. She thought he relaxed a little.

"Tell us where you go," she said.

"I'm going back down the path now. I'm at the place where it turns off. To the right coming from this direction."

Sarah watched as Bill picked up his paper and pen again.

"Yes, to the right," Sarah said.

"A few feet farther and it goes off to the left . . . Okay, now about ten feet more, yes, just a minute, off to the right again now and about another ten feet . . ."

Travers drew quickly, his forehead wrinkled in concentration.

". . . now right again. Okay, on for about ten feet and I've got another split. I can either go straight or off to the right. The path ahead goes for a long way. I think I'll take the right path. Okay, down the path five or six feet and off to the right. Five more feet and right again. Now three feet and right. Three feet again and right and . . ."

Travers scratched furiously for a second and stopped, his frown of concentration now turning to puzzlement and confusion. He looked up.

". . . dead end," Diana said.

Sarah watched Bill look from Diana to the paper and back again. At last he nodded, having reconciled the description to the map.

"I'm turning around now," Diana said. "Left . . . left . . . and left again. A little farther and left again. This could make you dizzy. Now up ahead is the branch. Left is back the way I came and right is the new path. Here I am, I'm turning right now. The path goes on for a long way, a good twelve or fifteen feet. I can't tell yet whether it turns or ends . . ."

Sarah sensed, even with no map, that if the path

veered to the left, Diana would enter a whole new section of maze. If it veered right, it would fold back in on itself, with limited room for expansion.

"Yes, it does turn," Diana said. "To the right . . ."

Limited room for expansion—the maze should be coming to an end.

"Okay, right and another quick right, so I'm essentially heading in the same direction I just came from. Parallel. It goes for about ten feet. Left now and a short corridor opening up ahead . . ."

Diana breathed with a slight pant. Sarah wondered whether her legs and feet would ache from this—*imaginary?*—walk. *At this point,* Sarah thought, *I wouldn't be surprised if she had blisters.*

". . . and this is it," Diana said. "The path ends in a little triangle-shaped clearing. I'm at one point of the triangle. There are people at each of the other points."

"Who are they, Di?" Sarah asked, suddenly tense. *This is the end of the maze. Now or never.* "Quickly," she added.

"I've seen them both before," Diana said. "The brunette from yesterday, the one who chased me. She's the one I saw in the corridor, too. The other is the blonde I saw in the corridor."

"The brunette's name is Nora," Sarah said. "The blonde is Lynn or Linda. You can trust Lynn. Don't trust Nora."

"Nora's at the point of the triangle to my right. Lynn's at the left point. Nora is smiling. Lynn is shaking her head."

"Ask Lynn what's wrong," Sarah instructed.

"I can't say anything, Sarah," Diana shouted. "Neither can the others. We try to talk and it's like the words are taken away. I see Lynn trying to tell me something, but I can't hear her. . . ."

Sarah sat silent, feeling helpless. Diana seemed to strain forward in her seat, her head tilting this way and that as if trying to hear some far-off conversation.

"I can't hear you," she whispered, her voice raspy and barely audible. "Please speak up," she said, but her own voice had faded to near-silence.

Sarah looked helplessly at Bill. Whatever was going on occurred in a triangular clearing in a boxwood maze; it was not a product of events in this living room.

Travers shot her a questioning glance. Sarah shrugged.

"Diana, what's happening?" Sarah asked sharply.

Diana's mouth moved in soundless whispers now. She showed no sign of hearing.

"Diana?" Sarah repeated.

I can't hear you, Diana mouthed.

Is she talking to me or Lynn? Sarah wondered.

Speak up, Diana's lips moved again.

Sarah could just make out the shape of the words. *To Lynn, then,* she thought. *She's talking to Lynn.*

"Sarah, Sarah, where are you?" Diana suddenly shrieked. Sarah, Travers, and even Mark sat up at once.

"I'm here, Di, I'm right here," Sarah answered.

"Where are you, Sarah?" she called again. "I can't hear you. Sarah?"

Sarah bounded out of her chair to kneel in front of Diana. She took the woman's hands in her own and reached up to touch her forehead.

"I'm right here, honey," she said. "Can you hear me?"

"Oh, Sarah," Diana said. "Please don't leave me here, alone," her voice choked off. "Nora's not alone. Oh, God, Nora's not alone."

"Good girl," Sarah said. "Keep talking."

"It's like looking into a fun house mirror. When Nora moves her head, I can see them lined up behind her in a row, one after the other. I can only see clearly the one behind her. She looks like me, only not like me, too. Her hair is dark but she's got my face, only her face is cruel. Oh, Sarah, where are you?"

"I'm right here," Sarah shouted. "I don't know if you can hear me, but I'm right here."

"Lynn is shaking her head again. I don't understand what she means. She looks sick and weak. I don't understand. Please tell me what . . ."

Diana's face changed as abruptly as a television tuned by remote control to another channel. Sarah recoiled involuntarily from the sudden onslaught.

"You little bitch, I've got you now . . ." the voice hissed.

Nora! Sarah recognized her immediately.

". . . you always were nothing, you know. Nothing to us and nothing to yourself. A shell is all you ever . . ."

". . . no, no, no," the voice changed abruptly. It was weak, yet the words carried an angry conviction.

Lynn, Sarah thought. *Lynn, please help Diana.*

". . . don't listen to her," Lynn continued. "You must help me, you must . . ."

". . . shut the fuck up, bitch," Nora interrupted again.

What the hell is happening? What was Lynn saying about helping?

". . . but not kill you," Nora was saying. "Take you into my soul and lock you away in the demon-filled recesses where the power dwells. Killing is too good for . . ."

"Sarah, where are you? Help me, I . . ." Diana's voice filled the room with panic.

"I'm right here," Sarah shouted. "I'm right here."

". . . in the dark places you have always loved so much," Nora jeered, "and you can fuck the demons all the time. They bring you such pleasure, don't they?"

". . . the children," Lynn's voice seemed to grow even weaker. "Where are the children?"

". . . could hear you for just a second, Sarah," Diana shouted, "I know you're there. For God's sake, can you hear me? *What's happeni—*"

"I'm here," Sarah shouted back. She was standing in front of Diana now, frantic with helplessness. *What in the name of God is going on? What is Lynn trying to tell Diana about the children? Keep talking to Diana and listen for Lynn when she comes around,* Sarah commanded herself.

"I can hear you, Diana," Sarah shouted. "Keep talking. I can hear everything you say."

". . . come be a part of us." Nora laughed a wild, pestilent laugh. "We *know* what you like. Come meet your destiny. Isis rules us all in the end . . ."

Sarah heard a groan and looked over at Mark. His face had gone pasty-white. *What the hell?* she wondered, then it hit her. He had just recognized Nora as the voice of Marcia. *Well, that's your little bridge to cross,* Sarah thought. *There are other things to deal with at the moment.* Then Sarah was suddenly and overwhelmingly angry. The voice of Nora inflamed her. She had seduced her husband, made it possible for evil men to abduct her, and now she was trying to suck the life out of her friend.

". . . and eat the sweet flesh of the helpless," Nora laughed again.

"Let her go, damnit, let her go," Sarah shouted.

". . . help me, Sarah, help me. She's getting closer, Sarah . . ."

"Let go!"

". . . and the flames burn bright, but you *like* the flames don't you, because it feels so good where it burns, doesn't it? Just like . . ."

"No! Let her go!"

". . . in the corridor, Diana. Remember the corridor? You've got to give me . . ."

"Let go, goddamnit!" Sarah shouted, then recoiled at a touch on her arm. She looked around. Bill touched her gently with his hand. He was saying something.

"Sarah, listen to Lynn," he said very softly. "She's trying to tell Diana something."

Sarah shook her head. *What have I been doing, yelling like a damn fool? Yes, Lynn. What is Lynn saying? Something about the kids. The kids and the corridor. The corridor Diana saw? With Lynn on one side and Nora on the other . . .*

". . . think of it, you know you like it, think of all the . . ."

Wait for Lynn, wait for Diana . . .

"Sarah, where are you? . . ."

"I'm here, Di. Listen to Lynn," Sarah said, her voice now just above a whisper, "Lynn knows what to do . . ."

". . . the Circle always waits for its daughters, you know that, and you are a daughter of the darkness, daughter of the Circle, one of us . . ."

". . . complete the triangle, Diana. I need them to balance the triangle . . ."

The triangle? What about the triangle? Wait. Put yourself there. See it like Di sees it now. Sarah forced her breathing to slow. *I'm at the point of an equilateral triangle. At one point, to my right, is Nora. Behind Nora are all the allies of the Circle, Isis and all the others. Nora is just the front. At the other point is Lynn. Lynn, who seems to be losing it, growing weaker . . .*

". . . not much time now, Diana. She's drawing her toward you. You can't resist her . . ."

"You *must* resist her," Sarah shouted. "Listen to Lynn."

". . . where you have lived all along, whenever you'd take off that cloak of sanctimony and recognize the way the universe really works . . ."

". . . trying to listen to Lynn, but she's so far away. Keep talking to me, Sarah, keep telling me what to . . ."

Nora on one side, Lynn on the other. Like the corridor. Nora with her charges behind her, Lynn with hers. But Lynn represents no one now. Is that why she is weak? Because she has given all the alters up to Diana? All her kids . . .

"Diana, listen to me," Sarah said with fierce urgency. "You must give all the others back to Lynn, you must . . ."

". . . bitch, come die a little death and live forever . . ."

". . . I need you, Diana, I need the . . ."

". . . I can't, Sarah. You said not to fragment again. I can't go back . . ."

". . . you must give them to her and trust her. Lynn can't fight without the kids, Di. You must . . ."

". . . quickly or it will be too late . . ."

". . . how do I do it? I don't know . . ."

". . . you must tell them to go. Tell them to run to Lynn. Tell them you set them free again . . ."

". . . free again to resume our place on the throne of Isis to rule over the house of . . ."

". . . go, go, go, please go. I'm scared, Sarah. I think this will kill me . . ."

". . . for there is no death within the Circle, for the Circle uses death and transforms . . ."

". . . send them to me, Diana . . ."

". . . send them to Lynn, Di, send them *now* . . ."

". . . go, go, *go now* . . ."

Sarah knelt again and for a moment buried her face in the fabric of Diana's jeans. The air seemed electric, the silence like the stillness of the summer air before it is rent by lightning. *What is happening?*

"They're with her, Sarah, they're with Lynn," Diana said.

"Can you hear me now, Di?" Sarah raised her head. Her cheeks were streaked with sweat and tears.

"Yes, Sarah, I can hear you," Diana said. "Lynn looks stronger now, Sarah. All the kids are lined up behind her. We're all back at our points now. Nora's no longer coming toward me."

"Good," Sarah breathed heavily. "Can you go to Lynn, Diana?"

"Then Lynn will win, won't she?" Diana asked softly. "I'm going to die, aren't I?"

"No, Di, I . . ." Sarah stammered. "I don't know."

"Thank you, Sarah, for telling me you don't know. I don't want to die, but I'll try." Diana panted, exhausted, silent for several seconds. "It's so hard . . .

Oh, oh, it worked. I took one step, and suddenly, Lynn is closer and Nora is farther away. But it's so hard."

"That's it, Di," Sarah shouted excitedly, "that's it. Go to Lynn."

"One more step. Uh . . . uh . . . there, I can almost touch Lynn now, and Nora is getting farther and farther away," Diana said. "Lynn is trying to say something, Sarah. She's shaking her head. Something's wrong, Sarah."

What could be wrong? Sarah looked to Bill, who looked back at her blankly.

"Balance," a small voice called from the corner of the room.

Both Sarah and Bill twisted their heads toward the source of the voice. Mark looked very pale now. He leaned forward as they turned.

"She said, 'balance the triangle,' Sarah," Mark whispered.

To Sarah, it seemed as if he struggled to speak. She wondered what was wrong with him. Perhaps in playing mute witness to Diana's ordeals, he was reminded of his own childhood demons. She didn't have time to worry about him now.

"You're losing the balance," Mark said, his whispered voice insistent.

Sarah looked at her husband, not understanding. She looked at Bill. He frowned.

Balance? But Nora is the counterweight. Balance may not be such a good idea.

"Di, step backward quickly," Sarah said. *Was Mark right? Is this what Lynn's trying to say?*

"No, Sarah, I'm almost there. I . . ."

"*Now,* damnit, step back."

"All right, all right, I'm back."

"What's Lynn doing?" Sarah asked.

"She's smiling and nodding," Diana answered.

"All right, now try this. Take one step forward, right

between the other two points of the triangle. Don't even look left or right. Take a step."

"I'll try, Sarah," Diana answered. "That was easier, Sarah, but it's brought Lynn *and* Nora closer to me."

"That's right, Di. They want to meet you in the center of the triangle. Walk ahead again."

"I can't, Sarah. What if Nora wins?"

"Nora's not going to win, Di." Sarah squeezed Diana's hands tightly. "Not if you all go together. You, and Lynn, and Nora."

"I'm taking another step, Sarah. I don't like this."

"All right, it's all right. Where are you? Talk to me."

"I'm one step away from them. For every step I take, they take one."

"Don't look at them, Di. Just put our your arms and take them in."

"But they're stronger than I am."

"No, they're not, Di."

"Yes, Sarah, they are. I know they are."

"No, Di. Listen to me. They have each watched the world through your eyes for many years. They have ridden on your shoulders. They took all the memories and the knowledge and the feelings. But they had to leave you the strength. You are the one who faces a world of uncertainty every day. They're both weak compared to that."

"Oh, Sarah, I love you," Diana whispered. "Whatever happens."

"Take the step, Di," Sarah said urgently. "Take it now."

"Wait."

"What is it?"

"Lynn is trying to say something."

"What is it?"

"Wait a minute, Sarah."

"What?"

Diana was silent. No one moved. The silence seemed to stretch on and on. Sarah watched as muscles moved in Diana's throat and mouth.

The voice was hoarse and barely audible. Sarah thought she heard triumph in it, as well as an infinite weariness.

"Goodbye, Sarah," it said.

It was the last time Sarah would ever hear the voice of Lynn. She tried to say "goodbye" in return, but the word choked in her throat. There was no time to dwell on losses.

"Now," Sarah said, "put out your arms and take them. Take them into you, Di. They are all your sisters. You have a place for all of them. They are all a part of you now."

Diana stepped forward, both in the boxwood maze and in the living room of the cabin. In the maze, her arms closed around two women, one blonde, one brunette, and when she held them in her embrace, a hundred others folded into them, like cards shuffled into a deck. Some were evil and ugly. Some were innocent and sweet. They were all a part of her, all daughters of the Circle.

In the cabin, Diana stepped into Sarah's arms. Sarah hugged Di tightly and let herself cry freely at last.

It was done. Whatever it was, it was done.

Chapter 30

Diana nearly collapsed, exhausted, in Sarah's arms. Sarah motioned to Travers, and together they carried her into her bedroom. They put her on the bed, and Sarah pulled a comforter over her. As she turned to leave, Diana's eyelids fluttered open.

"We did it, didn't we?" she asked sleepily.

"Yes, sweetie," Sarah said, "we did it."

Travers waited in the hallway. As Sarah closed the door, he asked, "Is she all right?"

Sarah smiled reassuringly. "I think so, Bill," she said. "I think she's doing fine for someone who just gave birth."

"Gave birth?"

"To herself."

Several hours later, Sarah went back to check on her. She knocked softly on the door, then opened it quietly and stepped in. To her surprise, Diana was out of bed. She had changed clothes and was just finishing buttoning up a fresh blouse.

"Come in," she said, and smiled at Sarah.

Sarah closed the door behind her.

"You look refreshed," she said.

"I am refreshed," Diana said. "Actually, renewed would be more accurate. Would you hit me if I said I felt like a new woman?"

Sarah smiled. "How are you really?" she asked.

Di walked across the little bedroom, stopping to stand in front of Sarah. She reached up to rest her hands on Sarah's shoulders and looked closely at her.

"I'm fine," she said. "And I think I owe you my life."

"Oh, nonsense," Sarah said.

Diana hugged her for a moment, then pulled away.

"Oh, yes," she said. "And you know it."

Sarah shook her head. "Whatever we did, we did together, Di," she said. "Is it all right if I call you Di?"

"Yes," she said. "I think I'll use that name from now on. How did you know to do that? To start calling me Di instead of Diana?"

"I didn't know," Sarah said, "but I thought it might be useful to have something new for you to identify with. Di seemed to be a good combination of the old and the new." Sarah paused a moment and looked wonderingly at Di. "I thought perhaps something based on the name Iris might be more appropriate, but I wasn't sure."

"You did well to choose Di. Even though she's a part of me now, in some ways Iris is dead. She was killed at the age of twelve, just as surely as they killed my friend Diana."

"What about Diana?" Sarah asked. "Do you remember?"

Di nodded. "Yes, I remember. They really did kill her, Sarah. Up until today, one part of me has always believed it was my fault."

"And you're going to keep the name?"

"Yes. I think Diana would like that." Di smiled. "In many ways, I'm as much her as I am Iris Morrison."

"And what about Nora and Isis?"

"They're here," Di said. "Nora was pretty insignificant, actually. She had no real emotions of her own.

She was the shell that the others used to watch the world from."

Di's face suddenly clouded over.

"Do you know that . . . what I mean is, do you have any idea about . . ."

"That she seduced my husband?" Sarah asked. "Yes, I know all about it, Di. It's all right."

A weight seemed to lift from Di.

"Oh, Sarah, I'm sorry."

"It's all right," Sarah reassured her. "It wasn't your fault. Mark and I have worked that all through. Now, tell me about Isis."

"Isis is a funny set of memories," Di said. "It's going to take some time to understand all this, I think, but basically Isis didn't exist except during the activities of the Circle. She knows ritual and protocol and doctrine and all that sort of stuff, but she really had no other life. That's why it was so important that they scare you off. There would have been a ritual for Isis to assume the memories of all the personalities."

"The metamorphosis. She would have become whole, in a sense," Sarah said. "She would have had the memories and emotions and knowledge of all the others."

"Yes," Di said. "But until it was time to do that, they were always vulnerable to me putting together all the pieces spontaneously."

"Or to assistance from meddlesome therapists."

"Yes. Which is why they keep close tabs on all the chrysalides."

"You're a real threat to them now, you know that?"

"Yes."

"Di, I'm planning on going public with what we know about the Circle and what happened to you. I need your permission to do it. I think it's the only way to get them to leave us alone."

"How will you go public?"

"I have to give a lecture soon. I'll start with that."

"So you think that if you tell everything, they'll leave us in peace?"

"That's the theory. What do you think?"

"I think it's a crazy idea," Di said, then laughed. "I also think it might work. Can I help?"

"You just have," Sarah said. "One more thing. You have all of Lynn's knowledge and memories?"

"Yes." Diana nodded, suddenly serious. "Lynn's a part of me. I know you cared about her."

"I cared about all of you." Sarah smiled. "But I was also wondering if you can do my hair when it starts growing out." Sarah pulled a handful of hair over her eyes and looked through it at Di. "Lynn did this to me, you know."

"I know," Di said.

She reached out in a gesture Sarah found startlingly reminiscent of Lynn and grasped a piece of Sarah's hair between her fingers.

"Yeah, doc," she said, "it's high time you did something about this stuff."

She was free, she was truly free. For the first time since infancy, a horrid, heavy weight had been lifted from her. It had been a weight so constant that only in its absence could she be aware that it had existed at all.

The past spread out before Di like a diorama in some roadside attraction. Mostly, it was a pictorial of victimization and abuse. The few good things that had occurred—the friendships, the innocent relationships—had been cut out, excised by the Circle like a tumor. But instead of curing her, they had left only malignancy, attempting to rid her of all connection to the world outside.

But she had experienced that world beyond the Circle. And when the pieces of her were shuffled for the final time, they allied behind that world. The manipulations, subterfuges, and violence of the Circle suddenly became things that she had miraculously endured, rather than lessons she had struggled to learn. The Circle was defeated within her.

Sarah had told her once that experts were discovering multiple personality disorder was much more common than had been previously suspected. Along with this came a recognition of the extent to which children have been subjected to the abuses of adults. Child abuse is far more common than you would believe, she had said.

True malignancy is the perversion of the natural trust and helplessness of a child by an adult, whatever the etiology or rationale of the act, Di thought. She looked over the shattered history of herself and resolved to do whatever she could to prevent such horror from being perpetuated on others.

Along with the memories of specific events, faces, names, and dates had fallen into place with the sudden integration of personalities. They stood before her, frozen in time.

She would not forget them.

Chapter 31

Week 19: Friday, December 8

Mark carefully eased out of the bedroom, leaving Sarah sleeping soundly. He found Di and Travers already up and drinking coffee at the kitchen table.

"Good, I wanted to talk to you guys before Sarah got up," he said.

"What's up?" Travers asked.

"I want to have a celebration tonight, for Sarah. She's worked so hard lately."

"Oh, what a wonderful idea," Di said.

"I want it to be a surprise," Mark said. "I'd like to go into town and buy her a present, maybe pick up a cake and some wine. But you'll have to help me. She'll get suspicious if I tell her I'm going off to town by myself."

Travers smiled. "I could tell her I want to talk with her alone."

"Yeah, that would be great." Mark turned to Di. "Maybe you'd like to come along? I could use some help finding a present."

"I'd love to," Di said excitedly. "I have a couple of ideas already. . . ."

* * *

Sarah sensed something was not right. Mark seemed distant, evasive somehow; he refused to look her in the eye. And Travers and Di seemed to be keeping some mutual secret from her. They looked like a couple of school kids about to burst into giggles. Travers wanted to talk to her privately, and there was much she wished to discuss with him. Sarah was beginning to wonder if the Circle really could be kept at bay by going public, and she needed Travers's ideas.

Mark wanted to go into town to check on some clients. Sarah was surprised that Di wanted to go with him, but they seemed to have it all worked out. Sarah thought all three of them looked like kids caught with their hands in the cookie jar, but she was willing to go along with the program. For once, they felt like friends rather than refugees.

Travers proposed that he and Sarah take a walk while the others went into town. He checked the doors to make sure they were all locked, then the four of them walked out to the Travel-All. Mark started up the vehicle.

"You drive carefully, Mark," Sarah said.

"I will. We'll be back in . . . Oh, damn," he said, climbing back out of the vehicle.

"What, Mark?"

"I forgot my address book. Bill, give me your keys. I'll just be a minute."

While Mark ran back inside, Sarah walked over to the passenger side. Di beamed happily at her. Her eyes were wide and shiny, and she seemed full of joyous energy.

"You look happy this morning," Sarah said.

"I am, Sarah. I've gotten a whole new chance at life, and it feels wonderful. Thanks to you."

Sarah shook her head. "It was a good job all around."

Mark emerged from the house, locking the door behind him. He tossed the keys to Travers, gave Sarah a quick kiss and a hug, then climbed into the Travel-All. Sarah and Bill watched the vehicle lumber down the mountain path.

"You ready to hike? Got enough cigarettes with you?" Sarah asked with a smirk.

"Yeah. You'll have to have mercy on me. Going down will be easy, but with my lungs, climbing back up could be a problem."

They headed off for the woods, away from the house and the road.

Di talked a reluctant Mark into letting her drive back from town. She felt joyous, intoxicated with the clear mountain air and the brilliant light of December. Each breath felt like a gift. She had never imagined she could feel this way. It was as if she had emerged from a lifetime spent in a cave.

When they reached the start of the narrow mountain road, Mark got out and set the vehicle's four-wheel drive. He tried to talk Di into letting him drive, but she would have none of it. With a laugh, she shifted gears and started up the logging trail.

She discovered that driving up a rocky, rutted track was a hell of a lot more fun than *riding* up the same track. Di enjoyed the slow, dependable lumbering of the Travel-All. Her body moved easily with the car's motions.

She recalled that roughly halfway up the path was a clearing where the track came very close to one side of the mountain. The view was breathtaking, as the tree line abruptly ended and the side of the road fell away to a sheer drop. On the western side of the clearing was an open, rubble-strewn field where they could park the car and walk around a bit.

As they neared the clearing, Di caught a flash of movement off to her left. She turned her head from the road for an instant, saw nothing, and figured it must have been a bird taking flight.

She eased the car out past the tree line, being careful to keep well to the left-hand side of the road. Di resisted looking out over the mountainside, knowing the view would make her dizzy. She concentrated on scanning the path and looking for a good stopping place.

About a hundred yards ahead, the clearing ended and the path disappeared inside stands of hickory and pine. Something obstructed the path ahead, just inside the trees.

What was it?

As they drew closer, Di saw that a tree had fallen across the path. "So much for a leisurely break," she said, glancing over at Mark. His gaze was fixed on the tree. He said nothing.

"There's a chain in the back, I think," she said. "Maybe we can pull it out of the way."

Mark had turned to look back down the path. He said nothing, but Di noticed his white-knuckled grip on the dashboard.

"Mark, what is it?" She twisted in the seat to follow his stare, and bile rose in her throat.

Another log lay across the path at the edge of the clearing. They had just come from there. The log had not been there. She had not gone over or around any log.

What are the odds of a tree falling within two minutes of passing it? she thought. Panic began to rise in her like a bird fluttering in her stomach.

Di eased the vehicle up to the edge of the clearing, turned it off, and carefully set the hand brake. She scanned the tree line, seeing nothing.

"Come on, Mark, let's move that log."

Mark also seemed to have grasped the incredible unlikelihood of two trees falling at virtually the same time, at either end of a mountain clearing. Di watched him step woodenly from the car and glance around tentatively, as if half paralyzed with fear. She understood the feeling.

Di began walking toward the log. The mountain seemed too quiet. Where were the birds, the rustle of leaves? She felt very cold. Something was wrong.

When they stepped out from behind the trees, Di thought at first that it was a trick of her eyes. The movement was so seamless and their clothing so well matched to the forest that they seemed to melt into view. When she realized that she was seeing half a dozen *people* emerging from the trees, Di turned to run back to the Travel-All.

And ran right into the man standing behind her. Di screamed. She turned to run, but the man wrapped his arms around her, locking her in a powerful bear hug.

Six people emerged from the forest ahead, three men and three women. Two additional men came up from behind, apparently having come out of the woods on the other side of the clearing. One of them moved behind Mark, who was still frozen in place by the Travel-All. The other man slipped into the driver's seat.

They were dressed ruggedly, in hiking boots, ski pants, and heavy parkas. Several carried large backpacks. Most had on dark glasses. All wore gloves.

Gloves don't leave fingerprints, Di thought.

All except one of the group appeared in their late twenties or early thirties and were healthy, attractive, if somewhat earnest-looking people. The exception was an older man with silver-streaked hair, ruggedly handsome features, and a generous crinkling of laugh lines around his eyes. Di recognized him. His ritual name, his name within the Circle, was Asmoday. She also knew him by another name. Nora, masquerading as Marcia, had called him Beiderbeck when she had gone to the Holiday Inn lounge on Thanksgiving.

Asmoday nodded to the man behind Mark, and before either Di or Mark could react, the man slipped a short blackjack out of his pocket and raised it high. Di screamed as he brought it down, but it was too late. The truncheon struck Mark behind the ear with a dull smacking sound. The man caught Mark as he crumpled and dragged him to the passenger seat of the Travel-All.

Asmoday smiled at her. "One down," he said.

"You're going to kill us, aren't you?" Di asked. She was breathing quickly, hyperventilating. In horror, Di suddenly realized that she was rocking. What she really wanted to do, what her body was screaming at her to do, was to lie down on the ground, tuck her legs up against her chest, wrap her arms around her legs, and rock herself into oblivion. That was the way it had always been. That had been her ticket, her magic carpet ride back to the safety of the maze. Sarah had warned her that she might try to dissociate again, and also that she might be able to fight it. Di bit fiercely on the inside of her cheek. With the sudden rush of pain, her head cleared. The seductive call of oblivion faded.

"You're already dead," Asmoday said contemptuously. "You were *almost* a fully-realized human being, if we'd just had time to complete your training."

"I *am* fully-realized," Di said, struggling to keep her voice even. "For the first time in my life."

"Where is Isis now?" Asmoday asked with genuine curiosity.

"Gone," Di said. "Gone but not dead. She's a part of the whole now." Di added as an afterthought, "A very small part."

"Do you have any idea how much we put into her training? Do you know how important she was, what a work of art Isis would have been? What you have done is a terrible thing."

"The terrible thing is what you do to innocent children," Di said. She forced the trembling from her voice. "You're wrong, you know. All of you."

Asmoday shrugged as if the matter were of little concern.

"How did you find us?" Di asked.

Asmoday smiled, and Di saw a look of cunning penetrate the mask of good humor he cultivated for his dealings in the world outside the Circle. "You did," he said. "You called us and told us where you were."

But Di knew he was lying. For once in her life, she was absolutely certain. Maybe he was testing her, seeing if there were still any dissociated fragments within her. Maybe he was just sowing seeds of doubt out of simple meanness. But he was lying, and she knew it. Di spat on the ground at his feet.

"Bullshit," she said.

Asmoday nodded to the man holding her. He turned her around and began walking her down toward the far side of the clearing, near the cliff's edge. The man in the Travel-All started it up. He drove it in reverse past them, to within twenty feet of the cliff.

When they reached the vehicle, Asmoday opened the door and gestured for Di to enter. She hesitated. What the Circle was going to do here on the cliff's edge seemed inescapable, but what were their plans for Sarah and Bill? Would they proceed on up the path to tie up the remaining loose ends? Di said a silent prayer, willing Sarah and Bill not to return to the cabin for a long time. If only there were some way to draw the heat off them.

The temptation to escape into trance was now greater than it had ever been. Di sensed that all she had to do was acquiesce, drop her guard a little, and the fragile edifice of her personality would shatter into a thousand pieces. A chorus of voices inside her screamed for oblivion. Di felt herself slipping into trance and bit her cheek again. *Help me,* she thought, calling out to all the voices.

Asmoday placed his hand on her arm to guide her into the car. In that instant, the hand became every hand that had ever held her down, that had clamped shut her mouth against the cries of pain and fear, that had ever struck her in malice or touched her in lust. For just an instant, she heard the cries of a thousand voices. They were the voices of all the dissociated fragments of her soul. But they were no longer frail, individual pieces, they were a union of selves. They were not the betrayal of her weakness, but rather, the source of her strength.

She shrugged out of Asmoday's grip. "Come on, then, let's get this damn thing over with," Di said with a bravado she did not feel. "I assume you want me in the car so you can push it off the cliff?"

Asmoday was clearly surprised. He hesitated before answering.

"Yes," he said, "that's right."

She climbed into the car. Mark was still slumped in the passenger seat, unconscious or dead.

As if it were an afterthought, Di said, "You know, she never understood."

Asmoday raised a hand, halting the preparations of his people. "Who? What?"

"Sarah," Di said. "It was in front of her all along, but she never really understood it. She thinks you're just a small group of isolated fanatics," she lied. "She doesn't understand that you're everywhere. She knows so little. She's no danger to you."

Asmoday shook his head in mock sadness. "I know what you're trying to do," he said.

"You can make our death look like an accident," Di continued. "If you kill *them,* it will be too much of a coincidence. Let them go. There's nothing they can do."

Asmoday paused. He held her gaze, looking genuinely thoughtful. Di prayed that he would heed her advice, but she knew enough not to expect him to tell her his plans.

"Please tuck your legs up under you," Asmoday said.

Di looked at him quizzically.

"Can't have you hitting the brakes at the last minute, can we?" he said. "Now, put your hands on the window ledge."

She placed her hands on the ledge. The big man who had held her earlier now placed his hands on top of hers. Di smiled at him. "What you do is wrong," she whispered.

At a signal from Asmoday, the remaining six men and women moved to the back of the vehicle and placed their hands against it as if they intended to push it up the path. One man then came around to the passenger side, opened the door, and reached in over Mark. He released the hand brake and pushed it to the floor.

"Goodbye, Isis," Asmoday said. "Goodbye, daughter."

"Burn in hell," Di answered through clenched teeth.

The man stepped away and slammed the door. He raised a hand and nodded. The six in back stepped away from the vehicle, and suddenly the Travel-All began rolling backward. Di tried to pull her hands away to grab the steering wheel, but the big man was still there, holding her hands and running alongside the accelerating vehicle.

She pulled as hard as she could, but the man held her tightly. His face never changed from a calm, dead expression until he released her at the cliff's edge. He smiled as he yanked his hands away.

As the Travel-All slipped over the edge of the cliff, Di closed her eyes. The thousand faces of her soul were all there before her. They lifted up their voices in a chorus, not of regret or defeat, but in a unified, clarion call of triumph. They had escaped the Circle. For once and for all time, they had beaten it. Di felt a rush of singular joy for what seemed like an eternity before the car made its first contact with the side of the mountain.

Sarah and Travers were late getting back to the cabin. They had wandered for hours, lost in conversation, and the walk back up the mountainside had taxed them both. They crested the deer path at last. The cabin lay before them, the Travel-All ominously absent from the clearing.

"They're not back yet," Sarah said.

"That's odd."

They crossed the clearing at a tired jog. Travers unlocked the door. They stood together in the foyer, both of them sensing a disturbance.

"Someone's been here," Sarah said.

"What makes you think so?"

"I don't know," Sarah said, unable to explain her feeling. "A smell, maybe, something missing. I don't know."

They searched the cabin quickly. Nothing seemed to be missing, nothing was disturbed. Travers ended the search in the kitchen, and he began making a pot of coffee. Sarah joined him a few minutes later.

"Anything?" he asked.

"Nothing."

He pulled his keys from a pocket, preparing to unlock the kitchen door leading out to the back deck. He grabbed the knob with one hand and was startled when it turned easily. Travers opened the door and began examining the lock and door frame.

"I locked this door."

"You're sure?"

"Damn right." He hesitated. "At least, I think so. I went through the house before we left. I'm almost certain I locked it."

"Any sign of forced entry?"

"No."

Sarah poured them both coffee but found herself too nervous to drink it. "Bill, we've got to do something. They should have been here hours ago."

Travers agreed. He didn't want to tell Sarah about the surprise party Mark had planned, but even with detours by the grocery stores and the little town's half-dozen specialty shops, they should have been back long ago.

"The Travel-All is ancient," he said. "It could have broken down."

"Maybe we should hike down the trail. If we meet them coming up, we get a ride back. If they're in trouble, we'll find them."

Travers wasn't keen about doing any more hiking, but he had no better idea. He reluctantly put his coffee down and began locking up.

"I'm worried now, I'm really worried."

It was after four o'clock and the winter sun was moving rapidly toward the tops of the pines. Bill and Sarah walked quickly, moving down the rutted path of the logging trail. The slope was steep enough to make the going slow. Both of them had already fallen several times, slipping on the scree.

"I'm worried, too," Travers said. "We'll be lucky if we've got an hour's light left. We may have to walk home in the dark."

"I don't care. We've got to find them."

"We will," Travers said grimly and wondered. He was beginning to feel that something was terribly amiss, and every step he took, his sense of foreboding deepened.

"There's the clearing up ahead," Sarah said. "That means we're about halfway down, right?"

"Yeah, that sounds about right."

The clearing was empty and seemed desolate in the late afternoon light. Travers's sense of impending disaster increased a notch.

They crossed the clearing, drawn by the magnificent view from the edge of the precipice. Both were winded, and they sat down to rest on a boulder near the edge of the cliff.

"You really think it's the car?" Sarah asked.

Travers nodded. "Could be. The damn thing's old enough. It probably broke down somewhere farther down the mountain." He felt no conviction when he said this.

Sarah handed him the plastic canteen she had filled before they left. Travers twisted the top off and took a small mouthful to rinse his mouth. He leaned forward to spit the water out over the side of the cliff and stopped as something down the mountain caught his eye. He swallowed the water slowly, closed his eyes, then opened them again.

Far, far below, a tiny flash of tan had trapped his attention. It was an odd color, a faded tan like the dust-covered paint of the Travel-All. Travers jerked his head to look back up the logging trail. His eyes traced the trail back to the edge of the cliff. There, where the ground fell away, were two unmistakable ruts—ruts made by the passage of a vehicle's four wheels over the edge of the precipice. Travers reached out and touched Sarah gently.

His voice choked when he tried to speak.

"They're dead," he said.

PART V

SONS AND DAUGHTERS

Chapter 32

Weeks 19–20: Friday–Sunday, December 8–10

The next twenty-four hours were a manic blur for Sarah. Most of it she would recall in tiny, fragmented glimpses as if memory, which most people seemed to experience as a seamless sequence of events like a motion picture, had suddenly developed a preference for still photography and displayed its recollections in random, arrested images. Nightmare glimpses of the rest of that horrible afternoon froze in her mind. She could see herself with Travers by her side, frantically running, sliding, and falling down the mountain trail, then hiking the deserted back roads looking for signs of habitation in the failing light. She could barely remember the farmhouse they eventually found and the cautious hospitality of the old farmer in his blue overalls. Someone made a call to the county sheriff's office—Sarah wasn't sure whether she had made the call or not—and the sheriff himself had arrived. Coordinating the search over his car's two-way radio, he had eventually driven them back up the mountain. Had Sarah told the sheriff her suspicion that the deaths were no accident? Again, she was not sure. She might have insisted that the sheriff have his men look for evidence of foul play. She thought she remembered trying to explain *why* Mark and Di might have been killed, but she wasn't sure if she remembered a conversation that actually took place or merely recalled her internal rehearsing for such a scene. Had it actually happened? Had she mentioned Satan worship? Multiple personality disorder?

She had no idea.

Neither did Travers.

Travers was a rock during most of the ordeal. He'd held her, listened to her, let her cry, let her scream, had even interceded as much as possible with the sheriff's men. She had almost been tempted to believe that he was unmoved by it all, until she'd looked closely at him in an unguarded moment. Then she'd seen the shock and the fatigue, the oscillation of his emotions, like hers, between disbelief and all-consuming grief.

At one point, he'd begun saying, "We shouldn't have let them go." It became a kind of mantra in the wee hours after they'd gotten back to the cabin. He said it over and over until Sarah had taken him by the hand and told him it was all right. They'd both cried then, for a little while.

Some time after dawn a man in uniform had informed them with regrets that the vehicle had been located and both passengers had been found dead at the scene. The man had not hidden behind euphemisms. It didn't matter; Sarah had known they were gone the instant Travers had pointed out the splash of tan on the valley floor.

That was when she had started bumming cigarettes off Travers. "Mark and I quit together four years ago," she explained as Travers held a lighter up to the trembling cigarette. "He'd understand me starting again now. Just to get through this."

Sarah remembered throwing their packed bags in a deputy's Jeep and being driven to town. At some point Travers left, returning later with a car he'd managed to rent. Sarah had Travers call a funeral home in Richmond to make tentative arrangements. The rest she'd handle later.

Their business with the sheriff's office had been long concluded. Sarah remembered the sad, kind face of one of the deputies who had helped load the car. He had given Sarah such a pitying look that she had almost felt sorry for him.

Travers started opening up on the drive back to Richmond. Some of the shock had worn off, or perhaps in the depths of his exhaustion he'd caught a second wind.

"How did they find us?" he asked, trying with little success to engage Sarah. When she wouldn't answer, he continued in a running monologue, his voice rising and falling with emotion as he began to acknowledge his anger.

"Somebody had to have tipped them off," he said. "They *had* to, goddamnit. They didn't follow us. At least, I don't see how. I'm no cop, but I would have sworn we weren't followed. Fisher knew we were in the mountains, but not exactly where. Did you tell anybody where we were?"

Sarah ignored him when he asked the question, but Travers persisted. Finally, she said that she had told Margie generally where they were going, but she hadn't known herself the exact location of the cabin.

"Margie, then," Travers said. "We've got to put Margie on our list of suspects."

Sarah looked at him as if he were crazy. He ignored her, continuing to rant.

"No one's exempt, no one's immune. Everybody's suspect except you and me. How did they do it, Sarah? How did they do it?"

Eventually, Sarah could stand it no longer. "Will you stop it, damnit," she exploded. "I've just lost my husband and a friend, and you're starting to sound like a paranoid schizophrenic. It's over. If the Circle killed them—and we can't even be certain of that—they got what they wanted. Case closed."

Travers managed to hold his tongue until they

reached the outskirts of the city. He waited till they had exited the interstate, then said as calmly as he could, "Sarah, you could still be in danger."

"What do you mean?" Sarah asked wearily.

"In my heart of hearts, I believe the Circle found Mark and Di, and killed them. They may have come to the house looking for us. Maybe they wanted to silence us, too. They may still think you're a threat to them, Sarah."

Sarah thought for a long time before answering. Events had reached a kind of finality. It was over, it had to be.

"No," she said. "If they act against us, it will make Mark's and Di's deaths look suspicious. Besides, they have no idea how much I know about them. There's nothing to worry about." A tiny part of her recognized that her reasoning was in large measure a mixture of exhaustion and fatalism. She just didn't want to worry anymore.

"I wish I could be as certain as you are," Travers said. "You know what I'd like to do?"

"No."

"Take you with me and get the hell out of town for a few days. Till we can sort things out. Make sure we're in the clear. I don't suppose I could interest you?"

Sarah shook her head. "Bill, I appreciate the concern. But I'm exhausted. I've got a funeral to arrange. I want to sleep in my own bed. I want to start dealing with this so I can put it behind me. I don't want to run away."

"But—" Travers began to protest, but Sarah shushed him. The only concession he managed to get from her was later, when he dropped her off at her house and helped her carry her bags in. He made her promise that if she needed anything, anything at all, she would call.

Sarah promised, mostly just to get rid of him. Before

he departed, Bill pressed a half-smoked package of cigarettes and a lighter into her hands, for which she was grateful. Then he left quickly.

As exhausted as she was, Sarah wondered if she would ever sleep again. After bidding Travers goodbye, she locked the doors, took a shower, put on her pajamas, and lay down on the bed. Within minutes, she was snoring softly.

It was late afternoon when she had gone to bed, and when she awoke, the clock told her that it was still late afternoon. She felt groggy, as if she had been drugged, certain she had been asleep for hours. She picked up her wristwatch from the dresser and checked the calendar. It was Sunday. She'd slept for nearly twenty-four hours.

Sarah dressed and began putting away the things from the mountain trip. She knew it was foolish to worry about such incidentals, but she felt lost, adrift. She desperately needed something to occupy her, something mindless. Soon, she would have to deal with the details of the funeral, and that meant dealing with her own grief. She wanted to put that off for as long as possible. For the moment, she felt numb. She wanted to stay that way for a little while.

Her emotions almost overwhelmed her when she carried Mark's portable computer into the den. Here she was surrounded by him. This had been his room; it was filled with his computers and books, with the essence of him. Sarah stood, the computer forgotten in her arms, gazing bleakly around the room.

She almost dropped the computer when the phone rang.

She took a deep breath, gathering her composure, reluctant to answer the phone. She picked it up on the fourth ring.

"Sarah?" a familiar voice said. "Where the hell have you been?"

"Jenny?" *My God,* Sarah thought, *it's been ages since I talked to Jenny. How will I explain to her what's happened?*

"Sarah Johnson, I'd almost given you up for dead," Jenny said. "Do you realize it's been three weeks since we talked last? Listen, if you're trying to get rid of me or something, just come right out and say it. Otherwise, you had better tell me what you've been up to."

"Oh, Jenny," Sarah said and stopped, choking on her words.

"What is it, Sarah? What's wrong? Are you all right?"

"Mark's dead, Jenny."

"Oh, my God," Jenny said. "You poor thing. What happened?"

Sarah began trying to tell Jenny about the accident, trying not to complicate the story with details of Diana or the Circle. But it was impossible to explain why they were in the mountains without filling her in on the case. Jenny listened patiently, making sympathetic clucking noises, reminding Sarah of an old hen. The more Sarah talked, the more complicated and convoluted her story became. Sarah suspected Jenny would fear for her sanity.

As she talked, Sarah began unpacking the portable computer from its nylon case. She put the computer on Mark's desk, then began rummaging through the case for the diskettes she had carried along. The case was empty; there were no diskettes. She checked the side pockets. Nothing.

She was in the middle of a sentence when the significance of the missing diskettes struck her. A quick thrill of fear jolted through her like an electric shock.

"Jenny," she said. "I've got to go."

"What. You can't—"

Sarah hung up on her and immediately began dialing Travers's number.

He answered on the second ring. He sounded as groggy as she had felt half an hour before. She explained about the missing diskettes.

"So they *were* in the house," Travers said. "I knew I locked the back door."

"Yes."

"What was on the diskettes? Anything important?"

Then Sarah remembered, and the shakes hit her. She struggled to hold the phone to her ear. "Jesus, Bill, I had my speech on one of them."

"Speech?"

"Yeah. The one where I reveal the existence of the Circle, the one where we were going to go public."

"Oh, no."

"Bill, now they know how much *I* know."

There was a silence for a few seconds while he pondered the implications. "Mother of God, Sarah. Hold tight. I've got one phone call to make, then I'm on my way."

With shaking hands, Sarah lit a cigarette from the package Travers had given her. She could barely hold the Bic lighter steady enough to do it. She inhaled deeply. *God,* she thought, *if ever there were a time that justified smoking, it's now.*

How long would it be before they examined the diskettes and found the speech? Did she have days, hours, minutes? Would they come for her immediately, or would they wait, choosing their time carefully?

Or would they come at all? Wasn't it still possible, Sarah mused, that they would choose to ignore her, knowing her story would not be believed? That was possible, wasn't it?

The sudden rush of adrenaline seemed to have cleared her head, and Sarah recalled with embarrassment just how perfunctorily she'd dismissed Travers's concerns yesterday. She'd been too tired to think clearly. But Travers was right. How had the Circle known where to find them? The only people who knew where they were had been right there on the mountain. Everybody. Everybody except . . .

Travers had asked about Margie. Could it have been her? *No, not Margie,* thought Sarah. But Margie had known when they were leaving, and Sarah had told her generally where they would be. But Margie was a friend, not a member of a satanic cult.

Margie could be a chrysalid, Sarah thought. *Margie could be just one cell of a cult-created chrysalid, just like Diana.* Her mind tried to deny it, but the thought kept returning with unrelenting insistence. *If she were a chrysalid, Margie herself wouldn't know about the cult, but inside her would be a cult-engineered alter. But for all those years, they couldn't have just planted her and left. Could they? Why?* Then Sarah remembered Helen Jenner, the woman who had killed herself. Diana had reminded her of Helen, and Sarah had wondered if Helen had been a multiple, too. What if Helen had not only been a multiple, but also a cult victim? Margie had started work shortly after Helen began therapy. A short time later, Helen had killed herself. Or been killed? *Oh God . . .*

And the key to the office. Margie had a key. The intruders had used a key. Not Margie, please, not Margie . . .

Sarah heard a car pull into the driveway. Relieved, she hurried out to the living room. Travers had made good time.

She put her hand on the front doorknob, then stopped. What if it wasn't Travers?

She rushed into the kitchen, straining to look out the window. She could just glimpse the front grill of the car. She couldn't tell if it was Travers or not.

She turned at the sound of glass breaking. Sarah watched in horror as a hand knocked out the broken pane in the kitchen door and reached in. She felt stuck in slow motion, while the movement of the hand and the man behind it seemed wildly accelerated. Before she could cross the kitchen floor, the door was opened and two men entered. One was in jeans, the other was dressed casually but expensively. He had impeccably styled silver hair. They were on her in an instant.

The first thing Travers did was pick the phone back up and call the police. He was in luck. Fisher was just going off duty. He explained the situation as quickly as he could. Fisher promised to pick him up in five minutes.

Travers waited nervously out on the lawn, chain-smoking and pacing. Seven minutes after he'd hung up on Fisher, the policeman pulled up to the curb in a battered seventies-vintage Ford sedan. Travers leapt into the front seat and they were off.

"Where did you get the ride?" Travers asked.

"This is my baby," Fisher said.

"It looks like shit."

"Yeah, but under the hood is raw, perfectly-tuned horsepower." As if to prove it, he goosed the accelerator and the car shot forward.

"Don't you have a flashing light?" Travers asked impatiently. "Can't you go any faster?"

"I'm off duty, for Christ's sake. What's your hurry, anyway?"

"Just a feeling," Travers said. And to himself, he thought, *A feeling like time is running out.*

They were just under fifteen minutes getting out to the suburbs. Travers directed Fisher down the street leading to Sarah's house. A late model Lincoln Continental, accelerating quickly, passed them going in the opposite direction.

"Slow down, jerk," Fisher muttered as the Lincoln passed.

Travers got out the door before Fisher had the car stopped. He bounded up the front steps, knocking and ringing the doorbell simultaneously. He waited nervously for Sarah to open up. Nothing happened. He knocked again.

"Come on, Sarah," he whispered. "Open the door."

Fisher appeared around the side of the house. "This way, Bill," he called. "Somebody broke in the back door. I'm going to check out the house and call it in."

They started around the side of the house. Then Travers remembered the speeding car. "The Lincoln," he shouted. "Come on, John, there's no time."

Fisher cranked the old car into life and made a quick U-turn. He punched the accelerator and the engine roared. When they reached the stop sign at the end of Sarah's street, Fisher hit the brakes just enough to throw them into a skid. He drifted through the intersection and hit the accelerator again. Travers began scanning the road ahead for Lincolns.

Beiderbeck drove. Sarah was sandwiched between him and the man in denim, Beiderbeck's helper. The helper had his arm wrapped around Sarah's shoulder. Sarah presumed this was intended to keep her from making any sudden moves, but what possible threat she could pose at this point, she had no idea.

Beiderbeck navigated the car through a series of secondary roads, but Sarah was so consumed with fear and shock that she took no notice of the route. She struggled to keep her breathing even. She would not show fear to these bullies.

"The Circle, I presume," she said, her voice sounding much calmer than she felt.

"A small part of it."

"You have me at a loss," Sarah said. "You know my name, but I don't know yours."

"What's in a name?" He glanced over at her. "Be at ease," he said. "From here on, the book is written quite clearly."

"You're going to kill me, aren't you?" Sarah asked.

"Oh, yes," he said. "Although there are those who

say that we all choose the time of our deaths. In that case, we are merely assisting you."

"As you assisted my friend and my husband? As you assist in the torture and abuse of helpless children?" Sarah added.

"As we assist in the development of fully-realized human beings, my dear." His smile never faltered. "Of course, you are not capable of understanding that."

"I understand enough," Sarah said.

"You understand too much," Beiderbeck replied. "Your speech made that all too clear. A shame you'll never have the opportunity to deliver it."

Beiderbeck turned his attention back to the road.

"Why?" Sarah asked. Maybe she could keep his attention diverted. He didn't drive quite so fast when he was talking. She supposed she was merely delaying the inevitable, but at that point any plan was a good plan. "Why such evil, such violence and inhumanity?" she asked. "It makes no sense to me."

"Power," Beiderbeck said.

"Power?" Sarah asked.

"Power to do whatever you wish in your short time on this earth," the man answered, and patted her on the knee as if he were her favorite uncle. It was all Sarah could do not to jerk away in revulsion. "Power to subject your Neanderthal cousin to your dominion with a stick sharpened by a flake of obsidian. Power to control as much of your destiny as you can wrap your little arms around. Power is what gets us up in the morning; power is what all men crave and only the bold know how to seek. And power is controlled by the forces of darkness."

Beiderbeck glanced her way, looking calmly triumphant. Sarah recognized that in spite of his look of perpetual amusement, he was quite serious.

Suddenly she was laughing.

It started as a giggle, erupted into a chuckle, and

quickly escalated into a full, unstoppable belly laugh. For the first time since she'd seen him, a look of uncertainty crossed the man's face. This struck Sarah as funny, too.

"What do you find so amusing?" the man asked.

Sarah thought she detected a note of irritation in his voice.

"You," Sarah said. "You and your little cult of power." Sarah laughed again. "You know what you sound like? Do you have any idea?"

The man looked at her blankly.

"A bunch of silly, self-centered yuppies," Sarah said. The impulse to laugh died as a cloud slipped over the face of the sun. The car seemed suddenly very cold. Its chill matched the icy blue of the driver's expressionless eyes. "Who'd have thought?" she asked.

"Who'd have thought what?"

"Who'd have thought that Satanism turns out to be the perfect yuppie religion," she said. "Gimme, gimme, gimme, more, more, more. Wealth, power, influence, it's all the same." Sarah shook her head, and a sudden wave of rage diminished the terrible fear that threatened to paralyze her. "You people aren't frightening, you're pathetic."

Beiderbeck flushed with anger. "You think you're so damned smart. You think you've got it all figured out. I believe I will tell you my name. One of them, anyway."

"I'm all ears," Sarah said.

"Beiderbeck," the man said. "John Beiderbeck. That's the name your husband knew me by."

Beiderbeck, Sarah thought, now totally confused. *Mark's customer? The man who had kept him so busy over the past few months? But why? . . .*

"Did your husband ever tell you about his little affair?" Beiderbeck asked. "Did he confess his indiscretion? I had such a wonderful time introducing the two of them."

"You bastard," Sarah shouted, but inside her mind was racing frantically. There was something she was missing, something that didn't quite add up.

"Of course, it didn't have the desired effect. I'd hoped it would distract you from meddling with our Isis." Without warning, Beiderbeck raised his hand from the steering wheel and slapped Sarah across the face with the back of his hand. "And you destroyed her, you bitch."

"Glad I could help." Sarah moved to rub her jaw, but the other man still held her tightly.

"Have you figured out how we found you on the mountain? Or how we got the keys to your office? By the way, you keep impeccable files."

"Margie's one of your chrysalides, isn't she?" Sarah asked, still not really believing it.

Beiderbeck looked genuinely surprised. "Margie? Oh, your secretary." He erupted into a belly laugh. "What an interesting idea. Sorry, but I'm afraid you're very cold on that guess. Very cold."

Sarah had no idea what he was talking about. She suspected he was playing games with her. She was tired and frightened. They were out in the country now, Beiderbeck driving at a steady sixty miles per hour, and every minute that passed took her farther from hope of rescue.

"Figured it out yet? Need a hint? It always pays to have an inside man."

The realization hit her at that moment as brutally as a fist to the stomach. Mark had gone to town two days before he and Di had been killed in order to check with some of his customers. He could have called anyone. And then there was the office break-in. Mark had had access to the spare key Sarah kept at the house. He could easily have had a copy made and passed it on to Beiderbeck.

But Mark couldn't have betrayed her. He had loved her. That was undeniable. But Diana had loved her, too, and at the same time Nora had regularly reported all that she knew to the Circle.

Sarah recalled that Mark had grown up as an orphan, shuttled from one facility to another. He'd been abused, that was how she had developed such sensitivity to the issues of child abuse.

"Mark?" she said, her voice choked and pathetically weak.

Beiderbeck laughed. "Now you're getting warm."

Could Mark have been a chrysalid? Sarah asked herself. The idea was absurd. Beiderbeck was just messing with her mind. She knew Mark as well as any person knows another. He wasn't fragmented, he didn't have MPD. *But wait a minute,* the therapist inside her spoke up. *The relatives of multiples usually have no idea what's going on. They just see mood swings and the chronic lateness and the missed appointments. Mark certainly had his share of those. And just a minute ago, I was willing to concede that Margie might be a chrysalid, a cult-produced multiple with no awareness of the fact. If Margie, why not Mark?*

Could Mark have had no knowledge of his connection to the Circle? He'd have been like Di, maybe not as fragmented, but fragmented nonetheless. *It can't be,* she thought, but even as she tried to drown the conclusion in doubt, it kept bobbing to the surface. It wasn't Margie who had betrayed Sarah; it was Mark.

They wanted a plant, just in case any of the chrysalides ever started having breakdowns. No, not just in case. When. They knew it would happen sooner or later. Helen Jenner was a multiple. A multiple and more.

They would have set it up years earlier. Mark had probably lived most of his adult life without contact with the Circle, but somewhere inside him was a dissociated fragment waiting to be reactivated. Di thought she'd pulled Sarah's name at random from the phone book. Instead, she'd been planted with Sarah's name as a contingency, like a posthypnotic suggestion: *If you ever feel yourself losing it, here's the therapist you'll find in the phone book.*

The certainty that this is what had happened overwhelmed her. *They wouldn't have wanted to leave a thing like that to chance,* she thought. *What security it must have given them, knowing they had me—their own chosen therapist—waiting in the wings. With such a dependence on induced multiple personality disorder, it was the kind of insurance they could hardly afford to be without. They knew they couldn't control everything, especially the kinds of mental health problems that are likely to surface with people who have been severely abused. So they settled for having some safeguards in place. Very effective safeguards.*

In a trembling voice, Sarah said, "Did you find me first and instruct Mark to marry me, or did you let him pick his own therapist?"

"Now you're hot." Beiderbeck grinned. "Oh, don't take it so hard. Mark was an insignificant player. He was just our ace in the hole. He had one other cell, and that cell simply acted on instructions to seek a mate in your profession. So you see," Beiderbeck sneered cynically, "love still makes the world go round. Mark was all yours, but a little bit of him was ours."

"Why did you bother having Nora seduce him, then?"

"Oh, that was for your benefit, and Diana's as well. If either of you found out what happened, I thought it might drive a wedge between you."

"Why did you kill him, then?"

Beiderbeck shrugged. "He had outlived his usefulness, as have you."

"Oh, God," Sarah said. She felt sick to her stomach. It was one thing for her husband to have been killed, quite another to discover that so much of her life had been . . . *engineered,* for want of a better word.

"Oh, God," she moaned again, wanting not to believe but knowing it was the truth.

The Lincoln sped on, into the gathering dusk.

* * *

Travers strained to see another car ahead of them on the winding road, but the distance between turns was too short and the view was blocked by houses and trees. He pounded his fists on his knees in frustration, trying to convince himself that Sarah would be all right. Fisher made a left-hand turn at the next intersection for no rational reason that Travers could see, then accelerated the car up to eighty. They were heading out into the country now, and the road opened up into longer stretches.

After several minutes, they pulled out of a sharp curve. The highway stretched ahead in a series of gentle hills, unbroken for several miles. Far ahead, at the limits of visibility, they saw the tail end of a car top a hill and disappear. Fisher goosed the old Ford up to eighty-five.

God, can it be? Can it really be? Sarah asked herself over and over. She felt horribly used. This monster sitting next to her had been an unsuspected but intimate part of her life for years. He, or men like him, had tortured and abused her client as a child, and had murdered both Di and her husband.

White-hot rage burned suddenly inside Sarah. He had to be stopped; if it was the last thing she did, he had to be stopped.

"How many know about me?" she asked.

Beiderbeck looked amused. "You mean what we're doing right now?"

"Yes." Sarah tried to inflect her voice with sarcasm. "Do you have to get clearance from Circle headquarters, or do they let you make your own decisions."

"This is my operation," Beiderbeck said. "I answer to no one."

Beiderbeck's arrogance stoked her fury, and Sarah

let the rage fill her up and sweep her away. The man restraining her had relaxed his grip. She reached out to the steering wheel and gave it a savage yank downward. She heard with satisfaction Beiderbeck's grunt of terrified surprise. She registered the fact that none of them were wearing seat belts, then looked up in time to see the car flying off the shoulder of the road and down a steep embankment, heading for a stand of enormous oaks.

Sarah dived for the floorboard as the two men screamed.

The highway swept them into a short length of forest, then opened up again. The road before them, a good mile stretch, was empty. To the left lay flat fields, while the road followed the edge of a steep embankment to the right.

At the speeds Fisher was driving, they should have narrowed the distance to the car ahead.

"Where the hell are they?" Travers shouted.

Sarah scrambled frantically around the coffin-sized space of the floorboards. She felt something wet and sticky on her face, wiped her nose on the back of her hand, and was not surprised when it came away slick with blood. That was the least of her concerns. The sensation of being trapped in the narrow space of the floorboards overwhelmed her. She tried to fight the panic, but the claustrophobia was too much. She fought her way out without regard for what was upholstery, dashboard, or the bodies of her abductors.

The car was cocked at a crazy angle. Sarah scrambled to the seat and pushed against something soft in order to reach the door on the driver's side. The latch resisted for a second, then she felt the door give. She climbed over something that might have been Beiderbeck and pushed the door hard to get it to open.

Sarah pulled herself up to the edge of the seat and looked out. The car was canted three feet in the air. She drew her feet up to jump, then felt a hand grasp weakly at her ankle. She gave a quick scream, like a person rousing from a nightmare, and kicked out with her foot. Her jogging shoes were still on her feet; she felt the heel connect with something solid, heard a moan, and the hand slipped away from her ankle. Without thinking, she drew her leg up and jumped from the car.

She must have blacked out for a few seconds. When she came to, she was lying on her back, not quite sure where she was or what had happened. She looked about dazedly. The sight of the Lincoln brought memory rushing back.

Sarah recoiled from the sound of movement in the car. She could hear the two men groaning in the wreckage. The smell of gasoline was heavy in the air. Sarah looked in horror at the pool of liquid spreading at the base of the overturned car. The Lincoln must have ruptured a fuel line.

Panic mounting from the need to escape both the gasoline and the men stirring in the wrecked car, she scrambled to her knees and began crawling up the slope toward the highway. The hillside was steep and wet from recent rains. Her feet could barely find purchase in the damp grass. She felt as if she were trapped in a nightmare, one of those dread-filled dreams of trying to escape a nameless monster while the ground turns to foot-deep mud.

Halfway up the hill, she stopped to catch her breath. She eased over onto her back and looked down at the wrecked car. She saw a hand emerge from the edge of the seat.

Sarah almost screamed. She wanted Beiderbeck to have died in the wreck. He didn't deserve to live. That was the hand that had tortured Diana and countless others, that had snuffed out the life of her friend at the very moment she was beginning to live. It was the hand that had directed the murder of her husband. Beiderbeck had to be stopped.

She had to stop him.

Get angry, a voice inside her shouted. *Fight.*

The smell of gasoline filled the air. Beiderbeck pulled himself up to the edge of the door, and his eyes met hers. Even from across the distance they seemed bottomless pools.

An idea occurred to Sarah.

Do it, a voice inside her shouted. She thought of Lynn and Iris and Diana. Of Di and Mark.

The cigarettes, along with Travers's lighter, were in her jeans pocket, where she'd put them during her phone call with Jenny. She pulled out the pack of Marlboros, shook one of the cigarettes out of the crumpled package, and smoothed it between her fingers. She fired up the Bic, her hands shaking so badly she could barely train the little finger of flame on the end of the cigarette. With some effort, she got it lit. She inhaled on the cigarette several times, until the coal on the end was long and hot. She took a final puff, then tossed it down the hill toward the Lincoln.

Beiderbeck's eyes grew wide in the instant before the cigarette hit.

They had lost the car somehow. The road was straight and flat now, the view ahead unimpeded, but there was no sign of the Lincoln. On impulse, Travers rolled down his window, as if that might somehow widen the view or allow him to hear over the roar of the Ford's stressed engine.

"Jesus, John, we lost 'em."

"I don't get it," Fisher said. "They've got to be here."

They both heard the whump of the ignited gasoline, followed a second later by a muffled explosion as the Lincoln's fuel tank caught fire. Fisher slammed on the brakes, bringing the car to a skidding halt. They scanned the horizon, looking for the source of the noise.

"There, behind us," Travers said.

A quarter mile back, an ugly ball of black smoke was rising in the air. Fisher turned the car around and accelerated. A few seconds later, he pulled onto the grassy shoulder of the road. Travers jumped out and ran across the highway.

They'd missed the Lincoln because of the wide verge and the steep slope of the hillside. Travers first caught sight of the burning car at the bottom of the hill and felt his heart drop down into his stomach. A moment later, his eye caught movement on the hillside where Sarah was still trying to crawl up the slope. In seconds, Travers had pulled her up to the side of the road and was cradling her head in his hands as he tried to gauge the extent of her injuries.

"Jesus Christ," Fisher said as he reached the couple, then surveyed the scene at the bottom of the hill. "I'll call for an ambulance, then we've got to get down there."

Sarah reached out and grabbed Fisher's arm. "No," she said.

The two men gazed at her incredulously. She looked from one to the other. "No," she repeated.

Travers was the first to understand. He nodded, then looked at his friend. The policeman took a deep breath. Travers knew that all of Fisher's instincts were telling him to get and give help, to slip into those finely trained emergency responses he relied on as a cop. Finally, Fisher whispered, "God have mercy," then nodded at Travers. Between them, they half carried Sarah across the road to the car, bundled her between them, and then were gone.

Chapter 33

Week 20: Wednesday, December 13

The sky was the ugly color of slate. Thick cloud masses threatened the season's first snow. Sarah thought the weather somehow appropriate as the limousine followed the hearse up the narrow road of the cemetery. At her request, both Travers and John Fisher had ridden with her. When the limousine stopped, they helped her out, then walked with her, one on each elbow, up the hillside to the grave site.

During the brief ceremony, large, lazy flakes of snow began to fall. By the time the service had ended, the flakes had gotten smaller and thicker, and snow was starting to cover the ground.

After the service, Sarah turned away from the grave, ignoring the muttered condolences of well-wishers. She began walking, steering Travers and Fisher farther up the hill. They stopped at the summit and stood looking down on the departing cars. A crew had already begun dismantling the canopy over Mark's grave.

"Sarah, I wish there were something I could say," Travers said.

Sarah patted his hand. "You of all people don't have to say a thing, Bill. You're perhaps the only other person who has an inkling how I feel right now."

He fished a package of cigarettes out of his pocket. "Care for one?"

"No," Sarah said. "I've stopped. You should, too."

Travers put the cigarettes away.

John Fisher stirred awkwardly at her side. "What are your plans, Sarah?"

"I'm going to get them, John," she said simply.

Fisher understood who *they* were. "How?"

"There are more like Di out there." She had to clear her throat before she could continue. "Like Di and Mark. More chrysalides. I'm going to find them. Then I'm going to expose the ones that made them like that."

"They play for keeps," the policeman said. "Are you sure you want to do that?"

"Not only that, Sarah," Travers added, "but if what Beiderbeck told you is true, you're safe at the moment. Do you want to change that?"

Sarah blinked away the flakes gathering on her eyelashes. She looked out over the cemetery and beyond, to the fields and woods. The air seemed unnaturally quiet, the sound muffled by the falling snow.

"I'm sure," she said. "We can't just walk away from the victims, not when we know they're out there, silent and helpless."

She started down the hill. The two men fell into step beside her. "Maybe I can interest you both in helping me."

Neither man said a word, but they both moved in closer to her, supporting her by the arms as they moved down the hillside.

Sarah stopped and turned when they reached the limousine. The snow swirled thickly about her. It lay like a blanket over the graves and had already hidden their tracks.

"The snow covers everything," she said. "But we remember what's under the snow, don't we? We won't forget."